PENGUIN

EXEMPLA

MIGUEL DE CERVANTES SAAVEDRA, the son of a
Spanish doctor, was almost certainly born in 1547. He
served in Italy when he was twenty-one, and as a regular
soldier he took part in the naval battle of Lepanto and
other engagements, until he was captured by pirates
while returning to Spain in 1575 and taken to be the
slave of a renegade Greek in Algiers; he attempted un-
successfully to escape three times, and was finally
ransomed in 1580. For the rest of his life he was preoccupied with the difficulties of making a living, and
spent several periods in prison. He had already written
some plays and a pastoral novel, *La Galatea*, when in
1592 he offered to write six plays at fifty ducats apiece.
He had no success until 1605, when the publication of
the first part of *Don Quixote* brought him immediate
popularity. The *Exemplary Stories* were published as a
collection in 1613, and in 1615 appeared the promised
continuation of *Don Quixote*. Cervantes died in 1616.

C. A. JONES was born in 1924 and educated at Milford
Haven Grammar School and Magdalen College, Oxford.
He taught at Launceston College in Cornwall before
returning to Oxford for a doctorate, and later to be a
university lecturer in Spanish and a fellow and Senior
Tutor of Trinity College. He taught at the University of
Pennsylvania (1959–60) and at Brown University, in
Providence, Rhode Island (1969–70). He was organizing
secretary of the First International Conference of Hispanists at Oxford in 1962, and President of the Association
of Hispanists of Great Britain and Ireland in 1967–9. He
edited plays by Lope de Vega and Calderón, and wrote
articles and reviews mainly on Golden Age drama and on
the nineteenth-century novelist Galdós.
   C. A. Jones died in 1984.

Cervantes

EXEMPLARY
STORIES

TRANSLATED BY
C. A. JONES

PENGUIN BOOKS

PENGUIN BOOKS

Published by the Penguin Group
Penguin Books Ltd, 80 Strand, London, WC2R 0RL, England
Penguin Putnam Inc., 375 Hudson Street, New York, New York 10014, USA
Penguin Books Australia Ltd, Ringwood, Victoria, Australia
Penguin Books Canada Ltd, 10 Alcorn Avenue, Toronto, Ontario, Canada M4V 3B2
Penguin Books (NZ) Ltd, Private Bag 102902, NSMC, Auckland, New Zealand

Penguin Books Ltd, Registered Offices: 80 Strand, London, WC2R 0RL, England

This translation first published 1972
18

Printed and bound in Great Britain by Antony Rowe Ltd.,
Chippenham, Wiltshire

CONTENTS

ACKNOWLEDGEMENTS

My thanks are due to Jane Clark and Sally Pether, who patiently typed and re-typed my versions of the stories, to my colleague F. W. Hodcroft, whom I consulted on several linguistic points and who read and made useful comments on some of my translations, and to my wife, who read them all and saved me from several stylistic blunders.

INTRODUCTION

Cervantes's *Novelas ejemplares* or *Exemplary Stories*, published in 1613 between the first and second parts of *Don Quixote* (1605 and 1615), are judged by critics to be the work of the author which most nearly approaches his masterpiece. Certainly, among the considerable volume of works of all kinds, poetry and drama as well as fiction, which Cervantes wrote, these stories most deserve to be rescued from the neglect from which all but the *Quixote* have suffered, except of course at the hands of the Cervantes specialist or the professional student of literary types.

The *Exemplary Stories* were certainly written over a considerable period of time, and at least two of them, and two of the best, were already in existence by the time Part I of the *Quixote* appeared, the first of them being in fact mentioned in the first part of the novel. These two stories were included, along with another which has often been attributed to Cervantes, *The Feigned Aunt*, in a miscellaneous collection of literary pieces prepared about 1604 by a certain Licenciate Porras de la Cámara for the entertainment of the Cardinal-Archbishop of Seville, during a summer vacation. The type of short story which we find in the 1613 collection made its appearance interpolated in the longer works of Cervantes, the most famous being perhaps *The Curious Impertinent*, which was included in the first part of *Don Quixote*. There is something to be said for the view that the short story in fact represents the essential unit of composition for Cervantes who, far from making novels out of plays, as one critic suggested, might well have turned some of his prose pieces into dramatic form for the sake of producing some at least of the *Interludes* which appeared in 1615.

The order in which the stories in the 1613 edition appeared is not chronological, and attempts to suggest other reasons for their arrangement are never very convincing, and sometimes frankly bizarre, one theory being that they represent the whole gamut of attitudes to love, set out according to a formula that is very deliberate and precise. Cervantes provided something of an excuse for this kind of interpretation when he suggested, in his prologue to the collection, that the stories contained some hidden mystery, and that one could derive wholesome profit not only from each but from all of them together. Cervantes was prone to this kind of mystification, and a good deal of time might be saved if we look for no principle more complicated than the search for variety through contrast.

The remark quoted from the prologue to the *Exemplary Stories* is only one of many found there which have been subjected to minute scrutiny by scholars, in an attempt to shed light on a work which has always puzzled specialists and general readers alike. 'I am the first', says Cervantes, 'to write *novelas* in the Castilian language.' The claim is glossed with the observation that the many *novelas* printed in Spanish are translated from other languages, while these are the author's own work. It is a claim which, if the nature of the Cervantine short story is understood, can be largely substantiated. Before Cervantes there had been translations and adaptations of stories of the Boccaccio type, few of them being as long as those of Cervantes, and concentrating fairly frankly on the anecdotal appeal, often enlivened by salacious details. (The dramatist known by his pseudonym of Tirso de Molina described Cervantes as 'our Spanish Boccaccio', and although this was perhaps meant as a compliment, it would not presumably have done much to warm Cervantes's heart.) On the other hand, there had been stories of the fable type, not differing very greatly from the *exempla* of the fourteenth-century writer, Don Juan Manuel, nephew of King Alfonso the Wise, short pieces with a fairly obvious moral distinctly stated at the end. Cervantes in some ways combined the best in the two traditions; and as far as the term *novela* is concerned, produced something which is longer and more complex than what is normally understood by a short story, and with a wealth of often realistic detail, a fair sprinkling of dialogue, and a breadth of understanding and sympathy, albeit ironically expressed, scarcely known in the works of his predecessors and rarely found again in those who came after him.

Part of the key to Cervantes's novelty lies too in the exemplary character of his stories. This epithet has been as much a stumbling-block as an aid to understanding; and the remarks in the prologue, although *prima facie* illuminating, lack the clarity which one might have wished for. It has been suggested that stories where vice is tolerated with remarkable ease, like the one about the card-sharper and the pickpocket, *Rinconete and Cortadillo*, or where slips from the path of strict morality are treated with a sympathy bordering on slackness, like *The Force of Blood*, can only be considered exemplary in the literary sense. Against this, however, there is a solemn declaration by Cervantes which is hard to gainsay. 'I have given them the title of "exemplary",' he writes, 'and if you look well there is not one of them from which some profitable example cannot be drawn.' This is followed by an even clearer statement of intention a little lower down, when he writes: '. . . if in any way it should come about that the reading of these *novelas* should induce the reader to any bad desire or thought, I would rather cut off the hand with which I wrote them than publish them. My age is not such that I can play fast and loose with the next life . . .' Cervantes had already lost the use of his left hand fighting against the Turks at the Battle of Lepanto in 1571, and as W. J. Entwistle suggested,[1] he would not lightly pledge his remaining hand, and his right one at that. Moreover, there was some substance in the point about his age: if, as is commonly accepted, he was born in 1547, he would be sixty-six at the time of publication of the *Novelas ejemplares*, a fact to which he obliquely alludes in the same prologue.

One answer to the problem of what Cervantes meant by 'exemplary' is to draw one's definition as widely as possible, including not only good examples to follow and bad ones to avoid, but those cases which provide honest recreation and entertainment. Here Cervantes again provides us with some justification in his prologue.

My intention has been to set up in the square of our republic a billiard table where each one can come to amuse himself without fear of injury; I mean, without hurt to soul or body, for honest and pleasant exercises bring profit rather than harm. For one is not always in church, places of prayer are not always filled, one is not always at one's business, however important it may be; there are times of recreation, when the troubled spirit may find rest.

1. *Cervantes*, Oxford, 1940, p. 87.

Even this answer leaves some important loose ends. Of the *Eight Plays and Eight Interludes* published in 1615, there are many among the latter which do not at all fit in with the moral intentions expressed for the *Exemplary Stories* published two years before. One of them, *The Jealous Old Man*, has very strong points of resemblance with *The Jealous Extremaduran*, but quite frankly exploits the more scabrous side of the story. We do not know when the Interlude was written; but we do know that it was published later than the *novela*, in the very year of his death. One cannot help wondering what had happened to Cervantes's scruples expressed in the prologue to his 1613 edition, even though it is well known that the morality of the theatre has rarely been so strict as that of the study or the drawing-room.

Another answer would be that Cervantes wrote many of his stories, not only some time before 1613, as we know to be the case, but before he came to formulate the ideas he had on the writing of exemplary tales, set out in the prologue of that year; and that when his formula was elaborated he collected together not only those stories which he had written with the prescription in mind, but those which were composed earlier and which could be fitted into the pattern, either with or without alteration. This could explain the two versions which exist of *The Jealous Extremaduran*. In the earlier version, included in the manuscript of Porras de la Cámara, adultery takes place between the young wife and the lover, whereas in the 1613 version it is avoided. Although the later form of the story may as a whole be superior to the original draft, as many modern scholars think, the idea that after a struggle in bed *both* parties fall asleep before the offence can take place might well draw the comment, 'A likely story'. The best explanation of this change is that Cervantes was thinking of the kind of assertion which he was to express in the prologue in the words: '... the love tales which you will find in some of them are so chaste and in accordance with Christian principles and ways of thinking that they are incapable of moving the careless or the curious reader to any evil thought.' The same consideration might well have deterred him from including *The Feigned Aunt*, a story which the majority, although by no means all, of Cervantes scholars have been inclined to attribute to the master. However, although it was in the Porras manuscript with two other stories eventually included in the 1613 collection, it could scarcely be fitted into a formula such as that which he had evolved, being a story of mutual deception even more scandalous than that related in *The Deceitful Marriage*. The subject might have done for an *Interlude*, in which the 'exemplary story' formula did not apply; but it was not fit for this new form of fiction, part of whose novelty lay, as I have suggested, in its exemplary character.

It has been pointed out that Cervantes inserted a number of short stories in such longer works as the first part of *Don Quixote*. The critics of this enormously popular work, to whom its author paid slightly reluctant attention in writing the sequel, complained of the abundance and irrelevance of the stories interpolated into the narrative of the Knight of the Sorrowful Countenance and his fat squire, on whose adventures and conversation they urged Cervantes to concentrate. Might it not be that in the period between 1605 and 1615, during which Cervantes must have been composing the second part of his masterpiece, he had already written and inserted in the work some short stories which he subsequently jettisoned, out of regard for the opinion of his critics? Some of these stories might well have found shelter under the umbrella of the exemplary story formula, which attempted to apply the recipe of honest entertainment to a *genre* where it had not been tried before. That they did not all fit too well under the cover may well be explained by the fact that a number of the stories had not originally been composed with the formula in mind.

Another factor is the great variety of the stories, difficult to fit into the formula which Cervantes devised, whether the stories or the formula came first. Among this great variety the bulk of the tales, although not among those here translated, could be more or less accurately described as romantic and Italianate in type. *The Little Gipsy Girl* and *The Jealous Extremaduran* are the nearest to this type among the stories included in the present volume, although the idealized pictures of gipsy life, contrasting with the more down-to-earth views expressed in *The Dogs' Colloquy*, give a peculiar flavour to the first; and the psychological interest to the second. More true to the Italianate type are *The Spanish English Lady* (which contains a remarkably tolerant view of Spain's greatest enemy and a flattering picture of the English Queen Elizabeth), *The Force of Blood, The Illustrious Kitchenmaid, The Two Maidens* and *Lady Cornelia*. Although excellent stories, they are not so original as the ones included in the present edition.

Among these, *Rinconete and Cortadillo*, one of the finest, is a splendid tale of low life in Seville, often described as a picaresque novel, but differing from most Spanish examples in that it is related in the third person and, more important, in its gently ironical tone which, after the first of these stories, the *Laẓarillo de Tormes*, rather deserted the *genre* and gave way to a more biting and sombre type of humour. There is social criticism in *Rinconete and Cortadillo*, if such a term means anything in the seventeenth century, but there is none of the gloomy seriousness which at least modern readers tend to find in *Guẓmán de Alfarche*. The two boys find the life of roguery so attractive that in spite of their recognition of its viciousness, they do not abandon it as soon as they feel they ought; but the reason for its attraction seems to be not its viciousness, but the amusement to be derived from it. (One recalls that in another of Cervantes's short stories, *The Illustrious Kitchenmaid*, two noble youths deliberately adopt the picaresque life for the sake of the pleasure and freedom it offered.) Cervantes's irony shows up the frightening gang of criminals under their awe-inspiring leader Monipodio for what it is, a scruffy mob of ignorant, self-important ruffians owing allegiance to an illiterate nonentity. But we are not left with a feeling of contempt towards them; rather, as so often in Cervantes, what we find is an infectiously tolerant smile at the foolishness of human beings, among whom he recognized himself to be no exception. He does not cover up or cloak in false colours the faults of his creatures, but his art manages to find and communicate a beauty in what could easily be seen as ugly and tawdry, in a way that calls to mind the paintings of Velázquez or Murillo, who can show sordid reality with complete frankness, and yet leave an impression of vivid artistic beauty.

Purely as fiction, *The Glass Graduate* is perhaps the least satisfactory of the stories. It is uncertain whether Cervantes wrote it before or after he conceived the idea of *Don Quixote*, but there is obviously a kinship between the two stories of madmen, despite the different ways in which the madness is induced. But whereas in the case of *Don Quixote* the idea proved so rich that, were it not for the appearance of a spurious second part, Cervantes might never have brought his novel to an end, in *The Glass Graduate* the whole thing fizzles out rather lamely after Thomas Rodaja has expressed a number of opinions on various professions and customs, which the dogs in the *Colloquy* would certainly have condemned as backbiting. Speculation that Rodaja was based on a real person, a Swiss doctor called Gustav Barth, rather loses its point when one learns that he did not visit Spain nor suffer from the affliction of believing himself to be made of glass until after the publication of the *Exemplary Stories*. A more likely source is Juan Huarte's *Examination of Wits*, which does describe, among other kinds of madness, one in which its victim thinks that he is made of some breakable material. It also makes the point that madmen are often exceptionally clear-sighted.[2]

Apart from the limited interest in Thomas Rodaja's madness, and the dubious appeal of hearing recited what are presumably Cervantes's rather acid views on a number of subjects, this tale has a certain autobiographical value, since there is little doubt that the Licenciate followed his creator in his journeys through Italy and Flanders, although it is not so certain that Cervantes started his career in the same fashion as Rodaja, as a student at Salamanca. The main interest of this tale, for me at least, is that it leads to speculation on what would have happened if Cervantes had not had the idea of sending Don Quixote home after his first sally, to be joined on his next journey by his comic squire Sancho Panza; or on what might have happened if Thomas Rodaja had found a companion like Sancho.

The Jealous Extremaduran is perhaps the tale which makes the most powerful appeal to modern taste, allowing for the difference of atmosphere and social customs. The calculating innocence of Carrizales, the timid innocence of Leonora, the calculating cunning of Loaysa and of the duenna Marialonso, the innocent stupidity of the Negro eunuch Luis are all exquisitely delineated, and the

2. cf. O. H. Green, '*El Licenciado Vidriera*: Its relation to the *Viaje del Parnaso* and the *Examen de Ingenios* of Huarte', 1964, reprinted in *The Literary Mind of Medieval and Renaissance Spain*, ed. J. E. Keller, Lexington, 1970, pp. 185–92.

reader who finds it difficult to condemn the various kinds of foolishness or vice which are revealed by this misguided collection of human beings, cannot say that anything but justice has been done at the end.

Fascination with the characters in this rich portrait gallery is matched by the curiosity and suspense aroused by Loaysa's efforts to accomplish a task which looks well-nigh impossible, but which leads to an outcome that is inevitable if one believes, as Cervantes did, that the will is free. The little song which so captivates the company listening to Loaysa ('Oh Mother, my mother, don't guard me so close,' etc.) is in some way the key to the moral lesson of this tale, a lesson which goes far beyond the circumstances that make up the story.

The last two stories translated here really need to be taken together, although they can stand on their own from the narrative point of view, and need to be read separately if one is to think of them as short stories at all. Most students of Cervantes have agreed that *The Dogs' Colloquy* is his best work apart from *Don Quixote*, but a dialogue of this kind, in its technique recalling the works of Erasmus and of his Spanish followers the brothers Alfonso and Juan de Valdés, and more remotely Apuleius' *Golden Ass*, could hardly survive in a collection of short stories if the way in were not provided by the story of *The Deceitful Marriage*, which by itself is a tale somewhat in the Boccaccio manner, and of distinctly dubious morality. Its justification is not so much the scarcely convincing repentance of Lieutenant Campuzano as the remarkable experience it offers of hearing the conversation of the dogs Scipio and Berganza, to which it leads.

Cervantes was always greatly concerned with verisimilitude, and the concern is shown here not only by the removal of the colloquy one stage from reality by transmitting it through the words of the stricken soldier, but by letting even him hint at some reservations. Before he came out of the hospital, where he was treated for a disease which might well have been accompanied by illusions, he heard and 'as good as saw' with his own eyes the two dogs talking; he has often doubted since whether what he witnessed was true; and his interlocutor lends no credence at all to this part of his tale. Moreover, the dogs might really have been human beings, transformed into animals through the power of witchcraft. In other words, the whole thing is, in relation to the normal realities of life, highly questionable. But Campuzano manages to persuade Licenciate Peralta that all the same it would be worth hearing the dogs' conversation recorded in the form of a colloquy, and whatever our own doubts might have been about the whole affair, we share his pleasure and profit in reading the results. For the colloquy is not only an invaluable indicator of Cervantes's opinions on subjects of both topical and permanent value, but it tells us an enormous amount about sixteenth-century and early seventeenth-century Spain. Also, somewhat surprisingly, it is a masterpiece of psychological observation, both in respect of the two dogs themselves, the backbiting Berganza and the censorious Scipio, and of the large number of people they meet – or rather whom Berganza meets, for we are never privileged to hear the full record of Scipio's life.

Not least of the appeals exercised by *The Dogs' Colloquy* lies in its style. In *Don Quixote* Cervantes told his readers that there were some stories which were attractive in themselves, while others required rhetorical arts and devices to put them over successfully. At the end of *The Deceitful Marriage* Campuzano tells us that he wrote down his story in every detail as he heard it, aided by an unusually sharp memory, the day after he had witnessed the dogs' conversation. He wrote it, he said, 'without looking for rhetorical colours to adorn it, or adding or subtracting anything to make it pleasing'. We may perhaps be allowed to doubt Campuzano's word, or that of his creator, for the whole exercise is in a sense a rhetorical device to make the reader accept what is a patent invention, itself devised presumably, at least in part, to persuade the reader to take as a short story what is as much an expression of opinions on life and customs as a narrative of the imaginary life of a dog.

However seriously we treat Cervantes's assertions with regard to the style of *The Dogs' Colloquy*, its clarity, rhythm and richness of vocabulary are undeniable, and although the style of other stories is very different, these qualities are apparent in all of them. The scenes and characters are painted vividly, and the dialogue is natural and always fitted to the personality of the speaker.

Some of the stories possess special features which broadly speaking come under the heading of style. *The Little Gipsy Girl* is interlarded with verses which are often charming, but can never be considered great poetry. Cervantes had a great respect for poetry, as this story and *The Glass Graduate* testify, but he was never appreciated as a poet, to his great chagrin. He may have derived a certain amount of wry pleasure from the praise which greeted Preciosa's recital or singing of the verses of the poet-page. In *Rinconete and Cortadillo* the thieves' slang is a feature which is extremely difficult for the translator; and the sententious note struck by Thomas Rodaja in *The Glass Graduate* gives a distinctive flavour to that story. Yet all these points of interest are subordinated to the flow of the narrative and the richness of the dialogue, which are nowhere better seen than in *The Jealous Extremaduran* and *The Deceitful Marriage*, stories otherwise lacking in obvious stylistic devices. It is in these tales, surely, that Cervantes, with an art that conceals art, has transformed what is basically commonplace material into literary pieces of the highest quality.

Describing his purpose in presenting these tales, Cervantes illustrated his claim to be providing recreation by comparing his efforts with the planting of groves and the cultivation of gardens. The wholesomeness of his entertainment is to be judged with these parallels in mind, and not by reference to narrow legalistic codes. Cervantes's generosity of spirit and mastery of language make the *Exemplary Stories* a worthy companion to what has been called the first European novel, *Don Quixote*. W. J. Entwistle, in his book on Cervantes, headed the chapter on the short stories 'Laboratory', and remarked: 'In the claim to have been the first writer of *novelle* in Spain Cervantes epitomized his contribution to literature; for out of the laboratory of the *novelle* or short stories came the first and best of novels.'[3] For this reason alone, putting aside their intrinsic value, the *Exemplary Stories* deserve to be more widely known and read. They were translated by James Mabbe, whose version was first published in 1640, and have been turned into most languages, including many versions in English since Mabbe's time.

The task of the translator of Cervantes is at the same time a rewarding and a frustrating experience. He realizes the wealth of

3. op. cit., p. 87.

linguistic resources which the author possessed and used with unerring skill. Cervantes wrote the Castilian of his age, many of whose features are now difficult of access, especially when he used jargon of any kind; but he wrote for all time. The nice balance of the colloquial and the majestic is almost impossible to recapture, and it would be a bold man who felt that he had come anywhere near to success. At the same time translating Cervantes, whatever the result, is something which enhances one's literary and linguistic experience; and the privilege of having been allowed to attempt the task may perhaps be the translator's greatest reward.

I am indebted to Mr John Rowlands for elaborating on footnote 5, p. 25 of this book. The relics (the grill and the blood and fat) of St Lawrence are apparently preserved at San Lorenzo in Lucina at Rome, one of the five churches in that city dedicated to the Saint. After the battle of St Quentin which began on St Lawrence's Day, 10 August 1557, the Spanish Royal House was closely associated with St Lawrence, so that it was not surprising that the Queen should give thanks for the birth in the Church of St Lawrence.

SUGGESTIONS FOR FURTHER READING

W. J. Entwistle, *Cervantes*, Oxford University Press, 1940.

A. F. G. Bell, *Cervantes*, Oklahoma, 1947.

E. C. Riley, *Cervantes's Theory of the Novel*, Oxford University Press, 1962.

F. Pierce (editor), *Two Cervantes Short Novels: El curioso impertinente and El celoso extremeño*, Oxford, Pergamon Press, 1970.

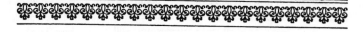

The Little Gipsy Girl

Gipsies seem to have been born into the world for the sole purpose of being thieves: they are born of thieving parents, they are brought up with thieves, they study in order to be thieves, and they end up as past masters in the art of thieving. Thieving and the taste for thieving are inseparable from their existence, and they never abandon them till they reach the grave. One of this tribe, an old gipsy who might have graduated in the school of Cacus,[1] brought up as her granddaughter a girl whom she called Preciosa and to whom she taught all her gipsy arts and frauds and thieving tricks. This Preciosa turned out to be the most accomplished dancer in all the gipsy world, and the most beautiful and discreet girl to be found, not only among the gipsies, but among all the most famous the world has ever known for their beauty and discretion. The heat of the sun, the winds and every kind of inclement weather, to which gipsies are more exposed than other folk, had failed to spoil the beauty of her face or to harden her hands. Not only that, but despite the rough upbringing she had received, she gave every sign of having been born of better stock than gipsies, for she was extremely polite and could talk well. And with all this she was a pert little thing; not that she showed any sign of immodesty, on the contrary, shrewd as she was, she was so virtuous that none of the gipsy women, old or young, dared to sing an improper song or say a bad word in her presence. The old woman soon realized the treasure she had in this grandchild, and like an old eagle, resolved to let her fledgling have her wings and to teach her to live by her wits.

Preciosa acquired a rich heritage of carols, songs, *seguidillas* and sarabands, and of other verses, especially ballads, which she sang with great charm. For her cunning grandmother realized that these tricks and graces, along with the youth and the great beauty of her granddaughter, would contribute to the increase of her fortune. So

1. In classical mythology, a famous robber, said to be three-headed and to vomit flames.

she sought out and got hold of these poems in any way she could, and there were plenty of poets to produce them: for there are poets who condescend to deal with gipsies and sell them their works, just as there are poets who write poems for the blind, and invent miracles for them to get a share of the profits. It takes all sorts to make a world, and hunger can drive clever people to do unheard of things.

Preciosa grew up in various parts of Castile, and when she was fifteen, her supposed grandmother took her back to Madrid to their old camp, which is where the gipsies usually settle, in the St Barbara fields; for they think they will sell their goods in the capital, where you can buy and sell everything. The day on which Preciosa first went into Madrid was the festival of St Anne,[2] the patroness of the city. She took part in a dance which was performed by eight gipsy women, four veterans and four girls, and a gipsy who was a greater dancer as leader; and although they were all clean and well dressed, Preciosa was so attractive that as time went on she won the hearts of everyone who clapped eyes on her. Amid the sound of the tambourines and the castanets, and the flurry of the dance, praises of the beauty and grace of the little gipsy girl brought the lads running to see her and the men to gaze at her. But when they heard her sing – for it was a dance with song accompaniment – that really was something! Then the little gipsy girl's reputation spread like wildfire, and by common consent of the directors of the festival she was singled out there and then as the star of the dancers; and when they performed in St Mary's Church, before the statue of St Anne, after they had all danced, Preciosa picked up the tambourine to the sound of which, gracefully pirouetting around, she sang the following ballad:

> Tree most precious
> slow to bear,
> ever barren
> standing there.
> Chaste desires,
> proving vain,

2. The mother of the Virgin Mary, whose festival takes place on 26 July. The doctrine of the Immaculate Conception of the Virgin involves the celebration of the virginity of her mother, which forms the burden of Preciosa's song.

consort's patience
starts to wane,
　Tired of waiting,
dark despair
drove from Temple
Man most fair.

　Sterile, holy,
from her came
God's abundance
worlds to claim.

　Die most sacred,
storehouse where
the godhead found
human care.

　Daughter's mother,
chosen then
shows God's greatness,
mankind's gain.

　Holy Anne, with
her to share
pain and suffering
humans bear.

　Your sway extends,
I dare swear,
o'er this grandchild,
kind and fair.

　Jointly guardian,
this domain
many would vie
now to gain.

　Daughter, grandson,
son-in-law!
Glory, honour
you shall know.

　You so humble
lesson gave,
learned by Mary
meek yet brave;

　now at God's side,
glory share,
and heaven's delights
rich and rare.

Preciosa's singing aroused the admiration of everyone who heard her. Some said, 'God bless you, my child.' Others said, 'What a pity this girl is a gipsy! She ought to be the daughter of some great nobleman.' There were others of a coarser kind who said, 'Let the kid grow up. She'll soon be up to some tricks. She'll grow up to be a fine snare for catching hearts.' Another one, of a more human and down-to-earth, less imaginative type, seeing her swirling so lightly as she danced, said to her, 'Go to it, lass, go to it! Come on, love, step lively!' And she replied, without stopping her dance, 'I'll step lively all right.'

When the eve and the day of St Anne were all over, Preciosa was rather tired, but she won such praise for her beauty, wit and discretion, and for her skill in dancing that she was the talk of the capital. Two weeks later she came back to Madrid with three other dancing girls, with tambourines and a new dance. All of them were equipped with ballads and songs that were lively but all perfectly proper, for Preciosa was unwilling for any songs to be sung in her company which were immodest, and she never sang them herself. People were very struck by this, and thought a lot of her for it. The old gipsy woman never left her side, and watched over her like Argus,[3] afraid lest anyone should run off with her. She called her her grandaughter, and Preciosa thought of her as her grandmother. They started to dance in the shade in the Calle de Toledo, and she soon had a great circle of followers. While they were dancing, the old woman would beg alms of the bystanders, and pennies and half-pennies would come pouring in like stones falling on a stage; for beauty has the power to awaken dormant charity.

When the dance was over, Preciosa said, 'If you give me four pennies, I'll sing you a song by myself, one that's extremely pretty, about when Our Lady Margaret[4] went to Mass in Valladolid, just after giving birth to her child, at the Church of San Llorente. It's a splendid one, by a poet of the top rank.'

Scarcely had she said this, when almost all those who were in the circle shouted out, 'Sing it, Preciosa, and here are your four

3. According to Grecian fable, Argus was a creature with a hundred eyes, charged by Juno to watch Io, of whom she was jealous.

4. Margaret of Austria (1584–1611), wife of Philip III of Spain and mother of Philip IV.

pennies.' And so the pennies came showering upon her like hail-stones, and the old woman could not keep up with them. When the harvest was gathered in, Preciosa shook the tambourine, and gaily sang the following ballad:

When Europe's fairest queen gave birth,
she went to Mass to celebrate.
Her courage and her fame shone forth
like jewels rich and delicate.

The eyes of all men follow her;
their hearts are captive to her spell.
They look and marvel at her grace,
and on her piety they dwell.

And just to show that she is part
of heaven come down on earth to stay,
on this side Austria's sun she bears,
and there Aurora's gentle sway.

Behind her comes the morning star
untimely, shining still and pale;
as night came forth upon that day
when heaven and earth Christ's death bewail.

And if in heaven stars can shine
and form a bright and moving trail,
her heaven is lit with other lights,
the living stars her beauty hail.

Here ancient Saturn limps along,
his beard though white still smooth and sleek.
His steps are slow, yet light and gay,
for pleasure makes old age less bleak.

The god whose silvery tongue speaks forth
in flattering and warm-hearted speech,
and Cupid with devices rare
in rubies and in pearls so rich.

And there goes Mars, the god of war,
his curious form you'll likely meet
in many a gallant youth, whose love
of battle soon admits defeat.

Look then, beside the sun's bright home
goes Jupiter; for none exceeds
the kind of favour which depends
on prudent works and valiant deeds.

There goes the moon whose beam divine
sheds light upon each human cheek;
Venus, whose purity is seen
upon this heaven-sent beauty meek.

The tiny Ganymedes go
crossing, wheeling and turning each,
a studded girdle there they form,
as round this wondrous sphere they reach.

And so that all may be amazed,
astonished at this heavenly feat,
all things their lavishness to show,
in prodigality compete.

Milan, its fabric rich and fine
shows off to startle curious eyes;
the Indies bring their diamonds rare;
Arabia richest scents supplies.

And biting envy shrinks away,
and ill will's banished from the scene,
leaving behind in Spanish hearts
kindness and loyalty serene.

While universal gaiety
flees from dull sorrow, runs apace,
speeding through every street and square
with mad, unhindered, carefree grace.

Then every tongue is loosed in praise,
where silent blessing used to reign;
and children's voices then repeat
the song that men begin again.

Then one says: 'Hail, thou fertile vine,
grow, soar aloft, touch and embrace
that elm which stands majestic there,
for ever offering shade, like grace;

to glorify your saintly name,
to honour and to prosper Spain,
to guard our Holy Mother Church
and terminate Mahomet's reign.'

Another tongue forthwith cries out:
'Long life to you, white dove of peace,
whose offspring shall be double-crowned,
imperial eagles to release

from birds of prey whose fury wild
the skies with terror long possessed,
and shelter timid virtue 'neath
your mighty wings for ever blessed.'

Another one, discreet and grave,
at once more lively and more rare,
speaks forth in joyous ringing tones
and eyes that sparkle with good cheer,

'This pearl, the gift of God to us,
Mother of pearl, from Austria came
defeating plans designed to harm,
and thwarting plots against His name.

What hope her coming will instil!
What base desires perish there!
What fears are increased as she comes!
And dread abortions, I dare swear!'

And now at last they reach that shrine [5]
where Holy Roman phoenix dwells,
whose body burnt, lived on in fame,
whose glory every tongue now tells.

Now to the one who bore our life,
now to the one who reigns in heaven,
now to the one who humble then
treads on the stars, adored by men,

To her who, Virgin, mother too,
to God's own daughter who became
God's very Spouse, upon her knees,
and reasoning thus, fair Margaret came!

5. Probably a reference to St Lawrence, to whom Philip II was devoted,
and in whose honour the Escorial was built. See p. 17.

'What you have given me I give
to you, most lavish generous queen,
whose favour once withdrawn, will leave
men in a misery doubly keen.

The first fruits of my love I bring
to you, most lovely Virgin; pray
receive them as a gift sincere,
guard and increase them day by day.

Their father to thee I commend,
who bent like Atlas 'neath the weight
of farflung realms in climes remote:
please keep them, thou so good and great.

Know then that even kingly hearts
in God's own hands securely dwell,
and know that with God's help you may
do all things merciful and well.'

This prayer now ended, other prayers
ascend from others gathered there,
and hymns and voices bring the news
that earth can now in Glory share.

The rites concluded royally,
the ceremony now complete,
this heaven on earth retired once more,
this lovely creature to her seat.

Scarcely had Preciosa finished her ballad, when with one voice
the illustrious audience and solemn assembly which heard her sing
cried out, 'Sing again, Preciosa, for pennies will fall on you like
showers!'

More than two hundred people were watching the dance and
listening to the song of the gipsies, and at the height of it there
happened to pass by one of the officers stationed in the city. Seeing
all that crowd of people he asked what it was, and was told that
they were listening to the beautiful little gipsy girl who was
singing. The lieutenant went up out of curiosity and listened for a
while, but for the sake of his dignity he did not listen to the ballad
to the end. The little gipsy girl quite captivated him and he sent
one of his pages to tell the old gipsy woman to come with the little

gipsy girls to his house that evening, for he wanted his wife Clara to hear them. The page did as he was told, and the old woman agreed to go.

They finished the dance and the song, and moved on, and at this moment a very smart page came up to Preciosa, and giving her a folded paper said to her, 'Preciosa, sing the ballad which is written on this paper, for it is very good, and I will give you others from time to time, so that you'll get the reputation of being the best ballad-singer in the world.'

'I will be very pleased to learn it,' answered Preciosa, 'and, sir, don't forget to give me the ballads you mention, so long as they are in good taste; and if you want me to pay for them, let's have an agreement that I pay you for every dozen sung, because if you think I'm going to pay you in advance you're very much mistaken.'

'I'll be satisfied with the price of the paper, lady Preciosa!' said the page, 'and what's more, any ballad that's not up to standard or in good taste, we won't count.'

'And it's up to me to choose them,' answered Preciosa.

And with that they went off up the street, and as they were passing a window some gentlemen called out to the gipsy girls. Preciosa looked in at the window, which was a low one, and saw a room which looked cool and richly furnished, with a great number of gentlemen, who were enjoying themselves, some walking about and others playing various games.

'Have you got any winnings for me, kind thirs,' asked Preciosa, who, like a good gipsy, spoke with a lisp, this being one of their tricks, and not a natural impediment.

When they heard Preciosa's voice and saw her face, those who were gambling left off playing and those who were walking about stopped, and one and all went up to the window to see her, for they had already heard about her. And they said,

'Come in, let the little gipsy girls come in, for we'll give them some of our winnings.'

'You'll be the losers,' replied Preciosa, 'if you take any liberties with us.'

'We are gentlemen,' answered one, 'so you can come in here all right, my dear, and be quite sure that none of us will touch so much as your shoe-string, I swear by the order whose insignia I wear.'

And he placed his hand on the insignia of the Order of Calatrava.[6]

'If you want to go in, Preciosa,' said one of the three little gipsy girls who were with her, 'you go in and good luck to you, for I don't intend to go in where there are so many men.'

'Look, Cristina,' replied Preciosa, 'what you need to beware of is one man by himself, and not of so many all together, because the fact that there are a lot of them means that you need not be afraid of being insulted. You can be sure of one thing, Cristina: that the woman who makes up her mind to keep her honour can do so among an army of soldiers. It's true that it's as well to avoid dangerous situations, but they are the secret and not the public ones.'

'Let's go in, Preciosa,' said Cristina, 'for you're wiser than a sage.'

The old woman urged them on and they went in, and as soon as Preciosa had entered, the gentleman who was a knight of Calatrava saw the paper which she had tucked into her dress. Going up to her he took it out, and Preciosa said,

'Don't take that, sir, for it's a ballad which I've just been given, and I haven't even read it yet.'

'And can you read?' asked one.

'And write,' replied the old woman, 'for I've brought up my granddaughter as if she were a scholar's daughter.'

The gentleman unfolded the paper, and seeing that there was a golden crown in it, he said,

'Indeed, Preciosa, this letter's got the cost of the carriage inside; take the crown which is wrapped up in the ballad.'

'Stop,' said Preciosa, 'for this poet has treated me like a pauper. All the same it's more of a miracle for a poet to give me a crown than it is for me to receive it. If his ballads are going to come with this bonus he can send me the whole *Romancero General*;[7] but let him do it one by one, and I'll try them, so that if they're hard, I'll certainly be softened when I receive them.'

Those who heard the little gipsy girl were astonished at her wit and at the graceful way she spoke.

6. The oldest Spanish Military and Religious Order, founded in 1158.
7. A comprehensive collection of traditional Spanish ballads first published in 1600.

'Read it, sir,' she said, 'and read it aloud. We shall see if this poet is as talented as he is generous.'

So the gentleman read as follows:

> Oh, loveliest gipsy maid so fair
> whom everyone congratulates,
> your heart in hardness emulates
> the stone whose 'precious' name you bear.
>
> The truth of this is guaranteed
> by evidence most clear in you,
> and herein there is nothing new –
> that beauty's cold, all are agreed.
>
> If in accordance with your worth,
> your pride increases equally,
> I will not praise too readily
> the day that gave your beauty birth.
>
> A basilisk was born in you,
> that kills the one on whom its eyes
> perchance do fall; you exercise
> a tyranny that's gentle too.
>
> How is it that such beauty came
> from gipsy camp so mean and poor;
> and humble Manzanares' shore
> produced a beauty of such fame?
>
> For this alone this lowly stream
> like golden Tagus now is known,
> more copious than the Ganges grown,
> made precious by Preciosa's name.
>
> Your name spells fortune, but alas,
> ill luck is all you ever bring:
> beauty and kindness never cling
> together as along they pass.
>
> For he who looks upon your face
> the risk of danger thereby courts,
> though pardon's there within your thoughts,
> your beauty deals out death apace.

They say that you and all your tribe
are skilled in witchcraft every one;
but your enchantment all alone
has power more than any bribe.

For havoc in his pathway lies,
whoever looks upon your charms;
enchantment straight away disarms
that one who looks into your eyes.

From strength to strength you go along,
and as you dance we marvel all,
your looks hold every heart in thrall,
and there's enslavement in your song.

A hundred thousand charms are yours,
in speech, in silence, song or glance;
should you approach, withdraw perchance,
love's flame you'll kindle without pause.

Your sway extends to every heart,
and from your charm there's none that's free;
the proof of this you see in me,
a slave content to play his part.

Jewel of love, my Precious one,
these lines are humbly penned for you,
by one whose love, though poor, is true;
who, humbly poor, loves you alone.

'The last verse ends in "poor",' Preciosa observed. 'A bad sign! Lovers must never say they are poor, because at the outset, it seems to me, poverty is a great enemy of love.'

'Who taught you that, girl?' asked one.

'Who do you think taught me it?' replied Preciosa. 'Haven't I got a soul in my body? Am I not fifteen years old? I'm not halt or maimed or deficient in understanding. The wits of gipsy girls are different from those of anyone else; they are always in advance of their years; you'll never find a stupid man, nor a slow woman among the gipsies; for as they depend for their livelihood on being alert and shrewd and up to all the tricks, they're always sharpening their wits, and never let the grass grow under their feet whatever happens. Do you see these girls with me here, silent and looking like stuffed dummies? Well, you put your finger in their mouths and feel their wisdom teeth, and you see what you find. There's not a girl of twelve who doesn't know what girls usually know at twenty-five, for they have the devil and long habit as their teachers, and from them they learn in an hour what you'd expect them to learn in a year.'

What the little gipsy girl said left the audience spellbound, and those who were playing gave them some of the winnings, and even those who were not gave them something. The old woman's box was heavier by thirty *reales*, and off she went, loaded with wealth and as pleased as Punch, with her lambs in tow, to the lieutenant's house, promising to come back with her flock another day to entertain those generous gentlemen.

The lady Doña Clara, the lieutenant's wife, already knew that the little gipsy girls were coming to her house, and she and her maids and ladies-in-waiting, along with those of a neighbour of hers, who had all gathered together to see Preciosa, were eagerly watching out for their arrival. As soon as the gipsy girls came in, Preciosa's beauty shone out like a torch among lesser lights; and everybody ran up to her, some kissing her, others staring at her; some blessing and some praising her.

Doña Clara said, 'There's golden hair for you, and her eyes are just like emeralds!'

Her neighbour was examining her closely, looking her carefully up and down. And struck by a little dimple that Preciosa had on her chin, she said,

'Ah, what a dimple! Everyone who sees her will fall, victim to that dimple!'

One of Doña Clara's attendants who was there, an old man with a long beard, said on hearing this, 'Is this what your ladyship calls a dimple? Either I don't know a dimple when I see one, or this is no dimple, but a tomb for men's desires. Good heavens, the little gipsy girl is so pretty that she couldn't be better if she were made of silver or of sugar. Can you tell fortunes, my girl?'

'In three or four different ways,' answered Preciosa.

'That too?' said Doña Clara. 'Then you must tell mine, for you're as lovely as gold, and silver, and pearls, and carbuncles – as heaven itself, and I can't say more than that.'

'Give the girl your hand and something to cross it with,' said the old woman, 'and you'll see what things she'll tell you, for she knows more than a doctor of medicine.'

The lady put her hand into her bag and found that she hadn't a sou. She asked her servants for a penny, and none of them had one, nor her neighbour either. When Preciosa saw this, she said,

'All crosses are good, simply because they are crosses, but silver or gold crosses are the best, and crossing the palm of the hand with a copper coin, you must know, reduces good fortune, at least, the good fortune I foretell; and so I prefer to make the cross first with a gold crown or with a silver *real*, for I'm like the sacristans, who are delighted when there is a good offering.'

'You have a ready wit, my girl,' said the neighbour.

And turning to the squire, she said to him,

'Señor Contreras, would you have a *real* on you? Give it to me, for as soon as my husband the doctor comes I will give it back to you.'

'Yes, I have,' answered Contreras, 'but I've given it in payment for a supper which I had last night, which cost me twenty-two *maravedis*. If you give me the *maravedis*, I'll go for my *real* straight away.'

'We haven't a penny among us,' said Doña Clara, 'and you ask us for twenty-two *maravedis*. Don't be silly, Contreras, you always did talk nonsense!'

One of the maids present, seeing how short of money they were in the house, said to Preciosa,

'Do you think it matters if you make the cross with a silver thimble?'

'On the contrary,' replied Preciosa, 'the best crosses in the world are made with silver thimbles, provided there are enough of them.

'I have one,' the maiden went on. 'If it's any good, here it is, provided my fortune is told as well.'

'All these fortunes for a thimble?' asked the old gipsy woman. 'Granddaughter, you must be quick, for it's getting dark.'

Preciosa took the thimble and the hand of the lieutenant's wife, and said,

Fairest lady, fairest one,
with hands of purest silver made,
your husband's love is dearer far
than Moorish king for Spanish maid.

Oh dove of sweetness unalloyed,
you still can show a strength as great
as lioness reared in Africa,
Hircania's tiger's worthy mate.

But straight away your anger's gone,
as quick as thought your furies fade,
and then you're just like sugar paste,
a lamb more gentle ne'er was made.

You scold more often than you eat,
you're somewhat jealous of your man;
your husband's playful, and is prone
to try his luck where'er he can.

In days gone by, before you wed,
you won the love of one so fair;
alas for meddlers, they who come
to ruin friendships bring despair.

If you perchance had been a nun,
an abbess now you'd surely be;
four hundred lines upon your hand
show signs of great authority.

I'd rather not tell you this news ...
but never mind, let's have no fear;
you'll be a widow, more than once,
and marry twice again, my dear.

But do not weep, my lady fair,
for gipsies do not always tell
the gospel truth, and so my dear,
please do not weep; all will be well.

For if indeed you die before
your husband, then be sure you may
that consolation for the woe
of widowhood will come his way.

You'll be an heiress, and ere long
you'll have great wealth, and great estate;
a canon of the church your son
will be, though where I hesitate

to say; but not Toledo, no.
A daughter beauteous and fair
you'll have, who if she takes the vow,
will also fill a prelate's chair.

If death does not first intervene,
before four weeks have passed away,
in Salamanca mayor he'll be,
or else in Burgos he'll hold sway.

You have a mole, a sheer delight,
the moon itself beside it pales;
a sun indeed, which carries light
to dark antipodean vales.

And many blind men would give all
to see this beauty here displayed;
and when you laugh, such beauty's there
I'd wish a thousand jokes were made.

Beware of falls, for falls bring ill
and danger most of all, you'll see,
to ladies who upon their hocks
do fall, and lose their dignity.

More things there are that I could say;
on Friday I shall tell them all;
Some are of pleasure, some of pain,
you'll hear them when again I call.

Preciosa finished her fortune-telling, to such good effect that all
those who were there were dying to know theirs, which they
begged her to tell; but she put them off to the following Friday,
when they promised her that they would have silver *reales* to cross
her palm. At this point the lieutenant arrived, and they sang the
praises of the little gipsy girl to him. He made them dance a little,
and was convinced that the praises showered on Preciosa were well
deserved. So, putting his hand into his pocket, he looked as if he

wanted to give her something, and after hunting and shaking and scratching several times, he took it out again, and said,

'By heaven, I haven't a cent! Doña Clara, give a *real* to little Preciosa, and I'll give it to you later.'

'Indeed, that's a good one, my lord! Yes, here's the *real* for you! We haven't been able to find a penny among the lot of us to make the sign of the cross, and here you are wanting a *real*!'

'Well, give her a necklace of yours, or some little thing, for Preciosa will come and see us another day, and we'll give her a better present.'

Doña Clara replied, 'Then to make sure she does come again, I shan't give anything to Preciosa now.'

'If you don't give me anything,' said Preciosa, 'I'll never come back here again! But I will really, just to oblige such distinguished ladies and gentlemen. I'll take it for granted that you're not going to give me anything, and save myself the trouble of expecting it. Take bribes, lieutenant, take bribes, and you'll have money, and don't try to change the customs or you'll die of hunger. Look, my lady, I've heard it said round here (and although I'm young, I realize that it's not just a saying) that one has to extract money from one's office to make good the claims at the end of one's term of service and to secure new appointments.'

'That's what they say, and indeed that's what the unscrupulous ones do,' replied the lieutenant, 'but the judge who carries out his duties properly will not have to pay any fine, and carrying out his duties properly will be the best recommendation he'll have to get him another post.'

'That's a very pious way to talk, lieutenant,' answered Preciosa. 'Go on like this and we'll cut off bits of your clothes as relics.'

'You know a great deal, Preciosa,' said the lieutenant. 'Just wait. I'll think of some way for you to meet their Majesties, for you're a piece fit for a king.'

'They'll want me as a buffoon,' answered Preciosa, 'and as I shan't know how to play the part, it'll be a disaster. If they wanted me for my good sense they might get me, but in some palaces buffoons get on better than clever people. I'm quite happy to be a poor gipsy, and let my fate lead me wherever heaven may decree.'

'Come, girl,' said the old gipsy woman. 'Don't talk any more, for you've talked a good deal, and you know more than I have taught you; don't get too subtle, or you'll get out of your depth; talk about things becoming to your age, and don't meddle with things which are above you, for there's always the risk of a fall.'

'These gipsies have the very devil in them,' said the lieutenant.

The gipsy girls said good-bye, and as they were going, the lady-in-waiting with the thimble said,

'Preciosa, tell my fortune or give me back my thimble, for I haven't got anything to do my sewing with.'

'My dear lady,' answered Preciosa, 'you can reckon that I've already told it, and get yourself another thimble. And don't do any sewing until Friday, when I'll come back and tell you more fortunes and adventures than you'll find in a chivalry-book.[8]'

So off they went, and joined up with the farm girls who leave Madrid at nightfall, to go back to their villages. The gipsy girls always joined up with a crowd of them for safety, for the old woman lived in continual fear lest her Preciosa be attacked.

One morning as they were going back to Madrid with the rest of the little gipsy girls to make a bit of money, in a little valley about five hundred yards before you reach the city they saw an elegant young man in rich travelling clothes. The sword and dagger he carried were a blaze of gold, as they say; his hat had an expensive-looking band and was adorned with plumes of various colours. The little gipsy girls were struck by the sight of him, and looked at him long and hard, amazed that at this time of day such a handsome youth should be in a place like this, on foot and alone. He went up to them, and speaking to the old gipsy, he said to her,

'Will you and Preciosa do me the favour of letting me have a word or two with you alone, for it will be to your advantage?'

'So long as we don't go far out of our way and are not delayed too much,' answered the old woman.

8. The romances of chivalry, of which the most famous was *Amadís de Gaula*, whose first extant edition dates from 1508, were highly imaginative tales of adventure enormously popular in the sixteenth century. It was through reading too many of them that the hero of Cervantes's masterpiece *Don Quixote* was reputed to have been turned mad.

She called Preciosa, they went on about twenty yards, and as they were standing there, the young man said to them,

'I come as a slave to the wit and beauty of Preciosa. In spite of all my efforts I can't help myself. I, my ladies (for I shall always give you this name, if heaven favours my purpose), am a gentleman, as this insignia will show' – and unfastening his cloak he revealed on his breast one of the most distinguished in Spain – 'I am the son of so-and-so' (his name is not disclosed here for good reasons) 'and am under his guardianship and protection; I am an only son, and can expect to inherit a reasonable estate. My father is here at court trying to secure an appointment, for which he has already been recommended, and which he is almost certain to get. And although my rank and nobility are as I've told you and as you can almost certainly see for yourselves, nevertheless I should like to be a noble of the highest rank to exalt my humble Preciosa, and make her my equal and my lady. I do not seek her hand in order to deceive her, for in the sincerity of the love which I have for her there is no room for any kind of deceit. I want only to serve her in the way that will please her best: her will is mine. As far as she is concerned my heart is made of wax, on which she may make whatever impression she wishes. But her wishes will be preserved, not in wax, but as if they were sculptured in marble, that will resist all the attacks of time. If you believe this to be true, my hopes will not suffer any discouragement; but if you do not believe me, your doubt will always keep me in fear. My name is this,' – and he said it – 'my father's name I have already told you; the house where he lives is in such and such a street, and the address is this; he has neighbours who can tell you about him, and even those who are not neighbours too; for the rank and name of my father, and mine, are not so obscure that they are unknown in the palace courtyards, and even throughout the capital. I have a hundred golden crowns here to give you as an earnest and indication of what I intend; because he who gives his soul won't withhold his property.'

While the gentleman was saying this, Preciosa was looking at him attentively, and there was no doubt that his arguments and his appearance made a good impression on her. Turning to the old woman, she said:

'Forgive me, grandmother, if I take the liberty of replying to this gentleman who is so much in love.'

'Answer as you wish, granddaughter,' said the old woman, 'for I know that you've enough sense to deal with anything.'

And Preciosa said,

'Sir, although I am a gipsy girl, poor and humbly born, I have a certain fancy inside me which carries me on to great things. I am not moved by promises, nor influenced by gifts, nor swayed by signs of submissiveness, nor by lovers' favours; and although I am only fifteen (or will be this Michaelmas according to my grandmother's reckoning), I am already grown up in my way of thinking, and am ahead of what my age would lead one to expect, more through my natural gifts than through experience. But at any rate, I know that passion in those who have only recently fallen in love is so impulsive and indiscreet that it quite unhinges one's will; and when this will comes up against obstacles, it hurls itself in the most crazy way after what it desires, and imagining that it is going to achieve the bliss that it sees, it lands instead in the hell of disappointment. If it achieves what it desires the desire diminishes with the possession of the desired object, and when perhaps as a result of this the eyes of understanding are opened one realizes that one should hate what previously was the object of adoration. This fear creates in me such caution that I have no faith in words and am often suspicious of deeds.

'Only one jewel I possess, and to me it is worth more than life itself; that jewel is my integrity and virginity, and I shall not sell it in exchange for promises or gifts, precisely because then it will be something you can get for money; and if it can be purchased it will be of very little value. Neither tricks nor frauds will take it away from me; for I am determined to go to the grave with it, and perhaps to heaven, rather than to risk the danger of exposing it to illusions and fancies which assail or threaten it. The flower of virginity is one which should not allow itself to be offended even by the imagination. Once the rose has been cut from the bush, how quickly and easily it fades! One touches it, another sniffs it, another strips it of its leaves, and it finally breaks in pieces in clumsy hands. If, sir, you come only in search of this prize, you shall have it only if it is wrapped in the bonds and ties of marriage; for if virginity is to be surrendered, it must be only under the sacred tie of marriage, which is not to lose it, but to use it in a kind of trade which promises rich profits.

'If you want to be my husband, I will be yours; but first there will have to be many conditions and inquiries. To begin with, I shall have to find out if you are who you say; then, when this has been proved true, you will have to leave your parents' house and exchange it for our camps, and taking gipsy garb, spend two years in our schools, during which time I shall satisfy myself as to what sort of person you are, and you will want to satisfy yourself about me. At the end of this time, if you are pleased with me and I with you, I will give myself to you as your wife; but until then I shall be like a sister and a humble servant to you. And you must bear in mind that during the period of this novitiate you might recover your sight, which you must have lost now or which at any rate must be blurred; and you might then see that you must flee from what you now so zealously pursue. And when once you've recovered your lost liberty, any fault can be pardoned if you truly repent. If on these conditions you want to be admitted as a soldier in our troop, it's up to you, for if you fall short of one of these conditions, you shall touch no finger of mine.'

The young man was astonished and dumbfounded at Preciosa's arguments, and stood looking at the floor as if he were wondering what to say in reply. When Preciosa saw this, she went on,

'This is not a matter of such slight importance, that it can or ought to be decided on in the short time we have now. Go back, sir, to Madrid, and consider at your leisure what seems to be the right thing for you, and you can speak to me at this very same spot on any feast day you like, on the way to or from Madrid.'

To this the nobleman replied,

'When heaven decreed that I should love you, Preciosa mine, I resolved to do for you whatever you might choose to ask of me, although the thought never occurred to me that you would ask what you are asking me now; but since it is your pleasure that my will should be adjusted and accommodated to yours, reckon me a gipsy from now on, and put me to all the tests you like, for you will always find me the same as I now declare myself to be. Let me know when you want me to change my dress. As far as I'm concerned I should like it to be straight away, for I'll deceive my parents on the pretext of going to Flanders, and get enough money to last for a few days; and it'll take me about a week to arrange to leave. I'll be able to hoodwink my companions so as to carry out my plan. What I ask of you is – if I may dare to ask or beg anything of you – that apart from today, when you will be finding out about my rank and that of my parents, you do not go any more to Madrid; for I should not like any of the all too frequent occasions which may arise there to deprive me of the good fortune which is costing me so much.'

'Indeed no, gallant sir,' answered Preciosa, 'you must know that my liberty must never be restricted, or disturbed and burdened by jealousy; and please understand that I shall never take such liberties that anyone can fail to see from miles off that my good character will not suffer because of my free and easy ways. And the first burden I wish to impose on you is that of asking you to trust me, and bear in mind that lovers who start by showing jealousy are either foolish or foolhardy.'

'You've got the very devil in you, girl,' said the old gipsy woman at this point. 'For you say things which you wouldn't expect from a student of Salamanca. You know about love, you know about jealousy, you know about confidence. How can this be? You amaze me, and I'm listening to you as to someone possessed, who speaks Latin without ever having learned it.'

'Be quiet, grandmother,' answered Preciosa, 'and remember that all the things you hear me say are nonsense and not to be taken seriously, compared with the serious ones that I'm keeping to myself.'

All that Preciosa said, and all the good sense she showed merely added fuel to the flames which burned in the heart of the lovesick young noble. They finally agreed to see each other in a week's time in the same place, where he would come to give an account of the state of his affairs, and the gipsies would have had time to verify the truth of what he had told them. The young man took out an embroidered purse, in which he said there were a hundred gold crowns, and gave them to the old woman. Preciosa was quite unwilling for her to take them, but the gipsy woman said,

'Hush, child, for the best indication that this gentleman has given that he has really surrendered is the fact that he has handed over his weapons, and giving, on any occasion, has always been the sign of a generous heart. Remember the proverb which says, "God helps those who help themselves." And what's more, I don't want gipsies to lose for my sake the reputation they've had for centuries of being grasping and on the make. Do you want me to reject a hundred crowns, Preciosa, real gold crowns, which can be sewn up in the tuck of a skirt worth no more than two *reales*, and kept there as quiet as can be? And if any of our children, grandchildren or relations should fall, through some misfortune, into the hands of the law, can there be any better favour to reach the ear of the judge or notary than these crowns, if they get to their purses? Three times, and for three different crimes, I've seen myself almost at the whipping-post, and on one occasion a silver jug brought me freedom, on another a string of pearls, and on another forty *reales* which I had changed into coppers, giving twenty *reales* overhead on the deal. Remember, girl, that we are in a very dangerous business, full of traps and dangers, and that no defence can help and protect us more readily than the invincible weapons of King Philip: no one can pass that "plus ultra". For at the sight of a doubloon with a double face the faces of the attorney and his deadly agents beam with delight – those persecutors of us poor gipsies, who would rather strip and flay us than a highwayman. For however torn and shabby we look, they never think we are poor, and they say that we are like the jerkins of the ruffians of Belmonte which are torn and greasy, but full of doubloons.'

'For heaven's sake, grandmother, don't say any more, for you look like producing so many laws in favour of keeping the money that you will use up all those in the codebooks. Keep them, and much good may they do you, and may it please God to bury them in a grave where they will never again see the light of the sun, or need to see it. We shall have to give our companions something, for they've been waiting for us for a long time, and they must be getting fed up.'

'They're as likely to see coins like these,' replied the old woman, 'as they are to see the Grand Turk[9]. Perhaps this good gentleman will look and see if he has some silver coins left, or coppers, which

9. The Sultan of Turkey.

he can distribute among them, for they won't want much to make them happy.'

'Yes, I have some,' said the young man.

And he took out of his pocket three *reales*, which he distributed among the three little gipsy girls, and which made them more pleased and happy than a theatrical producer who hears himself lauded to the skies with his rival looking on.

In short, they agreed, as we've said, that they would come there again in a week's time, and that when he was a gipsy the young man should be called Andrés Caballero, for there were already some in the company with that surname.

Andrés (for we shall give him this name from now on) did not dare to kiss Preciosa; instead, he looked at her in such a way that he seemed to leave his heart behind, and went back into Madrid; and they, delighted, went off too. Preciosa, more out of kindness than of love for the generous and handsome Andrés, was already anxious to find out if he was the person he said he was. She went into Madrid, and had only gone through a few streets when she met the poet page who had given her the verses and the crown, and when he saw her, he went up to her and said,

'How glad I am to see you, Preciosa. Did you by any chance read the verses I gave you the other day?'

To which Preciosa replied,

'Before I answer a word, you must give me an assurance about one thing, and swear it by whatever you love most.'

'This is an oath,' replied the page, 'which although it may cost me my life I shall not on any account refuse.'

'Well, what I want you to assure me about', said Preciosa, 'is whether you are by any lucky chance a poet.'

'If I were,' replied the page, 'it would indeed be by a lucky chance. For you must know, Preciosa, that very few deserve this name of poet, and I am not one of them, but simply one who is fond of poetry. And for my purposes, I am not going to ask or to look for poems by anyone else. Those I gave you are mine, and the ones I'm giving you now too; but I'm no poet, and God forbid that I should be.'

'Is it such a bad thing to be a poet?' asked Preciosa.

'It is not a bad thing,' said the page, 'but to be a poet alone doesn't seem a good idea to me. One must use poetry like a most precious jewel, whose owner does not wear it every day, or show it off to everybody all the time, but when it is appropriate and right to display it. Poetry is a maiden of great beauty, chaste, pure, discreet, shrewd, modest, and extremely circumspect. She is a friend of solitude: the fountains give her pleasure, the meadows consolation, the trees comfort, the flowers delight; and, in short, she brings pleasure and profit to all who come into contact with her.'

'Nevertheless,' replied Preciosa, 'I have heard it said that she is very poor, even to the point of beggary.'

'Rather the opposite,' said the page. 'There is no poet who is not rich, for they all live content with their lot, a philosophy which few attain. But tell me, Preciosa, what moved you to ask this question?'

'I was moved to ask it,' answered Preciosa, 'because as I consider all or most poets to be poor, I was astonished to receive that golden crown which you gave me wrapped up in your verses. But now that I know that you are not a poet, but one who is merely fond of poetry, I can see that you might possibly be rich, although I doubt it, because your taste for making verses must needs diminish whatever property you have; for there is no poet, they say, who can keep the property he has, or gain any if he has none already.'

'Well, I am not one of those,' replied the page. 'I write verses, and I am neither rich nor poor; and without regretting it or putting it down to business expenses, as the Genoese do with their guests, I can well afford to give a crown or two to anyone I wish. Take this second paper, my precious pearl, and the second crown which is wrapped up in it, without bothering to consider whether I am a poet or not. I only want you to bear in mind and to believe that he who gives you this would gladly possess the riches of Midas in order to give them to you.'

With that he gave her a paper, and when Preciosa felt it she found that the crown was inside it, and said,

'This paper will live for many years, because it has two souls: one belonging to the crown, and the other to the verses, which are always full of "hearts and souls". But, Mr Page, you must know that I don't want all these souls, and if you don't take the one out, you may be sure I shan't accept the other. I like you as a poet, and not for your gifts; and if you do this our friendship will be a lasting one; for one can more easily do without a crown, however useful it may be, than the making of a ballad.'

'Since, Preciosa,' replied the page, 'you want to oblige me to be poor, do not reject the soul which I am sending you in this paper, and give me back the crown; for if only you touch it with your hand, I shall consider it a sacred relic as long as my life shall last.'

Preciosa took the crown out of the paper, which she kept, not wishing to read it in the street. The page said good-bye, and went off as happy as could be, thinking that Preciosa was his, since she had spoken to him so kindly. And as her plan was to look for Andrés's father's house, without wishing to stop to dance anywhere, she soon reached the street where it was, a street which she knew very well; and when she had gone half-way along, she raised her eyes to some gilded iron balconies, which she had been given as a landmark. She saw there a gentleman of about fifty, wearing an insignia in the form of a red cross on his breast, and with a grave and venerable air. As soon as he saw the little gipsy girl, he said,

'Come up, girls, for they'll give you alms here.'

Hearing this, three other gentlemen came to the balcony, among them the lovesick Andrés, who, when he saw Preciosa, went pale and almost fainted, so startled was he at seeing her. All the little gipsy girls went up, but the old woman stayed down below to find out from the servants whether the things that Andrés had said were true. When the little gipsies came into the room the old gentleman was saying to the others,

'This must be the beautiful little gipsy girl they say is going round Madrid.'

'It is,' replied Andrés, 'and there's no doubt that she's the most lovely creature you've ever seen.'

'So they say,' said Preciosa, who heard it all as she came in, 'but indeed they must be exaggerating out of all proportion. I can well believe that I am pretty; but as beautiful as they say – not on your life.'

'By my son Don Juanico's life,' said the old man, 'you're even more beautiful than they say, my lovely gipsy.'

'And who is your son Don Juanico?' asked Preciosa.

'This young fellow beside you,' answered the gentleman.

'I thought', said Preciosa, 'that you were swearing by some child of two. This is a very dashing Don Juanico, upon my word! Indeed he could well be married and, according to the lines of his forehead, will be within three years, and very happy too, if he doesn't change his mind between now and then.'

'By Jove,' said one of the company, 'the little gipsy girl can tell fortunes by reading lines.'

Whereupon the three little gispy girls who were with Preciosa all made for a corner of the room, and huddled together in whispers so as not to be heard. Cristina said,

'Girls, this is the gentleman who gave us the three *reales* this morning.'

'Indeed it is,' they answered, 'but don't let us say so, or say anything at all, if he does not mention it. For all we know he doesn't want to be recognized.'

While this was going on among the three of them, Preciosa said in answer to the remark about fortunes,

'What I see with my eyes, I can confirm with my finger: I know that Don Juanico, even without the lines on his forehead, is somewhat amorously inclined, impetuous and hasty; and much given to promising things which appear impossible. God forbid that he should be untruthful in any way, for this would be worse than anything. He is going on a journey a long way from here, but things will turn out differently from what he thinks; man proposes and God disposes; he may think he's going to Oñez and end up in Gamboa.'

To this Don Juan replied:

'Indeed, my little gipsy, in many ways you have guessed right about the sort of person I am; but as far as being untruthful is concerned, *you* are very far from the truth, because I pride myself on telling it come what may. As regards the long journey, you have guessed right; for without doubt, God willing, I shall leave for Flanders in four or five days, although you threaten me with a change of direction, and I should not like any mishap to disturb my course.'

'Be quiet, young man,' answered Preciosa, 'and commend

yourself to God, for all will be well. Bear in mind that I know nothing about what I'm saying; and it's no wonder, since I talk a great deal and guess a lot, that occasionally I am right. I should like to succeed in persuading you not to go, but to stay put with your parents, to comfort their old age; because I am not in favour of these comings and goings to Flanders, especially for young men of such tender years as yours. Wait until you are a little older, when you can bear the trials of war, especially as there's plenty of warfare in your own house anyway. Your heart is assailed by many a battle of love. Keep calm, keep calm, you restless boy, and look what you are doing before you marry; and give us some alms for heaven's sake and your own, for I'm sure you are well born. And if in addition you are truthful, I shall boast that I've guessed right in everything I've said to you.'

'I have told you already, girl,' answered Don Juan, who was about to become Andrés Caballero, 'that you are right in everything except in your fear that I am not very truthful, for in this you are quite wrong, without any doubt. The promise I gave you in the country, I shall fulfil in the city or anywhere else, without having to be asked; for one who is in any way untruthful cannot pride himself on being a gentleman. My father will give you alms in the name of God and in my name; for the fact is that I gave everything I had this morning to some ladies, who if they were as amiable as they were beautiful, especially one of them, I don't know where it would lead.'

When Cristina heard this, she said to the other gipsy girls, taking good care again not to be heard, 'Girls, strike me down if he isn't talking about the three *reales* that he gave us this morning.'

'That can't be,' answered one of the other two, 'because he said they were ladies, and we are not ladies; and being as truthful as he says he is, he should not have lied about this.'

'A lie is of no great importance,' answered Cristina, 'if it is told without prejudice to anyone and to the advantage and credit of the person who tells it. But all the same, I see that they're not giving us anything, and we've not been asked to dance.'

At this point the old gipsy woman came up and said, 'Granddaughter, it's time to finish, for it's late and there's a lot to do and more to say.'

'What about, grandmother?' asked Preciosa. 'Is it a question of a boy or a girl?'

'A boy, and a very handsome one,' answered the old woman. 'Come along, and you'll hear some really wonderful things.'

'God grant that he does not die as soon as he's born,' said Preciosa.

'It'll all be taken good care of,' replied the old woman. 'At any rate so far this birth has gone well, and the child is a treasure.'

'Has some lady given birth to a child?' asked Andrés Caballero's father.

'Yes, sir,' replied the gipsy woman, 'but the birth was kept so secret that only Preciosa and I and one other person know of it; and so we can't say who it is.'

'And we don't want to know here either,' said one of the company, 'for the lady who trusts a secret to your tongues and puts her honour under your protection is in a sorry plight.'

'Not all of us are bad,' answered Preciosa. 'It may be that among us there are some who take as much pride in keeping secrets and telling the truth as the most upright man in this room. Let's be off, grandmother, for they don't think much of us here. But indeed we are no thieves and we don't ask favours of anyone!'

'Don't be angry, Preciosa,' said the father, 'for at least as far as you are concerned, I guess that no one could suspect anything amiss. For the goodness of your face vouches for you and is the guarantor of your good works. Please dance a little with your companions, for I have a gold doubloon here, with two heads, although neither head is as pretty as yours, even if they do belong to royalty.'

As soon as the old woman heard this, she said,

'Come on girls, hitch up your skirts, and let's give these gentlemen a treat.'

Preciosa took the tambourine, and they pirouetted about, linked arms and parted with such grace and ease that the eyes of all those who watched them were glued to their feet, and especially those of Andrés, which followed Preciosa as if his whole happiness was centred on her. But luck turned his happiness to torment, for it happened that in the flurry of the dance Preciosa dropped the paper which the page had given her, and as soon as it fell, the man who did not have a very high opinion of the gipsy girls picked it up, and opening it immediately, said,

'Well, we have a little sonnet here! Stop the dance and listen to it, for, if the first verse is anything to go by, it's not at all bad.'

Preciosa was upset, not knowing what was in it, and she begged them not to read it and to give it back to her. But her efforts simply spurred on Andrés's desire to hear it. Finally, the gentleman read it aloud, and this is how it went:

> When Preciosa plays the tambourine,
> And its sweet sound flows out upon the breeze,
> her hands drop pearls of music on the green;
> her lips shed flowers all the world to please.
>
> The soul remains enrapt, all sense departs,
> when harmony divine this goddess plays;
> her actions pure and wholesome win all hearts!
> Her reputation earns her heaven's praise.
>
> Suspended from the finest of her hair
> a thousand hearts hang helpless; at her feet
> love's arrows lay her victims powerless there;
>
> she blinds and dazzles with her two suns' light.
> Love through their power her sway for ever holds;
> gifts unsuspected she from sight withholds.

'By heaven,' said the man who read the sonnet, 'the poet who wrote this has some talent.'

'He is not a poet, sir, but a very gallant page and a man of honour.'

Mind what you've said, Preciosa, and what you are going to say, for these words are not just praises of the page, but lances which are piercing the very heart of Andrés, who is listening to them. Do you want visible proof, girls? Well, look there and you'll see that he's fainted in his chair, and he's sweating as if he were on the point of death. Don't make the mistake, young lady, of thinking that Andrés loves you so little that the slightest lack of thought on your part will not hurt and upset him. Go up to him straight away, and say something in his ear which will go straight to his heart, and bring him round again. If you go about with sonnets every day written in praise of you, just see what a state you'll have him in!

What you've read really happened; for Andrés, when he heard the sonnet, fell victim to a thousand jealous thoughts. He did not faint; but he lost his colour to such an extent that, when his father saw him, he said to him,

'What's the matter, Don Juan? You're so pale that it looks as if you are about to faint.'

'Wait,' said Preciosa at this juncture. 'Let me say a few words in his ear, and you'll see that he won't faint.'

And going up to him, she said to him, almost without moving her lips,

'That's a fine spirit for a gipsy! How will you be able to put up with the water test, if you can't stand a simple paper one?'

And making half a dozen crosses over his heart, she left him, and then Andrés came to and gave signs that Preciosa's words had done him good. Then the double-headed doubloon was handed to Preciosa, and she told her companions that she would change it and share it with them honourably. Andrés's father asked her to write down the words that she had said to Don Juan, for he was very keen to know them. She said that she was very willing to tell him what they were; and that he should realize that, although they seemed nonsense, they had a special power to do good to those who had weak hearts or suffered from dizziness in the head. The words were:

> Oh little head, oh little head,
> be steady, steady, don't you fall.
> Have patience, patience, that is all.
> Its blessings pray on you be shed;
> by trust be led,
> and never stray
> in thought away.
> Marvels you'll find
> that stun the mind;
> with God in front
> no giant shall you ever daunt.

'If you say just half these words, and make six crosses over the heart of the person who is suffering from dizziness in the head,' said Preciosa, 'he'll be as fit as a fiddle.'

When the old gipsy woman heard the incantation and the trick, she was amazed, and Andrés even more so, seeing that it was all her own clever invention. They kept the sonnet, because Preciosa did not want to ask for it back, in case she gave Andrés another bad turn; for she was well aware by now, without being told again, what it meant to give jealous shocks and starts to lovers.

The gipsy girls said good-bye, and as they went off, Preciosa said to Don Juan, 'Look sir, any day this week is suitable for departures, and there's not one that's unlucky. Set off as quickly as you can, for a pleasant, free and easy life awaits you if you are willing to adapt yourself to it.'

'The soldier's life is not so free, to my way of thinking,' answered Don Juan, 'that there's not a good deal more submission to authority than there is liberty; but all the same, I shall see what I can do.'

'You will see more than you think,' answered Preciosa, 'and God be with you and bring you to a happy end, as you well deserve.'

With these last words Andrés went off happily, and the gipsy girls even more happily. They changed the doubloon and shared it equally among them, although the old woman always took a share and a half of the pool, both because of her seniority and because she was the one who guided and directed them in their dances, games and even in their tricks.

Finally the day came when Andrés Caballero turned up one morning in the place where he had made his first appearance, on a hired mule, without any servant at all. He found Preciosa and her grandmother there, and as soon as they recognized him, they received him with great rejoicing. He asked them to take him to the encampment before daybreak and before his tracks could be discovered, in case anyone should try to follow him. The gipsies, who had deliberately come by themselves, turned round, and shortly afterwards reached their huts. Andrés went into one, which was the biggest in the camp, and straight away ten or twelve gipsies came to see him, all of them young and all handsome and well built. The old gipsy woman had already told them about the new companion who was coming to join them, and did not need to urge them to secrecy; for, as has already been said, you've never seen anyone so careful and so strict when it comes to keeping secrets. Then they looked at the mule, and one of them said,

'We can sell this one in Toledo on Thursday.'

'Indeed not!' said Andrés, 'because there's not a hired mule that isn't known to all the mule-boys who travel the length and breadth of Spain.'

'Good heavens, Señor Andrés,' said one of the gipsies, 'even if the mule had more distinguishing signs on it than those which are to precede the Day of Judgement, we should change it so that the mother who gave birth to it or the owner who reared it wouldn't recognize it.'

'All the same,' answered Andrés, 'this time my opinion must be accepted and followed. This mule must be killed, and buried where even the bones can't be found.'

'What a sin!' said another gipsy. 'Must one rob an innocent creature of its life? Don't let good, kind Andrés say such a thing. Just look carefully at it now so that all the distinguishing signs are imprinted on your memory, and let me take it away, and if you know it in two hours' time, let me be basted like a slave on the run.'

'I shall not give my consent on any account,' said Andrés, 'to the mule's remaining alive, however convincingly you disguise it. I am afraid of being discovered if she's not safely underground. And if it's a question of the profit which might arise from selling it, I'm not so short of cash that I can't pay as my entrance fee to this company the price of a mule or two.'

'Then since Don Andrés Caballero wishes it,' said another gipsy, 'let the innocent creature die, and God knows it grieves me, both because it's so young and hasn't got all its teeth (which is a most rare thing for a hired mule), and because it must be a fast one, for it has no scab on its flanks nor sores from spurs.'

The killing was postponed until nightfall, and for the rest of that day the ceremonies connected with Andrés's initiation as a gipsy were carried out. They cleared one of the best huts in the camp, and decorated it with branches and sedge; and when Andrés had sat down on the stump of a cork oak, they put a hammer and tongs in his hand, and to the sound of two guitars played by two of the gipsies, they made him caper about a few times. Then they bared one of his arms, and with a new silk ribbon and a stick they gave it a couple of gentle twists. Preciosa was present during all this, and many of the other gipsy women, old and young, some of whom looked at him with admiration, some with love; so dashing was Andrés that even the gipsy men were greatly taken with him.

When these ceremonies were over, an old gipsy took Preciosa by the hand, and standing in front of Andrés he said,

'This girl, who is the cream of all the most beautiful gipsy girls in Spain that we know, we give to you, as wife, or as mistress; because in this matter you can do whatever you best please, for our free and easy life is not subject to finicky ceremonial. Examine her well, and see if she pleases you, or if you see in her anything which you don't like, and if you do see anything, choose from among these girls here the one you like best, for we will give you whichever one you choose. But remember that once she has been chosen, you must not leave her for another, nor must you meddle or interfere with any married woman or unmarried girl. We keep inviolate the law of friendship: no one asks for what belongs to another; we live free from the bitter plague of jealousy. Among us, although there are many cases of incest, there is never one of adultery; and when adultery does take place with someone's wife, or there is some misdeed on the part of a mistress, we don't go to court to ask for satisfaction. We are the judges and executioners of our wives and mistresses; we kill them and bury them in the mountains and deserts just as readily as if they were beasts of prey. No relative will avenge them, and no father will ask satisfaction from us for their death. With this fear hanging over them they do their best to remain pure; and we, as I have already told you, live secure. We have few things which are not common to us all, except our wives or mistresses, for we want each to have the one destined by fate for him. Among us old age is as much a reason for divorce as death; anyone who wishes can abandon his aged wife, if he is young, and choose another who befits his years.

'With these and other laws and statutes we lead a happy life; we are lords of the fields and crops, of the forests, of the woods, of the springs and of the rivers. The woods offer us free fuel, the trees give us fruits, the vines grapes, the gardens vegetables, the springs water, the rivers fish, and the preserves game; the rocks give us their shade, the valleys fresh air, the caves houses. For us, the inclemencies of the weather are soft breezes, the snows bring us refreshment, the rain provides us with baths, the winds are music and the lightning torches; for us the hard earth is a mattress of soft feathers; the tanned skin of our bodies is an impenetrable armour to defend us; our fleetness of foot is unimpeded by fetters, never halted by ravines nor checked by walls; our courage is not daunted by bonds, nor damaged by pulleys, nor stifled by gags, nor held in check by the stocks. We make no distinction between yes and no when it suits us; we always take more pride in being martyrs than confessors; for our use beasts of burden are reared in the country and purses are cut in the city. No eagle or other bird pounces more swiftly on its prey than we pounce on opportunities for gain; and finally, we have many talents which come to our aid: for in prison we sing, in the stocks we are silent, by day we work and by night we steal, or rather, we take care that no one shall be careless about where he puts his property. We are not bothered by the fear of losing our honour, nor are we disturbed by the ambition to increase it; nor do we maintain factions, nor lose sleep trying to write petitions, or keep up with magnates, or ask for favours. We cherish these huts and camps of ours as if they were gilded roofs and sumptuous palaces; our Flemish scenes and landscapes are those which nature offers us in these lofty crags and snowy peaks, these broad meadows and dense woods which rise up before us at every step. We are homespun astronomers, because we almost always sleep under the open sky, and always know what time it is, whether it be day or night; we watch the dawn sweep away the stars from the sky, and fill the air with joy, cooling the water and moistening the earth; and then after her comes the sun, "gilding the heights" (as the poet said) and "curling the mountain tops". We are not afraid of being frozen when its rays fall fully upon us, nor burned when they strike us directly from above; we regard the sun and the frost with as much indifference as we face shortage and abundance. In short, we are people who live by our industry and our ready tongue, and without listening to the old saying "Church, Navy or Court are the only ways to get on"; we have what we want, for we are content with what we have. All this I have said, generous youth, so that you may not be ignorant of the life upon which you have entered and the customs you are to adopt, and which I have sketched for you. You will discover many many more things about it as time goes on, no less worthy of consideration than those you have heard.'

And having said this the eloquent old gipsy fell silent, and the novice said that he was delighted to have been taught such worthy statutes, and that he intended to make his profession in that order which was so well founded on reason and on political principles, his only regret being that he had not got to know this carefree life earlier; that from that very moment he renounced the profession of gentleman and the vanity of his illustrious lineage, and that he would submit it all to the yoke or rather to the laws whereby they lived, since they were satisfying his wish to serve them by offering such a rich reward, in the form of the divine Preciosa, for whom he would abandon crowns and empires, desiring them only that he might serve her.

To this Preciosa replied,

'Since these experts in the law have discovered through their laws that I am yours and have given me into your power, I have discovered by the law of my will, which is the strongest of all, that I do not wish to belong to you except on the conditions which we agreed between us before you came here. You must live for two years in our company before you may enjoy mine, so that you have no regrets at your haste, and so that I may not be deceived through wanting to go too fast. Conditions are stronger than laws; you know what conditions I have imposed on you: if you want to keep them, I may be yours and you mine; and if not, the mule has not yet been killed, your clothes are untouched, and not a mite of your money has gone. You have only been absent for one day, and what remains of it you can use as an occasion to consider what best befits you. These gentlemen may indeed hand over my body to you, but not my soul, which is free, and was born free, and will be free as long as I wish. If you remain, I shall think well of you for it; if you go back, I shall not despise you, because, as it seems to me, love's frenzy runs unchecked until it sees reason or is undeceived. I should not like you to treat me like the hunter, who, as soon as he catches the hare he is chasing, seizes it and then drops it to chase after another which is running away from him. There are eyes which are so easily deceived that at first sight tinsel seems to them as good as gold; but they soon come to recognize the difference between the true and the false. This beauty which you say I have, and which you esteem more highly than the sun and value above gold, how am I to know whether seen at close quarters it will not seem to you to be a shadow, and when you touch it, you will realize that it is a sham? I'm giving you two years to test and consider what you should choose or what it is right for you to reject; for the prize, which once bought one can only dispose of at death, must be looked at long and hard again and again, and its faults and virtues examined. For I am not governed by the barbarous and shameless licence which these relatives of mine have taken upon themselves to leave their wives, or punish them, when they fancy; and as I have no intention of doing anything which calls for punishment, I do not wish to associate with anyone who discards me simply because he pleases to do so.'

'You're right, Preciosa,' Andrés said at this point, 'and so, if you want me to set your fears and suspicions at rest by swearing that I shall not depart in one detail from the orders to which you subject me, consider what sort of oath you want me to take, or what other assurance I can give you, for you will find me ready for anything.'

'The oaths and promises that the captive makes in order to be given his liberty are rarely fulfilled once liberty is achieved,' said Preciosa, 'and it seems to me that those of the lover are of this kind, for to attain his desire he will promise Mercury's wings or Jupiter's thunderbolts, as a certain poet promised me, swearing by the Styx. I do not want oaths, Señor Andrés, nor do I want promises; I want only to submit the whole affair to the test of this apprenticeship, and it will be up to me to defend myself if you should attempt to offend me.'

'So be it,' answered Andrés. 'I ask only one thing of these gentlemen who are now my companions, and that is that they do not force me to steal anything, at least for a month or so, because it seems to me that I shall not succeed as a thief unless I first receive a good many lessons.'

'Don't worry, young man,' said the old gipsy, 'for here we shall instruct you so that you'll be a real past master in the profession;

and once you know it, you'll like it so much that you'll lick your fingers over it. It's great fun going out empty in the morning and coming back loaded to the camp at night.'

'I've seen some of those empty people come back loaded with lashes,' said Andrés.

'You can't catch trout, as they say,' replied the old man. 'Everything in this life is subject to its dangers, and thieving is subject to the risk of the galleys, of lashings and even of hanging. Just because a ship runs into a storm or sinks others are not expected to give up sailing the seas. A fine thing it would be if because war consumes men and horses there should be no soldiers! What's more, anyone in our company who is beaten by order of the court bears an insignia on his back which he considers better than the finest one he could wear on his chest. The point is not to land up kicking the air, in the flower of our youth and after only one or two crimes. For a blow on the back, or a bit of shovelling water in the galleys, we don't care a bean. Andrés, my boy, take it easy under our wings in this nest of ours, for in due course we'll let you fly, and to a place from which you'll certainly not return without a catch; and as I've said, you'll lick your fingers after every theft.'

'Well to make up', said Andrés, 'for what I might steal in this period you're letting me off, I want to share out two hundred gold crowns among the whole camp.'

Scarcely had he said this, when a crowd of gipsies rushed up to him and lifting him up in their arms and on to their shoulders, they sang out: 'Hurray, hurray, for Andrés the great!', adding, 'and long live Preciosa, his lovely prize!'

The gipsy girls did the same with Preciosa, not without some envy on the part of Cristina and of the other little gipsy girls who were there; for envy is to be found in the camps of barbarians and the huts of shepherds just as it is in the palaces of princes, and the business of seeing one's neighbour get on when he is no more deserving than oneself is a wearisome thing.

After this they ate a splendid meal; the promised money was distributed equitably and justly; the praise of Andrés was taken up again; Preciosa's beauty was lauded to the skies. Night came, they killed the mule and buried it, so that Andrés was satisfied that he would never be discovered because of it; and they also buried its trappings with it, such as the saddle, bridle and cinches, just like the Indians, who have their richest jewels buried with them.

Andrés was amazed at all he had seen and heard and at the ingenuity of the gipsies, and was even more determined to go ahead with and attain his object without becoming involved in their customs, or at least to avoid doing so in every way he could, trusting that he would, because of his money, be allowed exemption from the obligation to obey them in the unjust things which they might order him to do. The next day Andrés begged them to move on and get away from Madrid, for he feared he would be recognized if he stayed there. They told him that they had already made up their minds to go off to the woodlands of Toledo, and from there to go looting around throughout all the neighbouring territory. So they raised camp, and gave Andrés a donkey to ride, but he did not wish to, preferring to go on foot and to act as lackey to Preciosa, who rode on another donkey, delighted to see how she had her handsome squire under her thumb, and he no less delighted to see beside him the lady whom he had made mistress of his will.

Oh the power of this bitter–sweet god, as we call him in our unthinking way, and how truly he enslaves us, and with what little respect he treats us! Here is Andrés, a noble and intelligent young man, brought up almost all his life at court and spoiled by his rich parents, and all of a sudden he's changed to the point of deceiving his servants and friends, disappointing the hopes which his parents had for him, leaving the road to Flanders, where he would have been able to put to use his bravery and increase the honour of his family, and throwing himself at the feet of a girl, to be her lackey – a girl who, beautiful as she was, was a gipsy after all. Oh, the privilege of beauty, which rides rough-shod over and drags even the most fancy-free along the ground by the hair!

A few days later they came to a village two leagues away from Toledo, where they pitched their camp, first of all giving a few articles of silver to the mayor of the place, by way of guarantee that they would not steal anything either there or in all the area under his jurisdiction. When this had been done, all the old gipsy women, some of the young ones, and the men scattered about all through the villages, or at least those which were about four or five leagues from the one where they had encamped. Andrés went with them to receive his first lesson as a thief, but although they gave him several lessons on that expedition, none of them left any impression; on the contrary, as you would expect in one of his good breeding, every theft which his instructors committed tore him apart, and it came to the point where, moved by the tears of the victims, he paid out of his own money for the thefts of his comrades. The gipsies despaired at this, saying that it went against their statutes and ordinances, which did not allow charity to enter their hearts, for if it did, they would have to give up being thieves, a thing which would not do at all. So when Andrés saw this, he said that he wanted to go stealing on his own, without having anyone with him, because he could run fast enough to avoid danger and he was not lacking the courage to face it; and that he wanted the reward or the punishment for what he stole to be his.

The gipsies tried to dissuade him from this plan, telling him that he might come up against occasions when he would need company, both for attack and defence, and that one person alone could not make much of a haul. But however much they said Andrés determined to do his thieving by himself, so that he could get away from the gang and buy with his own money things that he could then say he had stolen, and in this way put the least possible burden on his conscience. So, using this device, in less than a month he brought more profit to the company than any four of the most accomplished thieves in it, at which Preciosa was very pleased, seeing that her devoted lover was such a fine and skilful thief; but all the same, she was afraid of some misfortune and would not have seen her Andrés in disgrace for all the treasure in Venice, so well disposed did she feel towards him for the many services and gifts that he had bestowed upon her.

They spent little more than four weeks in the Toledo area, making a rich harvest there during that month of September, and from there they went into Extremadura because, apart from being rich country, it was warmer. Andrés talked often with Preciosa, and these innocent conversations made her gradually fall in love with the good sense and good nature of her lover. His love too would have increased if it were capable of growing any stronger, such was the modesty, wit and beauty of his Preciosa. Wherever they went, he won the prize and the stakes as a runner and jumper; he played bowls and *pelota* with great skill; he could throw the bar with great force and accuracy: in short, his fame spread very quickly round the whole of Extremadura, and there was no place where the dashing gipsy Andrés Caballero and his charm and skill were not talked about, along with the beauty of the little gipsy girl; there was not a single town, village or hamlet where they were not in demand to take part in the local festivities or in celebrations of a private nature. So the camp grew rich, prosperous and happy, and the lovers were well pleased simply to gaze at each other.

It so happened that the camp was pitched among some oak-trees, a little way off the highroad. One night they heard the dogs barking much more loudly than usual. Some of the gipsies went out, and Andrés with them, to see what they were barking at, and they saw that it was a man dressed in white, who was defending himself from two of the dogs which had him by the leg. They went up to him and pulled the dogs off and one of the gipsies said to him,

'Who the devil brought you here, man, at this hour and so far off the beaten track? Have you come to steal, by any chance? Because you have certainly landed up in a good spot.'

'I haven't come to steal,' answered the man, 'and I don't know whether I am off the beaten track or not, although I can see quite well that I've lost my way. But tell me, gentlemen, is there some inn or place round here where I could find shelter for the night and get treated for these wounds your dogs have inflicted on me?'

'There's no place or inn to which we can direct you,' answered Andrés, 'but as far as treating your wounds and giving you lodging for the night is concerned, you'll be well cared for in our camp. Come with us, for although we are gipsies, we can still be charitable.'

'God be charitable to you,' answered the man, 'and take me where you like, for the pain in this leg is making me very weary.'

Andrés and another charitable gipsy (for even among devils there are some worse than others, and there is usually one good man among many who are bad) carried him between them. It was a bright moonlit night, so that they could see that the man was young and good-looking. He was dressed all in white linen, and round his shoulders and fastened round his chest was a sort of linen shirt or bag. They came to Andrés's hut or tent, and quickly made a fire and lit a lamp; then Preciosa's grandmother came to treat the wounded man, of whom news had already reached her. She took some of the hairs from the dogs, fried them in oil, and first washing with wine two bites which he had on his left leg, she laid the hairs with the oil on them, and on top a bit of crushed green rosemary; then she bound him up carefully with clean cloths, and making the sign of the cross over his wounds, she said,

'Sleep, my friend, for, with God's help, you'll be all right.'

While they were treating the wounded man Preciosa was standing by, and staring hard at him, and he at her, so much that Andrés noticed how attentively the young man was looking at her, which he attributed to Preciosa's great beauty. Anyway, after the young man had been treated, they left him alone on a bed made of dry hay, and for the moment they did not want to ask him any questions about his journey or anything else.

Scarcely had they left him when Preciosa called Andrés aside and said to him,

'Andrés, do you remember a paper which I dropped when I was dancing with my companions in your house, and which I think upset you a good deal?'

'Yes, I do remember,' answered Andrés. 'It was a sonnet in praise of you, and not a bad one either.'

'Well, Andrés,' Preciosa went on, 'the man who wrote that sonnet is this young man whom we have left in the hut. I'm sure I'm right, because he spoke to me in Madrid two or three times, and even gave me a very good ballad. He was going round there as a page, I think; not an ordinary one, but one who was under the patronage of some prince; and indeed, Andrés, he's a clever, intelligent, and most upright young man, and I don't know what to think of his coming like this and in these clothes!'

'What is there to think, Preciosa?' said Andrés. 'Only that the same power which has made me a gipsy has made him go round looking like a miller and coming in search of you. Ah, my Preciosa, I can tell that you want to boast of having more than one victim of your charms. And if this is so, finish me off first, and then you can kill this other one. Don't try to sacrifice us together on the altars of your deceitfulness, not to say of your beauty.'

'Heaven help me,' answered Preciosa, 'Andrés, how sensitive

you are, and how slender a thread your hopes and my reputation
hang on, that the fierce sword of jealousy has so easily penetrated
your heart! Tell me, Andrés: if there were any trick or deceit,
shouldn't I keep quiet and conceal who this young man is? Am I by
any chance so foolish as to give you an opportunity to cast doubt
upon my goodness and integrity? Be quiet, Andrés, for heaven's
sake, and try by tomorrow to get rid of this fear about where he
is going or what he has come for. Perhaps you are mistaken in your
suspicion, although I am sure I'm not mistaken in thinking that he
is the person I've said. And to satisfy you still further – since I've
got to the point of satisfying you – however and for whatever
purpose this young man has come, send him off straight away. And
see that he goes, since all our company obey you, and no one will
want to welcome him to our camp against your will. And even if you
don't do this, I give you my word that I shan't leave my hut nor let
myself be seen by him or by anyone whom you don't wish to see
me. Look, Andrés, I don't mind seeing you being jealous, but I
shall mind a great deal if I see you being stupid.'

'Unless you see me going mad, Preciosa,' answered Andrés,
'no proof will suffice to make you realize how bitter and wearisome is this endless jealousy. But all the same, I'll do what you say,
and if it is possible, I shall find out what this poet–page wants,
where he is going and what he is looking for; for it might be that
by pulling some thread which he's carelessly left showing I might
pull out the whole ball of yarn in which I fear he has come to
tangle me.'

'Jealousy, it seems to me,' said Preciosa, 'never leaves the understanding free to judge things as they are. Jealous people always
look at things with magnifying glasses which make small things
look large, make dwarfs look like giants and suspicions like cer-
tainties. By your life and mine, Andrés, act in this and in everything
relating to our agreements in a sane and sensible way; for if you do
I know that you will give me the highest award for purity, modesty
and truthfulness.'

At this she took leave of Andrés; and he, with his heart full of
confusion and a thousand conflicting fancies, waited for daylight,
when he could ask the wounded man to tell his story. He could not
persuade himself that that page had not come there attracted by the

beauty of Preciosa, for the thief thinks everyone is like him. On the other hand, the satisfaction that Preciosa had given him seemed so convincing that it reassured him and made him decide to leave his fate in her good hands.

Day came; he visited the injured man, asked him his name and where he was going, and how he came to be travelling so late and so far off the road, although he first asked him how he was and if the pain of the bites had gone. To which the young man replied that he was better and had no pain, and was fit to go on. To the question about his name and where he was going, he simply said that he was called Alonso Hurtado, and that he was going on business to Nuestra Señora de la Peña de Francia; that he was travelling by night to get there quickly, and that the previous night he had lost his way and come across the camp by chance, when the dogs which were guarding it had done to him what Andrés had seen.

This statement did not seem very straightforward, but distinctly devious to Andrés, and his suspicions once more began to torment him, so he said,

'Brother, if I were a judge and you had fallen under my jurisdiction for some crime, which would require me to put the questions which I have put to you, the answer which you have given me would oblige me to press you further. I do not want to know who you are, what your name is or where you are going, but I warn you that if it suits your purpose to lie about this journey of yours, lie with a little more plausibility. You say you are going to the Peña de Francia, and you've left it behind you on your right, a good thirty leagues from where we are; you are travelling by night to get there quickly, and you travel off the road among woods and oak-groves which have scarcely any tracks, let alone paths. Friend, get up and learn to lie, and good luck to you. But in exchange for this good advice I'm giving you, won't you tell me one true thing? I'm sure you will, since you are such a bad liar. Tell me, are you by chance one whom I have seen often at court, something between a page and a gentleman, who had the reputation of being a great poet, one who wrote a ballad and a sonnet to a little gipsy girl who was recently going about in Madrid, and who was regarded as outstanding for her beauty? Tell me, for I promise you on my word as a gentleman gipsy to keep whatever secrets you think proper. If you would deny the fact that you are the person I say, beware. It would get you nowhere, because the face that I see here is certainly the one I saw in Madrid. Without a doubt your distinguished reputation often made me notice you as someone outstanding, so that your face has remained in my memory. And so I have recognized you by it, although you are wearing clothes which are very different from those in which I saw you then. Do not be upset; take heart and do not think you have come to a den of thieves, but to a refuge which will guard and defend you from the whole world. Look: I have an idea, and if my idea is right, you have been very lucky in meeting me. My idea is that, being in love with Preciosa, the lovely little gipsy girl for whom you wrote the verses, you have come to look for her. For this I shall not esteem you any less, but rather much more; for, although I am a gipsy, experience has shown me to what lengths the power of love will go, and how it affects those whom it brings under its sway and command. If that is so, as I undoubtedly believe it is, the little gipsy girl is here.'

'Yes, she is here, for I saw her last night,' said the injured man. At this Andrés was dumbfounded, thinking that he had final confirmation of his suspicions. 'I saw her last night,' said the young man again, 'but I did not dare to tell her who I was, because it didn't suit my purpose.'

'So', said Andrés, 'you are the poet I talked of.'

'Yes, I am,' replied the youth, 'for I cannot and do not wish to deny it. Perhaps I have found my way when I thought I had lost it, if there is such a thing as loyalty in woods and a welcome in the wilderness.'

'Without doubt there is,' answered Andrés, 'and among us gipsies, the greatest secrecy in the world. With this assurance you can reveal your heart to me, sir; for in my heart you will find just what you see, without duplicity. The little gipsy girl is a relative of mine, and is subject to what I wish to do with her. If you want her as your wife, I and all her family will be delighted, and if as a mistress, we shall make no fuss, provided you have money, for greed is never far from our camps.'

'I have money,' said the young man. 'In this bag which I have strapped to my body there are four hundred gold crowns.'

This was another mortal shock for Andrés, who saw all this money as being intended simply to conquer and purchase his prize; and in a rather unsteady voice he said,

'That's a good deal of money; you must disclose who you are straight away, and get down to business, for the girl is by no means stupid, and will see how fitting it is that she should be yours.'

'Ah, my friend,' said the young man at this point, 'I want you to know that the power which has made me change my dress is not the power of love, as you say, nor the desire for Preciosa. For Madrid has lovely girls who can steal hearts and bring souls into subjection as well and better than the most lovely gipsies, although I confess that the beauty of this relative of yours is greater than that of any I have seen. But what puts me in this garb, on foot and bitten by dogs, is not love but my misfortune.'

While the young man was saying all this, Andrés was recovering his composure, seeing that what the young man said was not leading where he thought. Anxious to get out of the confusion he was in, he repeated his assurance that he could unburden himself, and so the young man went on,

'I was in Madrid in the house of a nobleman, whom I thought of not as a master but as a relative. This man had an only son and heir, and he, both because we were related and because we were of the same age and turn of mind, treated me with great familiarity and friendship. It happened that this gentleman fell in love with a noble young lady, whom he would very happily have chosen as his wife if his will had not been subject, like a good son, to that of his parents, who were anxious to achieve a better marriage for him. All the same, he paid court to her as secretly as he could, hidden from the eyes and ears of those who might have revealed his desires; only I was aware of what he was about. And one night, which ill luck must have chosen for the disaster of which I shall tell you, as the two of us were going along the street, and past the door where the lady lived, we saw two handsome-looking men. My relative wanted to see who they were, and he had scarcely made towards them when they put their hands with great speed to their swords and bucklers and came towards us, and we did the same, attacking each other with equal weapons. The quarrel did not last long, for the life of our two opponents came to a rapid end as a result of two thrusts aimed by my jealous relative and by me – an extraordinary thing the like of which you don't often see. In triumph then, in a cause we would not have chosen, we went back home and then secretly, taking all the money we could, we went to San Jerómino, waiting for daylight to reveal what had happened and who were under suspicion as the killers. We knew that there was no trace of anything of ours, and the prudent monks advised us to go home and not to give or arouse any suspicion against us by our absence. Since we were determined to follow their advice, they told us that the magistrates were holding the parents of the young lady and the young lady herself in custody in their house, and that one of the lady's servants whom they questioned told how my relative used to walk up and down outside her lady's room day and night. On the basis of this they had come in search of us, and not finding us, but finding many indications that we had fled, the whole court was convinced that we were the killers of those two gentlemen, who were in fact noblemen of great distinction. Finally, following the advice of the count my relative and that of the monks, after a fortnight during which we had remained hidden in the monastery, my companion, in the habit of a friar, and accompanied by another friar, went off towards Aragón, intending to cross to Italy and from there to Flanders, until he saw how the affair turned out. I wanted us to go separate ways, so that our fortune should not lead us both to disaster, so I went off a different way from him, and dressed as a friar's servant. I set off on foot with a monk, who left me in Talavera. From there I have come here alone and off the beaten track, until last night I arrived at this oak-grove, where you know what happened to me. And if I asked the way to the Peña de Francia, it was for the sake of giving some reply to the questions I was asked; for in fact I don't know where the Peña de Francia is, although I know it's beyond Salamanca.'

'That's true,' answered Andrés, 'and you've left it behind you on your right, almost twenty leagues from here, so you can see how well you would be doing if you were going there.'

'The road I thought of taking', replied the young man, 'is none other than the one to Seville, for I know a Genoese gentleman there, a great friend of the count my relative, who is in the habit of sending a great deal of silver to Genoa, and I want him to fix me up so that I can go along with those who usually take it. By this stratagem I shall certainly be able to get to Cartagena, and from there to Italy, because two galleys are due to come very shortly to take the silver on board. This, my good friend, is my story; you can see whether I am right in saying that it is the result of pure misfortune rather than of crossed love. But if these gipsies would be willing to take me in their company as far as Seville, if they are going there, I would pay them very well for it; for I realize that I should be safer in their company, free from the fear in which I now travel.'

'Indeed they will take you,' answered Andrés, 'and if not in our caravan, for I don't know yet whether we're going to Andalucia, you'll go in another which I think we'll be coming across in a day or two; and if you give them something of what you have with you, you'll pave the way to even greater favours.'

Andrés left him, and went to tell the other gipsies what the young man had told him, and what he hoped to do, with the offer he had made of good payment and reward. They all thought that he should stay in the camp; only Preciosa disagreed, and her grandmother said that she could not go to Seville or anywhere thereabouts, because in years gone by she had played a trick in Seville on a cap-maker called Triguillos, very well known in the city, whom she had had put in a pitcher of water up to his neck, stripped to the buff, and with a garland of cypress on his head, waiting for the stroke of midnight to get out of the pitcher and dig up a great treasure which she had led him to believe was somewhere in his house. She said that as soon as the good cap-maker heard the bell ring for mattins, he got out of the pitcher so quickly, so as not to miss the right moment, that he landed with it on the floor, and with the force of the blow and with the fragments of the pitcher he hurt himself, upset the water and was swimming about in it shouting that he was drowning.

She went on: 'His wife and his neighbours rushed up with lights and found him going through the motions of swimming, puffing, and dragging his stomach along the ground, waving his arms and legs for all he was worth and shouting out at the top of his voice, "Help, gentlemen, I'm drowning." He was so frightened that he really did think he was drowning. They got hold of him, and rescued him, whereupon he recovered, related my trick, and in spite of that, started to dig down a couple of yards in the same spot, even though everyone told him that it was a trick of mine. If a neighbour of his hadn't stopped him by telling him that he had got to the foundations of his house, and let him dig as much as he wanted to, he'd have had the whole house down. This story was known throughout the whole city, and even the children pointed their fingers at him and told the story of his credulity and my trick.'

This is the story the old gipsy told, and she gave this as her excuse for not going to Seville. The gipsies, who already knew from Andrés Caballero that the young man had plenty of money, readily welcomed him into their company and offered to protect him and keep him hidden as long as he liked, and they made up their minds to go off towards the left and get into La Mancha and into the Kingdom of Murcia. They called the young man and told him of all that they intended to do for him. He thanked them, and gave a hundred gold crowns to be distributed among them. With this gift they were ready to eat out of his hand; only Preciosa was not too happy that Don Sancho, as the young man said he was called, was going to stay. (The gipsies changed his name to that of Clemente, and that is what they called him from then on.) Andrés was also a bit upset and none too pleased that Clemente was staying, since he seemed to have changed his original plans for very little reason. But Clemente, as if he could read his mind, said among other things that he was glad to be going to the Kingdom of Murcia because it was near Cartagena, where if any galleys turned up, as he thought they would, he could easily cross over to Italy. Finally, in order to keep his eye on him better and to see what he was doing and how his mind was working, Andrés was very anxious that Clemente should be his companion, and Clemente considered this friendship a great favour to him. They always went about together, spent freely, distributed crowns like rain, ran, jumped, danced and threw the bar better than any of the gipsies, and were greatly beloved of the gipsy girls and highly respected by the gipsy men.

So they left Extremadura and went into La Mancha, and gradually made their way towards the kingdom of Murcia. In all the hamlets and villages they went through there were *pelota* and fencing matches, and contests in running, jumping, throwing the bar and other trials of strength, skill and speed; and in all of them Andrés and Clemente were the winners, just as Andrés was before. And during all this time, which was more than a month and a half, Clemente never had nor sought an opportunity to speak to Preciosa, until one day, when Andrés and she were together, they called him, and when he reached them Preciosa said to him,

'From the moment when you first came to our camp, I recognized you, Clemente, and I remembered those verses you gave me in Madrid, but I did not want to say anything because I didn't know for what purpose you had come to our camp. When I knew of your misfortune I was very sorry, and my mind was set at rest after the first shock, at the thought that as there were Don Juans in this world who changed into Andreses, so there could be Don Sanchos who changed their names to something else. I am talking to you like this because Andrés has told me that he has informed you who he is, and why he has turned into a gipsy.' (And this was true, because Andrés had told him his whole story, so that he could confide all his thoughts to him.) 'And don't imagine that it was of no advantage to you that I knew you, for on my account and because of what I said about you, the decision to welcome you and take you into our company was made, where God grant you may meet with all the good fortune you may desire. My wish is that you should compensate me for this good will by not making Andrés think ill of what he has decided to do, nor tell him what a bad thing it is to persevere in this way of life; for although I imagine that his will is subject to mine, I should nevertheless be sorry to give him cause, however slight, for any regret.'

To this Clemente replied,

'Do not think, peerless Preciosa, that Don Juan revealed to me who he was without due thought; I recognized straight away from the way he looked what he wanted. I was the first to tell him who I was, and I the first to guess that his will was not his own, as you say. He, very properly trusting me, confided his secret to me, and he will witness truly that I praised his resolution and his chosen way of life. For I am not, Preciosa, so lacking in intelligence that I do not realize the extent of beauty's power; and yours especially, since it surpasses all other beauty, is sufficient excuse for greater errors, if you call errors what one does with such overpowering reason. I am grateful to you, my lady, for what you have said in my favour, and I intend to repay the debt by wishing you a happy ending to your affair, and that you may enjoy your Andrés and Andrés his Preciosa, with his parents' consent, so that the world may see the offspring kindly Nature can produce from such a lovely couple. This is what I shall wish, Preciosa, and this is what I shall always say to your Andrés, and not anything which may turn him from his well-directed intentions.'

Clemente had said these things with such warmth of affection that Andrés was not sure whether he had spoken out of love or out of politeness; for this infernal disease of jealousy is of so delicate a nature that it gets attached to the tiniest specks of sunlight, and the lover grows anxious and almost despairs when they touch the adored one. But all the same his jealousy was unfounded, and he was reassured more by Preciosa's goodness than by his good fortune; for lovers always consider themselves unhappy as long as they do not attain what they desire. In short, Andrés and Clemente were comrades and great friends, their friendship sealed by Clemente's good will and Preciosa's modesty and prudence, which never gave Andrés cause for jealousy.

Clemente was something of a poet, as he showed in the verses which he gave to Preciosa, and Andrés also prided himself a bit on his talent in this direction; and both were fond of music. It so happened that one night, the camp being pitched in a valley a few leagues from Murcia, in order to amuse themselves the two of them were resting, Andrés at the foot of a cork-oak and Clemente at the foot of a holm-oak, each with a guitar. Affected by the silence of the night, Andrés began, and Clemente replied, and together they sang these verses:

Andrés   Clemente, see the starry veil
            whereby the night,
            than day more bright,
            renders day's beauty dull and pale.
            Compared with this
            your wit the truth can scarcely miss:
            that radiant face
            outshines the stars and sun in grace.

Clemente Outshines the stars and sun in grace;
while virtue pure
and goodness sure
join with the beauty of her face
to form one whole,
whose praise is sung from pole to pole.
If not divine,
all human virtues in her shine.

Andrés All human virtues in her shine.
Her beauty rare
e'en heaven thinks fair.
The world reveres this one of mine,
this gipsy girl,
whose name sets every head awhirl.
Her fame could well
heaven's utmost sphere with music swell.

Clemente Heaven's utmost sphere with music swell;
and justly so;
her praise should go
to heaven's lofty height as well
as here below,
where her sweet name all men do know,
and each tongue sings,
as peace and joy to souls she brings.

Andrés As peace and joy to souls she brings;
for her sweet voice
makes all rejoice,
like siren's song on airy wings.
Preciosa's charms,
her beauty every one disarms;
my lovely prize,
so witty, spirited and wise.

Clemente So witty, spirited and wise;
my gipsy maid,
dawn's freshness earlier will fade;
before your coolness summer flies.
See how love's dart,
through her will strike the hardest heart;
the force of love
through her its gentle power does prove.

This pair, one captive, the other fancy-free, were showing no sign of stopping; but then they heard behind them Preciosa's voice, for she had been listening to them. When they heard her they stopped singing, and without moving, they listened to her with rapt attention. I don't know whether she was improvising, or whether the verses she sang had been composed for her on some occasion, but she sang the following lines as if in answer to them:

> In these affairs of love, for me,
> I'd rather answer love's lament
> with modest words, sincerely meant.
> (Beauty's best friend is purity.)
>
> The humblest plant will surely grow
> to reach the skies, if only grace
> or nature speed it in the race,
> if always upright it will go.
>
> On this poor copper vessel I
> enamel of decorum wear,
> my every wish is pure and fair;
> no riches fate shall me deny.
>
> No pain for me to be unloved;
> esteem of men I count but vain,
> my own good fortune I would gain,
> good or ill luck leave me unmoved.
>
> If only I can do my best,
> and aim to be at all times good,
> heaven will provide my daily food,
> direct my paths and bring me rest.
>
> I'd gladly see if beauty's power
> suffices to exalt me so
> that I aspire more power to know,
> or rise to spheres unknown before.
>
> If souls of all men equal are,
> a ploughman's soul in worth can be
> as great as any and as free
> as those of king or emperor.

My soul will soar to glory there,
exalted to the highest sphere.
Together love will ne'er appear,
or throne with majesty will share.

Here Preciosa ended her song, and Andrés and Clemente got up and went to her. They engaged in lively conversation among themselves, and Preciosa in her speech revealed her good sense, her modesty and her intelligence in such a way that Clemente could understand Andrés's intentions with regard to her, which he hadn't done before, thinking that his rash resolution was to be attributed to youthful impulse rather than to rational thought.

That morning the caravan moved on, and they pitched camp in a place within the territory of Murcia, three leagues from the city, where Andrés suffered a mishap which almost cost him his life. What happened was that after having handed over a few vases and articles of silver in the village by way of guarantee, as was the custom, Preciosa and her grandmother, and Cristina, with two other little gipsy girls and the two friends Clemente and Andrés, stayed in an inn belonging to a rich widow. She had a daughter of seventeen or eighteen, who was more forward than she was beautiful, and who was called Juana Carducha. This girl, after seeing the gipsies dance, fell so madly in love with Andrés that she decided to declare her love to him and to have him as her husband if he would consent, however unhappy her relations might be about it. So she sought an opportunity to tell Andrés, and found one in a farmyard into which Andrés had gone to look at a couple of donkeys. She went up to him quickly, so as not to be seen, and said to him,

'Andrés,' (for she already knew his name) 'I am a maiden, and I am rich; my mother has no children besides me, this inn is hers, and besides this she has lots of vines and four more houses. I like you; if you want me as your wife, it's up to you. Answer me quickly, and if you are sensible, stay and you'll see what a good time we'll have.'

Andrés was astonished at the Carducha girl's boldness, and just as promptly as she had asked he replied,

'My dear young lady, I am engaged to be married, and we gipsies only marry gipsy girls; may God bless you for your good intentions towards me, of which I am not worthy.'

The Carducha girl nearly died when she heard Andrés's cold reply, and would have answered him if she had not seen that some of the gipsy girls were coming into the yard. She was very upset and rushed out, dying to have her revenge. Andrés, being a sensible fellow, decided to put some distance between them, and avoid the opportunity that the devil was offering him, for he could clearly read in the eyes of the Carducha girl that she would give herself to him completely, without bothering about the bonds of matrimony. He had no wish to stay and face the enemy on that particular battlefield, and so he asked the gipsies to leave the village that night. They always obeyed him, and so they did what he asked straight away, and collecting their pledges, went off that evening.

The Carducha girl, who seeing half her soul disappear with Andrés, and realizing that she had very little time to get what she wanted, contrived to have Andrés kept behind by force, since he was not willing to stay of his own accord. So, with the energy, subtlety and secrecy born of her evil intentions, she placed among Andrés's valuables some that she could recognize as her own, some costly coral necklaces and two silver lockets, and some other trinkets of hers, and as soon as they had left the inn, she began to shout out that those gipsies had stolen her jewels. Whereupon the police came, with all the villagers. The gipsies stopped, and all swore that they had no stolen property with them, and that they would open all the bags and supplies in their camp. The old gipsy was very upset by this, fearing that in that examination Preciosa's jewels and Andrés's clothes, which she was guarding with great care and caution, would come to light; but the good Carducha girl solved the problem very quickly, because they were only looking at the second bundle when she told them to ask which was the one that belonged to the gipsy who was a great dancer, for she had seen him come into her room on two occasions; and it might be he who had taken them. Andrés realized that she was referring to him, and said laughingly,

'My lady, this is my luggage and this is my donkey; if you find in the former or on the latter what you are looking for, I shall repay you sevenfold, apart from submitting to the punishment which the law prescribes for thieves.'

Then all the officers of the law came up to unload the donkey, and after rummaging about a bit they found the stolen property; at which Andrés was so startled and dumbfounded that he stood silent, like a stone statue.

'Wasn't I right in my suspicions?' said the Carducha girl. 'You can see that this handsome fellow is nothing but a thief.'

The mayor, who was there, began to hurl a thousand insults at Andrés and all the gipsies, publicly calling them thieves and highwaymen. Andrés, puzzled and bewildered, didn't tumble to the Carducha girl's treachery. Then a swaggering soldier who was the mayor's nephew came up to him, and said,

'Do you see how this miserable thieving gipsy is behaving? I'll bet he'll make a fuss and deny the theft, although he's been caught red-handed; you're mighty lucky that the whole lot of you aren't thrown to the galleys. This scoundrel would certainly be better there, serving His Majesty, instead of going round dancing all over the place and stealing right and left. By my soldier's honour, I've a good mind to knock him down.'

And without more ado he raised his hand and gave him such a slap that he brought him out of his reverie, and made him remember that he was not Andrés Caballero, but Don Juan and a gentleman; and attacking the soldier swiftly and angrily, he pulled the man's own sword from its scabbard and ran it through his body, leaving him dead on the ground.

The whole village was in an uproar, the old mayor was furious, Preciosa fainted, and Andrés was shattered when he saw her faint. They all seized their weapons and ran after the murderer. The confusion and the shouting grew, and Andrés, rushing to the fainting Preciosa, failed to rush to his own defence; and as luck would have it Clemente was not present at this disastrous affair, having already left the town with his baggage. They all fell on Andrés, arrested him and bound him up with two stout chains. The mayor would gladly have hanged him there and then, if it had been in his power; but he had to send him to Murcia, because he was within that jurisdiction. They didn't take him until the next day, and while Andrés was there he had to put up with innumerable insults, which the indignant mayor and his officers and all the villagers hurled at him. The mayor arrested all the other gipsies he could lay hands on, because most of them fled, among them

Clemente, who was afraid of being caught and recognized. At last,
armed with the indictment and followed by a great mob of gipsies,
the mayor, his officers and a mass of other people all armed went
into Murcia, among them Preciosa and poor Andrés, who was
bound in chains, on a mule and with handcuffs and iron collar. The
whole of Murcia came out to see the prisoners, for the news of the
soldier's death had already been spread abroad. But Preciosa was
looking so beautiful that day that no one looked at her without
blessing her, and the news of her beauty reached the ears of the
wife of the chief magistrate. She, curious to see her, got her husband
to order the little gipsy girl not to be put in prison, but all the rest
of the gipsies to be shut up. They put Andrés into a narrow cell, so
dark, and without the light of his Preciosa, that he thought he
would never get out of there except to go to his grave. They took
Preciosa off with her grandmother to see the magistrate's wife, and
as soon as she saw her she said,

'One can see why people praise her beauty so much.'

And going up to her, she kissed her tenderly, and couldn't stop
looking at her. She asked her grandmother how old the girl would
be.

'Fifteen;' answered the gipsy woman, 'a month or two more or
less.'

'That would be the age of my poor Constanza. Oh my friends,
this girl has reminded me of my misfortune,' said the magistrate's
wife.

Then Preciosa took the lady's hands, and kissing them again and
again, she bathed them with tears and said to her,

'My lady, the gipsy who is in prison is not to blame, for he was
provoked by being called a thief, which he is not. He was slapped
in the face, a face in which you can see what a good person he is.
For the sake of heaven and for your sake, my lady, let his case be
held up, and don't let my lord execute the punishment with which
the law threatens him. If my beauty has given you any pleasure,
preserve it by preserving the prisoner, for if his life comes to an end
mine will too. He is to be my husband, and just and proper impedi-
ments have been the cause of our not having got engaged up to
now. If money be needed to win pardon in this case, all our
caravan will be sold at public auction, and we'll give more than the

fine. My lady, if you know what love is, and were ever in love, and if you love your husband now, have pity on me, for I love mine tenderly and truly.'

All the time she was saying this she never let go of her hands nor took her eyes off her, shedding floods of bitter and pitiful tears. The magistrate's wife held her hands too, looking at her no less fixedly and with no fewer tears. At this moment the magistrate came in and finding his wife and Preciosa so tearful and clinging to each other like that, he was bewildered, both by their weeping and by Preciosa's beauty. He asked what all this commotion was about, and Preciosa's reply was to let go of the hands of the magistrate's wife and grasp the feet of her husband, to whom she said,

'My lord, mercy, mercy! If my husband dies, I shall die too! He is not to blame, but if he is, give me the punishment; and if this cannot be, at least put off this case until all possible means can be found to help him, for as he did not intend to sin he may be saved by heaven's grace.'

The magistrate was even more bewildered when he heard the little gipsy girl's clever arguments, and would have wept with her if he hadn't been afraid of showing signs of weakness. While this was going on, the old gipsy was pondering hard on a great many things, and after a long pause she said,

'Will you wait for me a little while, my lord and lady, for I shall make these tears turn to laughter, even if it costs me my life.'

And so she went quickly outside, leaving the company baffled by what she had said. While they waited for her return, Preciosa kept up her weeping and her appeals that her husband's trial should be delayed, so that his father might be informed and come and take part in it. The gipsy woman came back with a small chest under her arm, and told the magistrate and his wife to come into a room with her, for she had important things to tell them in secret. The magistrate, thinking that she wanted to tell him of some thefts by the gipsies, so that they could be taken into account in the prisoner's case, went off straight away with her and his wife into their dressing room, where the old gipsy, kneeling down in front of them, said to them,

'If the good news which I want to give you, my lord and lady, does not earn as a reward the forgiveness of a great sin of mine, I am ready to receive whatever punishment you may wish to give me; but before I confess to you I want you first to tell me if you recognize these jewels.'

And bringing out a small chest containing Preciosa's jewels, she put them into the magistrate's hands. When he opened them he saw some childish trinkets, but he did not realize what they might mean. The magistrate's wife also looked at them, but she didn't see what they meant either; she merely said,

'These are ornaments belonging to some tiny child.'

'That's true,' said the gipsy woman, 'and which tiny child you will learn from what's written on this paper.'

The magistrate opened it quickly and read the words, 'The child was called Doña Constanza de Azevedo y de Meneses; her mother Doña Guiomar de Meneses, and her father Don Fernando de Azevedo, Knight of the Order of Calatrava. Disappeared on Ascension Day, at eight in the morning, in the year 1595. The child wore the ornaments in this chest.'

Scarcely had the magistrate's wife heard what the paper said, when she recognized the ornaments, put them to her lips and kissing them time and time again, fainted. The magistrate rushed up to help her, before asking the gipsy woman about his daughter. When the lady had recovered, she said,

'Good woman, angel rather than gipsy, where is the owner, I mean the child to whom these trinkets belonged?'

'Where, my lady?' answered the gipsy. 'She's in your house. That little gipsy girl who brought tears to your eyes is the owner, and is undoubtedly your daughter, for I stole her in Madrid from your house on the day and hour this paper says.'

When the lady heard this, she rushed out distracted and as fast as she could go to the room where she had left Preciosa, and found her still weeping and surrounded by her ladies-in-waiting and servants. She rushed up to her and without saying a word quickly unfastened her dress and looked to see if she had a small birth-mark like a sort of white mole, under her left breast. She found that it was now quite big, for it had grown with time. Then, with equal speed she took off her shoe, and uncovered a foot so white that it looked like snow or carved ivory. There she saw what she was looking for, namely that the last two toes on the right foot were joined together by a small piece of flesh, which, when she was a child, they had never wanted to cut, so as not to give her pain. The breast, the toes, the trinkets, the day of the theft, the gipsy woman's confession and the shock and pleasure of her parents when they saw her, all went to confirm in the heart of the magistrate's wife that Preciosa was truly her daughter; so, taking her in her arms, she went back with her to the place where the magistrate and the gipsy woman were.

Preciosa, not knowing why she had had these things done to her, was still more bewildered when she saw herself in the arms of the magistrate's wife, who was covering her with kisses. At last, Doña Guiomar came back to her husband with her precious charge and transferring her to the magistrate's arms, she said to him,

'Here, sir, is your daughter Constanza, for it is she for certain: do not have the slightest doubt, sir, for I have seen the mark of the two toes joined together and the birth mark on her breast; and anyway, my heart has been telling me she is ours since the moment I set eyes on her.'

'I do not doubt it,' answered the magistrate, holding Preciosa in his arms, 'for she has affected me in the same way as you, and anyway, how could so many details coincide except by a miracle?'

All the people in the house were amazed, asking each other what could be happening; and they were all right off the mark, for who could imagine that the little gipsy girl was the daughter of their lord and lady?

The magistrate told his wife and his daughter and the old gipsy woman to keep the matter secret until he chose to reveal it, and that he forgave her for the injury she had done him in stealing the apple of his eye, since the recompense of having her back deserved greater reward, and he only regretted that, since she knew of Preciosa's rank, she had let her become engaged to a gipsy, especially one who was a thief and a murderer.

'Oh,' said Preciosa when she heard this, 'my lord, he is not a gipsy nor a thief, although he is a killer. But he killed one who robbed him of his honour, and could not help showing who he was and killing him.'

'How do you mean he is not a gipsy, daughter?' said Doña Guiomar.

Then the old gipsy woman briefly related the story of Andrés Caballero, and told how he was the son of Don Francisco de Cárcamo, a Knight of the Order of Santiago; and that his name was Don Juan de Cárcamo, of the same order, whose clothes she had had in her keeping ever since he changed them for gipsy dress. She also told the story of the agreement made between Preciosa and Don Juan to wait two trial years to see whether they should marry or not; she made due reference to the propriety of both of them and to the excellent character of Don Juan. They were as amazed at this as they were at finding their daughter, and the magistrate told the gipsy woman to go and bring Don Juan's clothes. She did so, and returned with another gipsy, who carried them.

While she was going and coming Preciosa's parents asked her a hundred thousand questions, and she answered them with such good sense and charm that even if they hadn't recognized her as their daughter, she would have won their love. They asked her if she was fond of Don Juan. She replied that she was no fonder of him than she was obliged to be by gratitude towards one who had been willing to undergo the humiliation of being a gipsy for her sake; but that her gratitude would not go beyond what her parents wished.

'Enough, Preciosa, my child,' said her father ('for I want you to stick to this name Preciosa, in memory of your loss and your recovery). I, as your father, take it upon myself to find you a match which will not be out of keeping with a person of your rank.'

When Preciosa heard this she sighed, and her mother, being a wise woman, realized that her sigh was caused by her love for Don Juan. So she said to her husband,

'Sir, as Don Juan de Cárcamo is as distinguished as he is, and since he loves our daughter so much, it wouldn't do us any harm to give her to him as his wife.'

And he replied, 'We've only found her today, and do you want us to lose her already? Let us enjoy her for a while, for once she's married she won't belong to us, but to her husband.'

'You are right, sir,' she answered, 'but do have Don Juan released, for he must be locked up in some dungeon.'

'Yes he is,' said Preciosa, 'for a thief and a killer and especially a gipsy will not have been considered worth any better quarters.'

'I want to go and see him and listen to his confession,' answered the magistrate, 'and I charge you once more, my lady, not to let any one know this story until I wish it.'

And kissing Preciosa, he went straight away to the prison and went into the cell where Don Juan was, and would not let anyone go in with him. He found him with both feet in the stocks and with handcuffs on his hands, and with the iron collar still on him. The room was dark, but he had them open a skylight in the roof, although it was a very small one; and as soon as he saw him, he said to him,

'How is our fine fellow? I'd like to see all the gipsies in Spain tied up like this, and get them all out of the way at once, as Nero wanted to do in Rome, and have done with it at one go! Let me tell you, my quarrelsome thief, that I am the chief magistrate of this city, and I have come to find out in confidence, whether a certain little gipsy girl in your company is your wife.'

When he heard this, Andrés imagined that the magistrate must have fallen in love with Preciosa (for jealousy is a fine substance which finds its way among other substances without breaking, separating or dividing them), but all the same he answered,

'If she has said I am her husband, it is quite true; and if she has said I am not, she has spoken the truth too, for it is impossible for Preciosa to tell a lie.'

'Is she so truthful?' replied the magistrate. 'That's no mean thing for a gipsy girl. Well, young man, she has said that she is your betrothed, but that she has never given you her hand. She realizes that since you are guilty, you must die for it, and she has asked that before you die I shall marry you to her, for she wants to have the honour of being the widow of this great thief.'

'Then sir, do as she requests; for as long as I marry her, I shall go as happily into the next life as I leave this one.'

'You must love her a great deal!' said the magistrate.

'So much,' answered the prisoner, 'that words could not express it. In fact, sir, let my trial be brought to an end. I killed one who wanted to take away my honour; I adore the gipsy girl; I shall be happy if I die in her favour, and I know that God's favour will not be lacking either, since we shall both have kept virtuously and faithfully what we promised each other.'

'Tonight I shall send for you,' said the magistrate, 'and in my house you shall be married to Preciosa, and tomorrow at midday you will be on the gallows; whereby I shall have fulfilled both the demands of justice and the desire of both of you.'

Andrés thanked him, and the magistrate went back home' and told his wife what had happened with Don Juan, and of the other things which he intended to do. While he was away Preciosa had told her mother of all that had happened in her life, and how she had always thought she was a gipsy and the granddaughter of the old woman; but that she had always thought more highly of herself than might have been expected of a gipsy.

Her mother asked her to tell her truly if she did indeed love Don Juan de Cárcamo. She, bashful and with eyes downcast, told her that since she had thought she was a gipsy, and that she was improving her fortune by marrying such a distinguished nobleman as Don Juan de Cárcamo, especially having seen for herself what a good and virtuous person he was, she had sometimes regarded him with affection; but that, after all, she had already said that she had no mind to do anything but what they wished.

Night came, and as it was almost ten o'clock they brought Andrés out of prison, without the handcuffs and the yoke, but bound hand and foot with a great chain. He came like this without being seen by anyone, except those who were taking him to the magistrate's house, and silently and cautiously they brought him to a room, where they left him alone. Shortly afterwards a priest came in, and told him to confess, because he was to die the next day. To which Andrés replied,

'I shall confess quite happily, but how is it that I'm not being married first? And if I am to be married, then the marriage bed which awaits me is certainly a wretched one.'

Doña Guiomar, who knew about all this, told her husband that the shocks he was giving Don Juan were too much; that he should go easy, because he might lose his life as a result of them. The magistrate thought this was good advice, and so he went in and called the confessor, telling him that they were going to marry the gipsy to Preciosa and that he would confess afterwards, and bade him commend himself to God with all his heart, for God often rains down mercies at a time when one is most parched of hope.

So Andrés was taken to a room where there were only Doña Guiomar, the magistrate, Preciosa and two of the household servants. But when Preciosa saw Don Juan bound with such a great chain, his face deathly pale and looking as if he had been weeping, she clutched her heart and leaned on the arm of her mother, who was at her side, and who kissed her and said,

'Don't be upset, my child, for you will see everything will turn out to your pleasure and advantage.'

Not knowing what was going on, she was inconsolable, and the old gipsy was alarmed, while the bystanders wondered how the affair would end.

The magistrate said, 'Curate, this gipsy man and girl are the people you are to marry.'

'I cannot do this unless the conditions required in this sort of case are first duly fulfilled. Where were the banns called? Where is the licence from my superior, so that the marriage can be carried out according to its terms?'

'It was an oversight on my part,' answered the magistrate, 'but I shall get the vicar to give it you.'

'Well, until I see it,' answered the curate, 'I must ask you ladies and gentlemen to excuse me.'

And without saying another word, in order to avoid any scandal, he went out of the house and left them all in confusion.

'The father was quite right,' said the magistrate, 'and this might be providential, so that Andrés's torture may be postponed, for in fact, he is to marry Preciosa and the banns must first be called. This will take time, which often solves our problems for us. By the way, I should like Andrés to tell me, if fate were to direct his affairs in such a way that he were to become Preciosa's husband without any of these shocks and alarms, whether he would regard himself as more fortunate to be Andrés Caballero or Don Juan de Cárcamo.'

As soon as Andrés heard himself called by his own name, he said,

'Since Preciosa chose to break her vow of silence and has revealed who I am, even if I should be fortunate enough to rule over the whole world, I should esteem her so much that she would be the end of my desires, and I should dare wish for no other blessing but that of heaven.'

'Then as a reward for the good spirit you have shown, Señor Don Juan de Cárcamo, I shall in due time make Preciosa your lawful wife, and for the moment I promise to give her to you as the richest jewel in my house and in my heart and soul. Value her as you say you will, for I am giving you the hand of Doña Constanza de Meneses, my only daughter, who if she is your equal in love is not unworthy of you in rank.'

Andrés was astonished, seeing the affection which they showed towards him. Briefly Doña Guiomar told how her daughter was lost and how she was found again, with the proofs that the old gipsy had given that she had stolen her; at which Don Juan was still more astonished and aghast, but unbelievably happy. He embraced his parents-in-law, and called them his parents and masters, he kissed Preciosa's hands, and she tearfully asked him for his.

The news of the affair was spread abroad by the servants who had been present. When the mayor, who was the uncle of the dead man, knew of it he realized vengeance was no longer possible, since the rigour of justice could not be brought to bear upon the chief magistrate's son-in-law.

Don Juan put on the travelling clothes which the gipsy had brought; captivity and iron chains were exchanged for liberty and chains of gold and the sadness of the imprisoned gipsies was turned to rejoicing, for the next day they released them on bail. The dead man's uncle received the promise of two thousand ducats which they gave him to make him withdraw his complaint and forgive Don Juan. The latter, not forgetting his comrade Clemente, gave orders that he should be searched for. But they could not find him or anything about him, until a few days later Don Juan learned that he had embarked in one of the Genoese galleys which were in the port of Cartagena, and had already set sail.

The magistrate told Don Juan that he had definite news that his father Don Francisco de Cárcamo had been appointed chief magistrate of that city, and that it would be a good thing to wait for him, so that the wedding could take place with his blessing and consent. Don Juan said that he would not quarrel with his decision, but that he wanted to be formally betrothed to Preciosa straight away. The archbishop gave permission for this to be done after the banns had been called only once. The city celebrated with illuminations, bullfights and tournaments on the day of the betrothal, for the magistrate was very popular. The old gipsy woman stayed indoors, for she did not want to be separated from her granddaughter Preciosa.

The news of the affair and the marriage of the little gipsy girl reached the capital and Don Francisco de Cárcamo was informed that the gipsy was his son and Preciosa the little gipsy girl whom he had seen. Her beauty was sufficient excuse for him for his son's fickle behaviour (for he had thought he was lost, when he found that he had not gone to Flanders), especially since he saw how right it was for him to marry the daughter of such a great and rich nobleman as Don Fernando de Azevedo. He set out with great speed, so as to see his son and daughter-in-law as soon as possible, and within three weeks he was in Murcia, his arrival being the occasion for renewed rejoicing. The wedding was celebrated, life stories were exchanged, and the poets of the city, of whom there are some very good ones, took it upon themselves to celebrate the remarkable affair, together with the matchless beauty of the little gipsy girl. The famous licenciate Pozo wrote verses that will make the fame of Preciosa last as long as time.

I forgot to relate that the love-struck innkeeper's daughter publicly owned that the story of Andrés the gipsy's theft was not true, and confessed her love and her guilt, for which there was no punishment. For in the happiness which followed the finding of the betrothed couple vengeance was buried and mercy revived.

Rinconete and Cortadillo

One hot summer day, two boys of about fourteen or fifteen turned up in the Molinillo inn, which is on the borders of the famous Alcudia plain, as you go from Castile to Andalusia. Certainly neither of them was more than seventeen, both of them were good-looking, but ragged, tattered and unkempt. They had no cloaks; their breeches were of drill and their stockings – of bare flesh. It's true that their footwear made up for it, because one of them wore rope sandals, but worn so much that they were in fact worn out, and the other had shoes which were full of holes and with the soles off, so that they were more like stocks than shoes. One of them wore a green hunting-cap; the other a hat without a band, low-crowned and broad-brimmed. In a bag on his back fastened round him one carried a greasy, chamois-coloured shirt; the other was empty-handed and with no baggage, although he had what looked like a big package inside his shirt-front, which turned out to be one of those so-called Walloon collars[1], stiffened with grease instead of starch, and so tattered that it seemed to be nothing but threads. Inside were some playing-cards of oval shape, for the corners had got worn out through use, and so that they would last a bit longer they had been clipped and left like that. The two were sunburnt, with long, dirty fingernails and hands none too clean; one had a cutlass, and the other a knife with a yellow horn handle, of the sort they call a cow-herd's knife.

The two of them came out to have their siesta on a sort of porch or shelter in front of the inn, and sat opposite each other. The one who appeared to be the older said to the younger one, 'What part of the country do you come from, noble sir, and where are you going?'

'I don't know, sir Knight,' replied the other, 'where I came from, or where I am going either.'

1. Walloon collar. Also known as a Vandyke collar: a deep, white collar extending over the shoulders and chest.

'Well, certainly,' said the older one, 'you don't appear to come from heaven, and since this is no place to settle, you will certainly have to move on.'

'That is so,' replied the younger one, 'but I have spoken the truth in what I have said, because the place I came from is not my own part of the country. All I have in it is a father who doesn't treat me as his son and a stepmother who treats me in the way stepchildren are usually treated. I am going where chance directs, and I shall stop wherever I find someone who will give me the wherewithal to get through this wretched life.'

'And do you know any trade?' asked the big one.

The younger one replied, 'All I know is that I run like a hare, and jump like a deer and can cut very neatly with shears.'

'All that is very good, useful and profitable,' said the older one, 'because you'll always find a sacristan who'll give you the All Saints' offering to cut the paper flowers for the monument on Maundy Thursday.'

'That's not my kind of cutting,' answered the younger one. 'My father, by God's mercy, is a tailor and hosier, and he taught me how to cut the sort of leggings which cover the instep like spats, and I cut them so well that I could easily pass my master's examination, if my wretched luck didn't always do the dirty on me.'

'That happens to the best of us,' answered the big one, 'and I have always heard that the finest talents are the ones which most often go to waste, but you are still young enough to improve your fortune. And if I'm not mistaken and my eyes don't deceive me, you have other hidden gifts which you don't want to disclose.'

'Yes, I have,' answered the younger one, 'but they are not for publication, as you have clearly pointed out.'

To which the older one replied,

'Well, I can tell you that I am one of the best keepers of secrets you'll find for miles around, and to make you open your heart freely to me, I am going to put you under an obligation by opening mine first. I do this because I imagine that there's some good reason why fate has brought us together here, and I think we are destined to be true friends from now until our dying day. I, noble sir, am a native of Fuenfría, a place well known and famous by reason of the illustrious travellers who continually pass through it. My name is Pedro del Rincón; my father is a person of quality, being an officer of the Holy Crusade, by which I mean that he is a seller of papal bulls, or a pardoner as the common people call them. I went with him on his rounds once or twice, and I learnt his trade so well that the man who is reckoned to be the best seller of bulls in the world couldn't beat me at it. But one day, being more fond of the cash from the bulls than the bulls themselves, I made off with a bag of money and ended up with it in Madrid. Taking advantage of the sort of opportunities that crop up there, I very soon took the stuffing out of that bag and left it with more creases than a bridegroom's handkerchief. The man who had charge of the money came after me; they arrested me and I hadn't any influence; although, when these gentlemen saw how young I was, they were satisfied just to let them tie me to the doorknob and tickle my back for a bit, and banish me from the capital for four years. I was patient, shrugged my shoulders, put up with my punishment and my beating, and set off to do my exile, so speedily that I did not have a chance to find a mount. I took what I could of my valuables and the things that seemed most necessary to me, and among them I took these cards' – and with that he took out the ones which we've mentioned, which he had wrapped up in his collar – 'with which I've earned my keep in the inns and taverns all the way from Madrid to here, by playing pontoon. Although you can see that they're all dirty and worn, they can do wonders if you know them. You never cut without finding an ace underneath and, if you are versed in this game, you'll see what an asset it is to know that you have an ace for certain with the first card you take, which you can use as one or eleven: for the good thing is that when you get twenty-one, you keep the money. Apart from this, I learned from an ambassador's cook some tricks to use in playing reversis and lansquenet, which is also known as *andabobo*, for just as you might pass an examination in cutting leggings, so I could qualify as a master in the art of card-playing. This is enough to ensure that I shall not die of hunger, because even if I come to a farm, there's always someone who's ready to spend a bit of time playing cards. We two must try this experiment – let's cast the net and see if one of these muleteer-birds about here will fall into it. I mean we'll play pontoon as if we were in earnest, and if anyone wants to make a third, he'll be the first to lose his cash.'

'A splendid idea,' said the other, 'and I'm most grateful to you for having told me about your life, and so obliged me to tell you about mine. To cut a long story short this is it: I was born in a respectable village between Salamanca and Medina del Campo. My father is a tailor; he taught me his trade, and having started cutting with shears, my natural talent soon taught me to cut purses. The restricted life of the village and my stepmother's unloving attitude made me fed up, so I left my village and came to Toledo to practise my trade. I've done wonders at it, for there's not a locket hidden in a head-dress nor a pocket so well concealed that my fingers do not explore or my scissors cut it, even though the owners may be guarding it like Argus.[2] And during the four months when I was in that city I was never once caught, attacked, chased by police, or split on by tale-bearers. It's true that about a week ago a double-crosser told the magistrate about my talents, and he, attracted by my gifts, wanted to see me; but I, being a humble person, and not wanting to have anything to do with such important people, contrived not to meet him, leaving the city so swiftly that I did not have time to fit myself out with a mount, money, hired coach, nor even a cart.'

'Forget it,' said Rincón, 'for now that we know each other, there's no occasion for these grand airs. Let's confess simply that we hadn't a bean, nor even any shoes.'

'All right,' answered Diego Cortado, for this is what the younger one said he was called, 'and since our friendship, as you, Mr Rinconete, have said, is destined to last for ever, let us initiate it with solemn and worthy ceremonies.'

And Diego Cortado, rising to his feet, embraced Rincón, and Rincón him, with equal affection. Then they both started to play pontoon with the aforementioned cards, free from dust and straw, but not from grease and cunning tricks; and after a few hands Cortado could turn up the ace as well as his teacher Rincón.

At this moment a muleteer came out to the porch to take the air, and asked if he could make a third. They welcomed him gladly, and in less than half an hour they won twelve *reales* and twenty-two

2. Argus, cf. above, *The Little Gipsy Girl*, note 3.

maravedís from him, which was the same as giving him twelve stabs with a lance and twenty-two thousand sorrows. And the muleteer, thinking that because they were boys they would not be able to stop him, tried to take the money from them; but they, one with his cutlass and the other with his knife with the yellow handle, gave him so much to think about that if his companions hadn't come out he'd certainly have had a bad time.

At that moment a company of travellers on horseback happened to pass by on their way to take a rest at the Alcalde inn, which is half a league farther on. Seeing the muleteer quarrelling with the two boys, they managed to calm them down and invited them, if they were by any chance going to Seville, to accompany them.

'That's where we're going,' said Rincón, 'and we'll serve you in any way you may command.'

And without further delay, they jumped in front of the mules and went off with them, leaving the muleteer in a sorry plight and in a great rage, and the innkeeper's wife amazed at the behaviour of the two rogues; for she had been listening to their conversation without their knowing. When she told the muleteer that she had heard them say that the cards they had were faked, he tore his hair and wanted to go to the inn after them to recover his property, because he said it was a great insult and slight on his honour that two boys had deceived a full-grown man like him. His companions stopped him and advised him not to go, if only to avoid broadcasting his clumsiness and stupidity. In short, they argued with him to such effect that although they did not manage to console him they persuaded him to stay.

Meanwhile Cortado and Rincón contrived to serve the travellers so well that they carried them on their horses for most of the way, and although they had some chances to rob the bags of their temporary masters, they didn't take them, so as not to lose the splendid chance of the journey to Seville, where they very much wanted to go. All the same, as they were going through the Aduana gate into the city at prayer time, Cortado, taking advantage of the inspection and the payment of duty, could not refrain from cutting the bag or valise that a certain Frenchman in the company was carrying on the crupper of his mule. So, with his yellow-handled knife he gave it such a long and deep wound that its insides were open for all to see, and he neatly took from it two good shirts, a sundial and a little memo book, things which they didn't much like the look of. They thought that if the Frenchman was carrying that valise on the crupper of his horse, it was a pity to have filled it with things of such little consequence as these trinkets, and they would have liked to give it another touch; but they didn't, thinking that it would already have been missed and the rest put in a safe place.

They had taken their leave of the party who had supported them so far on their journey before performing this robbery, and the next day they sold the shirts in the second-hand shop near the Arenal gate, and made twenty *reales* out of them. After this they went to look at the city, and were amazed at the size and splendour of its cathedral and the vast number of people by the river, because it was at the time when they were loading up the fleet. There were six galleys there, the sight of which made them sigh and dread the day when a mistake on their part would lead them to spend the rest of their lives in them. They saw the vast number of basket-boys who were running about there, and they inquired of one of them what sort of business they were engaged in, if it was hard work, and what they made out of it. An Asturian boy, who was the one they questioned, said that it was an easy trade and that you didn't pay any duty, and that some days he made five or six *reales* profit. With that he could eat, drink and live splendidly, without needing to look for a master to whom he would have to give guarantees; and knowing that he could eat at any time he wished, for he could find food at all times of the day in any cheap eating-house in the city.

The account given by the little Asturian didn't seem at all bad to them, and the trade seemed just made for them, for they could practise their own safely under cover of it, through the opportunity it offered of going into all the houses. They decided there and then to buy the necessary equipment to practise it, since they could engage in it without passing any examination. And the Asturian, in answer to their question about what they should buy, told them they would each need a small bag, clean if not new, and three palm baskets each, two big and one small, in which the meat, fish and fruit could be put, the bag being for the bread; and he took them to where they could sell it. They, with the money left from the loot from the Frenchman, bought the whole outfit, and in two hours, they were past masters at the new trade, such skill did they show in displaying their baskets and arranging their bags. Their guide showed them the places where they should go: in the mornings, to the meat market and San Salvador Square; on fish days to the fish market and the Costanilla;[3] every afternoon to the river; on Thursdays to the Feria.

They made a note of all this, and the next morning very early they stationed themselves in San Salvador Square. They had barely arrived when they were surrounded by other boys engaged in the same trade, who seeing their brand-new bags and baskets realized that they were new to the square. They asked them thousands of questions, and they answered all of them sensibly and politely. Then a student and a soldier came up, and attracted by the cleanness of the baskets of the two novices, the one who appeared to be a student called Cortado, while the soldier called Rincón:

'God be with you,' they said in unison.

'That's a good start to our business,' said Rincón, 'for you're the first to employ me, sir.'

To which the soldier replied, 'It's not a bad beginning, because I'm in funds and I'm in love, and I'm giving a dinner-party today for some friends of my lady-love.'

'Then load me up as much as you like, sir, for I've got the will and the strength to carry the whole square, and if you need my help to cook it, I'll do it very willingly.'

The soldier was very pleased with the boy's good humour, and told him that if he wanted to go into service, he would rescue him from that wretched trade; to which Rincón replied that as that was the first day he had practised it, he didn't want to leave it so soon, until he had at least weighed up the pros and cons. If he didn't like it, he gave him his word that he would rather serve him than a canon.

The soldier laughed, loaded him up well, showed him his lady's house so that he should know it from then on and so that he would have no need to go with the boy when he sent him again. Rincón promised to be loyal and treat him fairly; the soldier gave him three pennies and he rushed back to the square, so as not to lose

3. A hill on which a fishmarket stood.

the chance of another job. The Asturian had told him about this trick; and also that when they were carrying small fish, such as dace or sardines or plaice, they could take a few out by way of samples, at least against the day's expenses; but that this had to be done with care, so that one should not lose one's good reputation, which was what counted most in that trade.

Quick as Rincón was in getting back, he found Cortado already installed in the same spot. Cortado went up to Rincón, and asked him how things had gone with him. Rincón opened his hand and showed him the three pennies. Cortado put his hand into his shirt-front and took out a small purse, which gave signs of having been scented with amber in times gone by. It was rather bulky, and he said, 'This is what his reverence the student paid me with, and he gave me two pennies as well; but you take it, Rincón, in case anything happens.'

When the purse had already been handed over unobserved, the student suddenly arrived, sweating profusely and in a terrible state. Seeing Cortado he asked him if by chance he had seen a purse of such and such a kind, which he had lost, with fifteen real golden crowns and three *reales* and the same number of *maravedís* in pennies and half-pence, and whether he had taken it while he was going round with him doing his shopping. To which Cortado, dissembling with remarkable skill, and without showing any sign of being disturbed or changing his expression, replied, 'All I can say about this purse is that you must have been very careless to have lost it.'

'That's just it, wretch that I am!' answered the student. 'I must have been very careless with it, for it's been stolen from me.'

'That's what I say,' said Cortado, 'but while there's life there's hope, and your best hope is to be patient, for God made us out of nothing, one day follows another, and what they give they take away; and perhaps as time goes on, the one who took the purse may come to repent and return it to you smelling of incense.'

'We could manage without the incense,' answered the student.

And Cortado went on to say, 'Especially as there are papal letters of excommunication and there is diligence, which is the mother of good fortune. All the same, I shouldn't like to be the one who took that purse, because if you are in holy orders of any kind, I'd think I had committed some great incest or sacrilege.'

'He certainly has committed sacrilege,' said the disconsolate student; 'for although I'm not a priest, I am sacristan to some nuns, and the money in the purse was from the stipend of a chaplaincy, which a friend of mine who is a priest asked me to collect, and it is sacred and holy money.'

'That's his funeral,' said Rincón at this point. 'He asked for it. There's a day of judgement, when everything will come to light, and then we'll see whom we're dealing with, and who was the bold fellow who dared to take, steal and appropriate the stipend of the chaplaincy. And how much does he make a year? Tell me, Sacristan, for goodness' sake.'

'Make, be damned. Am I going to waste my time telling you about how much he makes?' answered the sacristan, bursting with anger. 'Tell me, brother, if you know anything; if not, God be with you, for I'm going to make a public declaration of the theft.'

'That doesn't seem a bad solution,' said Cortado, 'but be sure you don't forget what the purse looks like, nor the exact amount of money in it; for if you're a farthing out, it will never appear as long as the world lasts, and that's as true as fate.'

'There's no fear of that,' answered the sacristan, 'for it's more fixed in my memory than the peal of the bells: I shan't be a mite out.'

At this point he took out of his pocket a lace-edged handkerchief to wipe the sweat off his brow, for it was pouring off him, and as soon as Cortado saw it, he marked it down as his. So when the sacristan had gone, Cortado followed him, and caught him up at the Gradas, where he called him and drew him aside. Then he began to say such nonsense to him and tell him such tall stories about the theft and discovery of his purse, raising his hopes, without ever finishing any of the arguments he started, that the poor sacristan was quite bewildered as he listened to him; and as he couldn't manage to understand what he was saying to him, he made him repeat the argument two or three times. Cortado looked him straight in the face and didn't take his eyes off his; the sacristan was staring back at him, hanging on his words. This tremendous fascination gave Cortado a chance to finish off the job, and he neatly extracted the handkerchief from his pocket. Then, saying good-bye to him, he told him to try to see him in the same place in the afternoon, because he had an idea that a boy who followed the same trade and was about the same size as he, and who had thieving tendencies, had taken the purse, and that he undertook to find out, sooner or later.

The sacristan was somewhat consoled when he heard this, and left him. Cortado came up to Rincón, who had seen it all from a little way off; and farther on there was another basket boy, who saw all that had happened and how Cortado gave the handkerchief to Rincón. Going up to them he said,

'Tell me, gallant sirs, do you belong to the bad set or not?'

'We don't understand what you are on about, gallant sir,' answered Rincón.

'You don't understand when I say thieves?'

'We're not from Thebes nor from Murcia,' said Cortado. 'If you want anything else, say so; if not, be off with you.'

'Don't you understand?' said the youth. 'Well I'll make you understand, and I'll feed it to you with a silver spoon. I mean, gentlemen, are you thieves? But I don't know why I'm asking you this, for I already know you are. Tell me, how is it you haven't been to Mr Monipodio's customs-house?'

'Do you pay duty on thefts in this part of the country, gallant sir?' said Rincón.

'If you don't pay,' answered the boy, 'at least you register with Mr Monipodio, who is the father, master and protector of thieves; and so I advise you to come with me and pay your respects to him, or if not, don't dare to steal without his authority, or it'll cost you dear.'

'I thought', said Cortado, 'that stealing was a free trade, exempt from tax or tribute, and that if you do pay it, you pay wholesale, giving your neck and your back by way of settlement. But since things are this way, and every country has its customs, let us observe those of this country, which since it is the most important in the world will be the most proper as regards its customs. So you may conduct us to the place where this gentleman you mention is to be found, for I already have an idea, from what I've heard, that he is very well qualified and noble, and extremely skilled at his trade.'

'Indeed he is able, skilled and well qualified,' answered the youth. 'So much so, that during the four years that he's been our chief and our father not more than four of us have ended up on the gallows, only about thirty have had tannings and sixty-two gone to the galleys.'

'Indeed, sir,' said Rincón, 'I can no more understand what you are saying than fly.'

'Let's be on our way, for I'll explain as we go,' answered the young man; 'as well as other things which you ought to know like the back of your hand.'

And so as they walked on he explained to them other words belonging to what they call 'gipsy language' or 'thieves' slang', in the course of his talk, which was by no means short, for the road was long. On the way Rincón said to his guide, 'Are you by any chance a thief?'

'Yes,' he replied, 'in the service of God and all good folk, although not a very expert one, for I'm still in my novice year.'

To which Cortado replied, 'It's news to me that there are thieves in the world in the service of God and good folk.'

To which the boy replied, 'Sir, I don't get mixed up in things I don't understand; what I know is that each one in his profession can praise God, and especially when things are so well ordered as they are under Monipodio.'

'Without doubt,' said Rincón, 'it must be a good and holy order since it makes thieves serve God.'

'It is so holy and so good', replied the boy, 'that I don't know if it would be possible to improve on it in our craft. He has laid it down that out of what we steal we give something by way of alms to pay for oil for the lamp which burns in front of a most sacred image in this city, and indeed we have seen great things as a result of this good work. Some days ago they inflicted the *ansia* three times on a *cuatrero* who had stolen a couple of *roznos*, and although he was thin and sickly, he endured it without squealing, as if it were nothing. We in the profession attribute this to his piety, for he's not really strong enough to suffer the *primer desconcierto* of the torturer's rope. And because I know you are going to ask me about some of the words I've been using, prevention is better than cure, so I'll tell you before you ask me. You must know that a *cuatrero* is a horse-thief; *ansia* is a torture; *roznos* are asses, speaking with respect; *primer desconcierto* is the first twist of the rope. Other things we do, like saying our rosary once a week, and many of us don't steal on a Friday, nor do we speak to a woman called Mary on a Saturday.'

'All this seems delightful to me,' said Cortado, 'but tell me, is any other restitution or penance demanded apart from what you've said?'

'There's no question of restitution,' answered the boy. 'That is impossible; for the stolen goods are divided up, and each one of the members and contracting parties takes his share. So the one who first did the stealing cannot give anything back, especially since there is no one to make us do it, for we never go to confession. And if they excommunicate us, the news never reaches us, because we never go to church at the time when the decrees are read, except on feast days, for the sake of the profit which the crowds provide.'

'And do these gentlemen say', asked Cortadillo, 'that their life is holy and good just because they do things like that?'

'Well, what's wrong with it?' replied the boy. 'Isn't it worse to be a heretic or a renegade, or to kill one's father and mother, or to be a solomite?'

'You must mean "sodomite",' said Rincón.

'That's what I say,' said the boy.

'It's all just as bad,' Cortado went on. 'But since our fate has decreed that we should join this brotherhood, let's get moving, for I'm dying to meet Mr Monipodio, of whose many virtues I hear so much.'

'Your wish will soon be fulfilled,' said the boy, 'for you can see his house from here. Stay at the door, and I'll go in and see if he's free, because this is the time when he usually sees people.'

'All right,' said Rincón.

And going on a little, the boy went into a house, which didn't look very impressive – in fact it looked exactly the opposite – and the two of them waited at the door. He soon came out and called them, and they went in. Their guide told them to wait in a little courtyard paved with brick, which was so spotlessly clean that it shone as if it had been rubbed with the finest vermilion. On one side was a three-legged stool and on the other a pitcher with a broken lip, with a little jug on top, suffering from the same complaint as the pitcher; on the other side was a rush mat, and in the middle a pot, which they call a *maceta* in Seville, with sweet basil in it.

The boys examined the furnishings in the house with care until Mr Monipodio came down; and seeing that he was a long time, Rincón ventured into one of the two small rooms which led off the courtyard. In it were two fencing swords and two cork shields, hanging from four nails, and a big chest, without a lid or any kind of cover, and three more rush mats spread out on the floor. There was one of those badly-printed images of Our Lady stuck on the wall opposite, lower down a little palm basket and, fixed to the wall, a white bowl, from which Rincón concluded that the basket served as an alms box, and the bowl to hold holy water, as was in fact the case.

At this point, two youths of about twenty and dressed as students came into the house, and shortly afterwards, two basket-boys and a blind man. Without saying a word, they began to walk up and down in the courtyard. Soon after, two old men dressed in thick flannel came in, each wearing spectacles, which made them look venerable and respectable, and each with a rosary of jingling beads in his hand. After them entered an old woman with a long full skirt, and, without saying a word, she went into the room, and having taken holy water, knelt down very devoutly in front of the image. After some time, she kissed the ground and raised her arms and eyes to heaven three times. Then she got up, threw her offering into the basket, and went out with the rest into the patio. Within a short time there were about fourteen persons assembled in the patio in different dress and belonging to different professions. Among the last to arrive were two fine swaggering young fellows, with big moustaches, broad-brimmed hats, Walloon collars, coloured stockings, fancy garters, outsize swords, a pocket pistol each instead of a dagger, and with their bucklers hanging from their belts. As soon as they came in, these two cast suspicious glances at Rincón and Cortado, as if surprised to see them and not knowing who they were. And going up to them, they asked them if they belonged to the brotherhood. Rincón answered 'yes', and that they were at their service.

At last the moment arrived when Mr Monipodio came down, all

the more welcome for having been awaited so long by that virtuous company. He looked about forty-five or forty-six years old, tall, dark, beetle-browed, and with a very thick black beard and deep-set eyes. He was in his shirt-sleeves, and through the opening in front you could see a veritable wood, so thick was the hair on his chest. He wore a thick flannel cloak reaching almost to his feet, on which he wore a pair of shoes which he had left unfastened. His legs were covered by ill-fitting drill breeches, which were baggy and reached to his ankles. His hat was one of those worn by the gentry of the underworld, with a broad brim and a crown shaped like a bell, and he wore a shoulder-belt, from which hung a short sword with the 'little dog' mark. His hands were short and hairy, and his fingers fat, with fingernails splayed out and bent under. His legs were not visible, but his feet were enormously broad with bunions on them. In fact, he looked the most clumsy and hideous ruffian you've ever seen. The boys' guide came in with him, and seizing them by the hands, presented them to Monipodio, saying to him, 'These are the two good lads I told you about, Mr Monipodio. 'samine them, and you'll see how worthy they are to enter our fraternity.'

'I'll be very glad to do that,' answered Monipodio.

I forgot to say that as soon as Monipodio came downstairs, all those who were waiting for him bowed long and low to him, except the two toughs, who in a cool sort of way, as they put it themselves, took off their hats to him, and then went back to walking up and down one side of the courtyard, while Monipodio walked up and down the other, asking the newcomers about their trade, where they came from and who their parents were.

To which Rincón replied, 'The trade speaks for itself, since we have come to you; where we come from doesn't seem to matter much, nor who our parents are, because you don't have to provide this sort of information even to enter an order of nobility.'

To which Monipodio replied, 'You are right, my son, and it is a very proper thing to conceal these things, as you say; for if fortune doesn't turn out as it should, it is not a good thing that there should be an entry in the register with the notary's signature over it, with the words, "So-and-so, son of so-and-so, native of such-and-such a place, was hanged, or whipped on such-and-such a day," or something of that kind, for it sounds bad to sensitive ears. And so I repeat that it is a good idea to keep quiet about where you come from, to conceal your parentage, and to change your own name, although in our company nothing must be concealed. For the moment all I want to know is your names.'

Rincón told his, and Cortado too.

'Well, from now on,' said Monipodio, 'I wish and indeed insist that you, Rincón, shall be called "Rinconete", and you, Cortado, "Cortadillo", which are names just right for your age and our rules, which require us to know the names of the parents of our fellow-members. This is because it is our custom every year to have certain masses said for the souls of those who are deceased and for our benefactors, paying the priest's stupend with part of our takings, and these masses, once said and paid for, they say are profitable to the said souls by way of outrage. Under the heading of our benefactors we include the attorney who defends us, the bailiff who warns us, the executioner who has pity on us, the man who, when one of us is running away down the street and someone shouts after him, "Stop thief! Stop thief!", stands in the way and holds up the stream of people following him, saying, "Let the poor wretch go, he's been unlucky enough already! Let him get away; let his sin be his punishment!" The girls who take pains to help us both in prison and in the galleys are our benefactors too; and so are our fathers and mothers, who cast us into the world, and the notary, who if he is in a good mood plays down our crimes and gets us off lightly. For all of these that I've mentioned our brotherhood holds its adversary every year with the greatest pump and salinity we can manage.'

'Certainly,' said Rinconete, who had already adopted his new name, 'it is a task worthy of that most lofty and profound talent which, so we have heard, you, Mr Monipodio, possess. But our parents are still alive; if in their lifetime we should come across them, we shall immediately inform this most happy and friendly confraternity, so that they may benefit from this outrage or torment, or that adversary you mention, with the accustomed solemnity and pomp, if it wouldn't be more properly done with "pump" and "salinity", as you also noted in your statement.'

'It shall be done, or strike me dead,' replied Monipodio.

And calling the guide, he said to him, 'Come here, Ganchuelo. Are the guards posted?'

'Yes,' said the guide, whose name was Ganchuelo. 'There are three guards keeping watch, and there's no fear of our being caught unawares.'

'Returning then, to our business,' said Monipodio, 'I should like you to tell me, boys, what you know, so as to give you the duty appropriate to your inclination and talent.'

'I', answered Rinconete, 'know a bit about card tricks. I can keep a card back; I can recognize marked cards; I can play with one, or four, or eight; I'm not slow when it comes to marking cards so that you can recognize them by touch; I can make a gap in a pack as easily as I can get into my house, I'd sooner get together a band of sharpers than a regiment in Naples, and I'd slip a bad card to a chap faster than I'd lend him two *reales*.'

'That's a start,' said Monipodio, 'but all that is old stuff, and so well worn that every novice knows all about it, so it's no use except with people so green that they let themselves be killed before midnight. But time will tell, and we shall see what we shall see; for half a dozen lessons on top of this foundation I should think would make you a first-rate operator, and even a master of the craft.'

'All that will be in the service of your worship and the members of the brotherhood,' answered Rinconete.

'And you, Cortadillo, what do you know?' asked Monipodio.

'I', answered Cortadillo, 'know the trick called put in two and take out five, and I can explore a pocket with great accuracy and skill.'

'Do you know anything more?' said Monipodio.

'No, for my great sins,' answered Cortadillo.

'Don't be upset, my son,' replied Monipodio, 'for you have come to a refuge where you will not founder and a school from which you are bound to emerge with great profit in all those things that most concern you. And when it comes to spirit, how are you off, boys?'

'How do you think?' answered Rinconete. 'We've enough spirit to undertake anything to do with our craft and profession.'

'Good,' replied Monipodio; 'but I should like you also to be able, if necessary, to stand half a dozen *ansias* without opening your mouth, or saying a word.'

'We know already', said Cortadillo, 'what *ansias* means, and we're ready for anything. We're not so ignorant that we haven't grasped that what the tongue says the neck pays for, and heaven is kind to the man of courage, if we may use the term, when it leaves it to his tongue to determine whether he lives or dies. For after all, there's only a letter's difference between a "yes" and a "no".'

'Stop, that's enough,' said Monipodio at this point. 'This statement alone convinces me, and obliges me to let you become full members at once and dispense with the year of probation.'

'I agree to that,' said one of the toughs.

And with one voice all the company agreed, for they had been listening to the whole conversation, and they begged Monipodio to allow them straight away to enjoy the immunities of the brotherhood, because their pleasant bearing and good conversation well deserved this reward. He answered that, to please them all, he would grant this immediately, bidding them realize the importance of these immunities, since they involved not having to pay half the proceeds of the first theft they made, nor to do menial jobs all that year, such as taking bail to the prison for a senior member or going to the brothel on behalf of those who had contributed. They could drink wine without water in it, have a party whenever, however and wherever they wished, without asking leave of their chief; have a share straight away in the winnings of the senior members of the brotherhood; and other things which they considered to be a great privilege, and for which they thanked the company in the most civil manner.

At this point, a boy came running in out of breath, and said,

'The constable in charge of vagrants is coming towards the house, but he has no patrol with him.'

'Don't get excited,' said Monipodio, 'for he's a friend and never comes to do us any harm. Be calm, and I'll go out and talk to him.'

They were all rather frightened, but they calmed down, and Monipodio went out to the door, where he found the constable, to whom he stayed talking for a while. When he came back in again, he asked,

'Who was on today in San Salvador Square?'

'I was,' said the guide.

'Well, how is it', said Monipodio, 'that I haven't been shown a little amber purse which went astray there this morning, with fifteen gold crowns and two *reales* and I don't know how many pennies?'

'It's true', said the guide, 'that that purse was missing today; but I haven't taken it, nor can I imagine who did.'

'None of your tricks with me,' said Monipodio. 'The purse must be produced because the constable is asking for it, and he's a friend and does us thousands of favours every year!'

The boy swore again that he knew nothing about it. Monipodio began to get so angry that it looked as if he was shooting fire from his eyes, as he said, 'Let no one make light of breaking our rule in the slightest degree, or it'll cost him his life! Out with the purse, and if it's being concealed so as not to pay the dues, I will pay the lot on my own account, because the constable must be satisfied whatever happens.'

The youth swore and cursed again, saying that he hadn't taken the purse nor set eyes on it; all of which added fuel to the flames of Monipodio's anger, and made the whole gathering get excited, seeing that their statutes and good ordinances were being broken.

Rinconete, seeing all this dissension and excitement, thought it a good idea to calm it down, and to satisfy his chief, who was bursting with rage. So, taking counsel with his friend Cortadillo, with his consent he took out the sacristan's purse and said, 'Let's put an end to this quarrel, gentlemen, for this is the purse, and nothing is missing of what the constable has mentioned. My comrade, Cortadillo, took it, with a handkerchief belonging to the same owner, for good measure.'

Then Cortadillo took out the handkerchief and showed it to the company. When Monipodio saw this, he said, 'Cortadillo the good (for you must answer to this name and title from now on), you must keep the handkerchief, and I undertake to pay compensation for this. As for the purse, the constable must have it, for it belongs to a sacristan who is a relative of his, and it is only right that the proverb should be proved right which says: "The least you can do is give a leg of the chicken to the man who gave you the whole bird." This good constable covers up more in one day than we can or do give him in a hundred.'

By common consent, they all applauded the splendid behaviour

of the two newcomers and the judgement and decision of their
leader, who went out to give the purse to the constable. Cortadillo
was confirmed in his surname of 'Good', just as if he were Don
Alonso Pérez de Guzmán the Good – the one who threw the knife
over the walls of Tarifa to cut off the head of his only son.

When Monipodio came back, two girls came in with him, with
painted faces, reddened lips and their bosoms covered with white
lead. They wore short camlet cloaks, and were a brazen-looking
couple of hussies. As soon as they saw them Rinconete and Cortadillo recognized that they were from the bawdy-house, and they
were quite right. As soon as they came in, they went with open
arms towards Chiquiznaque and Maniferro, the two toughs (the
name Maniferro was because he had an iron hand in place of one
which had been cut off by order of the Court). They embraced the
girls with great delight, and asked them if they had brought anything to wet their whistle.

'Well, what do you think, my brave lad?' answered one of them,
who was called Gananciosa. 'Your boy Silbatillo will soon be home
with the laundry basket stuffed with what God has been pleased to
provide.'

And so it was, for immediately in came a boy with a laundry
basket covered with a sheet.

They were all delighted to see Silbatillo come in, and immediately Monipodio ordered them to get out one of the rush mats
which were in the room and to spread it out in the middle of the
courtyard. And then he ordered everyone to sit down in a circle;
because once they'd had a bite, they would get down to business.
Then the old woman who had prayed to the image said,

'Monipodio, my boy, I'm not in a mood for parties, for I have
had a dizzy head for two days and it's driving me mad. Anyway
before midday I must go and carry out my devotions and place my
candles before the altars of Our Lady of the Waters and the Holy
Crucifix of St Augustine, which I'd have to do even if it snowed or
blew a gale. What I've come for is to tell you that last night
Renegado and Centopiés brought a laundry basket to my house, a
bit bigger than this one, full of washing, and I declare with the soap
still on it and all. The poor things couldn't have had time to get rid
of it, and they were sweating so much that it was a shame to see

them come staggering in with the water streaming down their faces, like little angels. They told me they were going after a shepherd who had been weighing some sheep in the Carnicería[4] to see if they could get a touch from a magnificent bag of *reales* he was carrying. They didn't unpack or count the clothes, trusting my honesty; and as I hope that God will grant my good wishes and free us all from the power of the law I haven't touched the basket, and it's as sound as the day it was made.'

'We'll believe all you say, mother,' answered Monipodio, 'and let the basket stay there, for I'll go at nightfall, and examine what's in it, and give each one his due, as truly and faithfully as I always do.'

'As you decide, son,' answered the old woman; 'and as it's getting late, give me a swig if you have one to comfort this poor old stomach of mine. It's in such a poor state.'

'You shall have it, mother,' said Escalanta, Gananciosa's companion.

And when the basket was uncovered, there was a kind of leather bag with about eight gallons of wine and a cork measure which could take about a couple of litres easily; and when Escalanta had filled it, she put it in the hands of the devout old woman, who taking it with both hands, and blowing off some foam, said: 'You've poured a lot out, daughter Escalanta; but God will give me strength for all my tasks.'

And putting it to her lips, without taking breath, she transferred it from the measure to her stomach in one go, and said as she finished,

'It's from Guadalcanal, and the little chap still has a tiny trace of chalk in him. God comfort you, daughter, as you have comforted me; although I'm afraid it won't do me much good, for I had no breakfast.'

'It certainly won't, mother,' answered Monipodio, 'because it's extremely old.'

'By the Virgin I hope it is,' answered the old woman.

And she added, 'Girls, see if you have a penny to buy the candles for my prayers, because in my haste and eagerness to bring you the news about the basket I left my bag at home.'

4. Meat market.

'Yes, I have one, Señora Pipota' (for that was the name of the good old woman), answered Gananciosa. 'Here you are. I'll give you two pennies, and I beg you to buy a candle for me with one of them, and put it in front of St Michael; and if you can buy two, put the other one in front of St Blas, for they are my patrons. I should like you to put another in front of Santa Lucia, because I'm devoted to her too, for my eyes' sake, but I haven't any change. Never mind; we'll have enough to deal with them all another day.'

'Just you do that, daughter, and mind you're not mean; for it's very important to do your good deeds before you die, and not to wait until your heirs or executors do them.'

'Mother Pipota is right,' said Escalanta. And putting her hand in her purse, she gave her another penny, and asked her to put another couple of candles in front of the saints who in her opinion were most profitable and appreciative.

With that, Pipota said to them as she went off, 'Enjoy yourselves, children, while you have time; for old age will come, and then you will mourn the times you wasted in your youth, as I mourn them; and commend me to God in your prayers, for I am going to do the same for myself and for you, so that He may keep us free and safe, in our dangerous business, from the terror of the law.'

And with that, she left them.

When the old woman had gone, they all sat round the mat and Gananciosa spread out the sheet to serve as a tablecloth. The first thing she took out of the basket was a great bunch of radishes and about two dozen oranges and lemons, and then a big pan full of slices of fried cod; then she put out half a Dutch cheese, a pot of excellent olives, and a plate of prawns, a great dish of crabs, with a caper and pimento sauce, and three snowy white loaves from Gandul. There were about fourteen for lunch, and every one of them took out a knife with a yellow handle, except for Rinconete, who took out his cutlass. The two old men in flannel cloaks and the guide had the job of pouring out the wine from the cork measure. But they had barely begun to attack the oranges, when they were all startled by a knocking at the door. Monipodio told them to be calm, and going into the lower room, he took a buckler off a hook and went to the door with his hand on his sword, and in a deep and frightening voice asked,

'Who's there?'

The reply came from outside, 'It's nobody of consequence, Mr Monipodio; only Tagarete, on guard duty this morning; and I've come to say that Juliana La Cariharta is coming this way, all dishevelled and in tears, and she looks as if something terrible's happened to her.'

At that moment, the person mentioned arrived, sobbing, and when Monipodio recognized her, he opened the door, and told Tagarete to go back to his post and henceforth report what he saw with less noise and fuss; which he said he would.

Cariharta came in, a girl got up like the others and belonging to the same profession. Her hair was dishevelled and her face was all bruised, and as soon as she got into the courtyard she fell fainting on the ground. Gananciosa and Escalanta rushed to help her, and unfastening her blouse, found her all blackened and battered. They threw water in her face, and she recovered, and shouted out,

'Let the justice of God and the King fall on that shameless ruffian, on that cowardly thief, on that lousy rogue whom I've saved from the gallows more times than he has hairs in his beard! Woe is me! To think I've wasted my youth and the best years of my life for a soulless, wicked, incorrigible wretch like that!'

'Calm down, Cariharta,' said Monipodio at this point; 'for I'm here and I'll see that justice is done. Tell us what they've done to you, for it'll take longer for you to tell us about it than for me to see you revenged; let me know if you've had any trouble with your boy friend, for if this is the case and you want vengeance, you need only say the word.'

'Boy friend?' replied Juliana, 'I'd sooner have a boy friend in hell than that lion among lambs and that lamb among men. Do you think I'd ever eat or go to bed with that one again? I'd rather be eaten by jackals, after he's left me in the state I'm in now.'

And lifting her skirts up to her knees, and even a little higher, she showed that they were covered with weals.

'This is how that wretched Repolido has left me,' she went on, 'when he owes me more than the mother who bore him. And why do you think he did it? As if I gave him any occasion for it. Not on your life. All he did it for was because as he was gambling and started to lose, he sent me his boy Cabrillas to ask me for thirty *reales*, and I sent him only twenty-four, and may God grant that the labour and anxiety I had to get them may be set against my sins. And in payment for this kindness and good deed, thinking that I was keeping something back from the amount he imagined I had, this morning he dragged me out behind the Huerta del Rey,[5] and there, among some olive trees, he stripped me and with his belt, without bothering to hold the buckle (curse him and may I see him in fetters) he whipped me so many times that he left me for dead; and these weals that you can see will testify to the truth of my story.'

Then she began to shout again, and to demand justice; and Monipodio and all the toughs who were there promised again to satisfy her.

Gananciosa took her hand to comfort her, telling her that she would very willingly give one of the best jewels she possessed to have had the same thing happen to her with her boy friend.

'Because I want you to know, Sister Cariharta, if you don't know already, that to be beaten is a sign of affection; and when these rogues attack and beat and kick us, then they adore us. If this is not true, tell me this: after Repolido had punished you, and beaten you up, didn't he pet you a bit?'

'A bit?' she replied in tears. 'A hundred thousand times, and he'd have given his right hand to have me go back to his lodgings with him; and in fact I think he nearly wept himself after he had beaten me.'

'I don't doubt it,' replied Gananciosa; 'and he would weep now if he saw the state he'd left you in; for these men, in cases like this, have barely committed the sin when they are overcome by remorse. You'll see, sister, that he'll come and look for you before we leave here, and ask your forgiveness for all that has happened, as quiet as a lamb.'

'Indeed,' said Monipodio, 'the wretched coward will not darken these doors if he doesn't first do public penance for the crime he's committed. How dare he put his hands on Cariharta's face, or her flesh, a girl who's as clean and hard-working as Gananciosa herself, and I can't praise her more highly than that.'

'Oh, Mr Monipodio,' said Juliana, 'don't say anything against

5. Literally, the King's garden.

the wretch; for bad as he is I love him more than my own life, and the arguments that my friend Gananciosa has put forward in his favour have convinced me. In fact I'm inclined to go and look for him.'

'You won't if you take my advice,' replied Gananciosa, 'because he'll get all puffed up and be up to all sorts of tricks with you. Keep calm, sister, for you'll soon have him coming to say he's sorry, just as I've said; and if he doesn't come we'll write him some verses that will show him where he gets off.'

'Yes, indeed,' said Cariharta, 'for I've plenty of things to write to him!'

'I shall act as secretary when required,' said Monipodio, 'and although I'm no poet, if a man makes up his mind, he'll write a couple of thousand verses in next to no time; and if they don't come out as they should, I have a friend who's a barber and a great poet, who'll fill up the verses any time you like. But for the moment let's finish our lunch, for all the rest can wait till afterwards.'

Juliana was happy to obey her chief, so they all went back to their merry-making, and soon saw the bottom of the basket and the dregs of the wine-skin. The old men drank without stopping; the young ones freely; the ladies without stinting themselves. The old men then asked to be excused, and Monipodio gave permission immediately, telling them to come straight away and tell him anything that might be useful and profitable to the community. They replied that they would take good care to do so, and went off. Rinconete, who was curious by nature, having first begged leave, asked Monipodio what the use was to the community of this pair, who were so old, so broken down and seedy. To which Monipodio replied that these, according to their jargon and way of speaking, were called 'hornets', and that their job was to go round by day to see which houses they could break into by night, and to follow those who got money out of the Contratación, or Mint, to see where they went with it and even where they deposited it. When they found out they tested the thickness of the wall of the house concerned and marked the most suitable place to make the holes to enable them to get in. In short, he said that they were quite as valuable as anyone in the fraternity, if not more so, and that they kept a fifth of everything that was stolen through their efforts, like the King with treasure-trove; and that for all that, they were honourable and truthful men, who led a good life, and had a good reputation, feared God and their consciences, and heard Mass most devoutly every day.

'And there are some of them who are so frugal, especially these two who've just gone off, that they are content with much less than is their due according to our tariff. There are another two who are public porters, who, as they are always moving house, know how to get in and out of all the houses in the city, and which houses are worth while and which are not.'

'All this seems delightful to me,' said Rinconete, 'and I should like to be of some use to such an excellent brotherhood.'

'Heaven always favours good desires,' said Monipodio.

As they were talking, a knock came at the door, Monipodio went out to see who it was, and the answer came:

'Open up, Mr Monipodio; it's Repolido.'

Cariharta heard him, and screamed at the top of her voice, 'Don't answer, Mr Monipodio, don't open to that sailor from Tarpeia, that tiger of Ocaña.'[6]

Monipodio opened the door to Repolido in spite of all this; but when Cariharta saw that he was letting him in, she ran to the room where the bucklers were, and shutting the door behind her, she shouted from inside,

'Take this good-for-nothing away, this murderer of innocents, this frightener of tame doves.'

Maniferro and Chiquiznaque were holding Repolido, who was determined to get in to where Cariharta was; but as they didn't let him, he called from outside, 'Don't be angry any more; come down for goodness' sake, if you want to be married!'

'Married, you wretch?' answered Cariharta. 'That's a fine tune to play. You may want to marry me, but I'd rather marry a skeleton than you!'

'Come on, you stupid girl!' replied Repolido; 'let's stop this, for it's getting late. Don't get on your high horse because I'm talking to you so meekly and behaving so humbly, because, God

6. Ocaña. A town in the province of Toledo, which the illiterate Cariharta confuses with Hircania, a region of Asia, on the south-east coast of the Caspian Sea. Hircania's fierce tigers are mentioned by many classical authors, including Virgil, *Aeneid*, IV, 367.

knows, if my anger gets the better of me, the second attack may be worse than the first. Give in, let's eat our humble pie, and not give it all to the devil!'

'The devil can do what he likes with you,' said Cariharta, 'as long as I never see you again.'

'What did I say?' said Repolido, 'I'm beginning to think, Miss Strumpet, that I'm going to have to put a stop to this, whatever the consequences.'

At this Monipodio said, 'There must be no insolence in my presence. Cariharta will come out, not because of your threats, but out of regard for me, and everything must be done properly; for quarrels between persons who are fond of each other make it all the sweeter when they make up. Oh Juliana! Oh, my girl! Oh my Cariharta! Come out here, for my sake, and I'll make Repolido beg you for pardon on his knees.'

'If he does that,' said Escalanta, 'we'll all be on his side and beg Juliana to come out.'

'If I have to give in at the cost of my dignity,' said Repolido, 'I won't surrender to a bunch of ragamuffins; but if it's because Cariharta wishes it, I won't just kneel, but I'll be a slave and put a nail in my forehead for her sake.'

Chiquiznaque and Maniferro laughed at this, at which Repolido got so angry, thinking that they were making fun of him, that he said, looking absolutely furious, 'If anyone laughs or thinks of laughing at what Cariharta has said, or may say, about me, or I about her, I say he lies and will be lying every time he laughs or thinks of laughing.'

Chiquiznaque and Maniferro gave each other such a look that Monipodio realized that the whole thing would come to a nasty end unless he came to the rescue, and so placing himself straight away between them, he said,

'Don't go on, gentlemen, let's have no more threats; swallow your words, and since they don't amount to very much, don't let anyone take them to heart.'

'We are quite sure', answered Chiquiznaque, 'that this sort of warning has never been given or will be given on our account, for if anyone thought it was, the tambourine is in the hands of some- one who knows how to play it.'

'We've got a tambourine here too, Mr Chiquiznaque,' replied Repolido, 'and if necessary we can play the bells as well. As I've just said, anyone who pokes fun is a liar; and if anyone thinks differently, let him follow me, for I'll cut him down to size with my sword, and that's that.'

And saying this, he made for the door.

Cariharta was listening to this, and when she realized that he was going off in a huff, she rushed out, saying, 'Stop him, don't let him go, or he'll be up to his pranks. Can't you see that he's annoyed, and he's a real Judas Macabbeus when it comes to being tough. Come here, my hero, you apple of my eye.'

And closing in on him, she clutched him firmly by his cloak, and with the help of Monipodio, who came up, they stopped him. Chiquiznaque and Maniferro didn't know whether to be angry or not, so they stopped where they were, waiting to see what Repolido would do. When he saw Cariharta and Monipodio appealing to him, he turned round and said,

'Friends should never upset friends or make fun of friends, especially when they see that friends are upset.'

'There's no friend here', answered Maniferro, 'who wants to upset or make fun of any friend, and since we are all friends let us shake hands like friends.'

Whereupon Monipodio replied, 'You have all spoken like good friends, and being friends you must shake hands like friends.'

So they shook hands, and Escalanta, taking off one of her shoes, began to beat on it like a drum. Then Gananciosa took a new palm broom, which happened to be there, and scraping it made a noise which, although rough and harsh, harmonized with the music of the shoe. Monipodio broke a plate and made two clappers, which, placed between his fingers and clicked together at great speed, kept in tune with the shoe and the broom.

Rinconete and Cortadillo were amazed at the idea of the broom because until then they had never seen it. Maniferro noticed this, and said to them,

'Are you surprised at the broom? Well no wonder, because you couldn't find a cheaper and easier way of making music. Indeed I heard a student say the other day that not even Norpheus, who pulled his wife out of hell, nor Marion, who rode on a dolphin and

came out of the sea as if she were riding on a hired mule, nor that
other great musician who made a city which had a hundred doors
and as many posterns, ever invented a better sort of music, so
easy to learn, so simple to play, so free of frets, pegs and strings,
and with no need of tuning. And what's more I swear they say it
was invented by a fellow from this city, who prides himself on
being a real Hector where music is concerned.'

'That I can well believe,' answered Rinconete, 'but let's listen
to what our musicians want to sing; for you notice that Gananciosa
has cleared her throat, which is a sign that she wants to sing.'

And this was true, because Monipodio had asked her to sing
some *seguidillas* which were in fashion at the time; but it was
Escalanta who started first, and with a thin, quavery voice she sang
as follows:

> A sandy-haired lad from Seville
> has stolen my heart and my will.

Gananciosa went on to sing:

> To a dark handsome boy with green eyes
> every girl who has spirit will rise.

And then Monipodio, shaking the clappers at great speed, said:

> When lovers who quarrel make peace,
> past furies their pleasures increase.

Cariharta did not want her pleasure to be passed over in silence, so
picking up another shoe, she started to dance, and accompanied the
others with the words:

> Stop beating me, for you must see,
> You hurt your own flesh, striking me.

'Sing something straightforward,' said Repolido at this point,
'and don't bother with past history, for there's no sense in that;
let bygones be bygones, let's make a new start, and let it go at that.'

It looked as if the singing was not likely to end for some time,
but suddenly there came a quick knock at the door. Monipodio
went out to see who it was, and the guard told him that the Justice
of the Peace had appeared at the end of the street, preceded by two

constables, Tordillo and Cercnícalo. The people inside heard what
was happening, and they all got so excited that Cariharta and
Escalanta put their shoes on the wrong way round. Gananciosa left
her broom, Monipodio his clappers, and the music gave way to an
uneasy silence. Chiquiznaque didn't open his mouth, Repolido
was stunned and Maniferro was struck dumb. All of them, some in
one direction and some in another, disappeared, going up to the
rooftops to get away and escape over them to the next street. An
unexpected gunshot or a sudden clap of thunder never frightened
a flock of doves caught unawares more thoroughly than the news
of the arrival of the Justice of the Peace scared and threw into
confusion that gathering of good people. The two novices Rinconete and Cortadillo did not know what to do, and stood still,
waiting to see the outcome of that sudden storm. In fact the guard
came back to say that the Justice had gone by without stopping,
giving no sign or trace of any suspicion.

And as he was telling Monipodio this, a young gentleman came
to the door dressed, as they say, like a man about town. Monipodio
brought him in with him, and ordered Chiquiznaque, Maniferro
and Repolido to be called, and no one else. As Rinconete and
Cortadillo had stayed in the courtyard, they could hear all the
conversation that Monipodio had with the newcomer, who asked
Monipodio why his orders had been so badly carried out. Monipodio answered that he didn't even know what had been done, but
that the official in charge of the job was there, and that he would
give a very good account of himself. At this point Chiquiznaque
came down and Monipodio asked him if he had carried out the
fourteen-wound knifing job he had been charged with.

'Which one?' asked Chiquiznaque. 'Do you mean the one on
that merchant at the crossroads?'

'That's the one,' said the gentleman.

'Well, what happened', answered Chiquiznaque, 'was that I
waited for him last night at the door of his house, and he came
before prayer-time. I went up to him, had a good look at his face,
and realized that it was so small that it was absolutely impossible
to fit fourteen knife wounds into it; and finding that I couldn't
carry out my promise and do what was contained in my destructions . . .'

'"Instructions" you must mean,' said the gentleman, 'not "destructions".'

'That's what I meant,' answered Chiquiznaque. 'I say that as the wounds wouldn't fit into the small space available, so as not to waste my journey I knifed a lackey of his, and with the best quality wounds.'

'I'd rather', said the gentleman, 'that you'd given the master seven slashes than the servant fourteen. In fact, you haven't carried out my orders properly, but no matter; I shan't miss the thirty ducats I left by way of deposit. I'll bid you gentlemen farewell.'

And saying this, he took off his hat and turned round to go away, but Monipodio caught hold of the tweed cloak he was wearing and said to him,

'You stay here and keep your promise, for we have kept ours very honourably and to the best advantage; you owe us twenty ducats, and you won't leave here until you've given them to me, or some security worth the same amount.'

'Is this what you call keeping your promise?' answered the gentleman; 'knifing the servant instead of the master?'

'You're all at sea, sir,' said Chiquiznaque. 'You don't seem to remember that proverb which says, "Love me, love my dog!"'

'How does that proverb fit in here?' replied the gentleman.

'Well, isn't it all the same', went on Chiquiznaque, 'to say: "hate me, hate my dog"? So the merchant is the master, you hate him; the servant is the dog, and by hitting the dog you hit his master and the debt is settled and properly discharged. So all there is to do is to pay up straight away without further ado.'

'I'll swear to that,' added Monipodio; 'and you've taken the words right out of my mouth, friend Chiquiznaque. And so, my fine sir, don't you get mixed up in punctilios with your servants and friends, but take my advice and pay straight away for the work that's been done; and if you want the master to have another knifing, according to the number of slashes his face can carry, I can assure you that it's as good as done.'

'If that's the case,' answered the young man, 'I shall be very willing and happy to pay for both in full.'

'Have no more doubt about this,' said Monipodio, 'than about

being a Christian; for Chiquiznaque will give him a knifing that
fits him as if he were born with it.'

'Well, with this assurance and promise,' answered the gentleman,
'take this chain as security for the twenty ducats owing and for
forty which I'm prepared to pay for the knifing we've agreed on.
It weighs a thousand *reales*, and you might as well keep it, because
I have an idea that another fourteen slashes will be required before
long.'

With this he took a chain from his neck, and gave it to Monipodio, who from its colour and weight saw clearly that it was no
fake. Monipodio received it with every sign of pleasure and politeness, like the most well-bred man alive. Chiquiznaque was charged
with the execution of the deed, and undertook to do it that night.
The gentleman went off quite satisfied, and then Monipodio called
all the others, who had gone off in a fright. They all came down
and Monipodio, standing in the middle, took out a notebook which
he had in the hood of his cloak, and gave it to Rinconete to read,
because he could not read himself. Rinconete opened it, and on the
first page he saw that it said:

List of knifings for this week
The first, to the merchant at the crossroads; price fifty crowns.
Received thirty on account. Executor, Chiquiznaque.

'I don't think there are any more, my boy,' said Monipodio. 'Go
on and look under "List of beatings".'

Rinconete turned over, and saw on another page:

List of beatings

And underneath it said:

To the man who keeps the chop-house in Alfalfa: twelve top-quality
strokes, at a crown a piece. Eight given on account. Time limit six days.
Executor, Maniferro.

'You could cross that item off,' said Maniferro, 'for I'll have it
done tonight.'

'Any more, my boy?' said Monipodio.

'Yes, there is another,' answered Rinconete, 'and it says this:

To the hump-backed tailor known for his sins as Silguero, six strokes of the best, at the request of the lady who left the necklace. Executor, Desmochado.

'I'm amazed', said Monipodio, 'that this item is still on the books. Desmochado must be out of action, for it's two days after the time limit and he hasn't been anywhere near the job.'

'I met him yesterday,' said Maniferro, 'and he told me that because the hump-back had been laid up ill he hadn't carried it out.'

'I'm prepared to believe that,' said Monipodio, 'because I consider Desmochado to be so good at his job, that if it weren't for such a good reason he would have done even greater things. Any more, lad?'

'No, sir,' answered Rinconete.

'Then go on,' said Monipodio, 'and look where it says "List of miscellaneous offences".'

Rinconete went on, and on another page he found this:

List of miscellaneous offences
Namely, ink-throwings, juniper-oil smearings, fixing of *sambenitos* and horns, practical jokes, frights, and disturbances, threatened stabbings, publication of libels, etc.

'What does it say underneath?' asked Monipodio.

'It says:

Smearing with oil at the house ...

'Don't say which house, because I know where it is,' answered Monipodio, 'and I am the sine qua non and executor of this bit of nonsense, and there are four crowns paid on account, and the total charge is eight.'

'That's true,' said Rinconete, 'for all this is written down here, and lower down it says:

Fixing of horns.

'Don't read the name of the house nor where it is,' said Monipodio; 'for it's bad enough that the injury should be done, without its being published abroad, for it is a great load on one's conscience. At least, I'd rather fix a hundred horns and as many *sambenitos*, provided I'm paid for my work, than mention it once, even to the mother who bore me.'

'The executor of this is Narigueta,' said Rinconete.

'That's already done and paid for,' said Monipodio. 'See if there are any more, for if I remember rightly, there should be a twenty-crown fright, half paid for, and the executor is the whole community, and the time-limit the end of this month; if it's carried out to the letter, without missing a jot, it will be one of the best things that have happened in this city for a long time. Give me the book , young man, for I know there aren't any more, and I know too that business is very slack. But there are better times ahead and we'll have more to do than we want, for not a leaf falls without God's will, and it's not our business to force anyone to take his revenge. Anyway, everyone wants to do his own dirty work and no one wants to pay the cost of work which he can do himself.'

'That's it,' said Repolido in reply. 'But hurry up and give us our orders, Mr Monipodio, for it's getting late and the heat's coming up fast.'

'What you have to do,' answered Monipodio, 'is to go to your posts, all of you, and not to leave them until Sunday, when we'll all meet here and have a share out of anything that's come our way, without doing injury to anyone. Rinconete the Good and Cortadillo will have as their beat until Sunday from the Torre de Oro, outside the city, to the Alcázar gate, where they can sit on a bench and do their tricks. For I've seen others less clever than they getting away every day with more than twenty *reales* in small change, not to mention silver, with a single pack of cards, and with four cards missing at that. Ganchuelo will show you the beat; and it doesn't matter much if you go up to San Sebastián and San Telmo, although it's only right and proper that no one should encroach on someone else's territory.'

The two of them kissed his hand for the kindnesses done to them, and promised him to carry out their duty faithfully and well, with all diligence and caution.

Whereupon Monipodio took from the hood of his cloak a paper, on which was a list of the members of the brotherhood, and he told Rinconete to put his and Cortadillo's names on it; but as there was no inkpot he gave him the paper to take away and get it written at the first apothecary's, putting 'Rinconete and Cortadillo, members; probation, none; Rinconete, card sharper; Cortadillo, pickpocket'; and the day, month, and year, not mentioning parents or birthplace. As they were dealing with this, one of the old 'hornets' came in and said,

'I've come to tell you that I've just this minute met Lobillo from Málaga at the Gradas and he tells me that he's so much improved in his work that he can take money off the devil himself if he only has clean cards; and that because he's been beaten up he's not coming to register and swear the customary oath of allegiance at the moment; but that on Sunday he'll be here without fail.'

'I was always convinced', said Monipodio, 'that this Lobillo must be without equal in his craft, because he has the best hands for it that you could wish for; for to be a good tradesman in one's profession, one needs good instruments to practise it just as much as intelligence to learn it.'

'I also came across Judío', said the old man, 'in a lodging house in the calle de Tintores. He was wearing clerical dress, and had gone to stay there because he had been told that two wealthy Peruvians live in the same house. He wanted to see if he could get a game with them, even if only for small stakes, because it might lead to something big. He says that he will be at the meeting on Sunday too, and will give account of himself.'

'Judío is a great thief too,' said Monipodio, 'and knows what he's up to. It's days since I've seen him, and he's not behaving right. Indeed if he doesn't mend his ways I'll break his head; for he's no more in orders than the Grand Turk, and knows no more Latin than my mother. Is there any other news?'

'No,' said the old man, 'at least as far as I know.'

'Well, all right,' said Monipodio. 'Take this trifle' – and he distributed about forty *reales* among them – 'and don't let anyone fail to appear on Sunday, for there'll be a proper reckoning up.'

They all thanked him; Repolido and Cariharta embraced each other again, and so did Escalanta and Maniferro and Gananciosa and Chiquiznaque, agreeing that that night, after they had finished work at the house, they would see each other in Pipota's house, where Monipodio said he would also be going to inspect the laundry basket. Then he would have to go and do the oiling job and cross it off the books. He embraced Rinconete and Cortadillo, and giving them his blessing, dismissed them, charging them never to have any settled and fixed lodging, for the sake of every-one's safety. Ganchuelo went with them to show them their beat, reminding them not to fail to appear on Sunday, because, he believed, Monipodio was going to give them an important lecture on matters concerning their craft. With this he went off, leaving the two comrades amazed at what they had seen.

Rinconete, although only a boy, was very intelligent and good-natured. As he had accompanied his father in the business of selling bulls, he knew something about the proper way to speak, and he was highly amused when he thought of the words which he had heard Monipodio and the others of that blessed community say, especially when for '*per modum sufragii* . . .' he had said 'by way of outrage'; and 'stupend' for 'stipend', when referring to their winnings; and when Cariharta said that Repolido was like a 'sailor of Tarpeia and a tiger of Ocaña', when she meant 'Hir-cania';[7] with a thousand and one other absurdities like or even worse than these. He was especially amused when she said that heaven would offset against her sins the labour she had put into gaining the twenty-four *reales*. He was also amazed by the assur-ance they had and their confidence that they would go to heaven because they didn't fail to perform their devotions, when they were up to their eyes in stealing and murder and offences against God. And he laughed at the good old woman, Pipota, who left the stolen laundry basket safely in her house and went off to put wax candles in front of the images, and thought that by doing that she would go to heaven all dressed and shod. He was no less astounded by the obedience and respect they all felt for Monipodio, when he was such a barbarous, uncouth and soulless wretch. He thought of what he had read in the memorandum book and the practices in which they were all engaged. Finally, he was shocked by the slackness of the law in that famous city of Seville, where such pernicious and perverted people could live almost openly; and he made up his mind to advise his companion that they should not spend much time in that evil and abandoned way of life, so uncertain, lawless and dissolute. But all the same, carried away by his youth and lack of experience, he spent some months longer with the community, during which things happened to him which require more time

7. cf. above, note 6.

than this to tell; and so the account of their life and marvellous doings is left for another occasion, with those of their master Monipodio and the other events which took place in that infamous academy, all worth consideration and capable of serving as an example and warning to those who may read them.

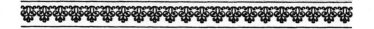

The Glass Graduate

Two gentlemen students were walking along the banks of the Tormes, when they found, asleep beneath a tree, a lad of some eleven years of age, in peasant dress. They sent a servant to wake him, and when he awoke, they asked him where he came from and what he was doing asleep in that deserted place. The lad replied that he had forgotten the name of his birthplace, and that he was going to the city of Salamanca to look for a master who, in exchange for his services, would give him the opportunity to study. They asked him if he could read, to which he said that he could, and write as well.

'So that it is not poor memory', said one of the gentlemen, 'that has made you forget the name of your country.'

'Whatever the reason,' answered the lad, 'no one shall know the name of my country or my parents until I can bring honour to them both.'

'And in what way do you propose to honour them?' asked the other gentleman.

'By the fame I win through my studies,' replied the boy, 'because I have heard that even bishops start off as men.'

This reply made the two gentlemen decide to accept him into their service, and take him along with them, so they did, giving him a chance to study according to the customary way with servants in that university. The lad said he was called Thomas Rodaja, whereby his masters inferred, from his name and dress, that he must be the son of some poor peasant. A few days later they dressed him in black, and after a few weeks Thomas showed signs of such extraordinary talent, serving his masters so faithfully, punctually and diligently that, although he never failed in any way to pursue his studies, he seemed to be solely occupied in serving them; and since a servant who gives good service gets treated well, Thomas Rodaja became his masters' companion, and no longer their servant. Eventually, in the course of the eight years he was with them, he became so famous in the university by reason of his keen intelligence and remarkable talents, that he won the esteem and affection of people of every kind. His principal study was law, but he was even more outstanding in the humanities; and he possessed such an astoundingly good memory, illuminated with such good judgement, that he became famous alike for both qualities.

The time came at last when his masters completed their studies and went off to their home, which was in one of the finest cities in Andalusia. They took Thomas off with them, and he stayed with them for a few days, but as he was anxious to return to his studies and to Salamanca, whose charms make everyone who has enjoyed the pleasure of living there determine to go back, he asked his masters' leave to return. They, being kind and generous, gave him leave, setting him up with the means to support himself for three years.

He thanked them, said good-bye, and left Málaga – for this was where his masters lived. As he was coming down the Zambra hill, on the road to Antequera, he met a nobleman on horseback, in splendid travelling clothes, with two servants also on horseback. He joined him and found out that they were going the same way; they shared lodgings, chatted about various things, and Thomas soon gave signs of his unusual talent and the gentleman of his magnificent and courtly bearing. He said that he was an infantry captain in the King's Guard, and that his ensign was recruiting in the Salamanca area. He praised the soldier's life, and gave him a vivid picture of the beauty of the city of Naples, the delights of Palermo, the prosperity of Milan, the banquets in Lombardy, and the splendid food in the inns. He gave a delightful and exact account of the way they shouted, 'Here, landlord', 'This way, you rogue', 'Let's have the *maccatella*, the *polastri* and the macaroni'. He praised to the skies the soldier's free life and the easy ways of Italy; but he said nothing to him about the cold of sentry duty, the danger of attacks, the horror of battles, the hunger of sieges, the destruction of mines, and other things of this kind, which some consider to be the extra burdens of a soldier's life, when in fact they are the main part of it. In short, he told him so many things and in such an attractive way, that our Thomas's judgement began to waver, and his will to be set on that way of life, where death is always so near at hand.

The captain, whose name was Don Diego de Valdivia, delighted with Thomas's good bearing, talent and free and easy manner, begged him to go with him to Italy, if he was interested in seeing it. He offered him his table and even a commission as ensign, a post which the present holder was about to give up. Thomas didn't need much pressing to take up the offer, and quickly persuaded himself that it would be a good thing to see Italy and Flanders and various other lands and countries. After all, travel makes men wise, and at the most he would spend three or four years which, considering his youth, would not be enough to prevent his returning to his studies. And thinking that everything would turn out as he wished, he told the captain that he was happy to go off with him to Italy, but only on condition that he need not take any commission or enlist as a soldier, for he did not want to be obliged to follow the flag. The captain told him that enlisting would not make any difference except that it would have the advantage of enabling him to enjoy the allowances and payments the company might receive, because he would give him leave whenever he requested it. But Thomas replied, 'That would be going against my conscience and against yours, captain; and so I would rather go as a free agent than be under an obligation.'

'Such a scrupulous conscience', said Don Diego, 'is more becoming to a monk than a soldier; but in any case, we shall go together.'

They got to Antequera that night and, by spending long periods on the road, in a few days they reached the place where the company was duly assembled. It was about to set out again for Cartagena, intending, with four other companies, to put up at such places as they should come across. Thomas took due note of the authority of the commissaries, the bad temper of some of the captains, the importunity of the billeting officers, the keenness of the paymasters, the complaints of the townspeople, the trading of passes, the insolence of the recruits, the quarrels of the tavern-keepers, the vast amount of excess baggage, and finally the way one more or less had to do all those things which he saw and disliked so much.

Thomas was now got up in all the finery of a soldier, having thrown aside his student garb, and was dressed to kill, as they say. He got rid of all his books with the exception of a copy of the *Hours of our Lady*,[1] and a Garcilaso[2] without commentary, which he carried in his pockets. They got to Cartagena more quickly than he would have wished, because life in lodgings is easy and has plenty of variety, and every day one comes across new and pleasing things. At Cartagena they embarked on four galleys going to Naples, and Thomas Rodaja was struck by the strange life that goes on in those floating houses, where most of the time one is pestered by the bedbugs, robbed by the galley slaves, annoyed by the sailors, gnawed by the mice and worn out by the heavy seas. He was terrified by the great squalls and storms, especially in the Gulf of Lyons, where they had two, one of which drove them as far as Corsica, while the other brought them back to Toulon in France. In short, deprived of sleep, soaked to the skin and hollow-eyed, they reached the beautiful city of Genoa. Disembarking in its sheltered harbour, they visited a church, and then the Captain with all his companions came to an inn, where they forgot all about the storms of the past in the merry-making of the present.

There they became acquainted with the smooth Trebbiano, the full-bodied Montefiascone, the strong Asprino, the generous Greek wines Candia and Soma, the great Five Vineyards, the sweet and gentle Vernaccia and the rough Centola, the lowly Roman wines never being allowed a place among these lordly creatures. And when mine host had gone through all these different wines, he volunteered to bring in, without recourse to trickery or sleight of hand, the genuine Madrigal, Coca, Alaejos and Cuidad Real, (which deserves to be called Imperial rather than Royal) which is sacred to the god of laughter; he offered Esquivias, Alanis, Cazalla, Guadalcanal and Membrilla, not forgetting Ribadavia and Descargamaría. In short, our host named and offered them more wines than Bacchus himself can have had in his vaults.

1. A devotional book illustrated with miniatures, very fashionable from the fifteenth century onwards.

2. The Toledan courtier-poet Garcilaso de la Vega, who lived from 1501 (or 1503) to 1536, and whose works, the first to be really successful in the Italianate style in Spain, became enormously popular. They were edited in 1580, with a learned commentary by Fernando de Herrera, the poet of Seville.

Our good Thomas was also fascinated by the fair hair of the girls of Genoa, the elegance and noble bearing of the men and the remarkable beauty of the city, whose houses are set on its hills like diamonds in gold. The next day all the companies which were to go to Piedmont disembarked; but Thomas did not want to go on this journey, but to go overland from there to Rome and Naples, which he did. He resolved to come back via the great city of Venice, through Loretto to Milan and then to Piedmont, where Don Diego de Valdivia said he would meet him, if they hadn't already been carried off to Flanders, as rumour said they might.

Thomas took his leave of the captain a couple of days later, and within five days reached Florence, having first seen Lucca, a small but very well-appointed city in which Spaniards are better received and entertained than in other parts of Italy. He was delighted with Florence, both because of its splendid situation and its cleanness, magnificent buildings, cool river and quiet streets. He was there for four days, and then set off for Rome, the queen of cities and mistress of the world. He visited its shrines, worshipped its relics and marvelled at its great size; and just as one realizes the greatness and ferocity of the lion by its claws, so he came to realize the greatness of Rome by its marble ruins, its statues, damaged or intact, its broken archways and ruined baths, its magnificent porticos and great amphitheatres, and by its famous and sacred river, which always fills its banks with water and blesses them with the countless relics of the bodies of martyrs which have been buried there; by its bridges, whose arches are like eyes looking at each other, and by its streets whose names alone make them superior to those of every other city in the world: the Via Appia, the Via Flaminia, the Via Julia, and others like them. But he was no less amazed by the way its hills were laid out within the boundaries of the city: the Caelian, the Quirinal and the Vatican, with the other four, whose names testify to the greatness and majesty of Rome. He was also impressed by the pomp of the College of Cardinals, the majesty of the Supreme Pontiff, the mass and variety of peoples and nations. He saw and took careful note of it all. And when he had gone the rounds of the Seven Churches, and made his confession to a penitentiary, and kissed His Holiness's feet, he decided to go off to Naples, loaded with *Agnuses* and beads. As it was unsettled weather, which made it dangerous to leave or enter Rome overland, he went off to Naples by sea, where he added to the delight of seeing Rome that of seeing Naples, a city which in his opinion, and in that of everyone who has seen it, is the best in Europe and even in the world.

From there he went off to Sicily, and saw Palermo, and then Messina. He was favourably impressed by the situation and beauty of Palermo, by the port of Messina, and by the abundance of the whole island, which is justly and truthfully called the granary of Italy. He went back to Naples and to Rome, and from there he went to Our Lady of Loretto, in whose holy shrine he did not see any walls at all, because they were all covered with crutches, shrouds, chains, shackles, manacles, switches of hair, wax busts, paintings and altar pieces, which gave testimony to the innumerable favours received by so many from God's hand through the intercession of His divine mother, to whose holy image He chose to give power and authority by many miracles, as a reward for the reverence which is shown to her by those who have adorned the walls of her house with these signs of devotion. He saw the very room and spot which witnessed the most exalted and important charge ever witnessed, though not comprehended, by the heavens, the angels, and all the dwellers of eternity.[3]

From there, embarking at Ancona, he went to Venice, a city which if Columbus had never lived would be unmatched by any in the world. Thanks be to heaven and to the great Hernando Cortés, who conquered the great city of Mexico, whereby this great city of Venice came to have something of a rival. These two famous cities are alike in that their streets are all water; the European one is the wonder of the old world; the American one, the marvel of the new. Its richness seemed to him to know no limits, and the way it was governed seemed a model of prudence, its situation impregnable, its prosperity vast, its surroundings delightful. In short, the whole and all the parts deserve the reputation they have in every part of the globe, and to which its famous arsenal, which is the place where the galleys, together with countless other craft, are made, add even further fame.

3. Presumably a reference to prophecy concerning the birth of Christ recorded in Matthew i, 20–21 and Luke i, 31.

The delights and pastimes our traveller found in Venice were nearly as dangerous as those of Calypso,[4] for they almost made him forget his original intention. But after he had been there a month, he came back by way of Ferrara, Parma and Piacenza to Milan, that Vulcan's forge and envy of the kingdom of France; a city of which it is said that they only have to think of something for it to be done. The size of the city and its great church and the marvellous abundance of everything necessary for human life are truly magnificent. From there he went off to Asti, and got there just a day before the regiment was leaving for Flanders. He was very well received by his friend the captain, and in his company went over to Flanders, and to Antwerp, a city no less worthy of admiration than those he had seen in Italy. He saw Ghent and Brussels, and he saw that the whole country was preparing to take up arms to go out on campaign the following summer. Having fulfilled the desire which prompted him to see what he had seen, he decided to go back to Spain and to complete his studies at Salamanca. It was no sooner said than done, to the great sorrow of his comrade, who begged him, as they parted, to let him know how he got on with his journey, how he was and what happened to him. He promised to do as he asked, and returned to Spain through France, without seeing Paris, since there was fighting going on there. He finally reached Salamanca, where he was warmly welcomed by his friends, and with the help they gave him he continued his studies until he finally graduated as a licenciate in Law.

It so happened that at that time there came to the city a certain lively lady who was up to all the tricks. Everybody rushed into the trap and fell for the decoy, and not one of the lads failed to pay her a call. They told Thomas that this lady said she had been in Italy and Flanders, and just to see if he knew her, he went to call on her. The result of this visit was that as soon as she saw Thomas she fell in love with him. He, not realizing it, would not have gone to her house unless he had been marched off to it by someone else. In the end she declared her love for him and offered him all she had. As

4. Calypso, known sometimes as the goddess of silence, reigned in the island of Ogygia, whose location is uncertain, but on whose coasts Ulysses is reputed to have been shipwrecked. Calypso received him with great hospitality and offered him immortality if he would remain with her as a husband.

he was more devoted to his books than to anything else, he did not respond at all to the lady's fancy, and she, seeing herself scorned, and, as she thought, hated, and realizing that she could not conquer the rock of Thomas's will by ordinary means, decided to look for other methods which seemed to her more effective and capable of achieving what she wanted. So, taking the advice of a Moorish woman, she gave Thomas one of those things they call love potions, hidden in a Toledo quince, thinking that by this means she would force his will to love her, as if there were herbs, charms or words in the world powerful enough to force free will. Those who give these aphrodisiac drinks or foods are called 'poisoners': because all they do is to poison those who take them, as experience has shown on many and varied occasions.

Thomas ate the quince to such ill effect that straight away he began to shake in his feet and hands as if he had epilepsy, and lost consciousness for many hours, after which he came to in a stupefied condition. He declared in a confused and stammering way that a quince he had eaten had done for him, and gave the name of the person who had given it to him. When the Officers of the Law learned of the affair, they went in search of the culprit; but she, seeing what had happened, had made herself scarce and was never seen again.

Thomas was in bed for six months, during which time he became completely dried up, and was nothing but skin and bones, as they say. Moreover, his senses seemed completely at sixes and sevens; and although they gave him all the treatment they could, they only managed to cure his bodily complaints, but not his mind. He got better but remained possessed by the strangest madness anybody had ever seen. The poor wretch imagined that he was all made of glass, and under this delusion, when someone came up to him, he would scream out in the most frightening manner, and using the most convincing arguments would beg them not to come near him, or they would break him; for really and truly he was not like other men, being made of glass from head to foot.

In order to relieve him of this strange delusion, many people, taking no notice of his shouts and pleas, went up to him and embraced him, telling him to look and he would see that in fact he was not getting broken. But all that happened as a result of this was that the poor wretch would throw himself on the ground shouting for all he was worth, and would then fall into a faint, from which he did not recover for several hours; and when he did come to he would start begging people not to come near him again. He told them to speak to him from a distance and ask him what they wanted, because being a man of glass and not of flesh, he would answer them all so much the more intelligently; for glass being a fine and delicate material, the mind could work through it more promptly and effectively than through an ordinary, solid, earthly body. Some wanted to experiment to see if what he said was true, and so they asked him many difficult things, to which he answered straight away, and very astutely too. It amazed the most learned men in the university and the professors of medicine and philosophy to see how in a person afflicted by such an extraordinary madness as to make him think he was made of glass there should be such a fund of knowledge that he could answer every question correctly and intelligently.

Thomas asked them to give him some sort of case in which he could place the fragile vessel of his body, so that if he wore any close-fitting clothes he would not break; and so they gave him a robe made of drab stuff and a very loose-fitting shirt, which he put on very carefully and tied with a cotton cord. He was not at all willing to put shoes on, and the arrangement he had for getting himself fed without people coming near him was to put on the end of a stick a basket, in which they would put whatever fruit was in season. He did not want meat or fish; he drank only from a fountain or a river, and then with his hands; when he went about the streets he went in the middle of them, looking up at the roofs, in fear lest some tile should fall on him and break him; in summer he slept in the country in the open, and in winter he would go into an inn, and bury himself up to the neck in the straw-loft, saying that that was the safest and most suitable bed for a man of glass. When it thundered, he would shake like a leaf and go off into the country, and would never go into the town until the storm was over. His friends kept him shut up for a long time; but seeing that his affliction showed no sign of being cured, they decided to do what he asked, which was to let him go free; and so they left him and he went about the city, arousing amazement and pity in all who knew him.

Then the boys flocked round him, but he would stop them with his staff, and beg them to speak to him from a distance, so that he did not break; for as he was a man of glass, he was very fragile. Boys, being the most mischievous creatures in the world, in spite of his pleas and shouts began to throw rags at him and even stones, to see if he really was made of glass as he said; but he shouted so much and made such a fuss that the men scolded and punished the children to stop them throwing things at him. But one day when they worried him a lot, he turned to them and said,

'What do you want, you wretched boys, who keep pestering me like flies, who are as dirty as bedbugs and as impudent as fleas? Do you think I'm Mount Testaccio in Rome, to hurl all these pots and tiles at me?'

When they heard him tell them all off they always followed him in crowds, and the boys thought it would be a much better game to listen to him than to throw things at him. On one occasion, when he was going through the old-clothes market in Salamanca, a woman who kept one of the stalls said to him,

'I'm sorry in my heart for you, Licenciate; but what can I do, for I can't shed any tears?'

He turned to her and very deliberately said to her,

'*Filiae Hierusalem, plorate super vos et super filios vestros.*'[5]

The woman's husband realized what a subtle answer it was and said to him,

'Brother Glass,' for that is what he said he was called, 'you are more of a rogue than a fool.'

'I don't care a bit,' he answered, 'as long as I'm not stupid.'

One day when he was going past the brothel he saw at the door several of the inmates, and declared that they were the baggage of Satan's army, lodging in the inn of hell. Someone asked him what advice or comfort he would give to a friend of his who was very sad because his wife had gone off with someone else. To which he replied,

'Tell him to thank God for having allowed his enemy to be taken away from his house.'

'Then shouldn't he go and look for her?' said the other.

5. 'Daughters of Jerusalem ... weep for yourselves, and for your children.' Luke xxiii, 28 (Authorized Version).

'Not on your life,' replied Glass, 'because if he found her he would be finding a true and everlasting testimony to his dishonour.'

'Since that is the case,' said the same man, 'what shall I do to live at peace with my wife?'

He replied, 'Give her what she needs; let her rule over everyone in the house; but don't allow her to rule over you.'

A boy said to him, 'Licenciate Glass, I want to leave my father because he's always beating me.'

To which he replied, 'Bear in mind, my boy, that the beatings that fathers give their children bring honour to them, and those which the executioner gives are the ones that cause offence.'

As he was standing at a church door, he saw one of those peasants who are always boasting of being old Christians go in, and behind him came another man who did not enjoy as good a reputation as the first. The licenciate shouted to the peasant,

'Domingo, wait for old Sabbath to pass.'

He used to say that schoolmasters were lucky, because they were always dealing with angels, and that they would be supremely happy if the little angels weren't so saucy. Someone else asked him what he thought of bawds. He answered that he had never known any who lived in seclusion, but only those who were neighbours.

The news of his madness and of his answers and clever sayings spread all through Castile, and when it came to the ears of a certain prince or gentleman of the court, he wanted to send for him. So he commissioned a nobleman who was a friend of his and who was in Salamanca to send him to him. When the gentlemen bumped into him one day, he said to him,

'Licenciate Glass, you know there is a great man at Court who wants to see you and has sent for you.'

To which he replied, 'Please offer my excuses to this gentleman, for I'm no good for palaces, because I'm bashful and don't know how to flatter.'

All the same, the gentleman sent him to court, and in order to get him there they used the following device: they put him into a wicker basket of the kind they use for carrying glass, filling in the spaces with stones, and putting some pieces of glass in the straw, so that he would get the impression that they were carrying him like a glass vessel. He got to Valladolid at night, and they unpacked him in the house of the gentleman who had sent for him, and who welcomed him with the words,

'You are very welcome, Licenciate Glass. How was the journey? How are you?'

To which he replied, 'There's no road so bad that it does not come to an end, except the one that leads to the gallows. As far as my health is concerned, I'm neither one thing nor the other, for my pulse and my brain are at odds.'

Another day, when he had seen a lot of falcons and hawks and other fowling birds on perches, he said that falconry was a fine thing for princes and great nobles; but that they should bear in mind that in this sport pleasure outweighed profit two-thousand-fold. Hunting hares he said was very pleasant, and especially when one was hunting with borrowed greyhounds.

The nobleman liked his brand of madness, and let him go out in the city, under the protection of a man to take care that the children did not harm him. In a week he was known to them and the whole court, and at every step, in every street and on every corner he would reply to all the questions they put to him. Among them was one from a student who asked whether he was a poet, since there seemed no limit to his gifts.

He replied, 'Until now, I have been neither so stupid nor so fortunate.'

'I don't understand what you mean by stupid and fortunate,' said the student.

And Glass replied, 'I haven't been so stupid as to be a bad poet, nor so fortunate as to be a good one.'

Another student asked him what he thought of poets. He replied that poetry he esteemed highly; but poets not at all. They went on to ask him why he said that. He answered that of the infinite number of poets in existence, the good ones were so few that they hardly counted, and so being unworthy of consideration, he did not hold them in any esteem; but that he admired and revered the art of poetry, because it contained within it all the other sciences put together. It makes use of all of them, and they all adorn it, so that it gives lustre and fame to their wonderful works, and brings great profit, delight and wonder to all the world. He added,

'I am well aware of the esteem in which a good poet should be held, because I remember those verses of Ovid which say:

> *Cura deum fuerunt olim regumque poetae.*
> *Praemiaque antiqui magna tulere chori.*
> *Sanctaque majestas, et erat venerabile nomen*
> *Vatibus, et largae saepe dabantur opes*[6]

And I am not unaware either of the great worth of poets, for Plato calls them interpreters of the gods, and Ovid says of them: *"Est Deus in nobis, agitanti calescimus illo."*[7] And he also says: *"At sacri vates, et divum cura vocamur."*[8] This is what they say of good poets; as for the bad ones, the mere windbags, what is there to say except that they are the most idiotic and arrogant creatures in the world?'

And he went on, 'What a thing it is to see one of these poets, when he wants to recite a sonnet to those of his circle, wheedling them with such words as, "Pray listen to a little sonnet which I composed last night for a certain occasion. Although it's of no value, I think it's quite nice in a way." And with that, he purses his lips, raises his eyebrows, and hunting about in his pocket, pulls out from the mass of grubby, torn papers, among which there are another thousand or so sonnets, the one he wants to recite, and finally pronounces it in mellifluous and sugary tones. And if by any chance his listeners, out of malice or not knowing any better, don't praise it, he says, "Either you haven't understood the sonnet, or I haven't recited it properly; so I'd better say it again, and you'd better listen to it more carefully, for there's no doubt at all that the sonnet is worth it." And then he starts to recite it all over again, with new gestures and new pauses. And have you seen the way they tear each other to pieces? You should see how these modern young puppies bark at the hoary old mastiffs. Not to mention those

---

6. 'Poets were once the care of chieftains and of kings, and choirs of old won great rewards. Sacred was the majesty and venerable the name of the poet; and oft-times lavish wealth was given them.' Ovid, *Ars amatoria*, III, 405–8, translated by J. H. Mozley (Loeb edition).

7. 'There is a god in us: when moved by him we are set on fire.' Ovid, *Fasti*, VI, 5, translated by J. G. Frazer (Loeb edition).

8. 'But we poets are called prophets and are beloved by the gods.' Ovid, *Amores*, III, IX, 17, translated by Grant Showerman (Loeb edition).

who snipe at some of those illustrious and worthy persons in whom the true light of poetry shines, and who find it a comfort and re-creation among their many serious occupations, who show the divine nature of their genius and the nobility of their thoughts, in spite of those meddlesome ignoramuses who pass judgement on what they do not know, and hate what they cannot understand; and those who only want praise for the stupid folk who sit beneath canopies, and the ignorant who cling to the seats of the mighty.'

On another occasion they asked him why it was that poets in general were poor. He replied that it was because they chose to be, for it was in their power to be rich, if they knew how to take advantage of the opportunity which they had at their disposal all the time; namely their ladies, who were all extremely rich, for their hair was gold, their brow burnished silver, their eyes green emeralds, their teeth ivory, their lips coral and their throats clear crystal, while their tears were liquid pearls. Moreover, where their feet trod, however hard and barren the earth, it would immediately bring forth jasmine and roses; and their breath was of amber, musk and civet; all these things being signs and proof of their great wealth. These and other things he said about bad poets; but he always spoke well of the good ones and praised them to the skies.

One day he saw on the pavement outside San Francisco church some badly painted figures, and this gave rise to the remark that good painters imitated nature, but bad ones vomited it up. One day he went up to a book shop, with the greatest caution lest he should break, and said to the bookseller,

'I should be very happy about this trade of yours if it were not for one drawback it has.'

The bookseller asked him to tell him what it was.

He replied, 'The fuss they make when they buy the privilege of a book, and the tricks they play on its author if by any chance he prints it at his own expense. Instead of fifteen hundred, they print three thousand books, and when the author thinks they are selling his, they're dispatching other people's.'

It happened that the same day there passed through the square six men who had been flogged, and when the crier said, 'The first one, for thieving,' Glass shouted to those who were standing in front of him,

'Keep out of the way, brothers, lest the list start with the name of one of you.'

And when the crier got to the point where he said, 'The last . . .,' he commented, 'That must be the one who goes bail for the children.'

A boy said to him, 'Brother Glass, tomorrow they're going to whip a bawd.'

He replied, 'If you told me they were going to whip a pimp, I'd assume they were going to whip a coachman.'[9]

One of those men who carry sedan chairs said to him, 'Haven't you anything to say about us, Licenciate?'

'No,' answered Glass, 'except that any one of you knows more sins than a confessor; but with this difference: that when the confessor knows them he keeps them secret, whereas you publish them in every inn.'

A mule-boy heard this (for all sorts of people used to come and listen to him all the time), and said to him,

'There's little or nothing to be said about us, Mr Flask, because we are honest folk, needful to the state.'

To which Glass replied,

'The master's honour is a sign of the servant's; and so you must look whom you serve, and then you'll see what honour you have. You boys are the scum of the earth. Once, when I was not made of glass, I went on a journey on a hired mule on which I counted a hundred and twenty-one marks, all big ones and harmful to humans. All mule-boys are scoundrels and thieves, not to say crooks: if their masters (which is the name they give to the people they take on their mules) are easily duped, they play more tricks on them than they've had in this city for years; if they are foreigners they rob them; if they're students they curse them; if they're monks, they hurl blasphemy at them; and if they're soldiers, they're afraid of them. These boys, like sailors and carters and muleteers, have a way of life which is unique and peculiar to them. The carter spends most of his life in the space of a yard and a half, for it can't be much farther from the yoke of his mules to the front of the cart; he sings half his time, and curses the rest, and spends a lot more time saying "stand back there"; and if by any chance he has

9. Coachmen had a legendary reputation for their activities as go-betweens, to which contemporary authors made very frequent references.

to get a wheel out of a ditch, he'd rather use two curses than three mules. Sailors are barbarous, ill-mannered folk who know no other language than that which is used on board ship; when it is calm they are industrious, and when storms come they are lazy; in bad weather there are lots to command and few to obey. Their god is their chest and their mess, and their favourite pastime is to watch the passengers being sick. Muleteers are people who have abjured sheets and become wedded to pack-saddles; they are so industrious and so quick that in order not to lose a fare they will lose their soul; their favourite music is the sound of the mortar; their sauce is hunger; their morning praises consist in getting up to feed the animals; and as for masses, they never go near them.'

As he was saying this, he was at the door of an apothecary's shop, and turning to the owner, he said to him,

'You'd have a healthy trade if only you weren't so hard on your lamps.'

'In what way am I hard on my lamps?' asked the chemist.

Glass replied, 'Because whenever you're short of oil you make it up with what's in the lamp nearest to hand; and there's something else in your profession which is enough to ruin the reputation of the most reliable doctor in the world.'

Asked what he meant, he replied that there were chemists who, so as not to say that they were out of what the doctor prescribed, put in substitutes for what they hadn't got, which they thought had the same properties and quality, when this was not in fact the case; and so the medicine which had been wrongly made up had the opposite effect to that of the proper prescribed one. Then someone asked him what he thought about doctors, and this is what he said:

'*Honora medicum propter necessitatem, etenim creavit eum Altissimus. A Deo enim est omnis medela, et a rege accipiet donationem. Disciplina medici exaltabit caput illius, et in conspectu magnatum collaudabitur. Altissimus de terra creavit medicinam, et vir prudens non abhorrebit illam.*[10] This is what Ecclesiasticus says about

10. 'Honour the physician for the need thou hast of him: for the most High hath created him. For all healing is from God: and he shall receive gifts of the king. The skill of the physician shall lift up his head: and in the sight of great men he shall be praised. The most High hath created medicines out of the earth: and a wise man will not abhor them.' Ecclesiasticus xxxviii, 1–4 (Douay version).

medicine and about good doctors; and of the bad ones you might say exactly the opposite, because there are no people more harmful to the State than they. The judge can distort or delay justice, the lawyer uphold an unjust cause for his own interest, the merchant can filch our property; in short, all those with whom we have to deal can do us some harm; but not one of them can take away our lives without fear of punishment; only doctors can and do kill us quietly without fear of trouble, without unsheathing any sword more powerful than a "prescription". And there's no way of uncovering their crimes, because they put them under ground straight away. I remember that when I was a man of flesh and not of glass, as I am now, a patient dismissed one of those doctors of the second class and went to another for treatment; and the first, a few days later, happened to go to the apothecary's where the second had his prescriptions made up. He asked the chemist how the patient whom he had left was getting on, and whether the other doctor had prescribed any sort of purge for him. The chemist replied that he had a prescription for a purge which the patient was to take the following day. He asked him to show it to him, and he saw that at the bottom of it was written: "Sumat diluculo", and so he said, "Everything in this purge seems all right to me, except for this 'diluculo', because it's too humid."'[11]

Because of all these things which he said about all the various professions, people ran after him, without doing him any harm, but without giving him any peace; all the same, he couldn't have defended himself against the boys if his guardian hadn't protected him. Someone asked him what he should do in order not to be envious. He replied, 'Sleep; for as long as you sleep you'll be the equal of the person you envy.'

Someone else asked him how he would set about getting away with a commission for which he'd been trying for two years. And he said to him, 'Ride off and watch out for the person who's got it, and go with him until he goes out of the city, and that's how you'll get away with it.'

On one occasion a court judge happened to pass by the place

11. 'To be taken first thing in the morning.' The doctor thinks it will be bad for him to take the medicine at this time, when it is too damp to be good for his health.

where he was, on his way to a criminal case, with two constables and a crowd of people. Glass asked who he was, and when they told him, he said,

'I'll bet that judge has enough vipers in his bosom, pistols in his belt and lightning in his hands to destroy everything within his jurisdiction. I remember that I had a friend who was working on a criminal charge and who gave a sentence which was far in excess of the crime. I asked him why he had given such a cruel sentence and committed such a manifest injustice. He replied that he intended to grant the appeal, and by this means he was leaving the field open to the members of the Council to show their mercy by moderating and reducing to its proper proportions the harsh sentence he had passed. I replied that it would have been better to have given a sentence which would save them this trouble, for in this way they would consider him to be an upright and just judge.'

In the circle which, as I've said, always crowded round to listen to him was an acquaintance of his dressed as a lawyer, whom someone addressed as 'Licenciate'; and as Glass knew that the man they called licenciate hadn't even qualified for his first degree he said to him,

'Take care, my friend, that the friars who devote themselves to ransoming prisoners don't get hold of your degree, or they'll take it off you as vagrant's property.'

To which the friend replied, 'Let's behave properly to each other, Mr Glass, for you know that I'm a man of lofty and profound learning.'

Glass replied, 'I know very well that you're a Tantalus[12] as far as learning is concerned, for it eludes you by reason of its loftiness and you can't reach it because of its profundity.'

Once when he was near a tailor's shop, he saw the tailor standing with his hands together, and said to him, 'Doubtless, master, you are on the way to salvation.'

'How do you arrive at that conclusion?' asked the tailor.

'How do I arrive at that conclusion?' answered Glass. 'I arrive

12. Tantalus, King of Lydia, and son of Jupiter by a nymph called Pluto, was said to be punished in hell with an insatiable thirst, and placed up to the chin in a pool of water which receded whenever he attempted to taste it.

at it by seeing that since you have nothing to do, you won't have any reason to tell lies.' And he added, 'Woe to the tailor who does not lie and who sews on a holiday; it's a marvellous thing that of all the members of that trade you'll hardly find one who'll make a suit fit, for there are so many sinners who make them.'

Of cobblers he said that never, in their way of thinking, did they make a bad shoe; because if the shoe was too narrow and tight for the person for whom they were making it, they told him that that was how it should be, for elegant people wore their shoes close-fitting, and that if they wore them for a couple of hours they'd be broader than sandals; and if they were too broad, they said that was how they should be, for the sake of the gout.

A bright boy, who was a clerk in a provincial office, and who pestered him a good deal with questions and requests, and brought him news of what was going on in the city (for he would discourse on and give an answer to everything), said to him on one occasion, 'Glass, last night a money-changer who was condemned to be hanged died in prison.'

To which he replied, 'He did well to hurry up and die before the executioner got his hands on him.'

On the pavement outside San Francisco church there was a group of Genoese, and as he walked by, one of them called him and said to him:

'Come here, Mr Glass, and tell us a tale.'

He answered, 'I'd rather not, lest you give me the bill for it in Genoa.'

On one occasion he bumped into a shopkeeper who was going along with a daughter of hers, who was very ugly, but covered in trinkets and finery and pearls, and he said to the mother, 'You've done very well to cover her with stones, to make her fit for walking.'

About pastry-cooks he said that they had been playing a double game for many years without paying any penalty, because they had charged fourpence for cakes worth twopence; eightpence for those worth four and half a *real* for those worth eight, just as they took it into their heads.

Of puppeteers he said thousands of bad things: he said they were vagrants, who treated divine things without due respect, because they made a mockery of worship with the figures they put on in their shows, and sometimes they would stuff in a sack all or nearly all the figures in the Old and New Testaments and then sit on the sack to eat and drink in the eating-houses and taverns. In short, he said he was amazed that the powers that be didn't put an end to their shows or banish them from the realm.

One day an actor happened to pass, dressed like a prince, and when he saw him, he said, 'I remember seeing this fellow come out of the theatre with his face covered with flour and wearing a sheep-skin inside out, and yet, off stage, he's always swearing by his noble blood.'

'He must be a nobleman,' answered one of the spectators, 'because there are many actors who are very well born and of noble blood.'

'That may be true,' replied Glass, 'but the last people you need in a farce are people who are nobly born; they need to be good-looking, elegant and well spoken. I can say this for them too: they earn their bread by the sweat of their brow with intolerable hard work, always learning things by heart. They're perpetual gipsies wandering from village to village and from inn to inn, losing sleep in order to give pleasure to others, because their own profit lies in the satisfaction they give to the public. They have this in their favour too: they deceive no one by their trade, for they are always showing their merchandise in public, for all to see and judge. The work of theatrical managers is incredible, and the worry they have remarkable, for they have to earn a great deal in order to avoid having so many debts at the end of the year that they have to go bankrupt. Yet they are necessary to the State, in the same way as woods, groves, restful landscapes, and all those things which provide honest recreation.'

He said that in the opinion of a friend of his anyone who paid court to an actress was the slave of a whole mass of ladies at the same time – a queen, a nymph, a goddess, a kitchenmaid, a shepherdess – and very often it also fell to his lot to serve a page and a lackey too; for all these roles and many more are normally played by actresses.

Someone asked him who had been the happiest person in the world. His answer was, '*Nemo*'; because '*Nemo novit patrem*;

nemo sine crimine vivit; nemo sua sorte contentus; nemo ascendit in coelum.[13]

Of fencers he said on one occasion that they were masters of a science or art which was of no use to them when they needed it, and that they were somewhat presumptuous, since they wanted to reduce to mathematical demonstrations, which are infallible, the movements and the angry intentions of their opponents.

He was particularly hostile to those who dyed their beards; and once when he came upon two men quarrelling, the one who was Portuguese said to the Castilian, grasping his beard, which had been heavily dyed:

'By this beard I name . . .'

Glass retorted:

'Hey man, don't say "I name", but rather "I stain".'

Another man had a beard that was a mixture of various colours, as a result of unskilful dyeing; and Glass told him that he had a beard like a speckled dungheap. To another man, whose beard was half black and half white because he hadn't bothered about it, and the natural colour was growing out, he said that he should not wrangle or quarrel with anyone, because he ran the risk of being told that he was lying by half his beard.

On one occasion he told how a bright and intelligent girl, in order to satisfy her parents' wishes, consented to marry a white-haired old man, who the night before the wedding went, not to the river Jordan, as the old women say, but to the phial of silver nitrate, with which he touched his beard up to such effect that when he went to bed it was like snow and when he got up like pitch. When the time came to plight their troth, the girl looked at him with his beard all dyed, and she asked her parents to give her the same husband that they had shown her; for she wanted no other. They told her that the man she was looking at was the same as the one they had shown to her and given her as a husband. She replied

13. '. . . neither knoweth any man the Father save the Son, and he to whomsoever the Son will reveal him.' Matthew xi, 27 (Authorized Version); 'No one lives free of crime'. Cato *Disticha*, 1, 5; 'No one is content with his lot', Horace, *Satires*, I, 1–3 (the full reading is: *Qui fit, Maecenas, ut nemo, quam sibi fortem,/Seu Ratio dederit, seu Fors objecerit, illa/Contentus vivat . . .*); 'And no man hath ascended up to heaven, but he that came down from heaven, even the Son of man which is in heaven.' John iii, 13 (Authorized version).

that he was not, and brought as evidence that the man her parents had given her was a venerable white-haired man, and as this one had no white hair, it wasn't the same one, and she was withdrawing on the ground that she had been tricked. She stuck to this, the man with the dyed beard was put to shame and the engagement was broken off.

Vidriera had the same antipathy towards duennas as he had towards those who dyed their hair; he talked endlessly of their *permafoy*,[14] the shrouds of their headdresses, all their affected ways, their scruples, and their extraordinary meanness; he was annoyed by the way they complained about their stomachs and about their dizziness in the head, the way they had of speaking, which had more frills than their headdresses, and their useless affectations.

Someone said to him, 'Why is it, Licenciate, that I've heard you speak ill of many professions and you've never said a bad word about notaries, when there is so much to be said?'

He replied, 'Although made of glass, I am not so fragile as to allow myself to be carried along by the crowd, which is usually wrong. It seems to me that notaries are what grammar is to backbiters and "la, la, la" to singers; because just as you cannot get at other branches of knowledge except by way of grammar, and just as the musician hums the tune over before he sings, so backbiters first show their tendency to slander by speaking ill of notaries and constables and other officers of the law, when the notary's profession is one without which the truth would be suppressed, abused and brought into disgrace. And so Ecclesiasticus says: "*In manu Dei potestas hominis est, et super faciem scribae imponet honorem.*"[15] The notary is a public figure, and the judge's profession cannot be carried out properly without his. Notaries must be freemen, not slaves, nor sons of slaves; legitimate, and not bastards, or born of inferior race. They swear to keep secrets, to be true to their word and not to make statements for payment; that neither friendship, nor enmity, profit nor injury, will prevent them from performing their duty with a good Christian conscience. If this profession

14. A corruption of French *par ma foi*, an affectation common among servants.

15. 'The strength of man is in the hand of God, and he will bring honour on the Scribe.' Ecclesiasticus x, 54 (Douay version).

requires so many good qualities, why should one think that from the more than twenty thousand notaries in Spain the devil should reap the reward, as if they were shoots of his vine? I have no wish to believe it, nor is it right that anyone should believe it; because the long and the short of it is that they are the most necessary people in a well-ordered state, and if they have made off with too many dues, they have also done many things which were not their due, and between these two extremes one could find a happy mean which could make them take care what they're about.'

On the subject of constables he said that it was not surprising that they should have some enemies, since their profession was either to make arrests, or to remove property from houses, or to keep people in their houses under custody and eat at their expense. He condemned the negligence and ignorance of attorneys and solicitors. As with doctors who get their fee, whether the patient gets better or not, so it is with attorneys and solicitors, whether or not the cause they are pleading is successful.

Someone asked him which was the best country. He replied that it was the one which gave prompt rewards.

The other replied, 'That's not what I'm asking, but which is the better place: Valladolid or Madrid?'

And he answered, 'Madrid, for the highest and lowest; Valladolid for the parts in the middle.'

'I don't understand,' said the questioner.

And he replied, 'In Madrid, the top and the bottom; in Valladolid, the part between.'

Glass heard one man telling another that as soon as he got to Valladolid, his wife had fallen very ill, because the place didn't agree with her. To this Glass said, 'It would be better if it had finished her off, if she's inclined to be jealous.'

About musicians and those who ran messages he said that they were limited in hopes and fortunes, because the messengers reached the end of theirs when they could go on horseback, and the others when they became musicians at the court.

Of ladies known as *courtesans*, he said that all or most of them were more *courtly* than they were *sanitary*.

One day when he was in a church he saw an old man being brought to be buried, a child to be baptized, and a woman to be

married, all at the same time; and he made the comment that
churches were battle fields, where the old meet their end, the
young win the day and the women triumph.

On one occasion a wasp stung him on the neck, and he did not
dare to shake it off, for fear of being broken: but all the same he
complained. Someone asked him how he felt the wasp, if his body
was made of glass. He answered that the wasp must be a backbiter,
and that the tongues and mouths of backbiters were enough to
penetrate bodies of bronze, let alone glass.

As a very fat monk happened to pass one of the bystanders said,
'The father is so weak he can't move.'

Glass said impatiently, 'Let no one forget what the Holy Spirit
says: "*Nolite tangere christos meos*".'[16] And getting more impatient,
he bade them consider that of the many saints canonized or included
in the ranks of the blessed by the Church in recent years, no one
had been called Captain So-and-So, or Secretary Such-and-Such,
or the Count, Marquess or Duke of such-and-such a place, but
Friar James, Friar Jacinto, Friar Raymond; in other words, they
were all friars and monks, because the religious orders are heaven's
garden, whose fruits are placed on God's table. He said that the
tongues of backbiters were like the feathers of the eagle, which
rub away and spoil those of all the other birds which come near
them.

He said some extraordinary things about keepers of gaming-
houses and about gamblers: that the former were a public menace,
because once they had extracted the winnings from those who were
in luck, they wanted them to lose and the cards to pass on, so that
their opponents should win and they should collect their pile too.
He had a lot to say about the patience of the gambler, who spent
the whole night playing and losing, and although angry as a
fiend, so that his opponent did not leave with his winnings, didn't
say a word and suffered like a martyr of the devil. He also had
great things to say about the conscientiousness of some honourable
gamblers who would not think of allowing their house to be used
for any other games but pool and piquet: and by this means,
slowly but surely, without fear of scandal, would find themselves

16. 'Touch not mine anointed.' Psalms cv, 15 (Authorized version).

at the end of the month with more winnings than those who played wilder games like *reparolo* and basset.

In short, he said so many things, that if it hadn't been for such sure signs of his madness as his cries when anyone touched him, or came up to him, and for his dress, his frugality, his way of drinking, his unwillingness to sleep anywhere but out of doors in summer and in straw lofts in the winter, as we've said, no one would have believed that he wasn't one of the sanest men in the world.

He suffered from this illness for some two years, and then a monk of the Jeromite order, who had a special gift for making deaf mutes hear and speak after a fashion, and for curing madness, out of charity took it upon himself to cure Glass. He managed to restore him to health, and to his previous good sense, intelligence and way of life. And as soon as he saw that he was sane, he dressed him up as a lawyer and sent him back to court, where, showing as many signs of sanity as he had previously shown indications of madness, he could practise his profession and make himself famous by it. This he did, and calling himself Licenciate Rueda, and not Rodaja, he went back to the court. As soon as he got there, he was recognized by the children; but as they saw him dressed so differently from the way he usually went about they didn't dare to hoot at him or ask him questions; but they followed him, and said to each other,

'Isn't this the madman Glass? Of course it is. He looks sane now. But he might still be just as mad when he's wearing good clothes as when he wore bad ones. Let's ask him something, and we'll find out the truth of the matter.'

All this the licenciate heard, but he kept silent, and was more bewildered and confused than when he was out of his mind.

The children passed on the word to the men, and before the licenciate reached the courtyard of the Consejos[17] he was being followed by more than two hundred people of all kinds. With this following, which was bigger than that of a professor, he reached the courtyard, where all the people there gathered round him. Seeing himself surrounded by such a crowd he spoke up as follows:

'Gentlemen, I am Licenciate Glass; but not the man I used to be: now I am Licenciate Rueda. Events and misfortunes which happen

17. 'Councils'.

in the world by heaven's design put me out of my mind, and God's mercies have now restored me to it. Bearing in mind the things they say I said when I was mad you can get an idea of what I shall say and do when I am sane. I am a Law graduate from Salamanca, where I was a poor student, and where I came out with a second; from this you can infer that I won my degree more by merit than as a result of influence. I have come here to this great sea of the capital to practise as a lawyer and to earn my living; but if you don't leave me alone, I shall merely sweat away and die at the end of it. For heaven's sake don't follow me to the point of persecution, and make me lose when I am sane the living I made when I was mad. What you used to ask me in the squares, ask me now at home, and you will see that the man who gave you good answers extempore, as they say, will give you better answers when he's thought them out.'

They all listened to him and some of them left him. He went back to his lodgings, with almost as many people as he had taken with him.

He went out the next day, and the same thing happened; he delivered another sermon, and it was no use. He lost a great deal and earned nothing; and seeing himself about to die of hunger, he decided to leave the court and go back to Flanders, where he thought he would avail himself of the strength of his arm, since he could get no advantage from that of his mind. And putting his decision into effect, he said, as he left the court,

'Oh court, you who build up the hopes of bold office-seekers, and cut short those of them who are virtuous and bashful; who keep shameful rogues in prosperity and starve modest and discreet men to death.'

This said, he went off to Flanders, where, accompanied by his good friend Captain Valdivia, he added eternal fame by deeds of arms to that which he had begun to acquire by his learning, leaving behind him after his death a reputation as a prudent and most valiant soldier.

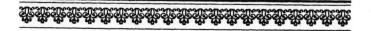

The Jealous Extremaduran

Not many years ago a gentleman born of noble parents set out from a village in Extremadura, and like a second Prodigal Son went off through various parts of Spain, Italy and Flanders, wasting his time and his substance. After much wandering, his parents having died and his inheritance spent, he came to live in the great city of Seville, where he found plenty of opportunity to get through the little that he had left. So, seeing himself so short of money, and with few friends left, he had recourse to the solution to which many ruined people of that city are driven, namely that of going to the Indies, the refuge and shelter of all desperate folk in Spain, the sanctuary of bankrupts, the safe-conduct of murderers, the protection and cover of those gamblers known by the experts in the craft as sharpers, the general decoy for loose women, where many go to be deceived, and few find a way out of their difficulties. In short, when there was a fleet leaving for Tierrafirme, he came to terms with the commander, got together a store of provisions and an esparto mat; and embarking at Cadiz, and saying good-bye to Spain, he set off with the fleet. Amid general rejoicing the ship hoisted sail, and was carried off by a fair wind that soon took them out of sight of land and opened up to them the broad and ample plains of that great father of all waters, the Atlantic Ocean.

Our passenger was thoughtful, turning over in his memory the many and varied dangers which he had passed through in the years of his wandering, and the lack of direction which had characterized the whole of his life; and from his stock-taking he came to a firm decision to change his way of life and to adopt another manner of looking after whatever fortune God might be pleased to give him. He also determined to proceed with more caution towards women than hitherto. The fleet was almost becalmed when Filipo de Carrizales, which was the name of the man who is the subject of our story, was passing through this storm in his mind. The wind blew again, driving the ships on with such force that everyone was

tossed hither and thither; and so Carrizales had to leave his ponder-
ings and allow himself to be preoccupied simply by the problems
of the voyage. This voyage was so successful that without suffering any set-back or shift in the wind they reached the port of
Cartagena. And to cut out all the details which have nothing to do
with our purpose, I should tell you that when Filipo went to the
Indies he would be about forty-eight years old, and during the
twenty he spent overseas, by his industry and diligence, he managed
to make a hundred and fifty thousand good solid pesos.

So, seeing himself rich and prosperous, and feeling the natural
desire which everyone has to return to his native land, he put off
the important business he had in hand, and leaving Peru, where he
had made such a rich harvest, he brought it all back to Spain in bars
of gold and silver, in bond to save trouble. He landed in Sanlúcar;
reached Seville, that ancient and wealthy city; collected his
property without any trouble, looked up his friends, found them
all dead, and decided to go off to his own part of the country,
although he had already heard that death had not left him any of
his relatives. If when he went off to the Indies, poor and in need, he
had been assailed by many thoughts which did not leave him a
moment's peace amid the waves of the sea, now in the calm of dry
land they assailed him no less, although for different reasons. For
whereas formerly he could not sleep because he was poor, now he
could find no rest because he was rich; for wealth is just as heavy a
burden for one who is not accustomed to bear it and does not
know how to make use of it, as poverty is to one who is continually
forced to endure it. Gold brings cares and so does the lack of it:
but the cares of poverty are alleviated when one attains a moderate
fortune, and those of wealth increase the more one gets.

Carrizales thought about his bars of gold and silver, not in any
miserly way, because he had learned to be generous in his years as
a soldier, but because he wondered what to do with them. To keep
them in the form of bars was pointless, and to keep them at home
was an incentive to the covetous and a stimulus to thieves. The urge
to return to the restless life of a merchant had gone, and it seemed to
him that in view of his age he had too much money. He wanted
to spend his days in his own country and invest his property,
passing his old age there in peace and quiet, giving to God what he

could, since he had given to the world more than he should. At the same time, he thought that his homeland and the people in it were very poor, and that to go and live there would be to make himself the target of all the importunity to which the poor subject the rich man who is their neighbour, and especially when there is no one else in the village to run to with their troubles. He wanted someone to whom he could leave his possessions at the end of his days, and with this wish in mind he looked into the state of his health, and it seemed to him that he was still fit enough to get married. But at the thought of this he was so terrified that he felt like a mist driven by the wind. By nature he was the most jealous man in the world, even without being married; the mere thought of marrying was enough to arouse his jealousy, weary him with suspicions and startle him with imaginary evils, so much so that he resolved at all costs not to marry.

And having made up his mind about this, but not about what he was going to do with his life, fate determined that one day as he was going along a street he raised his eyes and saw a young girl at a window, who appeared to be thirteen or fourteen years old, so pleasant to look at and so beautiful, that, unable to help himself, good old Carrizales surrendered the weakness of his old age to the youth of Leonora, which was the name of the beautiful girl. And immediately he began to make endless speeches to himself, saying such things as:

'This girl is beautiful, and from the look of this house she can't be wealthy; she is only a girl; her youth may be sufficient to set my suspicions at rest. I shall marry her; I shall shut her up and train her in my ways, and so that she won't know anything else but what I shall teach her. I am not so old that I need lose hope of having children to be my heirs. There's no point in worrying about whether she has a dowry or not, since heaven has given me enough for our needs. Those who are rich have no need to look for property when they marry, but merely to find pleasure, for pleasure prolongs life, and the lack of it between married couples shortens it. Enough then, the die is cast, and this is the girl that heaven wishes me to have.'

And so some days later, when he had gone through this soliloquy not once but a hundred times, he spoke to Leonora's parents, and learned that, although poor, they were noble; and telling them of his intention and of his rank and fortune, he begged them to give him their daughter as his wife. They asked him for time to verify what he said, and so that he too would have time to find out whether what they had said about their nobility was true. They took leave of each other, investigated each other's credentials and found that what both said was true. So at last Leonora became Carrizales's wife, after he had given her a dowry of twenty thousand ducats, so fired was the heart of the jealous old man with love. He had scarcely taken his marriage vow when he was suddenly attacked by a raging jealousy, and without any reason began to tremble and to be more worried than he had ever been in his life. The first sign that he gave of his jealous condition was his unwillingness to let any tailor measure his wife for all the clothes which he wanted made for her; and so he went in search of another woman of more or less the same figure and size as Leonora's. He found a poor girl, and had a dress made to her measurements, and trying it on his wife, he found that it fitted her well. So, using the same measurements, he had the rest of the clothes made, in such quantity and quality that the parents of the girl couldn't believe their luck in having found such a good son-in-law, for their own sake and their daughter's. The girl was astonished at the sight of so much finery, because she had never in her life had more than a serge skirt and a taffeta cloak.

The second indication of jealousy that Filipo gave was in not wanting to live with his wife until he had set up a separate house for her, which he arranged in this way. He bought one costing twelve thousand ducats, in one of the best parts of the town, with running water and a garden with lots of orange-trees; he shut up all the windows facing on to the street, and opened up skylights all over the house. At the street entrance which is called the 'house door' in Seville, he had a stable built for a mule, and above it a straw loft and a room for the man who was to be in charge of it, who was an old Negro eunuch; he raised the walls above the level of the roofs so that anyone going into the house had to look straight up to the sky, without being able to see anything else; and he made a revolving door, which led from the house door to the patio. He bought rich furnishings to decorate the house, so that with its

tapestries, furniture and canopies, it was obviously the property of
a gentleman of means; he also purchased four slave girls, whom he
branded on the face, as well as two newly-imported Negro girls. He
made arrangements with a caterer to supply him with food, on
condition that he did not sleep in the house nor come beyond the
revolving door – through which he would have to hand the things
he brought. When this was done, he leased some of his property in
several of the best parts of the city; he put some of his money in the
bank, and kept some for such contingencies as might arise. He also
had a master key made for the whole house, and bought in season
enough stores for the whole year. When he had arranged and set
everything up in this fashion, he went to the house of his parents-
in-law and asked for his wife, whom they handed over to him
amid much weeping, because it seemed to them that she was being
led off to her grave.

Poor Leonora did not know what had happened to her; and so,
weeping with her parents, she asked for their blessing, and saying
good-bye to them, surrounded by her slaves and maids and clutch-
ing her husband's hand, she came to her house, and when they
were inside Carrizales delivered a sermon to all of them, instructing
them to guard Leonora, and in no circumstances to let anyone
come in beyond the second door, even the black eunuch. And the
principal duty of guarding and looking after Leonora was en-
trusted to a wise and circumspect duenna, who was a sort of
governess for Leonora, with the duty of supervising everything
that went on in the house and overseeing the slaves and two other
girls of the same age as Leonora, who had been brought in so that
she should have the company of someone of her own age. He
promised that he would treat and look after them in such a way
that they would not regret their confinement, and that on saints'
days they would all without exception go to hear Mass; but so
early that the light of day would scarcely fall upon them. The
servants and slaves promised him that they would do everything
as he ordered, readily and willingly and without complaint; and
the new bride, shrugging her shoulders, bowed her head and said
that she had no will but that of her husband and master, to whom
she would always be obedient.

When all these arrangements had been made and the good

Extremaduran was settled in his house, he began to enjoy the fruits of marriage to the best of his ability, fruits which were neither pleasing nor disagreeable to Leonora, since she had no experience of any others; and so she spent her time with her duenna, her ladies-in-waiting and her slaves, while they found their enjoyment in eating sweetmeats; and rarely did a day pass without their making a hundred and one tasty things with honey and sugar. They had plenty of what was needed for this, and their master was very happy to give it to them, for he thought that they would be entertained and occupy their minds with all this and have no occasion to start thinking about their confinement. Leonora lived on terms of equality with her maids and took part in the same pleasures as they did, and in her innocence even started making dolls and other girlish things, which showed how simple-minded and childlike she was. All this was infinitely satisfying to the jealous husband, who thought that he had been happier in choosing his way of life than he could imagine, and that there was no way in which human ingenuity or malice could disturb his calm; so his only concern was to bring presents for his wife and remind her to ask him for anything that might occur to her, promising that he would see that she got all that she wanted.

The days when she went to Mass, which was, as we've said, at first light, her parents would come too and would talk to their daughter in church in front of her husband, who gave them so many gifts that although they were sorry for their daughter, on account of the confinement in which she lived, they were consoled by the many presents which Carrizales, their generous son-in-law, gave them.

He would get up early in the morning, and wait for the arrival of the caterer, who was told the night before, by means of an order which they put in the revolving hatch, what he was to bring the following day; and when the caterer came, Carrizales would set off, usually on foot, leaving the two doors shut, the street door and the middle door, with the Negro stationed in between. He would attend to his affairs, which were not very considerable, and was soon back. Then, shutting himself up, he would spend his time giving presents to his wife and treats to the servants, who were all very fond of him, because he was so easy-going and pleasant, and especially because he was so generous to all of them. In this way they spent their novice year, and went on to make their profession in that way of life, resolving to continue in it to the end of their days. And this is how things would have turned out if that cunning disturber of the human race had not upset things, as you shall now hear.

Let him who thinks himself prudent and cautious tell me now what more precautions old Filipo could have taken, for he did not even allow any male animal in his house. The mice in it were never chased away by a male cat, nor was the bark of a dog ever heard there; they were all of the female sex. By day he would be thinking; by night he would lie awake, patrolling and guarding his house, the Argus of his loved one; and no man ever came inside the patio door, for he would do business with his friends in the street. The figures on the hangings in his halls and rooms were all females, or else flowers and woodland scenes. His whole house had an air of virtue and seclusion; even in the stories which the servants told in the long winter nights by the fireside, nothing lascivious was ever mentioned when he was present.

The silver of the old man's hair was pure gold to the eyes of Leonora, because the first love of a maiden makes an imprint on her soul like that of a seal on wax. The close custody in which she was kept seemed like sensible caution to her; she thought and believed that all recently married wives went through the same experience as she did. Her thoughts did not stray beyond the walls of her house, nor did she wish for anything but what her husband desired. Only on the days when she went to Mass did she see the streets, and this was so early in the morning that except on the way back from church there was not enough light even to see them properly. Never was monastery more enclosed, nor nuns more withdrawn, nor golden apples more strictly guarded; but for all this, it was impossible to avoid falling into the danger he feared; or at least, thinking that he had fallen into it.

There is in Seville a class of useless idle people usually known as men about town; these are the richer young men from every parish, lazy, showy, plausible people, about whose dress and manner of living, and whose customs and rules of conduct a good deal could be said; but we'll leave that aside for good reason. One of these fellows, known in their own jargon as a *virote*, a young bachelor – the ones who are recently married are called *mantones* – happened to look at the house of the cautious Carrizales, and seeing it always shut up, he was anxious to know who lived in it. He was so curious and so energetic in his inquiry, that he soon found out everything he wanted to know. He learned what the old man was like, of his wife's beauty and how he guarded her; all of which stimulated in turn the desire to see if it would be possible to storm, either by force or by cunning, such a well-guarded citadel. Discussing it with two *virotes* and a *mantón* who were friends of his, they agreed to set to work on it; for there is never a shortage of advisers and helpers for this sort of task.

The difficulty was to find out how to set about such a hazardous exercise; and having discussed it several times, they agreed on this plan: that Loaysa, as the *virote* was called, pretending that he was leaving the city for a few days, should keep out of sight of his friends. This he did. He then put on some clean drill trousers and a clean shirt, but on top he put clothes which were so torn and patched that there wasn't a poor man in the whole city who wore such vile things; he cut off his beard, put a patch over his eye, bound up one of his legs tightly, and supporting himself on crutches, transformed himself effectively into such a broken-down wreck that not even the most genuine cripple could rival him.

In this guise he would station himself every night at prayer time at the door of Carrizales's house, which was already closed, the Negro, who was called Luis, being shut up between the two doors. Standing there, Loaysa would take out a rather grimy guitar with a few strings missing, and as he was something of a musician, he would begin to strum a few gay and merry tunes, changing his voice so as not to be recognized. Then he would go on to sing some cheerful Moorish ballads so pleasantly and with such spirit that everyone who went along the street would stop to listen to him, and always, as soon as he started singing, he would find himself surrounded by children. The Negro Luis, listening from his position between the doors, was spellbound by the *virote*'s music, and would have given his right arm to be able to open the door, and listen more easily; so strong is the love which Negroes have for music. And when Loaysa wanted those who were listening to him to leave him, he would stop singing, pick up his guitar and, taking up his crutches, would be off.

He had performed four or five times for the Negro – for it was merely for his sake that he did it, as it seemed to him that the way to begin the demolition of that edifice was and must be through the Negro – and his plans were not in vain, because one night, going up to the door as usual, he began to tune his guitar, and realized that the Negro was already waiting for him. So, going to the crack at the side of the door, he said softly,

'Do you think, Luis, that you could give me a drop of water, for I'm dying of thirst and I can't sing?'

'No,' said the Negro, 'for I haven't got the key to this door, and there's no hole through which I could give it to you.'

'But who has the key?' asked Loaysa.

'My master,' answered the Negro, 'who is the most jealous man in the world. And if he knew that I was talking to someone here and now, that would be the end of me. But who are you, asking me for water?'

'I'm a poor man with a lame leg,' answered Loaysa, 'and I earn my living begging from good folk in the name of God; and as well as this I am teaching some Negroes and other poor people to play. I've already got three Negroes, slaves of three of the city aldermen, whom I've taught so that they can sing and play at any dance and in any inn, and they've paid me very well indeed for it.'

'I'd pay you a good deal better,' said Luis, 'if I had the chance to take lessons; but it's impossible, because when my master goes out in the morning, he closes the street door, and when he comes back he does the same, leaving me shut up between the two doors.'

'By Jove, Luis,' replied Loaysa, who already knew the Negro's name, 'if you could find a way for me to get in at night now and then, in less than a fortnight I'd have you so expert at the guitar that you could play on any street corner without embarrassment; because I assure you I am a very skilful teacher. Moreover, I've heard that you are very talented, and from what I can judge by the sound of your voice, which is rather high-pitched, you must sing very well.'

'I don't sing too badly,' answered the Negro; 'but what's the use if I don't know a single tune except the one about the Star of Venus, and the one that goes:

> By a green meadow ...

and that one that's in fashion just now, which goes:

> With my trembling hand clutching
> The bars of a window.'

'Those are trifles', said Loaysa, 'compared with the ones I could teach you, because I know all the ones about the Moor Abindarráez, the ones about his lady Jarifa,[1] all the ones they sing about the story of the great Sufi Tuman-Bey;[2] and the ones that go with the sacred version of the saraband, which are so marvellous that they even make the Portuguese sit up and take notice. I teach all this by such easy methods, that even if you're in no hurry to learn, by the time you've eaten three or four pecks of salt[3] you'll be a fluent performer on every kind of guitar.'

At this the Negro sighed and said, 'What is the use of all this, if I can't get you into the house?'

'I have the answer,' said Loaysa. 'You try to take the keys from your master, and I will give you a piece of wax, on which you can take the imprint in such a way that the wards are marked on the wax; and as I've become rather fond of you, I'll get a locksmith who's a friend of mine to make the keys, and so I'll be able to get in at night and teach you better than Prester John of the Indies. I think it's a great pity that a voice like your should be wasted, simply for lack of support from the guitar; for you should know, brother Luis, that the best voice in the world goes off when it is not accompanied by an instrument, be it guitar or clavichord, organ or harp; but the one which most suits your voice is the guitar, being the easiest and least costly instrument.'

'This seems fine to me,' replied the Negro, 'but it can't be done,

1. Abindarráez and Jarifa. The hero and heroine of a romantic Moorish tale inserted into the 1561 edition of the *Diana*, the long pastoral romance by Jorge de Montemayor.

2. Tuman-Bey. The last Mamluk Sultan of Egypt, remembered for his bravery and misfortunes.

3. Presumably it takes a long time to eat such a large amount of salt, so Loaysa is not promising Luis any miracles.

because the keys never come into my possession. My master never lets them out of his hands during the day, and at night they're kept under his pillow when he's asleep.'

'Then think of something else, Luis,' said Loaysa, 'if you're keen to be an accomplished musician; for if you're not, it's not worth my taking the trouble to give you advice.'

'What do you mean, if I'm keen?' replied Luis. 'I'm so keen that there's nothing humanly possible that I won't do, in order to learn music.'

'Well, if that's so,' said the *virote*, 'I'll pass you some pincers and a hammer, if you will make room by taking away some of the earth by the hinge; and with them you'll be able to take the nails out of the lock very easily, and then just as easily we shall put back the plate so that no one can see that the nails have been taken out. Once I am inside, shut up with you in your loft or wherever you sleep, I'll be so quick doing what I have to do, that you'll see even more than I've told you, to my advantage and your satisfaction. And don't worry about what we shall have to eat: I'll bring enough supplies to last both of us a week, for I've pupils and friends who will see to it that I come to no harm.'

'As far as food is concerned,' replied the Negro, 'there'll be no cause for worry; for with the ration I get from my master and the leftovers I get from the slave girls there'll be plenty of food for two more people. Let's have this hammer and pincers you talk about, and I'll make room under the door by the hinge for you to pass it through, and then cover it up and seal it with mud; for even if I have to tap once or twice taking off the plate, my master sleeps so far from this door that it'll be a miracle, or hard luck on our part, if he hears it.'

'Then to work,' said Loaysa; 'for in two days from now, Luis, you will have all you need to carry out our plan; and take care not to eat things that cause phlegm, because they do more harm than good to your voice.'

'Nothing makes me more hoarse than wine,' answered the Negro, 'but I shan't give that up for all the voices on earth.'

'That's not what I mean,' said Loaysa. 'God forbid. Drink, Luis my boy, drink and much good may it do you, for wine drunk in moderation never did anyone any harm.'

'I do drink in moderation,' replied the Negro. 'I have a jug here which contains exactly two litres; the slaves fill this for me without my master knowing, and the caterer secretly brings me a little wineskin, which contains exactly four litres and which fills this up when it runs out.'

'That's excellent,' said Loaysa, 'for a dry throat can neither grunt nor sing.'

'God be with you,' said the Negro; 'but see that you don't fail to come here at night to sing while you're looking for the things you need to get in here, for my fingers are itching to have a go at the guitar.'

'You bet I'll come,' replied Loaysa. 'And what's more I'll bring new songs.'

'That's what I want,' said Luis; 'and now don't go without singing something for me, so that I may go happily to bed; and as far as payment is concerned, you may be sure, my poor sir, that I'll pay you better than any rich man.'

'I'm not concerned about that,' said Loaysa, 'for you can pay me as I teach you. For the moment listen to this little tune, and when I get inside you'll see wonders.'

'Splendid,' answered the Negro.

When this long conversation was over, Loaysa sang a brisk little ballad, with which he left the Negro happy and satisfied and hardly able to wait to open the door.

Loaysa had scarcely left the door when, more swiftly than you'd expect in view of his crutches, he went to tell his advisers of the good beginning he had made, an earnest of the good ending which he expected. He found them and told them what he had agreed with the Negro. The next day they found the instruments, so effective that they could break any nail as easily as if it were made of wood.

The *virote* did not fail to go and entertain the Negro with music again, nor did the Negro neglect to make the hole for the things his teacher was going to give him, covering it in such a way that if one weren't deliberately looking one would never realize there was a hole there. The second night Loaysa gave him the instruments, and Luis tried his strength, and almost without any effort found himself with the nails broken and the plate of the lock in his hands. He opened the door and welcomed his teacher inside like Orpheus himself. When he saw him with his two crutches and so ragged, with his leg all bandaged up, he was amazed. Loaysa wasn't wearing the patch over his eye, as it wasn't necessary, and as soon as he got in, he embraced his good pupil and kissed him on the face, and then put a big wineskin in his hands and a box of preserves and other sweetmeats, of which he had a good supply. And putting aside his crutches, as if there were nothing wrong with him, he began to caper about. The Negro was so surprised at this that Loaysa said to him:

'You must know, brother Luis, that my lameness and broken-down appearance are not the result of any affliction, but are contrived as a means of earning my food, begging for the love of God; and with the help of this and of my music, I have the best time in the world – a world in which all those who are not clever and scheming will die of hunger, as you will see in the course of our friendship.'

'Time will tell,' answered the Negro, 'but let's set about putting this plate back, so that no one can see what's been done to it.'

'Right ho,' said Loaysa.

He took some nails out of his bag and they fixed the lock so that it was as good as before, which delighted the Negro. Loaysa went up to the room in the loft, and settled down as best he could. Luis lit a taper, and without further ado, Loaysa took out his guitar, and playing softly he left the poor Negro quite carried away as he listened to it. After he had played a little, he took some food out again and gave it to his pupil, who drank with such a will from the wine skin that he was more carried away by the wine than the music. After this, he started Luis on his lesson; but as the poor Negro had a good load of wine on board, he couldn't get a note right. All the same Loaysa made him believe that he knew at least two tunes, and the funny thing was that the Negro swallowed it, and spent the whole night strumming the guitar out of tune and without touching the right strings.

They slept for what little of the night was left, and about six in the morning Carrizales came down and opened the middle door, and the street door also, and stood waiting for the caterer, who came shortly afterwards, and putting the food through the revolving door, went off again. Then he called to the Negro to come down and take the barley for the mule, and his own ration of food. When Luis had taken it, old Carrizales went off, leaving both doors shut, without seeing what had been done to the street door, at which both master and pupil were not a little pleased.

The master had barely left the house when the Negro grabbed the guitar and began to play so loudly that all the servants heard him and asked him through the revolving door,

'What is this, Luis? How long have you had a guitar, and who gave it to you?'

'Who gave it to me?' said Luis. 'The best musician in the world, and one who is going to teach me more than six thousand notes in less than six days.'

'And where is this musician?' asked the duenna.

'Not very far from here,' answered the Negro, 'and if it weren't that I'm embarrassed and afraid of my master, I might show him to you now, and I promise you'd be delighted to see him.'

'And where can he be for us to see him,' asked the duenna, 'if no man but our master has ever entered this house?'

'Well,' said the Negro, 'I don't want to say anything to you until you see what I know and what he has taught me in the short time I've said.'

'Certainly,' said the duenna, 'unless it's some devil who's going to teach you, I don't know who can make a musician out of you in such a short time.'

'You wait,' said the Negro, 'and you'll hear and see one of these days.'

'It's impossible,' said one of the maids, 'for we have no windows looking on to the street to be able to see or hear anyone.'

'That's all right,' said the Negro; 'for while there's life there's hope: and especially if you can and will keep quiet.'

'You bet we'll keep quiet, brother Luis,' said one of the slave girls. 'We'll be more quiet than if we were dumb; because I promise you, my friend, I'm dying to hear a good voice, for since we've been walled up here, we haven't even heard the birds singing.'

Loaysa was listening to all this conversation with great satisfaction, thinking that it was all directed towards the attainment of his ends, and that good fortune had been with him in guiding the conversation according to his wishes. The servants went off with a promise from the Negro that when they least expected it he would call them to listen to a very good voice, then, fearing that his master would return and find him talking to them, he left them and withdrew to his retreat. He would have liked to carry on with his lessons, but he did not dare to play during the day, lest his master should hear him. Carrizales came shortly afterwards, and closing the doors as his custom was, he shut himself up in the house. Luis told the Negress who happened to give him his food that night, that they should all come down to the hatch after his master had gone to sleep and that they would hear the voice without fail as he had promised them. It is true that before he said this he had begged his teacher earnestly to be so kind as to sing and play at the revolving door that night, so that he could keep the promise he had made to the maids that they should hear a remarkable voice, and assured him that he would be extremely well treated by all of them. The teacher pretended to be reluctant to do what he in fact most wanted to do; but finally he said that he would do what his good pupil asked, simply to give him pleasure. The Negro embraced him and gave him a kiss on the cheek, to show how pleased he was at this promised favour; and that day he fed Loaysa as well as if he had been eating in his own home, and perhaps even better, for he might well have been short of something there.

Night came, and at midnight or just before there were whisperings at the revolving door, and Luis realized that it was the crowd of servants coming. So he called his teacher and they came down from the loft, with the guitar well strung and tuned. Luis asked who and how many were listening. They replied that they were all there except their mistress, who was sleeping with her husband. Loaysa was sorry about this, but all the same, he wanted to get his plan under way and give pleasure to his pupil; so playing the guitar softly, he made such beautiful sounds that the Negro was amazed and the flock of women who were listening to him astounded. What shall I say about their feelings when they heard him play 'Woe is me' and finish up with the lively sound of the saraband, new to Spain at that time? Every one of the older women was dancing, and the young ones were beside themselves, although they all kept remarkably quiet, with guards and spies posted to give warning if the old man should wake. Loaysa also sang *seguidillas*, with which he filled to overflowing the cup of pleasure of the listeners, who pestered the Negro to tell them who this marvellous musician was. The Negro told them that he was a poor beggar, the nicest and finest-looking man you could find among all the beggars in Seville. They pleaded with him to arrange for them to see him, and not to let him leave the house for at least a fortnight, for they would look after him very well and give him everything he needed. They asked him how he had managed to get him into the house. He didn't say a word in answer to this; all he would say was that if they wanted to see him they should make a little hole in the revolving door which they could stop up with wax afterwards; and that as far as keeping him in the house was concerned, he would see what he could do.

Loaysa also spoke to them, putting himself at their service, and with such convincing arguments that they realized they were beyond the intelligence of a poor beggar. They asked him to come to the same place the following night, and said they would arrange with their mistress that she should come down and listen to him, although their master was a light sleeper, not because of his great age, but because of his great jealousy. To this Loaysa said that if they wanted to hear him without upsetting the old man he would give them some powder to put in his wine to make him sleep more heavily and for longer than usual.

'Heaven help us!' said one of the ladies. 'If this were true, what good fortune would have come to us unexpected and undeserved. It wouldn't be sleeping powder for him so much as life-giving powder for all of us and for my poor mistress Leonora his wife, for he doesn't leave her day or night and doesn't let her out of his sight for a single moment. Oh, sir, bring this powder and may God give you all the blessings you desire! Be off, and don't be long; bring it, sir, for I'll be happy to mix it with the wine and act as butler; and God grant that the old man sleeps for three days and nights, which would be heaven for us.'

'Well, I'll bring it,' said Loaysa, 'and it won't do any harm to anyone who takes it apart from making him sleep very heavily.'

They all begged him to bring it quickly, and having agreed to make a hole in the revolving door with a gimlet the next night, and to bring their mistress to see and hear him, they went off. Although it was almost day, the Negro wanted to have his lesson, which

Loaysa gave him, giving him to understand that not one of all his pupils had a better ear than he, when in fact the poor Negro didn't know, and never learned, how to play a note.

Loaysa's friends took care to come at night to listen at the street doors, to see if their friend had anything to say to them or if he needed anything. Giving a signal which they had agreed on, Loaysa found that they were at the door, and through the gap by the hinge he told them briefly of the good state in which affairs stood. He asked them earnestly to look for something to give to Carrizales which would induce sleep, for he had heard that there was a powder which did this. They told him they had a friend who was a doctor, who would give them the best thing he knew, if there was any to be had; and urging him to carry on with the plan, and promising to return the following night, with all caution and speed they left.

Night came, and the flock of doves came to the lure of the guitar. With them came innocent Leonora, fearful and trembling at the thought of her husband waking. Alarmed by this fear, she had not wished to come, but her servants, especially the duenna, said so many things to her about the soft tones of the music and the noble nature of the poor musician – for without having seen him she praised him and lauded him more highly than Absalom and Orpheus – that the poor lady, convinced and persuaded by them, was forced to do what she never wished or ever would wish to do. The first thing they did was to bore a hole in the revolving door to see the musician, who was no longer dressed as a poor beggar, but with breeches of tawny-coloured taffeta, full-cut like a sailor's; a doublet of the same stuff with gold braid, and a velvet cap of the same colour, with a starched collar with long points and lace on it; for he had brought all this with him in his knapsack, having an idea that the opportunity would come for him to change his clothes.

He was young, elegant and good-looking; and as all the ladies had been used to looking at their old master for such a long time, they thought they were seeing an angel. One would go up to the hole to look at him, then another, and so that they could see him better, the Negro moved the lighted taper up and down in front of him. And when they had all seen him, even the Negro slave girls, Loaysa took the guitar, and sang so exquisitely that night that they were all quite carried away, the old women and the girls alike. They all asked Luis to arrange for the teacher to come inside, so that they could hear and see him at close quarters, and not as if they were looking through a sextant; and moreover without being so dangerously far from their master, who could catch them suddenly and with the goods on them, which would not happen if they had him hidden inside.

Their mistress opposed this vigorously, saying that this must not happen and that he must not come in, because she would be very upset, and they could see and hear him safely from there, without danger to their honour.

'What honour?' said the duenna. 'The king has enough of that. You stay shut up with your Methuselah, and let us enjoy ourselves as best we can. Anyway, this gentleman seems so honourable that he won't want anything from us that we don't want to give him.'

'My ladies,' said Loaysa at this point, 'I came here simply to serve you with all my heart and soul, moved by your extraordinary isolation, and by the thought of the time you have to waste in this confined existence. Indeed, I am such a simple, inoffensive and good-tempered man, so compliant, that I shall do nothing but what I am told; and if any of you should say, "Maestro, sit here", "maestro, go over there", "lie down here", "come over here", I'd do it like a tame dog doing its tricks.'

'If this is so,' said poor, ignorant Leonora, 'how shall we arrange for you to get in here?'

'Well,' said Loaysa, 'you do your best to make a wax copy of the key of this middle door, and I'll arrange to get another made which we can use tomorrow night.'

'When you've copied that key,' said one of the ladies, 'you've copied every one in the house, because it's a master key.'

'That's all to the good,' replied Loaysa.

'It's true,' said Leonora, 'but this gentleman must first swear that all he will do when he gets in here is sing and play when he's asked, and that he'll stay shut up and quiet wherever we put him.'

'I'll swear that,' said Loaysa.

'That oath is worthless,' answered Leonora. 'You must swear by the life of your father, and on the Cross, kissing it so that all of us may see.'

'By my father's life I swear,' said Loaysa; 'and by this sign of the Cross, which I kiss with my unclean mouth.'

And making a cross with two fingers, he kissed it three times.

When he had done this, another of the ladies said, 'See that you don't forget about the powder, sir, for that's absolutely essential.'

With that the conversation ended for the night, everybody being very happy about the arrangement. And fortune, which was leading Loaysa's affair to a happy solution, just at that time, which was two o'clock in the morning, brought his friends along the street. They made the usual sign, which was to play a jews' harp, and Loaysa told them how things were, and asked them if they had brought the powder or something similar, as he had asked, to make Carrizales sleep; he also told them about the master key. They told him that the powder, or an ointment, would arrive the following night, so effective that, when the wrists and temples had been rubbed with it, it would induce a deep sleep, from which one would not awaken for two days unless one were bathed with vinegar in all the places where the ointment had been applied. They also asked him for the wax copy of the key, which they'd have made quite easily. With this they went off, and Loaysa and his pupil slept for what was left of the night. Loaysa longed for the next night to arrive, to see if they kept the promise about the key. And although time seems slow and dull to those who are waiting, in the end it catches up with one's thoughts and the desired end comes, for time never stands still.

So night came and with it the time at which they usually went to the revolving door, where all the house servants came, young and old, black and white, because they all wanted to see the musician in their seraglio. But Leonora did not come, and when Loaysa asked about her they replied that she was in bed with her husband, who had locked the door of the room where they slept, and after shutting it put the key under his pillow. They said that their mistress had told them that when the old man fell asleep she would try to take the master key from him and make a copy in wax, which she had made soft and ready; and that very shortly they were to go and get it through a cat's hole.

Loaysa was amazed at the old man's caution, but he did not lose heart nor his desire. At this point he heard the jews' harp so he went to the door and found his friends, who gave him a little jar of ointment of the sort they had described. Loaysa took it and told them to wait a little, and he would give them the master key. He went back to the revolving door and told the duenna, who was the one who most obviously wanted him to get in, to take it to her mistress Leonora, telling her how it worked and to try to rub it on her husband so that he didn't feel it, and that she would be amazed at what would happen. The duenna did this, and when she got to the hole, she found that Leonora was waiting for her lying flat on the floor, with her ear beside the hole. The duenna went up to it, and lying down in the same way, she put her lips to her mistress's ear, and whispered to her that she had the ointment and told her how she was to make it do its work. She took the ointment, and told her that it was quite impossible for her to take the key from her husband, as he hadn't put it under the pillow, as usual, but between the two mattresses and almost under the middle of his body; but told her to tell the teacher that if the ointment worked as he said, they would easily get the key whenever they wanted, so it wouldn't be necessary to make a wax copy of it. She told her to go and tell him immediately, and to come back to see if the ointment worked, because she intended to rub it on her husband straight away.

The duenna came down to tell Loaysa, and he sent away his friends, who were waiting for the key. Trembling and very gently, almost without daring to breathe, Leonora rubbed the ointment on the wrists of her jealous husband, and then on his nostrils. When she got to these she thought he shuddered and she was terrified, thinking she had been caught red-handed. But she finished rubbing the ointment as best she could in all the places which they told her were necessary, just as if she were embalming him for burial.

The opiate soon proved its effectiveness, because the old man straight away began to snore so loudly that he could be heard in the street, which was music more tuneful to the ear of his wife than that which the teacher played for the Negro. Still doubting her eyes, she went up to him and shook him a little, and then a bit more, and then a little more again, to see if he awoke; then she was so daring that she moved him about without his waking up. When she saw this, she went to the hole in the door, and not quite so softly as before, she called the duenna, who was waiting for her there, and said to her,

'Wonderful news, sister, Carrizales is sleeping like a corpse.'

'Then what are you waiting for to take the key, madam?' said the duenna. 'The musician has been waiting for it for more than an hour.'

'Wait, sister. I'll go and get it,' answered Leonora.

She went back to the bed, put her hand between the mattresses and took out the key without the old man's feeling it; and taking it in her hands, she began to jump for joy, and without more ado opened the door and handed it to the duenna, who received it with great delight. Leonora ordered her to go and open the door for the musician and bring him into the gallery, because she did not dare to move from there, for fear of what might happen; but first of all she insisted on his repeating the oath he had sworn, not to do anything but what they ordered; and that if he did not want to confirm his oath, they should not open the door to him on any account.

'I'll do that,' said the duenna, 'and indeed he shan't come in unless he swears and double-swears and kisses the Cross six times.'

'Don't be too rigid,' said Leonora. 'Let him kiss it as many times as he likes; but see that he swears by his father's and his mother's lives, and by everything he loves best, because then we shall be sure, and we'll hear him sing and play to our hearts' content, for indeed he does it beautifully. Now go on, and don't delay any longer, for we don't want to spend the night talking.'

The good duenna picked up her skirts, and rushed as fast as she could to the revolving door, where all the people in the house were waiting for her. When she had shown them the key she was carrying, they were so delighted that they lifted her shoulder high, like a professor, and shouted, 'Hurrah, hurrah!'; and even more so when she said there was no need to copy the key, because the old man was sleeping so soundly under the influence of the ointment that they could use the house key as often as they liked.

'Come on then, old friend,' said one of the ladies. 'Open the door and let this gentleman come in, for he's been waiting a long time, and let's have a bit of music without further delay.'

'But there must be further delay,' replied the duenna; 'for we have to make him swear an oath, like the other night.'

'He's so good,' said one of the slave girls, 'that he won't bother with oaths.'

The duenna then opened the door, and holding it ajar she called Loaysa, who had been listening to the whole thing through the hole in the revolving door. When he got up to the door, he wanted to come straight in, but the duenna put her hand on his chest, and said to him:

'You must know, sir, that by God and my conscience all of us in this house are virgins like the mothers who bore us, except my lady; and although I must look forty, when I'm two and a half months short of thirty, I am one too, for my sins; and if by any chance I look old, it's because all the upsets, the work and the hardships put years on you. And this being so, it would not be right that in exchange for listening to two or three or four songs, we should lose all this virginity that's shut up here; because even this Negress, who's call Guiomar, is a virgin. So, my dear sir, before you come into our domain, you must swear a very solemn oath that you will do nothing but what we command; and if you think this is a lot to ask, bear in mind that a lot more is being risked. If you come with good intentions you won't much mind swearing; for a good payer doesn't mind giving pledges.'

'Señora Marialonso is right, absolutely right,' said one of the ladies, 'as you would expect from one who is so discreet and *comme il faut*; and if the gentleman does not wish to swear, let him not come in here.'

Whereupon the Negress Guiomar, who wasn't very good at the language, said, 'For me, swear or not swear, let him come in and all devil too; for although he swear if you are here he forget all about it.'

Loaysa listened very calmly to Marialonso's harangue, and gravely and solemnly he answered as follows:

'Certainly, my sisters and companions, my intention never was and never will be any other than that of giving you pleasure and happiness in everything that is in my power, and so I shan't make heavy weather of this oath which you are asking me to swear. But I should like you to put some trust in my word, because the word of a person like me is equivalent to entering into a binding contract; for I want you to know that under the sackcloth there is something of substance, and that beneath a poor cloak there is usually a good drinker. But so that you may all be sure of my good intentions, I am resolved to swear as a Catholic and as a man of honour; and so I swear solemnly by the immaculate virtue and by the passes of the holy mountain of Lebanon, and by everything in the preface to the true history of Charlemagne, including the death of the giant Fierabras, never to depart from the oath I have sworn and from the command of the least and humblest of these ladies, the penalty being that if I should do or wish to do otherwise, from now henceforward and thenceforward till now I declare it to be null and of no effect or validity.'

Our good Loaysa got to this point in his oath, when one of the ladies, who had been listening attentively to him, shouted out:

'This is indeed an oath to move the very stones! God forbid that I should want you to swear any more, for with what you've sworn already you could go into the Cave of Cabra itself!'

And grasping him by the breeches she dragged him in, and then all the rest made a circle round him. Then one of them went to give the news to her mistress, who was standing guard over her sleeping husband; and when the messenger told her that the musician was on his way up, she was delighted and upset at the same time and asked if he had sworn the oath. She answered that he had, and using the most novel form of oath she had ever come across in her life.

'Then if he has sworn,' said Leonora, 'we've got him. How wise I was to make him swear!'

At this point the whole crowd arrived together with the musician in the middle of them, and the Negro and the Negress Guiomar lighting them on their way. And when Loaysa saw Leonora, he made as if to throw himself at her feet and to kiss her hands. She silently motioned him to get up, and they all kept their mouths shut, not daring to say a word lest their master should hear them. When Loaysa saw this, he told them that they could talk aloud without fear, for the ointment with which their master had been anointed was so powerful that, without actually taking his life away, it made a man seem just like a corpse.

'I can believe that,' said Leonora; 'for if it weren't so he would have woken up twenty times, so lightly does he sleep because of his many ailments; but since I rubbed the ointment on him, he's snoring like a beast.'

'Well, in that case,' said the duenna, 'let's go to that room opposite where we can hear the gentleman sing, and enjoy ourselves a bit.'

'Let's go,' said Leonora, 'but let Guiomar stay here on guard, so that she can tell us if Carrizales wakes up.'

To which Guiomar answered, 'I, black girl, stay; white girls go; God forgive us all.'

The Negress stayed behind, they went off to the drawing-room where there was a splendid dais, and placing the gentleman in the centre of it, they all sat down. And the good Marialonso took a candle, and began to look at the handsome musician from head to foot, and one said, 'What a splendid crop of hair he has, so handsome and curly!' Another said, 'Oh, what white teeth! You'd never find pine-kernels more white or more beautiful!' Another said, 'What eyes, so full and clear! And look how green they are, just like emeralds!' This one praised his mouth, that one his feet, and the whole lot of them together made a detailed study of him. Only Leonora was silent, and looked at him, and thought he was a finer-looking man than her husband. Thereupon the duenna took the guitar from the Negro, and put it in Loaysa's hands, begging him to play it and to sing some verses which were very popular in Seville at the time, and which went: 'Oh Mother, my mother, don't guard me so close.'

Loaysa did as she requested. They all got up and began to dance for all they were worth. The duenna knew the verses, and sang them with more vigour than talent, and they went like this:

> Oh Mother, my mother,
> don't guard me so close.
> I'll guard my own honour
> in the way I shall choose.
>
> They say it is written,
> well written I say,
> that privation well may
> cause men to be smitten,
> and girls to be bitten
> by a deep-hidden love.

If it's true then I move
that you no more time lose.
I'll guard my own honour, etc.

If a maiden's own will
will not keep her from harm,
fear'll not safeguard her charm,
rank no virtue instil.
The desire to fulfil
it will break down all walls:
death itself ne'er appals
when love asks its dues.
I'll guard my own honour, etc.

The girl who is ready
to fall victim to love,
like a moth round a stove
will hover unsteady,
for love's air is heady.
However well guarded,
your pains ill rewarded
I shall have to refuse.
I'll guard my own honour, etc.

Love's so strong in its power
that the most beauteous maid,
when its force is displayed,
will tremble and cower.
Her heart's soft as flour;
her desire's fierce heat
makes her hands and her feet
all their functions refuse.
I'll guard my own honour
in the way I shall choose.

The circle of girls, led by the good duenna, got to the end of
their song and dance, when Guiomar, who was on guard, came up
in great confusion, shaking as if she had a fit, and in a low hoarse
voice, said, 'Master's awake, lady; and lady, master's awake, and
get up and comes.'

If you've ever seen the way a flock of pigeons in a field calmly
eating what others have sown fly up when suddenly disturbed by
the angry sound of a gunshot, and wing their way through the air

in confusion and astonishment, forgetting their food, you can imagine how the circle of dancers was left in terror and alarm, when they heard the unexpected news that Guiomar had brought. Each one looked for an excuse and they all tried to find a way of escape, one here, one there, rushing off to hide in the attics and corners of the house, leaving the musician alone. He, abandoning his guitar and his singing, was so alarmed that he did not know what to do. Leonora wrung her beautiful hands; the lady Maria-lonso clapped her hands to her face, although not too hard; in short all was confusion, terror and alarm. But the duenna, being more shrewd and self-controlled, gave orders that Loaysa should go into one of her rooms, and that she and her mistress would stay in the hall for there would be no difficulty in finding an excuse to give to her master if he found them there.

Loaysa hid himself immediately, and the duenna listened care-fully to see if her master was coming. Not hearing any noise, her courage returned, and gradually, a step at a time, she went along to the room where her master was sleeping. She heard him snoring just as he had been earlier; so, being reassured that he was sleeping, she picked up her skirts and came running back to tell her mistress the good news, news which she was only too happy to hear.

The good duenna did not wish to lose the opportunity which fortune offered her of enjoying before anyone else the charms which she imagined the musician possessed; and so, telling Leo-nora to wait in the hall until she came to call her, she left her and went in to the room where he was waiting, his thoughts in a tur-moil, for news of what the old man was doing. He cursed the unreliability of the ointment, and complained of the credulity of his friends and his own lack of forethought in not trying it on someone else before he used it on Carrizales. Just then the duenna came in, and assured him that the old man was sleeping like a log. He calmed down and listened to the loving words that Marialonsa addressed to him, from which he deduced her evil intentions, deciding that he would use her as a hook to catch her mistress. And as they were both talking, the other servants who were hidden in various parts of the house, one here and one there, came back to see if it was true that their master had awakened. Seeing that everything was plunged in silence, they got as far as the hall where they had left their mistress, from whom they learned that their master was still asleep; and when they asked her about the musician and the duenna, she told them where they were, and they all went, as silently as they had come, to the hall, to listen at the door to what the two were talking about.

Among the gathering was the Negress Guiomar, but not the Negro, because as soon as he heard that his master had awakened, he clutched his guitar and went to hide in his loft, and taking cover under the blankets on his miserable bed, lay sweating with fear; yet he could not resist trying the strings of the guitar, so fond was the poor devil of music. The girls heard the old woman flirting with the musician, and they all started to curse her, calling her a witch and a hairy, bad-tempered old hag, and other things which out of respect we won't repeat; but what made everybody laugh more than anything were the things that the Negress Guiomar said. Being Portuguese and not very good at the language, the way she cursed the duenna was extraordinarily funny. In fact, the upshot of the conversation between the two was that he would fall in with her wishes if she first of all handed over her mistress completely to do with her as he wished.

The duenna was hard put to it to offer what the musician asked, but in return for satisfying the desire which had already taken possession of her body and soul, she promised him the most impossible things imaginable. She left him and went off to talk to her mistress. When she saw that all the servants crowded round her door, she told them to go to their rooms, for there would be a chance the next night to enjoy the musician's company without all this fuss: that night all the disturbance had taken away their pleasure.

They all understood quite well that the old woman wanted to be left alone; yet they had to obey her, because she was in charge of them all. The servants went off, and she hurried off to the hall to persuade Leonora to accede to Loaysa's wishes, with such a long and well-argued harangue, that it looked as if she'd had it worked out for days. She praised his politeness, his bravery, his wit and his many charms; she pointed out to her how much more pleasing would be the embraces of the young lover than those of the old husband, assuring her that she could enjoy her pleasure in secret for as long as she liked, with other arguments of the same kind, which the devil put into her mouth, so persuasive, convincing and effective that they would have moved not only the tender and innocent heart of simple Leonora, but even a marble statue. Oh you duennas, placed by birth and custom in the world to bring to naught a thousand good honest intentions! You with your long, pleated head-dresses, chosen to rule over the halls and drawing-rooms of illustrious ladies, how ill you exercise your function, a function which is now more or less unavoidable! In short, the duenna said so much, the duenna was so persuasive, that Leonora gave in, Leonora was deceived and Leonora was ruined, putting an end to all the precautions of wise old Carrizales, who was sleeping like the corpse of his own honour.

Marialonso took her mistress by the hand, and almost by force, she led Leonora, her eyes swollen with tears, to where Loaysa was. Having given them her blessing with a devilish laugh, she closed the door after her and left them shut up there, while she went off to sleep in the drawing-room. Rather, she went to wait for her reward, but exhausted after so many wakeful nights, she fell asleep.

At this point one might well have asked Carrizales, if one hadn't known that he was asleep, what had happened to all his prudent precautions, his fears, his counsels, his judgements, the high walls of his house, his care lest even the shadow of one bearing a man's name should enter it, the close-kept revolving door, the thick walls, the blocked-up windows, the close confinement, the great dowry which he had given to Leonora, the continual gifts he gave her, the kind treatment of her maids and slave girls, the way in which he had taken care not to neglect any detail of all that he imagined they needed or could desire. But we have already said that there was no occasion for such a question, for he was sleeping a good deal more than was good for him. If he had heard and had perhaps answered, he would not have been able to give any better answer than to shrug his shoulders and raise his eyebrows and say, 'All this was brought to the ground by the cunning, as I see it, of an idle and vicious young man, and the malice of a false duenna, together with the ignorance of a girl who had been won over by persuasive appeals: God deliver us all from enemies like this, against whom no shield of prudence nor sword of caution is effective.'

But all the same, Leonora's courage was such that the crucial moment showed her spirit in the face of the base attacks of her cunning assailant. They could not overcome her, so that he wore himself out in vain, she was victorious, and both fell asleep. And at this point heaven ordained that in spite of the ointment Carrizales woke up, and as his custom was, felt the bed all over. Not finding his beloved wife in it, he leapt out of bed in fear and astonishment, with more speed and more spirit than might have been expected of one of his great age. When he failed to find his wife in the room, and saw that it was open and that the key was missing from its place between the mattresses, he thought he would go mad. But pulling himself together a little, he went out to the gallery and from there, a step at a time so that no one would hear him, he came to the room where the duenna was sleeping, and seeing her alone, without Leonora, he went to the duenna's room, and opening the door very gently he saw what he would prefer never to have seen, what he would have been glad not to have had eyes to see; he saw Leonora in Loaysa's arms, sleeping as soundly as if the ointment were working on them and not on him.

Carrizales's heart stopped beating when he saw this bitter sight; his voice stuck in his throat, his arms hung helplessly at his side and he was like a cold marble statue; and although anger did what might have been expected, and stirred up his almost dying spirits, his grief was so strong that he could not breathe. Yet all the same he would have taken the vengeance which such a crime demanded if he had had the weapons wherewith to take it; so he resolved to return to his room to fetch a dagger, and to go back and remove the stains on his honour with the blood of his two enemies, and even with the blood of all his household. Having taken this honourable and necessary decision, he returned, as silently and cautiously as he had come, to his room, where grief and anguish so affected his heart that, unable to do anything else, he fell fainting on to his bed.

At last day came, and caught the adulterous couple entwined in each other's arms. Marialonso awoke, and was on the point of rushing off to claim what she thought was her due; but seeing that it was late, she decided to leave it for the following night. Leonora was alarmed when she saw that it was so late in the day, and cursed her carelessness and that of the wretched duenna. The two, full of alarm, went to the place where her husband was, praying silently to heaven that they would find him still snoring; and when they saw him lying quietly on his bed, they thought the ointment was still at work, for he was sleeping, and with great joy they embraced each other. Leonora went up to her husband, and grasping him by his arm she turned him from side to side, to see if he would wake up without their needing to wash him with vinegar, as they had been told was necessary for his recovery. But with the movement Carrizales recovered from his faint, and sighing deeply, in a feeble and sorrowful voice said,

'Woe is me, for to what a sad end my fortune has brought me!'

Leonora did not quite understand what her husband was saying, but seeing him awake and hearing him speak, she was surprised to see that the effect of the ointment had not lasted as long as they had told her, and went up to him. Putting her face close to his, and holding him in a close embrace, she said to him, 'What is the matter, my lord, for you seem to be in distress?'

The wretched old man heard the voice of his sweet enemy, and opening his eyes, in surprise and astonishment, he fixed them on her for a long time, at the end of which he said to her,

'Do me the favour, my lady, of sending straight away for your parents, because I feel a strange weariness in my heart and I am afraid I am soon going to die. I should like to see them before I go.'

Leonora was quite convinced that what her husband said was true, believing that the effect of the ointment, and not what he had seen, had reduced him to that state. She replied that she would do what he ordered, and sent the Negro to fetch her parents straight away. Then, embracing her husband, she caressed him more fondly than ever before, asking him how he felt, as tenderly and affectionately as if he were the person she loved best in the world. He looked at her in astonishment, as we have said, each word or caress being a sword-thrust that pierced his soul.

The duenna had told the household and Loaysa of her master's illness, impressing upon them that it must be serious, since he had forgotten to have the street doors closed when the Negro went out to fetch her mistress's parents. These folk were amazed at the summons too, because neither of them had set foot inside that house since their daughter had married. In short, they were all silent and baffled, not realizing the true cause of their master's illness. He would sigh every now and then so deeply and pitifully that his soul seemed to be torn from his body every time. Leonora wept when she saw him in that condition, and he laughed like one distracted at the thought of her false tears. At this point Leonora's parents arrived, and as they found the street door and the door into the patio open and the house silent and deserted, they were more than a little alarmed. They went to their son-in-law's room, and found him, as we've said, with his eyes still fixed on his wife, whom he held by the hand as they both wept, she at the mere sight of her husband's tears, he because he saw the deceit in hers.

As soon as her parents came in Carrizales began to speak, and this is what he said:

'Sit down, please, and all the rest of you leave the room, except for the lady Marialonso.'

They all did this, and when the five of them were alone, without waiting for anyone else to speak, Carrizales spoke calmly, wiping the tears from his eyes.

'I am quite sure, my parents and masters, that it will not be necessary to bring witnesses to make you believe the truth of what I want to tell you. You must well remember – for it is impossible that it should have slipped your memory – the love, the heart-felt emotion with which one year, one month, five days and nine hours ago you gave me your beloved daughter to be my lawful wife. You also know what a generous dowry I gave her, so lavish that it would have been enough to make more than three girls of her rank be considered rich. You must also recall the care I took to dress and adorn her with all that she desired and that I thought she ought to have. Furthermore you have seen, my lord and lady, how, as a result of my temperament, fearing that affliction from which I am doubtless going to die, and taught by the experience of my great age the many strange things that happen in this world, I tried to guard this jewel whom I chose and whom you gave me, with the greatest caution of which I was capable. I built up the walls of this house, I took the lights from the windows which looked on to the street, I doubled the locks on the doors, I put up a revolving door like a monastery, I banned from it for good and all everything which bore the sign or the name of a man, I gave her servants and slave girls to wait on her, I did not deny them or her anything they cared to ask of me, I made her my equal, I told her my most secret thoughts, I handed over my property to her. All these things were done, with due consideration, to ensure that I should enjoy without disturbance what had cost me such effort, and so that she should not give me any occasion for jealousy or fear of any kind; but as one cannot prevent by any human effort the punishment which the divine will chooses to inflict on those who do not centre all their desires and hopes in that will, it is no wonder that I should be disappointed in mine, and that I should myself have been the one to manufacture the poison which is killing me. But because I see that you are all puzzled as you hang on my words, I will bring to an end the long preamble to this speech of mine by telling you in one word what one could not properly say in a thousand. I declare then, ladies and gentlemen, that, after all I've said and done, this morning I found this girl, born into the world to destroy my peace and bring my life to an end – and here he pointed to his wife – in the arms of a handsome young man, who is now shut up in the room of this obnoxious duenna.'

Carrizales had scarcely finished speaking when Leonora was struck with anguish and fell fainting at her husband's knees. Marialonso turned pale, and Leonora's parents were speechless. But going on Carrizales said,

'The vengeance which I wish to take for this injury neither is nor should be of the usual kind, for it is my wish that, just as I went to extremes in what I did, the vengeance I shall take should be of the same kind, inflicted upon myself by my own hand as the one who is most worthy of blame in this crime, for I should have considered that this girl's fifteen years would harmonize ill with the nearly eighty years of my life. I was like the silkworm, making the house in which I was to die. I do not blame you, ill-advised girl – and saying this he bent and kissed the face of the fainting Leonora – I do not blame you, I say, because the persuasive tongues of crafty old women and the advances of enamoured youths easily conquer and triumph over the limited intelligence of those who are young. But so that all the world may see the extent of the good will and trust which I showed towards you, in these last moments of my life, I want to demonstrate it in a way that will be remembered in the world as an example if not of goodness, at least of unprecedented sincerity. So it is my wish that a notary be brought here immediately, so that I may make a new will, in which I shall have Leonora's dowry doubled, and shall beg her that after I am gone, which will be very soon, she make up her mind, which she will be able to do without effort, to marry that youth, whom the grey hairs of this dishonoured old man have never offended. In this way she will see that if in life I never for one moment departed from what I thought was her pleasure, in death I desire her to be happy with him whom she must love so much. The rest of my fortune I shall give to pious works; and to you, my lord and lady, I shall leave sufficient for you to live honourably for the rest of your lives. Let the notary come quickly, because my suffering is such that it will soon put an end to my life.'

When he had said this, he fell into a terrible faint, and dropped down so close to Leonora that their faces were together, a strange and sad sight for their parents, who saw their beloved daughter and their much loved son-in-law in this state. The evil duenna did not want to wait for the reproaches which she thought would be hurled at her by her lady's parents, so she rushed out of the room, and went to tell Loaysa of all that was going on, advising him to leave the house straight away, for she would take care to tell him through the Negro what happened, there being now neither doors nor keys to prevent it. Loaysa was amazed at what he heard, and taking her advice, he dressed up once more as a poor man and went to tell his friends of the strange, unprecedented turn his affairs had taken.

So while the couple were still unconscious, Leonora's father sent for a notary who was a friend of his, and who arrived by the time his daughter and son-in-law had recovered consciousness. Carrizales made a will in the terms he had mentioned, without declaring Leonora's guilt; and begging her moreover to marry, in the event of his death, the young man of whom he had privately spoken to her. When Leonora heard this, she threw herself at her husband's feet and, her heart beating furiously, said to him,

'May you live for many years, my dearest lord; for although you need not believe anything I may say, you should know that I have only offended you in thought.'

And beginning to make excuses and to tell the whole truth of the matter, she found she could not speak, and fainted again. The poor injured old man took her in his arms; her parents embraced her; and they all wept so bitterly that even the notary who was making the will was forced to weep too. In his will Carrizales left enough to keep all the servants in the house and let the slave girls and the Negro go free; and as for the false Marialonso, he simply ordered her to be paid her wages. A week later, overcome by grief, he was taken off to his grave.

Leonora was left to mourn him, a wealthy widow; and when Loaysa hoped to see fulfilled what he knew her husband had ordered in his will, he found instead that within a week she went off to be a nun in one of the most enclosed convents in the city. The young man went off in despair, and indeed in shame, to the Indies. Leonora's parents were desperately sad, although they found consolation in what their son-in-law had left them in his will. The servants were comforted too by what they inherited, and the slaves by their freedom; but the accursed duenna was left in poverty and disappointed of all her evil hopes.

And all I wanted was to get to the end of this affair, a memorable example which illustrates how little one should trust in keys, revolving doors and walls when the will remains free, and how much less one should trust youth and inexperience when confronted by the exhortation of these duennas in their black habits and their long, white head-dresses. The only thing that puzzles me is why Leonora did not make more effort to excuse herself and make her jealous husband realize how pure and innocent she was in that affair, but she was so confused that she was tongue-tied, and her husband died so soon that she could not find opportunity to explain herself.

The Deceitful Marriage

Out of the hospital of the Resurrection, which is in Valladolid beyond the Puerta del Campo, came a soldier, using his sword as a staff, and with legs so weak and his face so yellow that you could see quite clearly that, although the weather was not very hot, he must have sweated out in three weeks all the fluid he had probably got in an hour. He was tottering slowly along as if he were just getting over an illness, and as he went in through the gate of the city he spotted a friend of his coming towards him, whom he had not seen for over six months. The friend, crossing himself as if he were seeing a ghost, said when he got up to him,

'What is this, Ensign Campuzano? Are you really in this part of the world? Upon my word I thought you were trailing a pike in Flanders, not dragging your sword along here. What is the meaning of this awful colour and this weakness of yours?'

Campuzano replied, 'As for my being in this part of the world or not, Licenciate Peralta, the fact that you see me in it is sufficient answer; in reply to the other questions all I have to say is that I've just come out of that hospital, after sweating out fourteen buboes I got from a woman whom for my sins I took to myself.'

'So you got married,' observed Peralta.

'Yes sir,' answered Campuzano.

'It must have been for love,' said Peralta, 'and marriages of that kind have the path to repentance already built in.'

'I can't say whether it was for love,' answered the ensign; 'although I can assure you it was painful, because as a result of my marriage, or mismarriage, I was so afflicted with pain in both body and mind, that as far as my body is concerned, I've had to sweat it out forty times, and as for my mind, I can't find any cure for the pains. But I'm not in a fit condition for long conversation in the street, so I must ask you to excuse me. Some other day I'll tell you at leisure what has happened to me; for it is the most strange and unheard-of tale that you've ever come across in your whole life.'

'That won't do,' said the Licenciate; 'for I want you to come with me to my lodgings, and we'll do penance together there. Stew is just right for invalids, and although there are only enough helpings for two, my servant can make do with a pie; and if you're feeling sufficiently recovered, a few rashers of ham will serve as hors d'oeuvre and the good will with which I offer it to you is worth more than anything, not only on this occasion but whenever you may desire.'

Campuzano thanked him, and accepted the invitation and the offer. They went to San Lorenzo and heard Mass. Then Peralta took him off to his house, gave him what he had promised and offered him his services again, begging him as soon as he had finished to tell him the adventures he had said so much about. Campuzano was only too ready to oblige, and began as follows:

'You will remember, Licenciate Peralta, how I shared lodgings with Captain Pedro de Herrera, who is now in Flanders.'

'I remember well,' answered Peralta.

'Well one day,' Campuzano went on, 'as we had just finished a meal in that inn at La Solana, where we were staying, two good-looking women came in, with two maid-servants. One of them stood by the window and began to talk to the captain, and the other sat down on a chair beside me, keeping her veil lowered to her chin, and showing only what you could see through the thin material. Although I begged her out of courtesy to unveil herself, there was nothing doing, and this increased my desire to see her. It was still further increased by the fact that, whether by accident or design, she let me catch a glimpse of a snowy-white hand adorned with very fine jewels. At that time I was looking very smart, with that <u>big chain</u> which you must have seen me wearing, my hat with plumes and bands, my coloured army·uniform so dashing, to my crazy way of thinking, that it seemed to me that I could conquer a woman just by looking at her. Anyway, I begged her to unveil herself, to which she replied, "Don't pester me; I have a house; get a page to follow me, for although I'm a more respectable person than this answer implies, if I find you are as discreet as you are handsome, I shall be glad for you to come and see me."

'I kissed her hands out of gratitude for the great favour she was doing me, in return for which I promised her a heap of money. The captain finished his conversation, the ladies went off, and one of my servants followed them. The captain told me that what the lady wanted him to do was to take some letters to Flanders for her for another captain, who she said was her cousin, although he knew he was only her lover. I was inflamed with passion at the sight of those snowy hands, and dying to see her face; and so the next day my servant showed me the way, and I was allowed in quite freely. I found a very well-furnished house and a woman of about thirty, whom I recognized by her hands. She was not outstandingly beautiful, but she was sufficiently so for me to fall in love with her when I heard her speak, because her voice was so soft that when she spoke she touched my very soul. I had long amorous conversations with her; I boasted, wheedled, lied, offered, promised and went through all the motions I thought necessary to win her favours, but as she was used to hearing this sort of offer and argument, and even better ones, she appeared to be listening to me but without believing a word I said. The fact is that during the few days I spent visiting her our conversation was confined to trivialities, and I didn't manage to pick any of the fruit I desired.

'During the time I was visiting her I always found the house quite empty, with not a sign either of false relatives or real friends. She had as a servant a girl who was more crafty than stupid. In the end, treating my love-affair like a soldier who will soon be on the move, I put the pressure on my lady Doña Estefanía de Caicedo – for that's the name of the one who has reduced me to what I am – and she gave me this reply:

'"Ensign Campuzano, it would be sheer stupidity for me to pretend to you that I am a saint: I have been a sinner, and I still am; but not so much so that the neighbours gossip about me or that I attract the notice of the outside world. I inherited no property from my parents or from any other of my relatives, and yet my household effects are worth a good two and a half thousand crowns; and if they were auctioned would sell straight away. With this property I am looking for a husband whom I can cling to and obey; and apart from turning over a new leaf, I can promise him that I'll fall over myself to look after him and serve him. No prince has ever had a cook to make your mouth water more, or one more skilled in putting the finishing touches to the dishes I can give him when I'm in the mood for housekeeping and give my mind to it. I can act as butler, kitchenmaid and lady of the house. In fact, I know how to give orders and make people obey them. I waste nothing, and I manage to make a good deal of profit: I know how to make every *real* go a long way. My linen, of which I have a great deal and of the finest quality, is not from shops or drapers; it was spun by my own fingers and those of my maid-servants; and if it had been possible to weave it at home, it would have been woven there too. I am singing my own praises because it is only right that you should know these things. In short, what I mean to say is that I am looking for a husband to take care of me, give me orders and honour me, and not a lover to wait upon me and then hurl reproaches at me. If you are pleased to accept the prize you are being offered, here I am all ready to submit to any arrangement you choose, without offering myself for sale, which is the same as putting myself at the mercy of match-makers; for there's no one so well qualified to arrange things as the parties concerned."

'At that time I had my brains in my heels rather than in my head, and as the pleasure seemed just then greater even than I had imagined it, and all that property in front of me as good as cash already, without stopping to look for any arguments beyond my own wishes, which had quite overcome my reason, I told her that I was the most fortunate of persons to have been presented with this heaven-sent miracle, a companion like this to be the mistress of my will and my possessions. These were not so small for, taking into account the chain I had round my neck and some other small jewels at home, with what I could get from the sale of some of my soldier's finery, they were worth over two thousand ducats. This, together with her twenty-five hundred, was enough to enable us to live in retirement in the village where I was born, and where I still had some property. This, added to the cash, and by selling our produce at the right season, could allow us to live happily and at ease. In short, our betrothal was settled there and then, we contrived to have ourselves registered as bachelor and spinster, and the banns were called on the three holy days which happened to come together at Easter time. On the fourth day we were married, two friends of mine being witnesses, with a youth she said was her cousin, to whom I swore kinship in the most civil way; just as I had

behaved up to that moment with my new wife, though my intentions were so crooked and treacherous that I would rather not
speak of them; for although I'm telling the truth, it's not the whole
truth as I'd have to tell it at confession.

'My servant moved the trunk from my lodgings to my wife's
house. In front of her I locked up my splendid chain in it; I showed
her three or four more which, although not quite so big, were
superior in workmanship, as well as three or four hatbands of
various kinds; I let her see my finery and my plumes, and handed
over to her four hundred odd *reales* that I had, for household
expenses. The honeymoon lasted for six days, during which I took
my ease like a humble son-in-law in the house of his rich father-in-
law; I walked on rich carpets, slept on linen sheets, and basked in
the light from silver candlesticks. I breakfasted in bed, got up at
eleven, dined at twelve and at two took my siesta in the drawing-
room, while Doña Estefanía and her maid danced attendance on me.
My servant, who up to that time had always given me the impression of being lazy and slow, had become as swift as a deer. When
Doña Estefanía was not at my side, she was to be found in the
kitchen, preparing dishes to tempt my palate and stir up my appe-
tite. My shirts, collars and handkerchiefs smelt just like the
gardens of Aranjuez, with all the sweet-scented angel- and orange-
water she sprinkled on them.

'The days flew by, like all the years which are subject to the law
of time; and as they passed, seeing myself spoiled and waited on so
well, the evil intentions with which I had embarked on that affair
were changing. But it all came to an end one morning when, as I
was with Doña Estefanía in bed, there was a loud knocking at the
front door. The maid put her head out of the window, and withdrew it immediately.

' "Here's a fine sight!" she shrieked. "She's come sooner than
she said when she wrote the other day."

' "Who's come, girl?" I asked her.

' "Who?" she answered. "My lady Doña Clementa Bueso, and
she's got with her Don Lope Meléndez de Almendárez, with
two servants and Hortigosa, the duenna she took away with
her."

' "Hurry up, girl, for heaven's sake, open the door for them!", said Doña Estefanía. "And you sir, if you love me, don't be upset or answer anything you may hear against me."

' "And who will say anything to offend you, especially in my presence? Tell me: who are these people, whose arrival seems to have upset you so much?"

' "I've no time to explain to you now," said Doña Estefanía; "but you must know that everything that may happen here is a trick and is all part of a certain plan and purpose which you'll know about later."

'And although I should have liked to reply to this, I was not given a chance, because the lady Doña Clementa Bueso came into the room then, dressed in green satin lustre with lots of gold lace edging, a cape of the same material and the same trimmings, a hat with green, white and red feathers and a rich gold band, and with a fine veil covering half her face. She came in accompanied by Don Lope Meléndez de Almendárez, splendidly dressed in rich travelling clothes. The duenna Hortigosa was the first to speak.

' "Heavens! What is this? My mistress Doña Clementa's bed occupied, and occupied by a man? I can hardly believe my eyes. I must say Doña Estefanía has gone too far, taking advantage of my lady's good nature!" '

' "I should say she has, Hortigosa," replied Doña Clementa; "but it's all my fault! Will I never learn not to make the sort of friends who are only friends as long as it suits them?" '

'To all this Doña Estefanía replied, "Don't be upset, lady Clementa, and be sure that what you are seeing here in your home is not what you think. When the mystery is explained, I know I shall be blameless and you will have nothing to complain of."

'By this time I had put on my breeches and doublet, and Doña Estefanía led me off by the hand to another room, and told me that this friend of hers wanted to play a trick on this Don Lope who was with her, and whom she wanted to marry; and that the trick was to give him to understand that the house and all its contents were hers, so that she could get him to give her a written promise of marriage, and once the marriage was over she didn't mind if the deceit was discovered, so confident was she of this Don Lope's great love for her. "And then I'll get back my property, and no one will hold it against her or any other woman if she tries to get an honourable husband, even at the expense of a trick."

'I answered that the gesture of friendship she was proposing was extremely generous, and that she should think seriously about it, because she might later have occasion to resort to the Law to get her property back. But she replied with so many arguments, setting forth so many obligations that she was under to be of even greater service to Doña Clementa that, much against my will and better judgement, I had to fall in with Doña Estefanía's wish. She assured me that the game would last only a week, during which we would go to stay with another friend of hers. She and I finished dressing and then she went in to say good-bye to Doña Clementa Bueso and to Don Lope Meléndez de Almendárez. She told my servant to pack the trunk and follow her, and I followed on too, without saying good-bye to anyone.

'Doña Estefanía stopped at the house of a friend of hers, and before we went in she spent some time talking to her, after which a girl came out and told me and my servant to go in. She took us to a little room, in which there were two beds so close together that they looked like one, because there was no space between them, and the sheets on them were touching each other. There we stopped for six days, and not an hour passed without our quarrelling, I telling her how stupid she had been to leave her house and property in someone else's hands, even if it had been her own mother's. I kept on at her so much that the lady of the house, one day when Doña Estefanía said she was going off to see how her affairs stood, wanted to know why I quarrelled so much with her, and what she had done to make me scold her, accusing her of crass stupidity rather than friendship. I told her the whole story, and when I got to the point of saying that I had married Doña Estefanía, and mentioned the dowry she had, and how silly she had been to leave her house and property to Doña Clementa, even with such a worthy purpose as that of winning an excellent husband like Don Lope, she began to cross herself rapidly, and repeated to herself so many times the words "Lord, what a wicked woman", that I was completely confused. At last she said to me,

' "Ensign, I don't know whether I am going against my conscience in telling you what I think would be just as much on my conscience if I kept silent about it, but at all events I must tell the truth. And the truth is that Doña Clementa Bueso is the real lady of the house and owns the property which was given to you as a dowry; everything that Doña Estefanía has told you is lies. She has neither house nor property, nor anything but the clothes she stands up in. And what gave her the occasion to practise this fraud was that Doña Clementa went off to do penance at Nuestra Señora de Guadalupe, leaving her house in the hands of Doña Estefanía to look after, for they are in fact great friends. And indeed, you can't blame the poor lady, since she's managed to pick up someone like you as a husband, Ensign."

'Here she stopped speaking, and I was beginning to despair, and doubtless would have done so if my guardian angel hadn't come to the rescue at that moment by reminding me that I was a Christian and that the worst sin a human being could fall into was that of despair, for it was a devilish sin. This consideration or inspiration gave me some comfort, but not enough to prevent me putting on my cloak and sword and going off in search of Doña Estefanía, intending to inflict exemplary punishment on her. However luck, for better or worse, determined that I couldn't find Doña Estefanía, hard though I looked. I went to San Llorente, commended myself to Our Lady, sat down on a bench, and was so upset that I fell into a deep sleep, from which I shouldn't have stirred very quickly if I hadn't been awakened. Full of bitter thoughts I went to Doña Clementa's house, and found her completely at ease as the mistress of her house. I did not dare to say anything to her because Don Lope was there. I went back to my landlady's house, and she told me that she had told Doña Estefanía that I knew all about her plan and about the fraud, and that she had asked her how I had reacted to the news. She told her that I had taken it very badly, and that she thought I had gone to look for her, bent on doing her harm. Then she told me that Doña Estefanía had gone off with everything that was in the trunk, leaving me nothing but a single travelling suit.

'Here was a pretty kettle of fish! But I could feel the hand of God upon me again. I went to look at my trunk and found it open, ˝ke a tomb awaiting a corpse, and the corpse might well have been if my mind had been up to appreciating the full weight of my ˙une.'

'It certainly was a grave misfortune,' said Licenciate Peralta, 'that Doña Estefanía went off with all those chains and hatbands, for, as they say, you can bear any trouble with a full stomach.'

'I didn't mind the loss,' answered the ensign; 'for as they say: "Don Simueque thought he was deceiving me with his squinting daughter, but by jove, I'm lop-sided myself, so he met his match."'

'I don't know quite what the point of this is,' said Peralta.

'The point is', answered the ensign, 'that all that splendid pile of chains, hatbands and trinkets was worth no more than ten or twelve crowns.'

'That is impossible,' replied the licenciate. 'The one that you were wearing round your neck looked as if it was worth more than two hundred ducats.'

'Indeed it would have been,' answered the ensign, 'if truth matched appearance; but as all that glisters is not gold, the chains, hatbands, jewels and trinkets were in fact only artificial; but they were so well made that only a touchstone or fire could reveal it.'

'In that case,' said the licenciate, 'as far as you and Doña Estefanía are concerned, you're quits.'

'And so much so', answered the ensign, 'that we can shuffle the cards and start again; but the trouble is, Licenciate, that she can get rid of my chains, but I can't get over the dirty trick she played on me. The fact is that whether I like it or not I've got the consequences for keeps.'

'Give thanks to God, Mr Campuzano,' said Peralta, 'that she had feet and has gone off, and you're not obliged to look for her.'

'That's true,' replied the ensign. 'All the same, even without looking for her, she's always in my mind, and wherever I am my disgrace goes with me.'

'I don't know how to answer you,' said Peralta, 'except to remind you of a couple of verses of Petrarch, which go:

> *Che chi prende diletto di far frode,*
> *Non si de' lamentar s'altri l'inganna.*[1]

which being translated means: "He who takes delight in deceiving others must not complain when he is deceived himself."'

'I'm not complaining,' answered the ensign, 'but I am sorry for

1. *Trionfo d'amore*, Chapter 1.

myself, for the guilty man does not fail to feel the pain of punishment because he recognizes his guilt. I can well see that I wanted to deceive and that I was deceived, because I was caught in my own trap; but I can't help feeling sorry for myself. And to crown it all, and this is the main point of my story – for this is what one can call this affair of mine – I found out that Doña Estefanía had been carried off by the cousin who I told you was at our wedding, and who had been her steady lover for a long time. I had no wish to look for her, for I'd have been looking for more trouble. I left my lodgings and I lost my hair within a few days, because my eyebrows and eyelashes began to moult, and gradually my hair went too, so I went bald before my time, suffering from a complaint they call "alopecia", or in plain terms "loss of hair". I was really "fleeced", because I had neither hair to comb nor money to spend. My sickness kept pace with my need, and as poverty tramples honour under foot and brings some to the gallows and others to the hospital, just as it makes others go begging and pleading at their enemies' doors, one of the greatest misfortunes which can come to an unhappy man; so in order not to have to pawn, for the sake of paying for a cure, the clothes which would have to cover me and protect my honour when I was well again, I waited until the time when they put on the sweat treatment in the hospital of the Resurrection, and then went in. I've been sweated forty times, and they say I'll stay well if I look after myself. I have a sword, and as for the rest, may God help me.'

The licenciate, amazed at the things which he had told him, offered his sympathy again.

'What you say surprises you, Señor Peralta, is nothing,' said the ensign. 'There are things I could tell you which surpass all imagination, for they go beyond the bounds of nature. But I'd like you to know that they are of such a kind that I think all my misfortunes well worth while if only because they brought me to the hospital, where I saw what I shall now relate, which neither you nor any one else in the world will ever credit.'

All these preambles and commendations with which the ensign ~ed his account of what he had seen aroused the curiosity of ~o much so that he pressed him to tell him straight away of ~s things he had to relate.

'You will have seen', said the ensign, 'two dogs which go round with lanterns on them at night, accompanying the begging brothers, and lighting their way when they ask for alms.'

'Yes, I have,' replied Peralta.

'You will also have seen or heard', said the ensign, 'the stories that are told about them: that if by chance people throw alms out of the windows and it falls on the ground, they rush up straight away with a light to look for what falls, and stop in front of the windows where they know people usually give them alms; and although they go along so meekly that they are more like lambs than dogs, in the hospital they're like lions, guarding the house with great care and vigilance.'

'I've heard all this,' said Peralta, 'but there's no reason why that should surprise me.'

'Well, what I'm going to tell you now will; and you must be prepared to believe it without crossing yourself or raising objections and difficulties. The fact is that I heard and as good as saw with my own eyes these two dogs, one of whom is called "Scipio" and the other "Berganza", who were lying one night (the one before I had the sweat treatment for the last time) on some old matting behind my bed; and in the middle of the night, when it was dark and I was lying awake, thinking of my past adventures and present misfortunes, I heard talking close by. I was listening attentively, to see if I could find out who was talking and what they were talking about, and soon after I realized by what they said that it was the two dogs "Scipio" and "Berganza" who were talking.'

Campuzano had scarcely said this, when the licenciate got up and said, 'This is where I must part company with you, Mr Campuzano; for up to now I've been hesitating whether or not to believe all that you had told me about your marriage; and what you are now telling me about hearing the dogs speak makes me declare that I don't believe any of it. For heaven's sake, Ensign, don't tell this rubbish to anyone except a close friend like me.'

'Don't think I'm so ignorant', replied Campuzano, 'that I don't realize that it's only by a miracle that animals can speak. I'm well aware that if thrushes, magpies and parrots talk, it's only the words that they learn and get by heart, and because these creatures have tongues which are made in such a way that they can pronounce them. This doesn't mean that they can speak and answer back with reasoned speech as these dogs were doing; and so, many times since I have heard them, I have been unwilling to believe myself, and have preferred to take as something I dreamed what in fact wide awake and with all my five senses as God was pleased to give them to me, I heard, listened to, noted and finally wrote down all in due order, without omitting a word. From this you may have sufficient proof to convince and persuade you to believe the truth of what I say. The things they discussed were many and varied, and more suitable for discussion by wise men than to be in the mouths of dogs; so that, since I could not have invented them off my own bat, in spite of myself and against my better judgement I have come to believe that I was not dreaming and that the dogs were talking.'

'Good heavens,' said the licenciate, 'we're back to the time of Methuselah, when pumpkins talked; or Aesop's days when the cock conversed with the fox and animals talked to each other.'

'I should be one of them, and the biggest beast of the lot,' replied the ensign, 'if I believed that those times had returned, and I should be an animal too if I didn't believe what I heard, and what I saw, and what I shall dare to swear with an oath which will bind and compel the most incredulous person to believe it. But although I may be wrong, and what I think is true is a dream and to persist in it were nonsense, won't it interest you, Mr Peralta, to see written down in the form of a colloquy the things that these dogs, or whatever they were, had to say?'

'Provided you don't weary yourself further in persuading me that you heard the dogs speaking,' replied the licenciate, 'I shall be very happy to listen to this colloquy, which as it was written down from the notes of your ingenious self, Ensign, I already adjudge to be good.'

'Well, there's another point,' said the ensign. 'Since I was listening so attentively, my mind was in a delicate state, and my memory was also delicate, sharp and free of other concerns, thanks to the great quantity of raisins and almonds I had eaten, I learnt it off by heart and wrote it down the next day in almost the same words in which I had heard it, without looking for rhetorical colours to adorn it, nor adding or substracting anything to make it pleasing. The conversation did not take place all on one night, but on two consecutive nights, although I've recorded only one, when Berganza told his life story. I intend to write down his companion Scipio's, which was related on the second night, if I find that this one is credit-worthy or at least not deserving of scorn. I've got the colloquy tucked away in my shirt-front; I put it in the form of a colloquy to avoid the "Scipio said", "Berganza replied", which stretches out the narrative.'

And saying this he took out a notebook and put it into the hands of the licenciate, who took it, laughing and apparently making a joke of all that he had heard and of what he was expecting to read.

'I shall recline in this chair,' said the ensign, 'while you so kindly read these dreams or absurdities, whose only virtue is that you can leave them alone when they annoy you.'

'Take your ease,' said Peralta, 'for I shall soon get through my reading.'

The ensign lay back, the licenciate opened the notebook, and saw that it began with this title:

'Tale and Colloquy that took place between "Scipio" and "Berganza", dogs belonging to the hospital of the Resurrection, which is in the city of Valladolid, outside the Puerta del Campo, and commonly known as the dogs of Mahudes.'

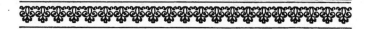

The Dogs' Colloquy

Scipio Berganza, my friend, let us leave the hospital for tonight to take care of itself and let's go off quietly over there to those mats, where we may enjoy unobserved this unprecedented blessing which heaven has granted to both of us at one and the same time.

Berganza Brother Scipio, I hear you speak and I know that I am speaking to you, and I cannot believe it, for it seems to me that our speaking goes beyond the bounds of nature.

Scipio That is true, Berganza, and this miracle is greater in that not only are we speaking but we are speaking coherently, as if we were capable of reason, when in fact we are so devoid of it that the difference between the brute beast and man is that man is a rational animal, and the brute irrational.

Berganza All you say, Scipio, I understand, and the fact that you are saying it and that I understand it makes me even more amazed. It is indeed true that in the course of my life I have often heard of the great prerogatives which we possess; so much so, that it seems that some have believed that we have a natural instinct, so lively and acute in many things, that it almost seems to demonstrate that we possess some sort of understanding which is capable of reasoning.

Scipio What I have heard praised and extolled is our good memory, our gratitude and our great loyalty; to such an extent that they often depict us as the symbol of friendship. You will have noticed perhaps how on alabaster tombs, where they put figures of husbands and wives who are buried there, between the two, at their feet, they place the figure of a dog, as a sign that in their lives their friendship and fidelity to each other were inviolable.

Berganza I am well aware that there have been dogs so filled with gratitude that they have thrown themselves into the same grave with their masters' dead bodies. Others have stood on the graves where their masters were buried, never leaving them nor taking food for the rest of their lives. I also know that after the elephant, the dog has the highest reputation for seeming to possess under-standing; then the horse, and finally the ape.

Scipio That is true; but you will have to admit that you have never seen or heard of any elephant, dog, horse or monkey speaking. That leads me to believe that this unexpected gift of speech which we possess comes under the heading of those things which they call portents. When they appear, experience shows that some great catastrophe threatens.

Berganza This makes me think that what I heard the other day from a student who was passing through Alcalá de Henares was a portent.

Scipio What did you hear him say?

Berganza That of the five thousand students at the university that year, two thousand were reading medicine.

Scipio Well, what do you infer from that?

Berganza I infer either that these two thousand doctors must have patients to treat – which would be a calamity and a great mis-fortune – or that they must die of hunger.

Scipio Well, anyway, we are speaking, whether it's a portent or not; for what heaven has ordained should happen, no human endeavour or wisdom can prevent; and so there is no point in our starting to dispute about how or why we are speaking. Let us make the most of this happy day, or happy night, and since we are so comfortable on these mats and we don't know how long this good fortune of ours will last, let us take advantage of it, and talk all night, without allowing sleep to rob us of this pleasure, which I have so long desired.

Berganza And I too, for ever since I was strong enough to gnaw a bone I have had the desire to speak, to say many things which were stored up for so long in my memory that they were going mouldy or getting forgotten. However, now that I see myself so unex-pectedly endowed with this divine gift of speech, I intend to enjoy it and take advantage of it as much as I can, making haste to say everything I can remember, even if it is all jumbled up and confused, because I don't know when this blessing, which I consider to be on loan, will be revoked.

Scipio Let us agree, friend Berganza, that tonight you will relate the story of your life and the adventures through which you have come until you have reached the point where you are now; and if tomorrow night we should have this gift of speech, I shall relate the story of my life; for it will be better to spend the time in relating our own life stories than in trying to find out about other people's lives.

Berganza Scipio, I have always considered you to be a sensible friend, and even more so now, since you are willing to tell me your adventures as a friend and to hear mine. Your good sense is shown in the way you have apportioned the time in which we may be allowed to tell them. But see first if anyone is listening to us.

Scipio No one, I think; although there is a soldier just here who is undergoing sweat treatment; but at the moment he will be more interested in sleeping than in listening to anyone.

Berganza Well, if I can speak with this assurance, listen to me; and if what I tell you wearies you, check me or tell me to be quiet.

Scipio Speak till morning, or until someone hears us; for I'll listen to you very willingly, without stopping you unless I see that it is necessary.

Berganza As far as I know I first saw the light of day in Seville, in the slaughter-house, which is outside the Puerta de la Carne. This makes me think – were it not for what I shall say later on – that my parents must have been mastiffs, reared by the practitioners of that wretched trade, the people they call slaughterers. The first master I knew was one called Nicholas the Flat-nosed, a robust fellow, sturdy and bad-tempered, like all those who follow this trade. This Nicholas taught me and some other pups to go with the old mastiffs and attack the bulls and nip their ears. It didn't cost me much effort to become an expert at that.

Scipio I'm not surprised, Berganza, for since wrong-doing comes naturally, one easily learns it.

Berganza The things I could tell you, brother Scipio, about what I saw in that slaughter-house, and about the extraordinary things which go on there! First of all, you must bear in mind that all those who work there, from the youngest to the oldest, are people with easy consciences, without mercy or fear for the king or his law. Most of them are living with concubines, and they're like birds of prey, maintaining themselves, along with their mistresses, on what they steal. Every meat day there are vast numbers of girls and youths in the slaughter-house before daybreak, all with bags which are empty when they start, but which are full of pieces of meat when they go home; while the servant-girls go away with offal and with practically whole shoulders of lamb. Not a beast is killed without these people carrying off their tithes and first-fruits from the best and tastiest parts. And as there is no meat purveyor in Seville, everyone can bring what he likes, and the first to be killed is either the best or the lowest-priced, and by this arrangement there is always plenty. The owners trust their affairs to these fine folk I've mentioned, not so that they won't steal from them – for that's asking the impossible – but so that they go easy on the cuts and on the tricks they carry out on the carcasses, which they clean and prune as if they were willows or vines. But nothing shocked me more than to see that these slaughterers will kill a man as easily as they kill a cow. For a trifle, and without a thought, they put a knife in a man's stomach as readily as if they were killing a bull. It's a rare thing for a day to pass without quarrels and wounds, and sometimes deaths; they all take pride in being tough, and even boast of being ruffians. There isn't one of them without his guardian angel in San Francisco Square, whose favours are bought with shoulders of lamb and ox tongues. In short, I've heard it said by a wise man that the king still had three things to win in Seville: the Calle de la Caza, the Costanilla and the slaughter-house.[1]

Scipio If you're going to be so long in telling me about the habits of the masters you've had and the bad things about their professions as you have been this time, friend Berganza, we shall have to ask heaven to grant us speech for at least a year; and even then I'm afraid that at the speed you're going, you won't get half-way through your story. And I want to point out to you something which you'll be able to test when I tell you of the adventures of my life; and that is that some stories contain their appeal in themselves, others in the way they are told. In other words there are some which, even without preambles and elegant language, give pleasure; and there are others which need to be decked out with words; and with gestures of the face and hands and changes in the tone of voice, something comes out of nothing, and instead of being

1. Presumably a reference to the extreme lawlessness of these parts of the city.

weak and feeble they become witty and pleasing. So don't forget to profit from this warning in the rest of your story.

Berganza I will, if I can and if the great urge which I have to speak will allow me; although I think it will be extremely difficult for me to restrain myself.

Scipio Look to your tongue, for the greatest evils in human life come from it.

Berganza I tell you, then, that my master taught me to carry a basket in my mouth and to defend it from anyone who tried to take it from me. He also showed me his mistress's house, and so avoided her maid's having to come to the slaughter-house, for I would take to her in the morning what he had stolen during the night. And one day when, just at daybreak, I was duly going off to take her her rations, I heard my name being called from a window. I raised my eyes, and saw a very beautiful girl. I stopped for a moment, and she came down to the front door, and called me again. I went up to her, to see what she wanted, and what she did was to take what I was carrying in the basket and put in its place an old shoe. Then I said to myself, 'Flesh to flesh'. When she had taken the meat, the girl said to me, 'Go on, Gavilán, or whatever you're called, and tell your master, Nicholas the Flat-nosed, not to trust animals, and that one must take from a miser anything one can get.' I could easily have got back what she took from me; but I didn't want to touch those pure white hands with my dirty slaughter-house mouth.

Scipio You did quite right, for it's the prerogative of beauty always to be respected.

Berganza That's what I did; and so I went back to my master without the rations and with the shoe. He thought I was back quickly, saw the shoe, guessed the trick and, taking out a knife, lunged at me so that, if I hadn't dodged, you'd never have heard this story or any of the others which I intend to tell you. I hoofed it at top speed behind San Bernardo, and simply followed my nose. That night I slept in the open air, and the next day I was lucky enough to come across a herd or flock of sheep and lambs. As soon as I saw it, I thought that I had found my resting-place. For it seemed to me to be the natural function of dogs to guard cattle, because it's a task which calls for great virtue, consisting in the protection and defence of the humble and helpless from the mighty and the proud. One of the three shepherds who looked after the flock had scarcely clapped eyes on me when he called out to me, and I, wanting nothing better than this, went up to him with my head down, and wagging my tail. He ran his hand over my back, opened my mouth, spat into it, looked at my teeth, sized up my age and told the other shepherd that I showed all the signs of being a thorough-bred. At this point, the owner of the sheep came up, trotting along on a grey mare, with lance and shield, and looking more like a coastguard than a sheep-owner. He asked the shepherd, 'What dog is this? He looks like a good dog.' 'You can be sure of that,' replied the shepherd, 'for I have examined him closely and he shows every sign of being a great dog. He's just arrived here, and I don't know who he belongs to, although I know he doesn't belong to the flocks round here.' 'In that case,' answered the gentleman, 'put Leoncillo's collar on him straight away, the dog that died, and give him the same rations as the rest, and pet him, so that he gets attached to the herd and stays with it.' And saying this he went off, and the shepherd straight away put a mastiff's collar with lots of studs round my neck, having first of all given me a good helping of bread and milk in a bowl. And then he gave me the name of Barcino. I was delighted with my second master and my new job; I was careful and diligent in looking after the flock, never leaving it except at siesta time, when I would go and lie down in the shade of a tree or of some bank or rock, or a bush, beside one of the many streams which flowed in those parts. And I wasn't idle in these periods of rest, because I would be exercising my memory in recalling many things, especially about the life I had led in the slaughter-house, and the life my master led, along with all those who, like him, have to pander to the trifling pleasures of their mistresses. Oh, the things I could tell you that I learned in the school of my butcher—master's lady! But I must be silent or you'll think I'm a tedious backbiter.

Scipio As I've heard that one of the great poets of antiquity said that it was difficult not to write satires, I will let you do a bit of backbiting so long as it's only in fun, just to mark but not to wound or kill anyone. Backbiting is not a good thing even though it makes many people laugh if it mortally wounds a man; and if you can be amusing without it, I shall think all the better of you for it.

Berganza I shall take your advice, and anxiously await the time when you tell me of your adventures; for from one who is so good at recognizing and correcting the faults I reveal in relating mine, one can certainly hope that he will relate his in such a way that they will give instruction and pleasure at the same time. But, to take up the broken thread of my story, I was saying that in the silence and solitude of my siestas, I would reflect among other things that what I had heard about the life of shepherds could not be true; at least, about those that my master's lady read of in books when I used to go to her house. They were all about shepherds and shepherdesses, and they told how they spent their whole lives singing and playing on bagpipes, whistles, rebecks and shawms, and other extraordinary instruments. I would stop to listen to her reading how Amphrysus' shepherd sang divinely well as he praised the peerless Belisarda, there being not a single tree in the whole of the Arcadian mountains at whose foot he had not sat down to sing from the moment the sun came forth in the arms of Aurora until it set in the arms of Thetis. Even after night had spread over the face of the earth its black wings of darkness, he did not cease from his beautifully sung and tearful laments. She did not forget to mention incidentally the shepherd Elicio, more amorous than bold, of whom it was said that, heedless of his love and of his flock, he entered into the cares of others. She also told how the great shepherd of Filida, an unrivalled painter of portraits, had been more confident than fortunate. Of the swooning of Sireno and the repentance of Diana she declared that she thanked God and wise Felicia, who with her enchanted water undid that maze of entanglements and cleared up that labyrinth of problems. I would recall many other books of this kind which I had heard her read; but they were not worth mentioning.

Scipio You are making good use of my advice, Berganza; do your backbiting, sting, and pass on; and make sure your intentions are pure, even if your tongue does not seem to be.

Berganza In affairs like this the tongue never stumbles unless the intention first gives way. But if by chance I do any backbiting, either inadvertently or through malice, I shall say in reply to anyone who reproaches me for it what that stupid poet Mauleon, the mock academician of the Academy of Imitators, said in answer to someone who asked him what *Deum de Deo* meant: 'Do as you like'.

Scipio This was a fool's answer, but if you are or want to be wise, you must never say anything for which you will have to apologize. Now carry on.

Berganʒa I tell you that all the thoughts I've mentioned, and many more, made me realize how different the manners and habits of my shepherds and all the rest of their crew were from those that I had been told about the shepherds in books. If my shepherds sang, it wasn't harmonious and properly composed songs, but 'Mind the wolf, Jenny', and other things of that sort; and all this to the accompaniment not of shawms, rebecks or pipes, but to the sound of one shepherd's crook hitting another or of the clapping of a couple of tiles between their fingers; not with delicate, tuneful and pleasing voices, but with hoarse cries which, whether they sang solo or together, gave the impression of shouts and grunts rather than songs. Most of the day they spent de-lousing themselves or mending their sandals. There were no Amaryllises, Filidas, Galateas or Dianas among them; nor were there Lisardos, Lausos, Jacintos or Riselos; they were all Antones, Domingos, Pablos, or Llorentes. All this led me to realize what must be commonly accepted: that all those books are well-written inventions for the entertainment of idle folk, with not a grain of truth in them. For if they were true, there would be bound to have been some trace among these shepherds of mine of that blissful life, and of those pleasant pastures, spacious forests, sacred mountains, lovely gardens, clear streams, and crystal fountains, and of those modest and elegant love-tales with a swooning shepherd here and a shepherdess there, and the bagpipe of a shepherd on this side and the flageolet of another on that.

Scipio That's enough, Berganza. Back to the beaten track, and on with the story.

Berganʒa Thank you, Scipio my friend, for if you hadn't warned me, I'd have got so warmed up that I shouldn't have stopped until I'd filled a whole book about those deceitful shepherds. However, the time will come when I'll tell you the whole story in better order and more eloquently than now.

Scipio Look at your feet, and you'll come to earth, Berganza. I mean you should remember that you are an animal without powers of reason, and if you are giving signs of possessing it, we've already agreed that it is something unprecedented and beyond the bounds of nature.

Berganza I'd accept that if I were still in a state of innocence, but now that I recall what I ought to have said to you at the beginning of our conversation, I am not only amazed at what I am saying ,but alarmed at what I'm failing to say.

Scipio But can't you tell what you do remember?

Berganza It's a true story of what happened to me with a great witch, a disciple of Camacha of Montilla.

Scipio Then tell me before you go any further with the story of your life.

Berganza That I shall not do, I promise you, until the proper time; be patient, and listen to what I have to tell you in order, for you'll be better pleased that way, unless you insist on knowing the middle before the beginning.

Scipio Be brief, and say what you like and how you like.

Berganza Very well, what I say is that I was getting on fine at the business of looking after sheep, for it seemed to me that I was earning my bread by my labour and by the sweat of my brow, and that idleness, the root and source of all vices, had no claim on me, because if I rested during the daytime, I did not sleep at night, for the wolves were constantly attacking us and rousing us to action. And scarcely had the shepherds said, 'Barcino, wolf,' when up I ran before all the other dogs, to the place where they said the wolf was. I would run through the valleys, search the woods, ransack the forests, leap over ravines, cross roads, and the next morning I would come back to the flock, without having found a trace of a wolf, panting, weary, torn to pieces and with my feet cut open by splinters, and I would find a dead sheep among the flock, or else a lamb with its throat torn open and half eaten by the wolf. I was in despair at the thought of how little use my effort and trouble were. The owner of the flock would come; the shepherds would go out to meet him with the skin of the dead animal; he would blame the shepherds for their negligence and order the dogs to be punished for their laziness; blows would rain down on us, and reproaches on top of them.

So, one day, seeing that I was being punished for nothing and that all my trouble, swiftness and courage were of no avail to catch the wolf, I decided to change my tactics. So I didn't go off away from the flock to look for him, as I usually did, but stayed nearby; for as the wolf came there, it was there that I should be more sure of catching him. Every week they would call us out, and one very dark night I saw wolves which the flock could not possibly guard against. I crouched down behind a bush, the other dogs went on ahead of me, and from there I watched and saw two shepherds catch hold of one of the best lambs in the fold, and kill it, in such a way that the next morning it really looked as if the wolf had done the killing. I was amazed and quite taken aback when I saw that the shepherds were the wolves and that the very ones who were supposed to guard the flock were tearing it to pieces. They told their master immediately of the wolf's attack, gave him the skin and some of the meat, eating the bigger and better part themselves. The master scolded them once more, and the dogs were once more punished. There were no wolves, but the flock was dwindling. I wanted to say what was going on, but was dumb; and all this left me bewildered and distressed. 'Good heavens!' I said to myself. 'What is the answer to this? Who is going to reveal the truth and say that it is the defenders who are causing the offence while the watchmen are sleeping, that the people in charge are the thieves and the guardian is the killer?'

Scipio And you were quite right, Berganza; because there's no greater or more subtle thief than the one within one's own doors; and so the trusting are killed in far greater numbers than the cautious. The worst of it is that it's impossible for people to get on in the world if they don't trust others. But let's stop here, for I don't want it to look as if we were preaching. Go on.

Berganza I shall go on, and what I want to say is that I decided to leave that job, although it seemed so good; and to choose another where if I got no reward, at least I shouldn't be punished. I went back to Seville, and entered the service of a very rich merchant.

Scipio What method did you use to get a master? Because, as things are nowadays, it's very difficult for an honest fellow to find a master to serve. The lords of this world are very different from the Lord of heaven: they, when they take a servant, first of all scrutinize his pedigree, test his skill, take note of his appearance, and even want to know what clothes he has. But to enter God's service the poorest is the richest; the humblest is the man of most exalted lineage; and so long as he sets out with a pure heart to serve him willingly, he orders his name to be written in his wage-book, and assigns him such rich rewards that in number and excellence they surpass all his desires.

Berganza All this is preaching, Scipio my friend.

Scipio I agree with you, and so I'll be quiet.

Berganza As regards your question as to how I set about finding a master, all I can say is that, as you already know, humility is the basis and foundation of all the virtues, and without it there is no virtue worthy of the name. It smooths obstacles, overcomes difficulties, and is a means which never fails to lead us to glorious ends. It makes enemies into friends, calms the anger of the irate, and brings down the arrogance of the proud; it is the mother of modesty and the sister of moderation. In short, with humility vices can win no profitable victory, for the shafts of sin are blunted and dulled by its softness and meekness. So I took advantage of this same humility when I wanted to enter service in a house, having first of all considered and looked very carefully to see if it was a house which could maintain and accommodate a big dog. Then I would go up to the door, and when some stranger, as I thought, was going in, I would bark at him, and when the master came I would lower my head and, wagging my tail, would go up to him and lick his shoes with my tongue. If they beat me and sent me away, I would bear it, and would come back as meekly as ever and fawn on those who beat me, for no one ever did it again when they saw my persistence and my nobility of bearing. In this way, after two attempts I would settle in the house. I would give good service, then they'd get to like me, and no one sent me away, unless I took my own leave or went off of my own accord; and sometimes I would get a master so good that if it hadn't been for my bad luck, I'd have still been with him.

Scipio I used to use the same method to enter the service of the masters I had: you'd think we'd read each other's thoughts.

Berganza In things like this we have had the same experiences, unless I'm mistaken, and I'll tell you about them in due course, as I have promised you. Now listen to what happened to me after I left the flock in the care of those rogues. I went back to Seville, as I said, which is a shelter for the poor and a refuge for the outcast, for in its vast expanses not only can the humble find a place, but the great are unable to make their presence felt. I went up to the door of a big house belonging to a merchant, and went through my usual motions, and in next to no time I was a fixture there. When they'd got me in they kept me tied up behind the door in the daytime, and loose at night; and I was very careful and diligent in my service. I used to bark at strangers and growl at people who weren't very well known at the house; I would stay awake at night, and go round the yards and up on the terraces, making myself the general guardian of my own and other people's houses. My master was so pleased with my good services that he gave orders that I should be treated well and given a ration of bread and the bones which were picked up or thrown down from his table, as well as the kitchen leftovers. I showed how grateful I was for this by jumping up and down incessantly when I saw my master, especially when he came back after a journey and, as a result of all the signs of pleasure I gave and all the jumping up, my master ordered me to be untied and allowed to run loose day and night. As soon as I saw that I was loose I ran up to him and all round him, without daring to touch him with my paws, remembering the fable of Aesop about the ass who *was* such an ass that he wanted to caress his master in the same way as a spoiled lapdog of his, and who was rewarded by being beaten. It seemed to me that in that fable we were meant to understand that the airs and graces of some don't go down well in others; let the jester make jokes, let the clown practise his sleight of hand and his somersaults, let the rogue talk nonsense, let the low fellow who has made a speciality of it imitate the song of the birds and the various antics and actions of animals and men; but don't let a man of distinction do these things, for none of these achievements will bring credit or honour to his name.

Scipio That's enough; get on, Berganza, for we know what you mean.

Berganza I wish I were as well understood by those on whose account I'm saying this as I am by you. For I think so well of people that it upsets me terribly when I see a gentleman behave like a buffoon and boast that he knows how to juggle with Chinese boxes and pine cones and that nobody can dance the chaconne like him. I know a gentleman who used to boast that, at the request of a sacristan, he had cut out thirty-two paper flowers to place on top of the black drapes on a monument. He made such a fuss about these things that he would take his friends to see them as if he were taking them to see the banners and spoils of enemies upon the tombs of his parents and grandparents. Well, this merchant had two sons, one of twelve and the other of about fourteen, who were studying grammar in the Studium of the Company of Jesus. They would go about in great state, with their tutor and their pages to carry their books and what they called their portfolios. Seeing them go about with such show, in sedan chairs if it was sunny, in a coach if it rained, made me consider and reflect upon the very simple way in which their father would go to the Exchange to conduct his affairs, because the only servant he took was a Negro, and occasionally he would go so far as to ride on a rather shabby mule.

Scipio You should know, Berganza, that it is the custom of the merchants of Seville, and of other cities too, to display their power and wealth, not in their own persons, but in that of their children; because these merchants are greater by reason of the shadow they cast than they are in themselves. As it's unusual for them to pay any attention to anything else but their agreements and contracts, they live modestly; but since ambition and wealth cry out for display, they burst forth in their children, and so they treat them and give them privileges as if they were the sons of princes. There are some who seek titles for them and try to place on their breasts the insignia which so clearly mark out important people from the plebs.

Berganza It is ambition, but a generous kind of ambition, which sets out to improve their position without harming anyone else.

Scipio Rarely if ever can one fulfil ambition without harming someone else.

Berganza We've already said that we must not backbite.

Scipio Yes, but I'm not backbiting about anybody.

Berganza Now you convince me of the truth of what I've often heard said. One wretched backbiter will ruin ten families and slander twenty good folk, and if anyone reproaches him for what he has said, he replies that he has said nothing, and that if he did say anything he didn't mean it, and that if he thought that anyone would take offence, he wouldn't have said it. Indeed, Scipio, anyone who wants to keep up a conversation for two hours without lapsing into backbiting has got to be very wise and very careful; because I can see that as far as I am concerned, although I am an animal, I've only got to open my mouth a few times to find words rushing to my tongue like flies to wine, all full of malice and backbiting. And so I say again what I've said before: that we inherit the tendency to do and speak evil from our first parents and absorb it with our mother's milk. You can see this clearly in the fact that the child has barely got his arm out of his swaddling clothes before he raises his hand as if he wanted to have his revenge on the person who he thinks has offended him; and almost the first word he utters is an insult to his nurse or his mother.

Scipio That is true. I confess my error, and beg you to forgive me, for I have forgiven you for so many. Let bygones be bygones, as the children say, and don't let's do any more backbiting from now on. Carry on with your story, which you left off when you were describing the showy way your master the merchant's sons used to go to the Studium of the Company of Jesus.

Berganza To whom I commend myself whatever befall. Although I consider it difficult to refrain from backbiting, I intend to use a device which I was told was used by a man who was always swearing, and afterward repenting of his evil habit. Every time he swore after he had repented he would give himself a pinch in the arm, or would kiss the ground, by way of penance for his sin; but would swear all the same. So every time I go against your precepts about backbiting, and against my own intention not to backbite, I'll bite the tip of my tongue in such a way that it hurts and reminds me of my sin and so that I don't do it again.

Scipio If that's your remedy, my guess is that you'll bite your tongue so often that you won't have any tongue left, and so you won't be able to backbite.

Berganza At least I'll try as hard as I can, and hope that heaven will make up for my failures. Anyway, I was saying that one day my master's sons left a satchel in the courtyard, where I was at the time; and as I was trained to carry the basket for my master the slaughterer, I got hold of the satchel and went off after them, determined not to let go of it until I got to the Studium. Everything turned out as I wished; and my masters, who saw me coming in with the portfolio in my mouth, carefully held by the ribbons, ordered one of the pages to take it from me; but I did not let him, and wouldn't let go of it until I got into the classroom with it, which made all the students laugh. I went up to the elder of my masters, and put it into his hands in a very well-bred manner, as I thought, and then stayed squatting on my haunches at the classroom door, gazing attentively at the master who was delivering his lesson. I don't know what it is about virtue, since I have remained practically untouched by it, but I was delighted to see the loving care and the solicitude and diligence with which those blessed fathers and masters taught those boys, training the tender young shoots so that they did not turn aside or stray from the path of virtue, which they were taught along with their letters. I noticed how gently they scolded them, with what forbearance they punished them, how they urged them on with examples, encouraged them with prizes and prudently bore with them; and finally, how they depicted for them the ugliness and horror of vice and portrayed for them the beauty of virtue, so that hating the former and loving the latter, they might attain the end for which they were created.

Scipio You're quite right, Berganza, because I've heard it said of these blessed folk that as statesmen there are none so prudent anywhere as they, and as guides and leaders on the path to heaven, there are few who can approach them. They are mirrors reflecting uprightness, Catholic doctrine, uncommon prudence, and deep humility, the foundation on which the whole edifice of happiness is constructed.

Berganza All this is as you say. And, to continue my story, I must tell you that my masters were delighted that I always carried their portfolio for them, which I did very gladly; and as a result I lived like a king, and even better, for my life was an easy one. The students took to playing games with me, and I got so tame with them that they would put their hands in my mouth, and the smaller ones would get on my back; they would throw their caps or hats, and I would put them neatly back in their hands with every sign of pleasure. They got into the habit of feeding me with anything they had, and were delighted to see that when they gave me walnuts or hazelnuts I would crack them like a monkey, leaving the shells and eating the soft part. There was even one who, to test my skill, brought me a great mass of salad in a handkerchief, which I ate as if I were a human being. It was winter-time, when you can get muffins and butter in Seville, with which I was so well supplied that several Nebrijas[2] were pawned or sold so that I could have my fill. In short, I lived the life of a student, free of hunger and of the itch, which is as much as one need say by way of proof that it was a good life. For if hunger and the itch were not so much a part of a student's life, no life would be more pleasant and agreeable, for virtue and pleasure go there hand in hand, and one spends one's youth in learning and in enjoying oneself.

I was removed from this state of glory and tranquillity by one of those ladies whom I think they call reasons of state in these parts, a lady with whom one complies at the expense of every other sort of reason. The fact is that those masters got the idea that the half hour between lessons was spent by the students not in going over what they had learned, but in playing with me; and so they ordered my masters not to take me to the Studium any more. They obeyed, and took me back home to my old job of guarding the door; and as the old merchant had forgotten his kind decision to let me run loose day and night, I had to submit my neck to the chain once again and lie down on a little mat which they put behind the door for me. Oh, friend Scipio, if you knew how hard it is to have to pass from a happy state to a wretched one. For when wretchedness and misfortune continue over a long period, they either come to a speedy end with death, or the continual suffering of them becomes a habit and a custom, which acts as relief, even when they are at their most severe; but when one emerges suddenly and unexpectedly from a state of calamity and misfortune to the enjoyment of a prosperous, fortunate and happy state, and then shortly afterwards goes back to suffering one's original fate and enduring one's earlier labours and misfortunes, the pain is so harsh that if one's life doesn't come to an end it is an even greater torment to go on living.

So, as I say, I went back to my dog-food and to the bones which

2 Antonio de Nebrija was the author of a famous Latin Grammar first published in 1481, and in wide use as a text book.

a Negress living in the house used to throw to me, and even these were filched by two tabby cats which, being fast movers and not tied up like me, would easily run off with what did not fall within the circuit of my chain. Brother Scipio, God give you all you desire if you will let me philosophize a bit without getting annoyed; because if I didn't tell you straight away the things that happened to me then and which have come into my mind at this moment, I don't think my story would be complete or of any value at all.

Scipio Beware, Berganza, lest this desire to philosophize which you say has come over you be a temptation of the devil. Backbiting has no finer veil to excuse and conceal its wickedness than for the back-biter to maintain that all the things he says are the wise observations of philosophers, that malice is reproof, and revealing others' defects is merely laudable zeal. And there is no backbiter whose life, if you look at it carefully, is not full of vice and impudence. If you bear this in mind, go ahead and philosophize as much as you like.

Berganza You may be sure, Scipio, that I shan't backbite any more, because I'm determined not to. The fact is then that as I was idle all day and idleness breeds thought, I began to go through in my mind some of the Latin phrases which stuck in my mind from the time when I heard them from my masters in the Studium, and as a result of which, it seems to me, I became somewhat wiser. I decided that if ever I knew how to speak, I would take advantage of them when the occasion arose, but not in the way that some ignorant folk use them. There are some Spanish writers who now and then insert bits of Latin phrases into the conversation, giving the impression to those who do not understand that they are great Latinists, when they scarcely know how to decline a noun or conjugate a verb.

Scipio I consider them to be less harmful than those who really do know Latin, of whom there are some who are so lacking in sense that when they are talking to a cobbler or a tailor they throw in Latin phrases like water.

Berganza From that we may infer that one who speaks Latin in front of those who don't know it is as bad as one who speaks it without knowing it.

Scipio There's another thing you can bear in mind, and that is that there are some who are no less fools for knowing Latin.

Berganza There's no doubt about that. The reason is clear, for when in the time of the Romans everyone spoke Latin as their mother tongue, there must have been some fools among them, who would be no less stupid by reason of the fact that they spoke Latin.

Scipio In order to know how to be silent in one's mother tongue and speak in Latin one needs to be wise, brother Berganza.

Berganza That is true, because it is as easy to say something stupid in Latin as in the vernacular, and I have seen educated men who are fools and learned men who are bores, people whose Spanish is studded with Latin words which can easily cause annoyance, and not once but many times.

Scipio Let us leave that, and start telling me your philosophical opinions.

Berganza I've already told you them, in fact I've just been telling them now.

Scipio Which are they?

Berganza The ones about Latin and Spanish, which I began and you finished off.

Scipio Do you call backbiting philosophy? So that's how it is. That's the way, Berganza, make a virtue out of this cursed plague of backbiting, and give it whatever name you like, for it will earn us the name of cynics, which means backbiting dogs. Now for heaven's sake shut up and get on with your story.

Berganza How am I to get on if I shut up?

Scipio I mean get on quickly, without adding tails to it, and making it look like an octopus.

Berganza Talk properly; for you don't talk about tails on octopuses.

Scipio That is the mistake made by the man who said that there was nothing rude or vicious in calling things by their proper names, as if it weren't better, if you have to name them, to refer to them by circumlocutions and round-about phrases which temper the unpleasantness of hearing them referred to by their own names. Proper words show the propriety of those who speak or write them.

Berganza I'm prepared to believe you; and I would add that my luck, not content with having taken me away from my studies and my happy and well-ordered life, putting me on a leash behind a door, and exchanging the students' generosity for the Negress's meanness, this same fortune took it upon itself to rob me of the bit of ease I had. Look Scipio: be quite sure, as I am, that ill luck pursues and finds the unlucky man, even though he hides himself in the utmost corners of the earth. I say this because the Negress in the house was in love with a Negro, also a house-slave, and this Negro used to sleep in the porch, between the street door and the middle door, behind which I used to be. They could only see each other at night, and in order to do so had stolen or copied the keys. So on most nights the Negress would come down, and shutting my mouth with a bit of meat or cheese, would open up for the Negro, with whom she used to enjoy herself, aided by my silence, which was purchased by all the things that the Negress would steal. For some days the things the Negress gave me played havoc with my conscience, for I thought that without them I should have a pretty thin time, and would change from a mastiff into a greyhound; but in fact, carried away by my natural goodness, I decided to do my duty to my master, for I was drawing my wages from him and eating his food. After all, this is the duty not only of honest dogs, who are famous for their gratitude, but of all who serve.

Scipio Now this I grant, Berganza, *can* pass for philosophy, for these are arguments which stand by their truth and good sense; but get on, and don't dawdle too much over your story.

Berganza To begin with I'd like to ask you to tell me, if you know, what philosophy means; for although I use the word I don't know what it is, though I'm given to understand that it's a good thing.

Scipio I'll soon tell you. The word is composed of two Greek nouns which are 'philos' and 'sophia'; 'philos' means 'love', and 'sophia' means 'knowledge'; so 'philosophy' means 'love of knowledge' and 'philosopher' means 'lover of knowledge'.

Berganza You know a great deal, Scipio. Who the devil taught you Greek words?

Scipio You are simple, Berganza, if you take any notice of that; these are things that every schoolboy knows; and there are those who pretend to know Greek when they don't, just as there are those who pretend to know Latin.

Berganza That is what I'm saying. I'd like to see people like that put in a press and the juice of what they really know squeezed out of them, so that they didn't go about deceiving everybody with the tinsel of their torn breeches and their bogus Latin phrases, like the Portuguese with the Negroes in Guinea.

Scipio Now indeed, Berganza, you can bite your tongue, and I too; because all we're saying is backbiting.

Berganza Yes, but I'm not obliged to do what I've heard it said that a certain Tyrian called Charondas did. He made a law that no one should go into the Council Chamber of his city armed, on pain of death. He forgot about this, and one day went into the council meeting with his sword on; they pointed it out to him, and recalling the penalty he had prescribed, he straight away unsheathed his sword and ran it through his breast, so being the first to make and break the law, and the first to pay the penalty. What I said wasn't intended as a law, but a promise that I would bite my tongue when I was guilty of backbiting; but nowadays things aren't as strict as they used to be in times gone by. Today you make a law, and tomorrow you break it, and perhaps it's right that it should be so. Nowadays one promises to give up one's vices, and in no time one falls into worse ones. It is one thing to praise discipline and another to impose it on oneself; in fact there's many a slip twixt the cup and the lip. Let the devil bite himself, but I don't want to bite myself or do my good deeds behind a mat, where I can't be seen by anybody who can praise my honest intention.

Scipio According to this argument, Berganza, if you were a human being, you would be a hypocrite, and all the works you performed would be just for appearance, and merely false and artificial, covered with the cloak of virtue, just so that you might win praise, as all hypocrites do.

Berganza I don't know what I'd do then; but I know what I want to do now, and that's not to bite myself, when I have so many things left to say that I don't know how or when I can get through them, especially as I'm afraid that when the sun comes up we'll be left in the dark, deprived of speech.

Scipio Heaven will order things better than that. Carry on with your story, don't go off the track with irrelevant digressions and, however long the story is, you'll soon get to the end that way.

Berganza I tell you, then, that having seen the impudence, the thieving and indecent behaviour of those Negroes I decided, like a good servant, to put a stop to it, as best I could; and I did so to good effect. The Negress would come down, as you've heard, to take her pleasure with the Negro, trusting that the pieces of meat, bread or cheese which she threw to me would keep me quiet. Gifts count for a lot, Scipio!

Scipio Yes, they do. But stick to the point, and get on.

Berganza I remember that when I was a student I heard the master say a Latin proverb, which they call an adage, and which went 'Habet bovem in lingua'.

Scipio Oh, how inaptly you've brought in this Latin of yours! Have you forgotton so soon what we said a short time ago about those who insert Latin phrases into conversations in Spanish?

Berganza This bit of Latin fits in just right here; for you must know that one of the coins used by the Athenians was stamped with the figure of an ox, and when a judge failed to say or do what was right and just, because he had been bribed, they would say: 'He's got an ox on his tongue.'

Scipio I don't see the point.

Berganza Isn't it quite clear, if the gifts of the Negress kept me silent all those days when I didn't want or dare to bark when she went down to see her Negro lover? This is why I repeat that gifts can do a great deal.

Scipio I've already agreed that they can, and if it wasn't that I didn't want to make a long digression, I could prove to you by a thousand examples just how much they can do; but perhaps I shall tell you some day, if heaven grants me time, opportunity and speech to relate the story of my life.

Berganza May God give you what you desire, and listen to me. In the end, my good intentions triumphed over the Negress's wicked gifts; and one very dark night, as she was coming down to her usual pastime, I attacked her without barking, so that the household shouldn't be disturbed. In a moment I had torn her chemise to shreds and ripped a bit out of her thigh, a trick which kept her safely in bed for more than a week, pretending to her master and mistress that it was goodness knows what illness. She got better, came back the next night, and I attacked her again, and without biting her scratched her all over as if I'd been carding wool. Our battles were conducted in silence, I was always the winner, and the Negress got badly knocked about and very cross. But her anger showed up in the condition of my coat and my health. They took away my rations and my bones, and my own bones gradually began to stick out. All the same, although they took away my food, they couldn't take away my power to bark. But the Negress, in order to finish me off for good and all, brought me a sponge fried in butter. I realized what she was up to, and knew that it was worse than eating poison, because the stomach of one who eats it swells up and he never gets away alive. So, as it seemed to me impossible to protect myself against the tricks of these savage enemies, I decided to put myself out of reach and out of sight of them.

One day when I was loose I went out into the street without saying good-bye to anyone, and in less than a hundred yards I had the good fortune to meet the police officer I mentioned at the beginning of my story, who was a great friend of my master, Nicholas the Flat-nosed, and who, as soon as he saw me, recognized me and called me by my name. I recognized him too, and when he called me I went up to him with my usual ceremonies and caresses. He grabbed hold of my collar, and said to his constables: 'This is a famous guard-dog, who belonged to a great friend of mine; let's take him home.' The constables were delighted, and said that if I was a guard-dog I would be very useful. They wanted to grab hold of me and take me away, but my master said there was no need to hold me, as I would go because I knew him. I have forgotten to tell you that the steel-pointed collar which I took with me when I upped and left the sheep was taken off me by a gipsy in an inn, and by the time I got to Seville I was rid of it; but the police officer put one on me which was all studded with Moorish brass. Think, Scipio, how the wheel of fortune turned for me: yesterday I was a student and today a constable.

Scipio That's the way of the world, and there's no reason why you should start exaggerating the swings of fortune, as if there were much to choose between serving a butcher and a constable. I haven't the patience to put up with listening to the complaints which some men make about fortune, when the best fortune they ever had was the hope of becoming a squire. What curses they hurl at her! How they abuse her! And only so that those who listen to them might think they have known better days and fallen on hard times.

Berganza You are right; and you must know that this police officer was friendly with a notary, whom he used to consult. The two of them had as concubines two women who were no better than they should have been, but in fact far worse; it's true they were fairly pleasant-looking, but they had all the brazenness and viciousness that goes with whores. These women acted as a net or hook to make their catches for them, in this way: they would dress in such a manner that anybody could see a mile away that they were loose-living women. They were always on the hunt for foreigners, and when the fair came to Cadiz and Seville they would smell profit, and no foreigner was safe from their attacks. When one of these greasy fellows fell in with these fair creatures, they would tell the police officer and the notary to what inn they were going, and when they were together they would pounce on them and arrest them for consorting with concubines; but they would never take them to prison because the foreigners would always settle the affair with cash.

It so happened that Colindres, which was the name of the officer's girl friend, got hold of one of these foreigners who was a really dirty customer. She arranged to have supper and spend the night with him in his lodgings. She tipped off her boy friend; and they'd scarcely got undressed when the police officer, the notary, two constables and I descended upon them. The lovers were covered with confusion; the officer made a great deal of the crime, and ordered them to get dressed quickly to be taken off to prison. The foreigner got very upset, the notary, moved by charity, intervened, and by dint of his pleading reduced the penalty to a mere hundred *reales*. The foreigner asked for some chamois trousers which he had put on a chair at the foot of the bed, in which he had the cash to pay for his freedom. But the trousers failed to appear, nor were they in a position to do so, for as soon as I went into the room a smell of bacon reached my nostrils, which raised my spirits considerably. I tracked it down by following the scent, and ran it to earth in one of the pockets of the trousers. So, having found this fine piece of ham, in order to enjoy it and to get it out without being detected I took the trousers out into the street, and there I settled down to enjoy the ham to my heart's content. When I got back to the room I found the foreigner calling out for his trousers in his outlandish speech, the import of which was nevertheless clear, for he had fifty real gold crowns in them. The notary imagined that either Colindres or the constables had stolen them. The officer thought the same, and called them aside; but none of them owned up, and they all swore like mad it was not they.

When I saw what was happening, I went back out to the street where I had left the trousers, to bring them back, for the money was of no use to me. But I couldn't find them, because some lucky passer-by had gone off with them. When the officer saw that the foreigner had no money for bribes, he got very annoyed, and thought he'd get out of the landlady the money that the foreigner no longer had. He called her, and she arrived half dressed; and when she heard the foreigner's shouts and complaints, and saw Colindres undressed and in tears, the officer furious, the notary in a rage, and the constables helping themselves to whatever they could find in the room, she was none too pleased. The officer ordered her to get dressed and come with him to the prison, because she was harbouring in her house men and women of loose habits. There was a fine to-do! The shouting and confusion grew greater every moment; and finally the landlady said,

'Mr Police Officer and Mr Notary, don't try your fancy tricks on me, for I can see exactly what's going on. Let's have less of your shouting; shut your mouths and be off with you. If not, I swear I'll lose my temper and let everybody know all about this game. I know Mistress Colindres very well and I know that the police officer has been keeping her for some months. And don't ask me to say any more, but give the money back to this gentleman, and let's keep our good reputation. I'm an honest woman and I have a husband with his letters patent of nobility, and his *ad perpetuam rei memoriam*[3] and his leaden seals. God knows I carry on my trade in a decent manner and without doing any harm to anybody. I've got my tariff posted where everybody can see it, and don't come to me with tall stories, for by heaven I won't stand any nonsense. Am I responsible if women come in with my guests? They have the key to their rooms, and I'm not a lynx to see through walls.'

My masters were astounded when they heard the landlady's

3. 'In perpetual memory of the affair', a motto which appeared on the patent of nobility.

harangue and realized that she knew all about them; but as they saw
that if they didn't get money out of her, they weren't going to get
it from anyone else, they insisted on taking her to prison. She
appealed to heaven against the injustice which they were inflicting
upon her, with her husband away and he such an important
gentleman. The foreigner was roaring for his fifty crowns. The
constables insisted that they hadn't seen the trousers, and God
forbid that they should. The notary, on the quiet, was urging the
officer to examine Colindres's clothes, for he had reason to suspect
that she must have the fifty crowns, since she was in the habit of
looking round the hiding-places and pockets of those who had
dealings with her. She said that the foreigner was drunk and must
have lied about the money.

In short: everything was confusion, shouting and swearing, and
there was no prospect of anyone calming down; nor would they
have done so if at that moment there had not come into the room
the deputy chief of police, who was on his way to visit that inn,
and was attracted by the shouts to the place where all the commotion was. He asked the reason for the shouting. The landlady
explained it in great detail, telling him all about the nymph
Colindres, who was now dressed. She revealed the girl's open
friendship with the police officer. She made a public pronounce-
ment about his tricks and methods of stealing; and insisted that no
woman of ill repute had ever entered her house with her consent.
She made herself out to be a saint and her husband scarcely less;
and shouted orders to a servant girl to run and fetch from a chest
her husband's letters patent of nobility, so that the lieutenant could
see them. When he saw the patent he would realize that the wife of
such an honourable husband couldn't do anything bad, and that if
she traded as a boarding-house keeper it was out of sheer necessity.
God knew how she hated it, and how she wished she had some
income and means of sustenance to live without exercising that
calling. The lieutenant, annoyed at her incessant talking and her
pretensions to nobility, said to her,

'My dear landlady, I'm willing to believe that your husband has
a patent of nobility if you'll admit to me that he's a noble innkeeper
all the same.'

'And a very honourable one,' replied the landlady. 'And what family is there in the world, however good it be, which hasn't got some skeleton in the cupboard?'

'I tell you, sister, you'll have to get dressed, for you're coming to prison.'

This news was too much for her; she tore her face, and started shrieking; but despite all this the lieutenant, with a show of great severity, took them all off to prison, that is the foreigner, Colindres and the landlady. I found out afterwards that the foreigner lost his fifty crowns and ten more by way of costs; the landlady paid the same amount, and Colindres got away scot free. And the very day they let her go she hooked a sailor, who made up for the foreigner by the same trick of the tip-off; so you can see, Scipio, all the difficulties that my greediness caused.

Scipio Rather your master's wickedness.

Berganza Well, listen, and I'll tell you the lengths he went to, although I don't like speaking ill of police officers and notaries.

Scipio Yes, for they're not all tarred with the same brush. Indeed there are many, very many, notaries who are good, faithful and law-abiding, and ready to do favours without compromising anybody. Yes, not all of them put off lawsuits, or advise both the parties; nor do they all take more than their due, nor go searching and prying into other people's lives to get them involved with the law; nor do they all gang up with the judge on the 'you scratch my back and I'll scratch yours' principle; nor do all police officers make bargains with vagabonds and crooks; nor do all have girl friends like your master's to help them with their frauds. There are many, very many, who are noble by birth and by nature; there are many who are not rash, insolent, ill-bred, and thieving, like those who go round inns measuring strangers' swords, and if they find them a shade longer than the regulation allows, ruin their owners. Yes, they don't all let people go as soon as they catch them and act as judges and advocates as the fancy takes them.

Berganza My master aimed higher; he was on another tack, and had pretensions to being a real tough and making first-class hauls; although he acted the tough at no risk to himself, but at the cost of his purse. One day at the Jerez gate he attacked single-handed six notorious ruffians, without my being able to give him any assistance at all because I had a muzzle on my mouth, which he kept on me in the day time, and took off at night. I was amazed to see his daring, his spirit and his courage; he dashed in and out among the six swords of those toughs as if they were osier twigs. It was wonderful to see how swiftly he attacked, the thrusts, the parries, the way he calculated and watched out for attacks from behind. In short, in my opinion, and in that of all those who witnessed the fight, he was a second Rodamonte,[4] taking his enemies from the Jerez Gate to the columns of the Colegio de Maese Rodrigo, a distance of more than a hundred yards.

He locked them up, went back to pick up the trophies of the battle, which amounted to three scabbards, and then went off to show them to the chief officer who, if I remember rightly, was at that time Licenciate Sarmiento de Valladares, famous for the destruction of Sauceda.

They used to look at my master as he went along the streets, pointing at him as if to say: 'That is the brave man who single-handed dared to fight with the biggest thugs in Andalusia.'

He spent the rest of the day parading round the city, just to be seen, and at nightfall we found ourselves in Triana, in a street near the powder mill; and when my master had had a dekko – as they say in the song – to see if anyone could see him, he went into a house, and I after him, and we found in a courtyard all the toughs from the fight, without their cloaks and swords, and all taking their ease. One who must have been the host had a great jug of wine in one hand, and in the other a big tavern cup, which he filled to the brim with rich sparkling wine and then toasted all the company. As soon as they saw my master, they all rushed towards him with open arms, and all toasted him, and he returned all their toasts, and would have done it for twice as many if it had been worth his while, so friendly was he and anxious not to offend anyone for a trifle.

If I were to try to tell you now what went on then, the supper they had, the fights they related, the robberies they recounted, the ladies who came up to their standard and those who failed to pass their test, the praises they sang about each other, the absent thugs whose names were mentioned, their skill in fencing, with folk getting up in the middle of the supper to practise the thrusts which

4. Rodamonte. A character in Boiardo's *Orlando Innamorato* famous for his arrogance.

happened to occur to them and making fencing moves with their hands; the delightful terms they used; and finally, the appearance of the host, whom they all respected as lord and father: all this would get me into a maze from which I couldn't possibly escape, however hard I tried.

In short, I was assured beyond doubt that the master of the house, who was called Monipodio, kept a refuge for thieves and was a fence for hired killers, and that my master's great fight had been pre-arranged with them, down to the detail of retreating and leaving their scabbards, which my master paid for in cash there and then, with what Monipodio said was the cost of the supper, which did not finish until almost daybreak, to the great delight of all present. And by way of dessert they gave my master the tip-off about a brand-new ruffian, just arrived in the city. He must have been a bigger tough than they, so they squealed on him out of envy. My master seized him the following night, when he was naked in bed; for if he had had his clothes on I could see from the look of him that he wouldn't have allowed himself to be taken off in such a docile way. With this capture, which followed the fight, my cowardly master's fame grew apace – for he was in fact as cowardly as a hare – and with his free meals and drinks he kept up his reputation as a tough, and all that he gained from his profession and his brains went down the drain to support it.

But be patient and listen now to a story of what happened to him, without a word of exaggeration. Two thieves stole a very good horse in Antequera; they brought it to Seville, and in order to sell it without risk they used a stratagem which I think was very sharp and clever. They went to stay in different inns, and one went off to court and put in a claim that Pedro de Losada owed him four hundred *reales* which he had borrowed, as was proved by a certificate signed in his name, which he duly presented.

The deputy officer ordered the said Losada to acknowledge the certificate, and if he did so, to give security for the amount in question, or else he would be put in prison. It fell to my master and his friend the notary to carry out this job. One of the thieves took them to the inn where the other one was staying, and he immediately acknowledged his signature and owned up to the debt, offering the horse by way of guarantee that he would pay up. When my master saw this, he took note of it and marked it down for himself in case by any chance it were to be sold. The thief waited until the time fixed by the law had passed, the horse was put up for sale and the deal closed at five hundred *reales*, through an agent that my master employed to buy it for him. The horse was worth half as much again as what they gave for it; but as the vendor's concern was to make a quick sale, he clinched the deal after the first bid. One of the thieves recovered the debt which was not owing to him, and the other the receipt which he did not need; and my master was left with the horse, which as far as he was concerned was more of a menace than the horse of Sejanus to his masters.

There and then the thieves cleared off, and two days later, by which time my master had made good the horse's harness and other trappings, he appeared on him in San Francisco Square, looking more vain and stuck-up than a peasant in his Sunday best. They congratulated him heartily on his splendid purchase, assuring him that it was worth a hundred and fifty ducats just as sure as an egg was worth a *maravedí*; and he, turning and wheeling the horse, played out his act in the theatre provided by the afore-mentioned square. And as he was prancing and turning about, two good-looking and well-dressed men came up, and one said: 'Heavens, this is Piedehierro, my horse, who was stolen from me a few days ago in Antequera.' The four servants who were with him swore that that was the truth, that this was Piedehierro, the horse that had been stolen from him. My master was stunned, the owner complained, proofs were produced and those of the owner were such clear ones that the verdict went in his favour and my master was dispossessed of the horse. The clever trickery whereby the thieves had sold what they had stolen through the medium of the law itself all came out, and nearly everyone was delighted that my master's greed had been his undoing.

And this was not the end of his misfortune, for that night, as the chief officer himself was going out on patrol, having received information that there were thieves in the San Julián district, just as they were passing a crossroads they saw a man running away. The officer immediately caught hold of my collar and set me off, shouting, 'Stop thief, Gavilán: come on, Gavilán, my boy, stop thief,

stop thief.' I, being already weary of my master's misdeeds, did what
the chief officer ordered without any hesitation, and set upon my
own master. Before he could stop me I had him on the ground, and
if they hadn't hauled me off I should have avenged a good few
scores. As it was they pulled me off to the great chagrin of both me
and my master. The constables would have liked to punish me
and even beat me to death, and would have done it if the chief
officer hadn't said to them: 'Don't let anyone touch him, for the
dog did what I ordered.' Everybody realized the trick, and I, without
saying good-bye to anyone, escaped through a hole in the wall out
into the country, and before dawn I was in Mairena, which is a
village four leagues from Seville. By good luck I found there a
company of soldiers who, I heard, were going to set sail at
Cartagena. In the company were four ruffians who were friends of
my master, and the drummer had been a constable, and a great
showman, as drummers usually are. They all recognized me and
spoke to me; and naturally enough they asked about my master
just as they'd ask a human being about a friend; but the one who
was most kind to me was the drummer. So I decided to come to
an arrangement with him if he was willing and go on the expedition,
even if it took me to Italy or to Flanders, because it seems to me,
and I dare say you'll agree, that although the proverb says: 'A
fool at home is a fool the whole world over', travel and meeting
different people teaches men wisdom.

Scipio That is very true. Indeed I remember hearing a very clever
master I had say that the famous Greek called Ulysses gained a
reputation for prudence simply because he had travelled a lot and
met various people from different nations. And so I applaud your
decision to go wherever they might take you.

Berganza The fact is, then, that because the drummer now had the
means of showing off his tricks better than before, he began to
teach me to dance to the sound of the drum and do other tricks,
which no other dog but I could possibly learn, as you will hear
when I tell you about them. As we were nearing the end of our tour
of duty we didn't kill ourselves with marching; there was no
quarter-master to keep us in check; the captain was young, but a
real gentleman and a thoroughly good fellow; the ensign hadn't
left the court and the banqueting-hall many months; the sergeant

was cunning and quick, and very skilled at leading troops from base to point of embarkation. The company was full of ruffians and leadswingers who used to get up to some fine tricks in the villages we went through, which brought curses on one who did not deserve them. It is the misfortune of the good prince to be blamed by his subjects for the faults of his other subjects, because they do harm to each other, through no fault of their master. And however much he may want and try he cannot put these injuries to rights, because all or nearly all things connected with war bring with them bitterness, hardship and inconvenience.

In short: in less than a fortnight, through my own talent and the effort of the man I had chosen as my master, I learned how to jump for the King of France and not to jump for the bad landlady; he taught me how to prance like a Neapolitan charger, and to go round in circles like a miller's mule, as well as other things that, if I had not taken care not to show them off too soon, would have made people wonder whether it was some devil in the form of a dog which was performing them. He gave me the name of the 'Wise Dog', and we had barely got to our lodgings when, playing his drum, he would walk through the whole village, announcing that all those who wished to come and see the marvellous tricks and accomplishments of the Wise Dog could see them in such and such a house or in such and such a hospital at eight or four *maravedís* a head, depending on the size of the town. As a result of these advertisements everybody in the place came to see me, and not one of them went away without being amazed and delighted at having done so. My master was very pleased with the huge profit he was making, and was keeping six of his friends living like kings on the proceeds. Greed and envy made the ruffians decide to steal me, and they looked round for an opportunity to do it. For this business of getting a living by doing nothing has many adherents and supporters, which is why there are so many puppeteers in Spain, so many who exhibit pictures, so many who sell pins and ballads, whose property, even if they sold all of it, is not enough to live on for a single day. And all the same they never leave the eating-houses and taverns the whole year round. Hence I conclude that their constant drinking bouts are paid for by something other than the professions they pursue. All these people are useless and good-for-nothing vagrants, sponges who soak up wine and grubs who consume bread.

Scipio That's enough, Berganza; let bygones be bygones; carry on with your story, for the night is nearly over, and I shouldn't like us to be overshadowed by silence when the sun rises.

Berganza Be quiet, then, and listen. As it is an easy matter to add to what has already been invented, when my master saw how well I could imitate the Neapolitan charger, he made me some embossed leather coverings and a little saddle, which he fitted over my back, and on it he put a dummy figure of a man with the sort of small lance which you use to tilt at the ring. He taught me how to run straight at a ring which he placed between two poles, and when the day came for me to do my tilting he announced that on that day the Wise Dog was going to tilt at a ring, and perform other new and unprecedented feats of skill, of my own invention, as they put it, so as not to make my master look a liar.

So we came, by easy stages, to Montilla, the seat of that famous and great Christian, the Marquess of Priego, head of the house of Aguilar and of Montilla. They put my master up in a hospital, as he arranged; he made the usual announcement, and as the news of the skill and the tricks of the Wise Dog had already got round, in under an hour the courtyard was full of people. My master was delighted when he saw that he was in for a rich harvest, and surpassed himself with his games that day. The show began with my jumping through the hoop of a sieve which looked as if it had come from a cask; he started me off with the usual questions, and when he lowered a cane which he held in his hand it was the sign for me to jump; and when he held it up, it was the sign for me to stay put. The first order that day, which I shall remember as long as I live, went as follows:

'Come on, Gavilán, my boy; jump for that old fellow you know who dyes his beard; and if you don't want to, then jump for the pomp and show of Doña Pimpinela de Plafagonia, who was a friend of that Galician girl who used to serve at table in Valdeastillas. Don't you like that order, Gavilán my boy? Then jump for Pasillas, the undergraduate who signs himself as a licenciate when he has no degree at all. Oh, you are a lazy hound! Why don't you jump? Ah, now I get your games: now jump for the wine of

Esquivias, which is as famous as that of Cuidad Real, San Martin and Ribadavia.'

He lowered the cane and I jumped, and took note of his malicious tricks. Then he turned to the people, and said aloud,

'Don't imagine, worthy public, that what this dog knows is something to be taken lightly. I have taught him twenty-four tricks the least of which is worth going miles to see; he can dance the saraband and the chaconne better than the man who invented them; he can drink two litres of wine without leaving a drop; he can sing a "sol fa mi re" as well as a sacristan: all these, and as many again which I could tell you about, you will see during the days that the company is here. For the moment let's see our Wise Dog do another jump, and then we'll get down to serious business.'

At this point he left the audience in suspense, and made them determined not to miss all the things I could do. My master turned to me and said, 'Come back, Gavilán, my boy, and go through again all those jumps you've done so nimbly and skilfully; but you must take your orders from the famous witch who they say came from this village.'

As soon as he had said this the hospitaler, who was an old woman who looked over seventy years old, said, 'Scoundrel, charlatan, cheat and son of a whore, there's no witch here. If you were thinking of Camacha, she has paid for her sins, and is God knows where; and if you were thinking of me, you coarse lout, I am not and have never been a witch in my life, and if I've ever had the reputation of being one, thanks to false witnesses and an arbitrary law and to a hasty and ill-informed judge, everyone knows the sort of life I lead, as penance not for the sorcery I was never guilty of, but for the many other different kinds of sins I've committed, like the sinner that I am. So, you crafty drummer, get out of this hospital; if you don't by heaven I'll make you get out at top speed.'

At this point she began to shout such a stream of insults at my master that he was left in a state of alarm and confusion; and the long and the short of it was that the show simply came to a standstill. My master wasn't at all upset by the disturbance because he made off with the money and postponed to another day and another hospital what had had to be put off in that one. The people went off cursing the old woman, adding the name of witch to that of sorceress, and saying not only that she was an old hag but that she was a hairy old goat to boot.

Despite all this we stayed in the hospital that night, and when the old woman met me alone in the yard, she said to me, 'Is it you, Montiel my boy? Is it you by any chance, my son?' I looked up at her steadily; and when she saw that, she came up to me with tears in her eyes, and threw her arms round my neck, and she'd have kissed me on the mouth if I'd let her; but she was so repulsive that I didn't allow her to.

Scipio You were right, for it's no pleasure but sheer torture to kiss or let yourself be kissed by an old woman.

Berganza What I want to tell you now I ought to have said at the beginning of my story, and then we shouldn't have been so surprised at finding that we could speak. Because what the old woman said to me was,

'Montiel, my boy, come with me and I'll show you my room. See if you can arrange for us to see each other alone there tonight. I'll leave the door open: and remember that I have many things to tell you about your life, and to your advantage.'

I lowered my head as a sign of obedience, which made her quite sure that I was the dog Montiel that she was looking for, as she afterwards told me. I was astonished and perplexed as I waited for night to come so that I could see what the end of this mystery or marvel that the old woman had spoken about would be; and as I had heard her called a witch, I was expecting great things when I saw and heard her speak. At last the moment arrived when I found myself with her in her room, which was dark, narrow and low, and only lit by the dim light of an earthenware lamp. The old woman trimmed it, and sat down on a little chest, pulling me towards her. Without saying a word, she embraced me again, and I took care once more to make sure that she didn't kiss me. The first thing she said to me was,

'I hoped that heaven would grant that before these eyes of mine closed for the last time I should see you, my boy, and now that I have seen you, let death come and take me away from this weary life. You must know, my boy, that in this town there lived the most famous witch in the world, who was called Camacha de Montilla. She was so unrivalled in her profession that the Erichthos, Circes

and Medeas of whom I'm told the history books are full were no
match for her. She would freeze the clouds when she wanted to, and
blot out the face of the sun with them; and when she felt like it, she
would make the stormiest sky clear. She would bring men in a
moment from far-off lands, would repair in a marvellous way the
maidenhood of girls who had been careless about guarding their
integrity; she would act as cover for widows so that they could
behave as they liked without losing any of their respectability; she
would arrange and undo marriages just as she wanted to. In Decem-
ber she had fresh roses in her garden and in January she would be
harvesting wheat. Making watercress grow out of a trough was one
of the least of her achievements, and she could make you see in a
mirror or a baby's finger-nail anyone you cared to mention whether
living or dead. It was said that she could change men into animals,
and that she had used a sacristan as an ass for six years. I've never
managed to find out how it's done, because the stories they tell
about those old magicians who changed men into beasts only
amount, according to those who know most about it, to the fact
that by their great beauty and their charms they attracted men,
made them fall deeply in love with them, and kept them in subjection to such an extent that, by making them do whatever they
wanted, they seemed like beasts. But experience indicates the
opposite in you, my boy; for I know you are a rational being and
yet I see you in the form of a dog, unless this is being done by
means of that art they call *tropelia*, which makes one thing appear
to be another. At all events, what grieves me is that neither I nor
your mother, who were pupils of the good Camacha, ever knew as
much as she did; and not for want of intelligence, or skill, or
determination, for all these things we had in abundance, but
because she was so sly that she never wanted to teach us the most
important things, all of which she kept for herself.

'Your mother, my boy, was called Montiela, and was nearly as
famous as Camacha. My name is Cañizares, and if I'm not so clever
as the other two, I've at least as much desire to do well as either
of them. It is true that as far as your mother's determination to get
into a circle and be shut up in it with a legion of devils was concerned she was not even second to Camacha herself. I was always a
bit timid, and was quite content to conjure up half a legion; but

with due respect to both of them, when it came to concocting the ointments with which we witches anoint ourselves, I was not inferior to either of them, nor am I to any of those who nowadays follow and observe our rules. For I would have you know, my boy, that as I have seen and now see that life, which rushes by on time's swift wings, is coming to an end, I have wanted more and more to abandon all the vices of witchcraft in which I was engulfed many years ago, and all I have left is the fancy to be a witch, a vice which is extremely difficult to give up. Your mother was the same: she abandoned many vices and did many good works in this life; but in the end she died a witch. She did not die of any illness but out of chagrin when she found that Camacha, her teacher, was envious because she was reaching the point of knowing as much as herself, or through some other jealous quarrel that I could never get to the bottom of. So when your mother was pregnant and about to give birth, Camacha acted as midwife for her and showed her what she had given birth to, which was two puppies. And as soon as she saw them she said:

'"There's some evil, some mischief here! But sister Montiela, I'm your friend: I will keep this offspring of yours hidden, and you give your mind to getting well. You can be sure that this misfortune of yours will be veiled in silence: don't be at all upset by what has happened, for you know I'm perfectly well aware that you've been going round with no one else but Rodríguez, that porter friend of yours, for days. So this doggy offspring comes from somewhere else, and there's some mystery here."

'Your mother and I, who was present all this while, were amazed at this strange affair. Camacha went off and took the pups with her: I stayed with your mother to make her comfortable, and she couldn't believe what had happened to her. When Camacha came to the end of her days, at the eleventh hour she called your mother and told her how she had changed her children into dogs because of some complaint she had against her; but said she should not be upset, for they would revert to their natural form when they least expected it; but that it could not happen until they had seen with their eyes what follows.

> They will return to their true form
> when they see the mighty speedily brought down

and the humble exalted
by that hand which has power to perform it.

'This is what Camacha said to your mother at the time of her death, as I have already told you. Your mother took it down in writing and learned it by heart, and I fixed it in my mind in case I should ever get a chance to tell one of you. And in order to find you I call all the dogs of your colour that I see by your mother's name, not because I think the dogs will know the name, but to see if they answer when they're called by names which are so different from those of other dogs. And this evening, when I saw you do all those things and heard you called the Wise Dog, and when I saw you look up to me when I called you in the yard, I thought you must be the son of Montiela. So it is a great pleasure to tell you what happened to you and how to get back your original form. I wish it were as easy as the way they say Apuleius did it in *The Golden Ass*, simply by eating a rose. But your metamorphosis depends on others' actions and is not a question of your own efforts. What you must do, my boy, is commend yourself to God in your heart, and wait for these divinations, which I'd rather not call prophecies, to come about quickly and happily; for as the good Camacha pronounced them, they will undoubtedly come to pass, and you and your brother, if he is still alive, will see yourselves in the form you desire.

'What I regret is that I am so near my end that I shall not have a chance to see this happen. I have often wanted to ask my goat how your affair will end; but I have never dared, because he never gives a straight answer to what we ask, but answers in a roundabout and obscure way. So it's no good asking this lord and master of ours anything, because he mixes a thousand lies with one truth; and from his answers, he knows nothing of the future with any certainty, but only by guesswork. All the same he's got all us witches fooled to such an extent that, even though he plays a host of tricks on us, we can't leave him. We go to see him a long way away from here, in a big field, where a whole host of us assemble, wizards and witches; and there he gives us wretched food to eat, and other things happen there that for the sake of truth and of God and of my soul I dare not tell, so filthy and loathsome are they; and I don't want to offend your pure ears. Some people think we go to these gatherings only in our imagination, and that through it the devil presents to us images of all those things which we say afterwards have happened to us. Others deny this, and say that we really go, body and soul. I myself hold that both these views are true, for we don't know whether we go in imagination, or in reality, because everything that happens to us in our imagination happens in such an intense way that it can't be distinguished from the times when we go really and truly. The inquisitors have made some experiments on some of us whom they have apprehended, and I think that they have found that what I say is true.

'I should like to get rid of this sin, my boy, and for this purpose I have done what I could. I have had recourse to becoming a hospitaler; I look after the poor, and some of them when they die provide me with enough to live on with the things they bequeath to me or with what they leave among their rags, which I go through very carefully. I pray little and in public; I do a good deal of back-biting and in secret; I get on better by being a hypocrite than by sinning openly; the sight of the good works I do now blots out from the memory of those who know me my evil deeds in the past. Indeed false sanctity never harms anyone but those who practise it. Pay heed, Montiel my boy, to this advice I'm giving you: be good in every way you can, and if you must be bad, try not to appear so any more than you can help. I am a witch, and I don't deny it: your mother was a witch and a sorceress, and I can't deny that either; but the good appearance we both put on gave us a good reputation everywhere.

'Three days before she died we had both been in a valley in the Pyrenees on a great jaunt; and yet she died so calmly and peace-fully that were it not for the faces she made a quarter of an hour before she gave up the ghost, you'd have thought she was lying on a bridal bed strewn with flowers. She was heart-broken over her two sons, and even at the hour of death could not bring herself to forgive Camacha, such was her unswerving integrity of purpose. I laid her out; and I went with her to the grave. There I left her, never to see her again, although I haven't abandoned hope of seeing her before I die, because it's been said in the village that she's been seen wandering about the cemeteries and crossroads in different forms. Perhaps I shall come across her some day, and then I shall ask her if she wants me to do anything to ease her conscience.'

Every one of these things which the old woman told me in praise of the woman she said was my mother was like a dagger thrust at my heart, and I should have liked to attack her and tear her to pieces with my teeth; and if I refrained from doing so it was only in order that death should not come to her in the state she was. In the end she told me that she intended to anoint herself that night to go on one of her usual outings, and that when she was there she intended to ask her master for news about what was going to happen to me. I wanted to ask her what anointing she was talking about, and she seemed to read my wishes, for she answered me as if I had really asked the question.

'This ointment,' she said, 'with which we witches anoint ourselves is composed of the juices of herbs, very cold, and not, as is commonly said, of the blood of the children we suffocate. You might ask me what pleasure or profit the devil gets out of making us kill tiny babes. He knows that if they are baptized, since they are innocent and without sin they go straight to heaven, and he gets a special punishment for every Christian soul which escapes his clutches. The only comment I can make on this is what the proverb says: that there are some who will cut out both their eyes if their enemy will cut out one; and he does it for the sake of the grief which he inflicts on their parents in killing their children, which is the greatest imaginable. But what matters most to him is to make us commit these cruel, perverse crimes all the time; and all this God allows because of our sins, for without His permission experience has shown me that the devil cannot harm an ant. This is so true that once when I asked him to destroy a vineyard belonging to an enemy of mine, he replied that he could not even touch a leaf of it because it was against God's will.

'So you will be able to understand, when you become a man, that all the misfortunes which befall people, kingdoms, cities and villages; sudden deaths, shipwrecks, falls, in short all those misfortunes which are called damages come from the hand of the Almighty and by His leave; and the injuries and misfortunes which are called crimes come from and are caused by ourselves. God is incapable of sin; hence it follows that we are the authors of sin, by forming it in our intention, and in our words and deeds, with God's leave because of our sins, as I have said. Now, my boy, you'll be asking, if by any chance you can understand me, who made me a theologian, and you might even say to yourself, "Curse the old whore! Why doesn't she give up being a witch, since she knows so much, and turn to God, when she knows that He is more ready to forgive sins than to allow them?" To this my answer would be, if you were to ask me, that the habit of vice becomes second nature, and this business of being a witch becomes a thing of flesh and blood. Even when you are fired by it, as you really are, it carries with it a chill which freezes the soul and benumbs it even in its faith, so that it forgets itself and doesn't even remember the terror with which God threatens it or the glory which He invites it to share. And in fact, since it is a sin of the flesh and of sensual pleasure, it must of necessity deaden all the senses, and charm and beguile them, without allowing them to fulfil their functions as they should. So the soul, becoming useless, weak and dispirited, cannot rise to the consideration of a single good thought and, allowing itself to be sunk in the deep abyss of its wretchedness, it does not want to reach out its hand to the hand of God, who offers it, for His mercy's sake, so that the soul may rise. I have a soul such as I have described to you; I see and understand everything, but as sensual pleasure has fettered my will, I have always been and always shall be evil.

'But let us leave this and come back to the business of anointing. As I said, the ointments are so cold that when we anoint ourselves with them we are deprived of all our senses, and lie stretched out naked on the ground, and then, they tell us, we go through in our imagination all that to us seems really to happen. On other occasions, as soon as we have anointed ourselves, we change form, as it seems to us, and transformed into cocks, owls or crows, we go to where our master is waiting for us. There we recover our original form and enjoy pleasures which I refrain from telling you about, because they are such that one's memory is scandalized when one recalls them, and so one's tongue tries to avoid relating them.

'In spite of all this I am a witch, and I cover up all my many faults with the cloak of hypocrisy. It is true that though I am esteemed and honoured by some on account of my goodness, there are plenty who upbraid me within my hearing with the names with which we were branded through the fury of an angry judge. This judge dealt with your mother and with me in times gone by, passing on his fury to an executioner who, not having been bribed, used all his powers without reserve upon our backs. But this has passed, as everything does pass; memories fade. You can never live your life over again, people's tongues get tired of gossip, new things make one forget the old ones. I am a hospitaler: my conduct is a credit to me; I have a good time when I anoint myself and I am not so old that I may not have a year left to live, although I am seventy-five. Now that I can't fast because of my age, or pray because I go dizzy, or go on pilgrimages because of the weakness of my legs, or give alms because I am poor, or think good thoughts because I am addicted to backbiting (and in order to do good one must first think good thoughts), all my thoughts are bound to be evil. Nevertheless, I know that God is good and merciful and that He knows what is to become of me, and that is enough.

'Now let's put an end to this conversation which is making me very sad. Come, my boy, and watch me anoint myself. Every trial is easier to bear when you've a full stomach; make hay while the sun shines, for you can't weep while you're laughing. What I mean is that although the pleasures that the devil gives us are false and illusory, they still look like pleasures, and it's better to imagine pleasure than to enjoy it, although it ought to be the other way round where true pleasures are concerned.'

When she had finished this long harangue she got up, and taking the lamp went into another, smaller room. I followed her, tormented by a thousand thoughts of all kinds, and amazed at what I had heard and at what I expected to see. Cañizares hung the lamp on the wall, and with great speed stripped herself down to her shift. Then, getting a glass pot out of a corner, she put her hand into it, and muttering to herself, she anointed herself from head to foot, for she was not wearing a headdress. Before she had finished anointing herself she told me that whether her body remained senseless in that room, or whether it disappeared, I should not be afraid, nor fail to wait there until the next day, because I should learn what I had to go through until I became a man. Lowering my head, I indicated that I would do this, and thereupon she finished anointing herself, and stretched herself out on the ground as if she were dead. I put my mouth to hers, and saw that her breathing had stopped altogether.

I must confess, Scipio my friend, that I was very frightened to find myself shut up in that little room with that creature in front of me. I will describe her to you as best I can. She was more than seven feet tall; her bones stuck out all over, covered with dark, hairy, hard skin; her private parts were covered with the folds of skin from her stomach which was like a sheepskin and hung half-way down her thighs; her nipples were like the udders of wrinkled, dried-up cows; her lips were black, her teeth worn down and her nose hooked and all askew. With her staring eyes, her dishevelled hair, her hollow cheeks, her shrunken neck and shrivelled breasts, she was as hideous and repulsive as could be. As I looked at her, all of a sudden I was overcome by fear, as I thought of the ugliness of her body and the evil to which she had abandoned her soul. I wanted to bite her, to see if she would recover consciousness. I couldn't find anywhere on her person where I could do it without feeling revulsion, but all the same, I did grab her by her heel and drag her out into the courtyard, and not even then did she show any sign of consciousness. Out there, where I was in the open and could see the sky, I lost my fear; or at least it lost its hold on me sufficiently to allow me to wait and see the end of that evil old woman's doings and what she intended to tell me about my affairs.

And as I waited I asked myself, 'Who made this evil old woman so knowledgeable and so wicked? How does she know all this about harmful and culpable evil? How does she understand and talk so much about God and do so much of the devil's work? How does she sin so deliberately without the excuse of ignorance?'

Thinking about these things the night passed and day came, and found the two of us in the middle of the courtyard – she still unconscious and I crouching beside her on the alert, staring at her ugly and frightful form. The people from the hospital came out, and when they saw the scene, some said, 'Old Cañizares is dead; look how skinny and disfigured her penances have left her.' Others, more practical, took her pulse, and finding that her heart was beating, and that she wasn't dead, came to the conclusion that she was in an ecstasy, and that sheer goodness had caused her to fall into a rapture. There were others who said: 'There's no doubt this old whore must be a witch, and that she's been anointing herself, for saints never go into such indecent raptures, and she's always been better known to us as a witch than as a saint up to now.' Some curious people went as far as to stick pins right up to the head into her flesh; but not even then did our sleeping beauty stir. She did not come to until seven o'clock in the morning. And when she saw herself riddled with pinpricks, and the bites on her heels, and the bruises from being dragged out of her room, and exposed to the sight of so many eyes staring at her, she thought, and thought rightly, that I had been the cause of her dishonour. So she attacked me and putting both hands round my throat, she tried to strangle me, shouting, 'Oh you ungrateful, ignorant, malicious rogue! And is this then the reward for the good things I did for your mother and which I intended to do for you?' I, seeing myself in danger of losing my life in the claws of that fierce harpy, shook myself, and grabbing her by the long folds of her belly I pushed her and dragged her all round the courtyard, while she cried out to be released from the teeth of such a malignant spirit.

Influenced by what the evil old woman said, most of the by-standers thought that I must be one of those devils who bear a perpetual grudge against good Christians, and some came and threw holy water over me, while others did not dare to come near me to pull me off, and others shouted out that I should be exorcized. The old woman was grunting, I was holding on with my teeth, the confusion was growing, and my master, who had by now arrived, attracted by the noise, was most upset when he heard people saying that I was a devil. Others, who knew nothing about exorcisms, got hold of three or four clubs, with which they began to beat my back. I got tired of the game, let the old woman go, and in a few strides was out in the street, and in not many more out of the town, pursued by a host of children, who ran along shouting at the tops of their voices,

'Look out, the Wise Dog has gone mad!' Others said: 'He's not mad; he's the devil in the form of a dog!' In the midst of all this fuss, I left the town with the bells ringing, followed by a crowd who undoubtedly thought that I was a devil, as much because of the things they had seen me do as of the words the old woman spoke when she awoke from her wretched sleep. I took to my heels and got out of sight so quickly that they thought I had disappeared like a devil. In six hours I travelled twelve leagues, and got to a gipsy camp in a field near Granada. There I stopped for a while, because some of the gipsies recognized me as the Wise Dog, and were delighted to welcome me. They hid me in a cave, so that I could not be found if anyone came to look for me, intending, as I gathered afterwards, to make a profit out of me, like my master the drummer. I was with them for three weeks, during which time I got to know and observe their life and customs, which I must tell you about since they are so remarkable.

Scipio Before you go on, Berganza, we ought to take notice of what the witch told you and find out if the great lie you are prepared to believe can be true. For look, Berganza, it would be the most utter nonsense to believe that Camacha could change men into beasts and that that sacristan could serve her for all the years they say he did in the form of a donkey; all these things and others like them are frauds, lies or manifestations of the devil. And if we seem now to have some understanding and power of reason, since we are speaking when we are in fact dogs, or have the form of dogs, we have already said that this is a marvellous and unprecedented thing, and that although we are experiencing it we must not be taken in by it until the outcome shows us what we ought to believe. Do you want it more clearly? Think on what vain and absurd premises Camacha based her argument about our transformation back to human form; and then you will see that the things that look like prophecies to you are nothing but fairy stories or old wives' tales, like the ones about the headless horse and the magic wand, with which people while away the time by the fireside on long winter nights. Because otherwise it would have happened; unless her words are to be taken in a sense I've heard called allegorical, which means that the sense isn't as it sounds, but something else which, although different, may resemble it. So to say

> They will return to their true form
> when they see the mighty speedily brought down
> and the humble exalted
> by that hand which has power to perform it,

in the sense I have mentioned, seems to me to mean that we shall recover our form when we see that those who yesterday were at the summit of fortune's wheel are today trampled down and cast at the feet of misfortune and held in low esteem by those who valued them most; and likewise, when we see that others who a couple of hours ago had no place in this world but as a cipher to increase the number of its inhabitants are now so lifted up by prosperity that we can no longer see them; and if to begin with we could not see them because they were so small and timid, now we cannot get near them because they were so great and exalted. And if recovering our form consisted in this, we have already seen it happen and it happens all the time, from which I gather that it is not in the allegorical but in the literal sense that Camacha's verses are to be taken. However, the answer to our problem does not lie here either, for we have often seen what they say and we are still dogs as much as ever we were.

So Camacha was a false deceiver, and Cañizares a liar, and Montiela a foolish, malicious and wicked woman, begging your pardon, if she is by any chance the mother of either of us both or just of you, for *I* certainly don't want her as a mother. I tell you then that the true meaning is just a game of ninepins, in which those who are standing are quickly knocked down and those who fall down get up again, and this by the hand of him who is able to perform it. Consider then whether in the course of our lives we have ever seen this game of ninepins and whether in doing so we have become men again, if indeed that is what we are.

Berganza I declare you are right, brother Scipio, and that you are cleverer than I thought, and from what you have said I truly think and believe that all that we have experienced up to now and are experiencing is a dream, and that we are dogs. But don't let us for that reason fail to enjoy this blessing of speech which we have and the great honour of possessing the gift of speaking like humans for as long as we can. So don't get bored with hearing me tell you what happened to me with the gipsies, who hid me in their cave.

Scipio I am very willing to listen to you, so that you may be obliged to listen to me when, if heaven wills, I tell you of my life's adventures.

Berganza The life I led with the gipsies made me think about all their wickedness, their trickery and their frauds, the thieving in which the women as well as the men take part, from the moment they leave their swaddling clothes and learn to walk. Have you noticed the enormous number of them who are scattered about Spain? Well, they all know each other and know what the others are doing, and they pass the things they steal from one to the other.

They owe more loyalty than they owe to their king to one whom they call Count, and he, and all his descendants, have the surname of Maldonado. It is not because they come from that noble family, but because a page of a gentleman of this name fell in love with a gipsy girl, who would not return his love unless he became a gipsy and took her to be his wife. The page did this, and the other gipsies were so pleased that they promoted him to be their lord and declared their allegiance to him; and as a sign of loyalty, they bring him a share of their thefts, if they are of any consequence.

In order to cover up their lack of occupation, they busy themselves in making things in iron, instruments to help them in their thieving; and so you will always see them in the streets with tongs, drills and hammers for sale, and the women with trivets and shovels. All the women are midwives, and in this they have the advantage over ours, because without any expenses or any assistants they give birth to their offspring, and wash the babies in cold water as soon as they are born. From the moment they are born until they die they are hardened and exposed to the inclemencies and rigours of the elements; and as you will see they are all excellent at running, dancing and acrobatic feats. They always marry among themselves, so that their evil ways don't come to the notice of the outside world; they are respectful to their husbands, and rarely do they cause them offence by having dealings with anyone outside their own group. When they ask for alms, they use tricks rather than prayers, and on the grounds that no one will trust them, they don't enter into service, and end up by being idlers. And rarely if ever have I seen, so far as I can remember, any gipsy woman taking Communion at the altar rail, although I have been into churches many times. All they think about is how they can deceive and where they can steal: they compare notes on their thefts and their methods of stealing.

One day a gipsy in my presence told another one of a thieving trick that he had played one day on a peasant. The gipsy had a bob-tailed ass, and on the bit of his tail which had no hair he tacked a piece of another with hair, which looked like its own. He took it to the market, a peasant bought it from him for ten ducats, and after he had sold it to him and got the money, he told him that if he wanted to buy another ass which was the brother of this one, and quite as good, he would sell it to him for a more favourable price. The peasant told him to go and fetch it and he would buy it from him; and then while he was waiting for him to come back, he would take the animal to his lodgings. The peasant went off, the gipsy followed him, and somehow or other the gipsy contrived to steal from the peasant the ass that he had sold him, and immediately he took off the false tail, and it was left with its own bald one. He changed its saddle and halter, and had the nerve to go and look for the peasant to persuade him to buy it; and finding him before he had missed the first ass, in next to no time the peasant bought the second.

He went to his house to get the money to pay, and there the silly ass found the real donkey missing; and stupid as he was, he suspected that the gipsy had stolen it from him, and did not want to pay him for it again. The gipsy went in search of witnesses, and brought the people who had charged him the tax on the first donkey, and they swore that the gipsy had sold the peasant an ass with a very long tail and very different from the second ass he was selling. The whole thing was witnessed by a police officer, who took the gipsy's side with such conviction that the peasant had to pay for the ass twice.

They told me about a lot more thefts, and all or most of them were of animals, for they are most practised experts at this. In short, they are bad people, and although many wise judges have come out against them, they don't mend their ways at all.

After I had been with them three weeks they decided to take me to Murcia. I went through Granada, where my master the drummer's captain was living. As soon as the gipsies found out about it, they shut me up in a room in the inn where they lived. I heard them discussing their plans, and didn't think much of the journey they were proposing, so I decided to break loose, which I did. On my way out of Granada I came upon a garden belonging to a Moor, who was very ready to take me in, and I was even more ready to stay, for it seemed to me that he would only want me to keep watch over his garden, a job which to my way of thinking involved less work than keeping sheep. And as there was no question of pay to discuss, it was easy enough for the Moor to find a servant to obey his orders and I a master to serve.

I was with him for more than a month, not because the life I had with him was all that pleasant, but because it gave me a chance to get to know the sort of life my master led, and thereby that of all the Moors living in Spain. The things I could tell you, Scipio, about this Moorish rabble, if I weren't afraid that it would take me more than a fortnight to get through it! And if I had to go into detail, it would take me two months. But in fact I shall have to say something, so I'll give you a general account of what I saw and noted down in detail about these fine folk. You will rarely find among them one who sincerely believes the holy law of Christianity. Their whole object is to make and keep money, and in order to get it they work and eat nothing. Once a coin gets into their hands, if it's worth anything at all, they condemn it to perpetual captivity and eternal darkness; so that by always earning and never spending they collect and amass most of the money in Spain. Where money is concerned, they are treasure-chest, moth, magpie and weasel; they get hold of it, hide it and swallow it up. Bear in mind that there are a lot of them and that every day they earn and hide a certain amount of money, and that a slow fever finishes a person off just as effectively as a quick one. And as they are increasing in number, so the number of those who hide money away grows, and will go on growing without stopping, as experience shows. Among them there is no such thing as chastity, nor do any of them, men or women, take religious orders. They all marry and multiply because frugal living makes them all the more fit for procreation. They do not get exhausted by wars, nor do they take any employment which wearies them unduly. They rob us, without going out of their way at all, and on the fruit of our properties, which they sell back to us, they grow rich. They have no servants, because they all act as their own. They don't spend money on schooling for their children, because all the learning they want is to know how to rob us. From the twelve sons of Jacob who I hear tell went into Egypt, when

Moses brought them out of their captivity, there came out six hundred thousand men, not to mention women and children. Hence you can infer how the wives of these will multiply, for they are incomparably greater in number.

Scipio People have looked for remedies for all the injuries you have pointed out and hinted at; and I am well aware that those you don't mention are much greater in number and kind than the ones you've recounted; yet up to now the right remedy hasn't come to light. But our state has wise watchmen, who, bearing in mind that Spain is rearing and harbouring in its bosom all these Moorish vipers, with God's help will find a sure, quick and certain way out of this harmful situation. Now carry on.

Berganʒa As my master was mean, like all those of his breed, he would feed me on millet bread and some leftover gruel, which is what they normally live on. But heaven helped me to bear this wretched fate in the strange way of which I will now tell you. Every morning, at day break, a youth would appear, seated at the foot of one of the many pomegranate trees in the garden. He looked like a student, dressed in flannel, no longer black and sleek but drab and threadbare. He would write busily in a notebook, and from time to time would slap his brow and bite his nails, as he looked up to the heavens; and then he would become so lost in thought that he would move neither hand nor foot, nor even bat an eyelid, so absorbed was he.

Once I went up to him without his noticing me. I heard him muttering between his teeth, and after a long while he shouted out, 'By heaven that's the best octave I've ever composed in my life!' And writing quickly in his notebook, he would give signs of great satisfaction; all of which led me to believe that the poor fellow was a poet. I made the usual fuss of him, to assure him of my tameness; I lay down at his feet, and he, reassured by this, went on with his thoughts and his head-scratchings, and his ecstasies, and his scribbling down of what he had thought up. While he was at it another youth came into the garden, an elegant, well-dressed young fellow with some papers in his hand, from which he would read from time to time. He came up to where the other youth was, and said to him,

'Have you finished the first act?'

'I've just put the final touches to it,' replied the poet, 'and it's as elegant as you could wish.'

'How does it go?' asked the second.

'Like this,' answered the first. 'His Holiness the Pope comes on fully robed, with twelve cardinals, all dressed in purple, because when the action of my play took place it was the time of the "mutatio caparum", when the cardinals don't wear red, but purple. So it is most essential in order to conform to the rules of propriety that these cardinals of mine should come on in purple; and this is a point which is very important for the play and would certainly be noticed, and if it weren't done would give rise to thousands of impertinent absurdities. I couldn't go wrong on this, because I've read the whole book of the Roman ceremonial just to get these vestments right.'

'And where,' replied the other, 'do you think my manager is going to get purple vestments for twelve cardinals?'

'Well, if you just take one of them away,' answered the poet, 'you've as much chance of getting my play as of flying. Good heavens, do you think I'm going to waste such a splendid scene? Just imagine the effect in a theatre when you get a Supreme Pontiff with twelve solemn cardinals and all the other attendant ministers they are bound to have with them. By heaven, it will be one of the greatest and most noble sights ever seen in a play, even the *Ramillete de Daraja*!'[5]

At this point I came to the conclusion that one was a poet and the other an actor. The actor advised the poet to cut down a bit on the cardinals if he didn't want to make it impossible for the manager to put on the play. To this the poet replied that they ought to be grateful that he hadn't put on the whole conclave that attended that memorable event which he intended to recall to the memory of the audience in his splendid play. The player laughed, and left him to his task while he went off to do his own, which was to study a part in a new play. After he had written a few verses of his magnificent comedy, the poet slowly and calmly took out of his pocket some crusts of bread and twenty-odd raisins as I calculated, or perhaps

5. *Ramillete de Daraja*. A sixteenth-century play on a Moorish subject, now lost and of unknown authorship, but frequently mentioned by authors of the period for its fantastic and extravagant character.

not quite so many, because there were some crumbs of bread with them which made up the bulk. He blew on the crumbs to separate them from the raisins, which he ate one by one, complete with stalks, not one of which he threw away as far as I could see, adding the crusts which, through being in contact with the fluff from his pockets, looked as if they were mouldy, and were so hard that although he tried to soften them by moistening them in his mouth several times, they couldn't be persuaded to abandon their rock-like character. All this was to my advantage, because he threw them to me with the words, 'Here boy, and may they do you good.'

'Look,' I said to myself, 'what nectar or ambrosia this poet is giving me, food which they say the gods and Apollo himself live on up in heaven!' In short, on the whole, the lot of the poet is a wretched one; but my need was greater, since it forced me to eat what he rejected.

All the time he was composing his play he came every day to the garden and I got crusts to eat, because he shared them with me very generously, and then we would go off to the water-wheel, where we would slake our thirst like kings, I lying down and he with one of the buckets.

But the poet went missing, and my hunger anything but; to such an extent that I decided to leave the Moor and go into the city to seek my fortune, for he who changes his situation often finds good luck. On my way into the city I saw my poet coming out of the famous monastery of San Jerómino, and as soon as he saw me he came up to me with open arms, and I went to him with renewed signs of pleasure at having found him. He immediately began to unload pieces of bread, not so hard as the ones which he used to take to the garden, and to feed me with them without first tasting them himself, a kindness which added pleasure to the satisfaction of my hunger. The soft bits of bread and the fact of seeing my poet coming out of the monastery made me suspect that he had turned his back on the muses, like many others. He set off for the city, and I followed him, determined to have him as my master if he were willing, and guessing that I should be able to live on the crumbs that fell from his table, because there is no greater or better purse than that of the charitable person, whose generous hands are never affected by poverty. I don't agree with the proverb which says:

'The hard-hearted man gives you more than the one who's hard up,' as if the miser would give as much as the generous pauper, who at least gives his good will when he has nothing more to give.

By degrees we got to the house of a theatrical manager, who, so far as I can recall, was called Angulo the Bad, to distinguish him from another Angulo, who was not a manager but an actor, the most amusing you've ever come across in the theatre. The whole company gathered together to listen to my master's play (for such I already considered him to be), and half-way through the first act they all began to leave, one by one and two by two, except for the manager and me, who were the only audience. The play was so bad that, although I am a complete fool where poetry is concerned, I thought Satan himself must have written it, just to ruin and humiliate the poet, who was speechless when he saw that he had been deserted by the audience. It was not surprising that his prophetic soul gave him secret warning of the misfortune which was threatening him. In fact all the players came back, more than a dozen of them, and without a word grabbed hold of my poet, and if the manager hadn't used his authority to intervene with pleas and shouts, they would certainly have given him a tossing. I was amazed at the affair, the manager was pretty annoyed, the players delighted, and the poet peeved. With great patience, although with a rather wry face, he took his play, and tucking it under his coat, he went off muttering, 'It's no use casting pearls before swine.' And then he went quite calmly away.

I was so ashamed I neither could nor wished to follow him; and I did right, because the manager made such a fuss of me that I felt obliged to stay with him, and within a month I turned out to be a great composer of sketches and a great mummer. They put a fancy muzzle on me and taught me to attack anyone they chose in the theatre. As the sketches usually ended in beatings, in my master's company they ended up by setting me loose on the crowd, and I would knock them all over and trample on them, which made the ignorant mob laugh and brought a good deal of profit to my master.

Oh, Scipio, I wish I could tell you all the things I saw in this and two other companies of players I was with. But as it's impossible to reduce it to a short and succinct account, I shall have to leave it to

another day, if indeed we have another day when we can communicate with each other. Do you see how long my discourse has
taken, and how many and varied adventures I have had? Have you
considered the journeys I have made and all the masters I have had?
Well, all you have heard is nothing compared with what I could tell
you about the things I noted, found out and observed among these
people; where they come from, their life and customs, their practices, the work they do, their idleness, ignorance and wit, together
with countless other things, some of which are suitable for private
communication and others for public proclamation, and all well
worth noting for the enlightenment of the many who take delight
in imaginary figures and fake beauties artificially contrived.

Scipio I am well aware, Berganza, of the range of things you had to
cover in your discourse, and in my opinion you ought to reserve it
for telling in private on an occasion when we shall not be interrupted.

Berganza I agree, so just listen. With one of the companies I got as
far as this city of Valladolid, where in one of the sketches they gave
me such a blow that it nearly finished me off. I couldn't have my
revenge, because I had my muzzle on at the time; and later, in cold
blood, I didn't feel like it; for premeditated vengeance is a sign of
cruelty and ill will. I got bored with this occupation, not because it
was difficult, but because I could see that it involved things which
called for reform and censure; and as, however much I deplored
these things, I could do nothing to put them right, I decided to turn
a blind eye, and took refuge in a safe place, like those who leave
their vices when they can no longer practise them (although
better late than never).

So, then, one night when I saw you carrying the lantern in company with that good Christian Mahudes, I thought how happy you
were, and how justly and virtuously employed. So full of righteous
envy I decided to follow in your footsteps, and with this laudable
intention I went up to Mahudes, who chose me straight away to be
your companion, and brought me to this hospital. What has
happened to me here is not so slight a matter that it does not
require some time to relate it, especially what I heard from four
sick men whom fate and necessity brought together to this hospital,
and to four adjacent beds. Forgive me, for it's a short story, which
I shan't dwell on, and is very much to the point.

Scipio Of course I'll forgive you. Finish quickly, because it seems to me that daylight isn't very far off.

Berganza What I want to tell you is that in the four beds at the end of this infirmary, there were respectively an alchemist, a poet, a mathematician and one of those people they call schemers.

Scipio I can remember seeing these good folk.

Berganza Well, one afternoon last summer, when the windows were closed and I was trying to get a breath of air under the bed belonging to one of them, the poet began to complain pitifully about his fate; and when the mathematician asked him what he was complaining about, he replied that it was about his bad luck.

'And haven't I good reason to complain?' he went on. 'Having kept to the rules that Horace lays down in his *Art of Poetry* that one shouldn't publish a work until ten years after it is finished, I have one which took me twenty years to write, not to mention twelve more I had it by me, a work with a vast subject, an admirable and novel plot, dignified lines and entertaining episodes, marvellously balanced, with the beginning matching the middle and the end: so that the poem is lofty, tuneful, heroic, pleasing and substantial; yet I can't find a noble patron to whom I can address it. I mean a nobleman who is intelligent, liberal and magnanimous. What a wretched age and depraved century we live in!'

'What is the work about?' asked the alchemist.

The poet replied, 'It's about what Archbishop Turpin didn't get round to writing about King Arthur of England, with a further supplement to the "Story of the quest of the Holy Grail". It's all in heroic verse, partly in octaves and partly in free verse; but all in dactyls and nouns at that, without a single verb.'

'Personally,' replied the alchemist, 'I don't know much about poetry; and so I can't properly appreciate the misfortune you are complaining of. But, however great, it could not equal mine, which consists in the fact that, since I lack instruments, or a patron to support me and make available the things required by the science of alchemy, I am not, as I should be, rolling in riches and wealthier than all the Midases, Crassuses and Croesuses who ever lived.'

'Have you, Mr Alchemist,' said the mathematician at this juncture, 'carried out the experiment of extracting silver from other metals?'

'Up to now,' replied the alchemist, 'I haven't managed to extract it; but I do know that it can be extracted, and I only need a couple of months to get the philosopher's stone, with which it is possible to make gold and silver out of stones.'

'You have certainly been exaggerating your misfortunes,' said the mathematician at this point, 'for after all, one of you has a book to dedicate to someone and the other is very near to extracting the philosopher's stone; but what about my misfortune, all alone and with no one to turn to? I've been looking for the fixed point for twenty-two years, and within an ace of finding it; and when I think I've found it and that it can't escape me come what may, all of a sudden I find I'm so far away from it that I'm absolutely amazed. The same thing happens to me over squaring the circle: I've got so near finding the final answer, that I don't know and can't think how I haven't already got it in my pocket, and so I suffer the tortures of Tantalus,[6] who was within reach of fruit and yet dying of hunger, and right beside water and yet perishing of thirst. At times I think I'm on the point of arriving at the truth, and the next minute I'm so far from it that I'm climbing up the hill which I've just come down, with the stone of my labours on my back, just like Sisyphus.'[7]

Up to this point the schemer had been silent, but now he broke out with the words, 'Poverty has brought together in this hospital four of the most miserable wretches you've ever seen, and I'm fed up with trades and occupations which are no fun and which don't bring anything to eat. I, sir, am a schemer, and at different times I've presented many and varied schemes to His Majesty, all to his advantage and with no detriment to the Kingdom. I have now written a memorandum in which I beg him to put me on to someone to whom I can pass on a new scheme I have, so effective that it will help him to pay off all his debts; but from what has happened to me with other memoranda, I can guess that this one will end up like them on the rubbish-heap.

'But just so that you don't think I'm a crackpot, although my

6. Tantalus, cf. above, *The Glass Graduate*, note 12.

7. After his death the Greek prince, Sisyphus, was condemned in hell to roll to the top of a hill a large stone, which had no sooner reached the summit than it rolled back.

scheme will be public knowledge, I'm going to tell you what it is. There is to be a petition in the Cortes[8] that all His Majesty's vassals, from the ages of fourteen to sixty, shall be obliged to fast once a month on bread and water, on a day chosen and appointed, and that all the expenditure on other food in the form of fruit, meat and fish, wine, eggs and vegetables, shall be turned into money and be handed over under oath to His Majesty without a copper being taken off. By this means, in twenty years he will be free of fund-raising devices and clear of debt. Because if you calculate, as I have done, there are a good three million persons of this age in Spain, not counting invalids and those who are over or under the age limits, and not one of them will fail to spend a *real* and a half a day, at least; but I'm willing to put it at no more than a *real*, for it can't come to less even if they eat hay. Do you think it would be worth nothing to have three million *reales* every month served up on a plate? And this would be to the advantage rather than the detriment of those who do this fasting, because by fasting they would please heaven and serve their king; and for some of them this fasting might even be a good thing for their health. This is the bare bones of the scheme, and you could collect by parishes, without the expense of commissaries, who ruin the State.' They all laughed at the scheme and the schemer, and he laughed himself at his crazy ideas; as for me, I was amazed to hear them and to find that most people like this finished their days in hospitals.

Scipio You're right, Berganza. Are you sure you have nothing more to say?

Berganza Just two things, with which I will bring my speech to a close, for it seems to me that daylight is on its way. One night when my boss was going to beg for alms at the house of the chief magistrate of this city, who is a great gentleman and a man of integrity, we found him alone. I thought I would take advantage of this to pass on to him some remarks which I had heard from one of the old patients in this hospital about the way in which one could get rid of the notorious menace of those 'tramps', girls who so as not to enter service come to a bad end, so bad that every summer they fill all the hospitals with the wretches who go after them; an intoler-able scourge which calls for a quick and effective remedy. As I was

8. The Spanish Parliament.

saying, I wanted to tell the magistrate, and as I opened my mouth, thinking that I could speak, instead of uttering coherent arguments, I barked so quickly and so loudly that the magistrate got angry and called his servants to give me a beating and drive me out of the room. And one of the lackeys who rushed up at his master's call (would that he had been deaf just then) caught hold of a copper pot which happened to come to hand, and whacked my ribs with it so hard that I still have the marks of those blows to this day.

Scipio And is that what you're complaining about, Berganza?

Berganza Well, haven't I reason to complain, if it still hurts, as I said, and if in my opinion my good intention called for no such punishment?

Scipio Look, Berganza, no one should interfere without being asked, or meddle with matters which don't concern him. And bear in mind too that no one ever took any notice of a poor man's advice, however good, and a man who is poor and humble must never presume to give advice to the great and those who think they know everything. Wisdom in a poor man is always overshadowed; for necessity and poverty are the shadows and clouds which blot it out; and if by any chance it comes to light, people think it is foolishness and treat it with scorn.

Berganza You are right, and learning by my own mistakes, from now on I shall follow your advice. Another night, in the same way, I went into the house of a distinguished lady, who had in her arms one of those little dogs they call lapdogs, so small that she could hide it in her bosom. When the dog saw me, it jumped out of its mistress's arms and attacked me, barking fiercely; and it wasn't satisfied until it had bitten me in the leg. I looked at it with a mixture of respect and anger, and said to myself, 'If I were to catch you in the street, you wretched animal, I should either ignore you or tear you to pieces with my teeth.' I couldn't help thinking how even cowards and mean-spirited creatures are bold and insolent when they are in a position of favour, and ready to insult those who are better than themselves.

Scipio One sure sign of the truth of this is provided by those little men who under the shadow of their masters dare to be insolent; and if by any chance death or some other accident of fortune destroys the tree under which they are sheltering, then their worthlessness is revealed and shown up because, in fact, their claims are worth no more than the value given to them by their masters and protectors. Virtue and understanding are one and indivisible, whether naked or clothed, alone or in company. Of course it is true that these things can suffer as far as people's estimation of them is concerned, but not in their real merit and worth. And with this let us bring to an end this conversation, for the light coming through these cracks shows that day is coming on, and tomorrow night, if we haven't been deserted by this great blessing of speech, will be mine, so that I can tell you my life story.

Berganza So be it, and be sure to come to this same spot.

The end of the 'Colloquy' related by the licenciate coincided with the ensign's awakening, and the licenciate said,

'Although this colloquy may be a fake and may never have happened, it seems so well put together that you may continue with the second, Ensign.'

'Since you think that,' answered the ensign, 'I shall pluck up courage and prepare to write it, without disputing any more with you about whether the dogs did speak or not.'

To this the licenciate replied, 'Ensign, don't let's return to this argument. I appreciate the art of the colloquy and the invention you've shown, and that's enough. Let's go off to the Espolón and refresh our eyes, for my mind's been well refreshed.'

'Let's go,' said the ensign.

And with that, off they went.